THE

DANCE OF DEATH;

OR,

THE HANGMAN'S PLOT.

A THRILLING ROMANCE OF TWO CITIES.

LONDON:

THE NEWSAGENTS' PUBLISHING COMPANY, 147, FLEET STREET,

AND ALL BOOKSELLERS.

THE
DANCE OF DEATH:
OR
The Hangman's Plot.

BY DETECTIVE BROWNLOW AND MONSIEUR TUEVOLEUR, SERGEANT OF THE FRENCH POLICE.

"MERCY! THERE'S MERCY FOR YOU, DESPICABLE HOUND!"

CHAPTER I.

A HAPPY HOME—A FEW PARTICULARS—TWO OLD ACQUAINTANCES—A COMFORTABLE SMOKE—A GOOD MAN, AND A SHEEP IN WOLF'S CLOTHING—DICK SPALDINGS, THE FARMER—CARROTTY NAT, THE SECRET FOE—AN INTERESTING CONVERSATION—A WIFE'S HONOUR AT STAKE.

IN a comfortable, but plainly furnished room of a pretty cottage, which stood near the edge of the high road which led from Bournemouth, in Hampshire, to London town, two men were seated at the time when our story begins.

They were sipping together their hot gin, and puffing their long clays, which are commonly denominated "Churchwardens," which, it must be confessed, were exactly in accordance with the popular, and also too often abused, beverage before them.

From the costumes which they wore, it was no

difficult matter to guess that they derived their resources—whatever they might be—from the cultivation of the soil, and that they rejoiced in the name of farmers; a supposition on our part which would have been fully confirmed in the minds of those who, with a knowledge of the country, would have gazed upon the professional taste with which the sloping patch of ground at the back of the abode was laid out, upon the fatherly care which seemed to have been bestowed upon the numerous plants, vegetables, and fruit trees, which grew luxuriously in a garden of which the owner was known to be somewhat proud.

Dick Spaldings, the tenant of the farm, and of the two hundred acres of ground appertaining to it, was thriving in the world, and had hitherto been thoroughly happy.

He was a tall, wiry, slim-built man, the very picture of health; and were it not for his sunburnt countenance and his coarse hands, rendered so by manual labour, he might, indeed, have aimed at the appearance of one far above his calling in life; but he was not ambitious: he had a pretty wife and a darling boy, with bright eyes and soft curls; he could boldly walk up to the squire's agent, when the rent became due, and pay it without asking time; he could enjoy his home without going to the public house to forget troubles he never had—and he felt satisfied.

When on Sundays he walked to the parish church, with his darling wife, Jenny, leaning upon his arm, and his handsome son running before him, gathering daisies along the road-side, Dick's features glowed with those marks of satisfaction which are to be noticed with those who, having in their youth felt the pangs of hunger, can appreciate the blessings of ease and comfort shine upon them; and all the neighbours envied the lucky husband, and every one was jealous of his prosperity in Bournemouth.

There was, however, a determination in his grey eye, which denoted a will of iron; and the tightly-compressed lip showed that when he took something in his head—a very nasty personage to whom a civilised author may be permitted to allude—would not drive it out.

His companion, to whom we must now revert our attention, was far from being prepossessing in his appearance.

He had, once upon a time, we must inform you, reader, been one of Jenny's suitors.

And how did it come to pass, you may well ask, that these two men happened to meet, and to be on friendly terms?

Our answer is simple: business brought them together; and you know perfectly well—at least, you ought to know, if you do not—that business transactions, whether in town or country, often compel men to shake hands together, to have a drink together, which the two individuals were doing at the time we make their acquaintance; and to swear to each other protestations of friendship which neither means.

But this is how the world wags; it has been so for centuries, and no one can ever change the acknowledged ways of society.

Nat Smith was a strange fellow; some thought him foolish, but he was worse than that.

As the story proceeds, we dare say, that many will think the same as ourselves.

He was a disagreeable-looking man, dressed in a shabby suit of velvet; and his altogether slovenly appearance was far from being relieved by an evil countenance, which was covered with deeply-set marks of small-pox, a disease which had kept him laid up for several weary weeks, and which,

depend upon it, had not been calculated to improve a naturally morose and back-biting temper, which, more than once, had involved him in quarrels, out of which he had always managed to make his exit with flying colours.

Lucky fellow, you see, was Nat Smith!

He was endowed, besides, with a shuffling cuteness, and a tongue which he could either render honeyed or bitter, and which, considering all the harm it had done, ought by rights to have been long ago extracted by the root out of his wicked old throat!

The boys in the village used to call him "Carrotty Nat;" a cognomen which he was far from relishing, but the truth of which he was bound to admit when quizzed about it in friendly confab; for, notwithstanding his attempt to make people believe his head of hair was fair, they would reply, that if their sight did not belie them, it resembled a great deal too much the useful vegetable above alluded to, for any one to make a mistake about it.

Nat Smith had formerly made love to Jenny Hayward, when a maiden and unmarried, of course, but now Mrs. Spaldings; and as she was then, and up to the present period of our story, generally acknowledged to be the prettiest lass in the town, and could pick and choose for herself, she had spurned his advances; nay, not only had she refused to have him, but she always had disliked him, and the sexton laughed very loud one day that Jenny had offended her unlucky suitor by a casual remark, of which she scarcely knew the real purport at the time, but which had, nevertheless, fallen like molten lead upon the disappointed heart of the rejected lover, who still felt its bitter weight.

Hence revenge had sprung up within him.

If he found an opportunity to harm the girl, he was not the one to lose it.

Besides, how he would have chuckled, how his vitiated, selfish nature would have rejoiced could he have thrown discord and sorrow in a quiet, peaceful home!

Of late he had watched his friend's wife carefully—narrowly—and now he knew something.

What was that something?

"Dick," he began, in a leering way, "you are happy, aint you?"

"Happy? Well, mate, I think so. What can make you think otherwise?"

"Oh! if you are happy, that is so far right."

And Nat Smith blew clouds from his clay, and taking the decanter, helped himself to a fourth draught of the cordial on the table.

He seemed to be fond of it, for when he brought the tumbler to his lips and drained off its contents, he smacked them like one who felt perfectly satisfied with the imbibing process which he had just undergone.

Perhaps he rejoiced at the communication which he was about to make.

Such men ought to be swept away from the surface of the earth—partaking of a man's hospitality, and profiting by the same to change his blood to gall, his heart to ashes.

Shame upon such creatures calling themselves Christians!

Dick looked inquisitively at his companion.

"What mean you?" he asked at length, in a cool, unsuspecting tone of voice.

"Oh! nothing, nothing, Dick; I asked you if you were happy."

"You did."

"You said yes."

"Well, that's all right."

"What's all right?"

"What I said I repeat."

"There's an end of it, then."

And the two men smoked in silence.

"You returned earlier from the fair than you anticipated, didn't you, Dick?" his companion resumed, in a drawling sort of way, which, however, geered strongly upon the farmer's hearing.

"I did, and what matters about it?"

"I suppose you could make no good bargain?"

"I could not."

"And you thought it better to come back?"

"Even so," sullenly retorted Dick Spaldings.

Here Nat rose.

"Good-bye," he said, holding out his hand to the late speaker, "I'll be off."

Dick Spaldings looked puzzled.

But, in no ways noticing his friend's consternation, Nat coolly went to fetch his hat, which he had placed upon the cupboard upon entering the room, and, without another word, placed it upon his head.

It was a big, slouched, beaver sort of covering, and he looked a monster in it.

There was something decidedly repulsive in his general appearance.

And he walked towards the door slowly and steadily.

One minute more, and he would be outside the abode.

Now, we must state, that Dick Spaldings had become suddenly plunged in a deep reverie, but when he saw that his friend was not joking, as it had been his first impression, and that he really meant to depart, he rose suddenly, and, grasping him by the shoulder, drew him back by the side of the chair, which he had just quitted.

"What are you arter, man?" asked Nat, rubbing his shoulder as if the tightness of the late grip still caused him pain. "Darn my buttons, if you don't hurt a fellow."

"Sit down," said the husband, in a tone which admitted of no reply.

Like a snarling cur, who submits to superior authority, the ruffian did as he was bid.

CHAPTER II.

A YOUTHFUL VISITOR—A HARSH RECEPTION—HEART-RENDING REMEMBRANCES—BITTER SUSPICION—SAD FOREBODINGS—GROWING ANXIETY—A VILLAIN SPEAKS AT LAST—THE WARNING—THE OUTRAGED HUSBAND—THE FIERCE STRUGGLE—THE VICTORY—THE SUDDEN DEPARTURE—NAT'S SOLILOQUY.

No sooner had Nat complied with the peremptory request which had been made to him, than the sound of footsteps were heard cracking against the gravel walk which led to the cottage entrance, and a boy, of about thirteen years of age, made his appearance.

This was Dick Spaldings' son.

How his heart did beat.

Oh! if it had only been his wife.

He loathed the presence of his son now.

Harrowing thoughts were entering his mind, and what he suspected might be true after all!

Now, had he followed the first impulse of his nature, he would have welcomed his boy like a good devoted father should have done.

But reflection came.

"Harry," he asked, sternly, "what have you been doing all this time, idling your time at school, I suppose, instead of learning your lessons?"

"No, Pa, I have not been idle," the lad replied in a faint voice, "I am sure to get a prize at Midsummer!"

"What's that to me? Where's your mother?"

How could the poor boy tell?

He remained silent.

Never before had his father spoken so roughly to him.

Dick Spaldings gazed upwards.

The presence of his son seemed to work upon him like electricity.

It produced upon him the same effect as a bitter draught; and quickly the blood flew to his cheeks.

"Away, away, from me!" he exclaimed at last. "Away from me! The sight of you is irksome to me; it recals to my mind scenes of bygone love; ah! my happiness has fled; away, and do not come again under this roof, you son of——"

And here he stopped.

The boy felt that his mother was insulted.

His youthful pride had received a lasting shock.

Defiant and trembling, he looked the farmer in the face.

He was now upon the threshold of the room.

But his glance cowed before that of him who had reared, and hitherto loved him, and, without saying a word, he left.

And so, in a few minutes, Harry was out in the country.

Sadly he gazed upon the pretty cottage which had once been his home.

A change was now taking place within his breast.

For he did not go gathering daisies with a light and merry heart as he did of yore, but he walked on thoughtfully, with his eyes bent downwards.

He had made up his mind to do a certain thing.

He had taken a resolution which, at the time, he fully intended to carry out.

What that was, and whether he succeeded or not, remains to be told.

But return now, we must, to his father.

Dick Spaldings was, as yet, unacquainted with the news which he was about to hear.

Nat Smith smiled with a satanical, fiendish smile.

He had enjoyed the scene above related.

He felt at home whenever there was mischief going on, and still more so when it was his own work.

Dick Spaldings was now deadly pale.

His companion wished he had left the matter alone, but he had gone too far to retreat; and he felt that he should make the most of the plight in which he had willingly placed himself.

"You hurt me just now, Dick," the coward began, in a submissive manner; "of course, I am not accustomed to the off-handed way in which you treated me, and feeling offended, I thought it better to leave you quietly, instead of falling out with an old acquaintance."

A cleverer being than the farmer would have been unable to discern the deep and scheming nature of the speaker; no wonder, then, that he fell into the trap which was so cleverly laid open beneath his feet.

Nat noticed the advantage and the ground which he had gained.

What was Dick about to hear?

Alas! he had been too happy, and this was not to last for ever.

The dazzling rays of the congenial sun, which for years past had shone upon the thriving artizan's home, would ere long disappear before the impending blast.

Yes; they were gradually coming on; those dark inky clouds, which were to break out upon the poor unfortunate husband, in a pelting storm, which would either annihilate his nature, prostrate him to the ground like the tree struck by the vivid lightning, or rouse within his frame feelings of despair, hatred, and revenge; over which the angels in Heaven would weep, and Satan glorify from his fiery throne of ingratitude and infamy.

"Stay, Nat, stay," he exclaimed wildly, "stay your speech until I tell you to go on."

Here there was a pause.

It was hard to see one's dreams dashed to the ground, for Spaldings could love, dote upon his once dear Jenny, the sweet girl whom he had led to the altar as his bride!

What would he not have done, had she remained faithful to him?

Willingly would he have incurred any punishment, however ignominious, for her sake. He would not have minded days of the most abject suffering, were she by his side to smile on him. What would have been the empty cupboard, the fireless grate, the excruciating pangs of hunger, the sickening feelings of thirst, if she was there to smile upon him, and help him to struggle against the world's vicissitudes?

But without her.

Without Jenny.

Without his darling wife!

And when, too, she had become his own—when he had trampled upon all his rivals—when Jenny had said to him—

"I am yours!" to see her snatched away from him.

Oh! this was too much for him to bear!

And he remembered her on her bridal couch, when those lips, so moist and rosy, had met his—when her sweet breath, like enervating perfume, had mingled with his own—when her warm hair had rested upon his forehead, and bashful and blushing, her heaving bust had told a woman's tale; when, in the thrilling embrace of love, he had pressed her quivering frame to his burning heart, and yielded to the desires of an absorbing mutual passion.

*	*	*	*	*

Oh! how cruelly heaven punished him now; for, having thought that his bliss was superhuman—and that had the archangel's trumpet sounded then, it would have failed to summon him before its supreme tribunal!

Now he could endure his anxiety no longer.

"Tell me the worst, Nat," he shrieked, "I am ready to listen to you."

The yell which he gave sounded like that of some wild beast, and clashed strangely with the meaning of the sentence.

"I am sorry, Dick," Nat began slowly, "that you did not make a good week's work."

"So am I," muttered the farmer, sullenly. "But enough, you wished to tell me something, I know."

Previously, Dick had asked his companion whether he could inform him where his wife was; but dreading to become aware of a truth which he still took pleasure in doubting, he had not reverted to the subject again.

"You know I am your friend, don't you, Dick?" Nat resumed, guessing his friend's curiosity.

"I have no reasons to doubt it."

"Do you think it is a friend's duty to prove a friend, Dick."

He accentuated his last words meaningly.

"That depends," chimed the farmer, thoughtfully, and he buried his head in his hands, for he began to fear that he would not be able to summon sufficient strength to listen to that man who came into his house to be the bearer of an information which, to the longest day of his life, he would never forget.

That man who called himself his friend!

He remembered him as a rival, and somehow, although he was compelled to admit him beneath his roof, he would have wished him far away from his sight.

"Mine is a painful duty, Dick."

Cold drops of perspiration oozed from the husband's forehead.

"Proceed," he muttered inaudibly, becoming livid.

He appeared like a clammy corpse, and none would have believed that the blood of life still flowed in the veins of one who was about to hear of his shame, of his dishonour.

"I have noticed your wife," Nat Smith began slowly.

"Jenny?" muttered the listener.

There was still a spark of affection lingering in the intonation which he had placed upon a name, which had never sounded so sweet to his ear.

"Yes, ere now I have noticed Jenny's partiality to William Spanton."

"The schoolmaster?"

"Aye."

"Oh, is that all?"

"Quite enough, I should think."

A ray of hope illuminated the husband's countenance.

"He is very handsome," ventured Nat.

"So they say."

"She might speak to him about the boy."

"Exactly."

"That would account for being on terms of friendship."

"Yes, friendship," returned the informant, meaningly.

Here Dick Spaldings clenched his fist threateningly.

But Nat Smith was not easily frightened.

On the contrary, the husband's sorrow caused him to grow bold.

His eyes leered villainously from under his beetling brow, and he cracked satisfactorily the joints of his fingers.

"Why are you standing in that stupid way, Nat, looking at me as if I was a gorilla?" the farmer now resumed, in an impatient tone of voice; "if you have anything to say, say it, or else you may go, and be d—d."

Nat laughed loudly.

"Dick," he said, "you are using strong language."

"Enough of your palaver, man; go on, I order you."

So peremptorily had Spaldings spoken, that further delay would have been dangerous.

Nat Smith was not slow in perceiving the growing excitement of his listener.

"Your wife's behaviour, mate," he went on, in a friendly tone, which he had assumed for the occasion, "might be prompted by friendship certainly—there, I agree with you; but—"

"I'll have no ' buts!'" hissed the farmer, between his clenched teeth. "Speak out! Now, like a good fellow," he continued, in a tone which trembled with anxiety, "let us hear what you have to tell me."

"Jenny's ways of late," Nat resumed, taking up the subject where he had left it, "have given rise to my suspicions. I watched her; and now I can speak without laying myself open to a denial. I have noticed familiarity."

"Familiarity!" repeated the husband, as if loth to believe his hearing.

"Yes, familiarity, that is the word I used."

Dick Spaldings drew breath.

"Now, look here, Dick," the informant resumed, "I do not know whether I must go on."

The farmer rose on hearing those words, and paced up and down the room.

"I have noticed more than familiarity," Nat continued.

"And that is ?" the husband asked, quietly.

"Love !"

"Ah ! ah !"

"Love, yes, love, if you like; but others call it adultery."

"*Adultery !*" moaned the husband, and heavy drops of perspiration oozed from his brow.

"Yes, that be it," replied Nat, with a leer.

This was too much for the outraged husband.

"You lie, you lie, you cursed hound !" he exclaimed, foaming with rage.

Thus speaking, he sprang upon his companion.

The coward tried to escape.

But he had no time to do so.

It was now the husband's turn.

With one heavy blow, he fell Nat to the ground; but with the quickness of a roused blood-hound, he sprung upon his feet, and made a bold onslaught upon his assailant.

And now began a severe, bloodthirsty struggle.

There was something fearful in the contest of these two men, with their arms surrounding each other's waists, both uttering groans of rage, impelled by their craving for blood.

And down they fell; and away went the table, the crockery smashing in a thousand pieces upon the floor with a heavy crash, mingling with Nat's cries, who was now beginning to shriek for mercy.

But no one came to his rescue, for the cottage was far from the road, and his exclamations remained unheard.

And again they fought and they struggled, and their limbs became entwined like knotted serpents in the tight embrace of hate.

The veins and arteries of their necks rose like chords.

Their eyes protruded from their sockets.

And rapidly did the blows follow each other, while thick drops of blood chased their feverish and swollen cheeks.

"Oh, mercy ! mercy !" howled Nat.

"Mercy ! There's mercy for you, despicable hound !" retorted the farmer, and up went the fist, and down it came upon the cowardly scoundrel.

Uneven was now the contest.

Dick Spaldings had the best of it.

Nat's strength was fast giving way.

And presently, with a heavy groan, he sank upon the ground, apparently senseless; but he would not confess himself beaten, for he was not so hurt but that he could utter words in an audible tone.

He knew that his tongue could lacerate his antagonist's heart, far more keenly than ought else would have done.

And so, in his half-consciousness, he kept on muttering:

"Oh, they will rejoice at the happy farmer's downfall. I know they will! I have seen them: Jenny, once the sweet, innocent Jenny, and her infatuated lover exchanging fulsome showers of kisses at the back of the haunted mill. Oh, they aint afraid of the ghosts, not they; and to-night, I feel convinced they will be there !"

With breathless suspense the husband listened.

"He raves ! he raves !" he soliloquized, "still it must be true."

And he mused for awhile.

"Get up, you hound !" Spaldings said at last, gazing upon his companion, whose presence filled his heart anew with loathing. "Get up !"

But Nat, making no reply, the husband's rage kindled once more, and he kicked his prostrated companion with his heavy boot, which sounded ominously on the fellow's back.

A painful sigh, and hideous contortions soon told the husband that his conquered foe was now a prey to intense suffering.

But he could wait no longer, and under the impulse of some sudden thought he left the room, sallied to the stable, saddled his horse, and was soon afterwards galloping along the high road, spurring his steed's flanks, and hurrying on towards the destination which he had just heard, towards the haunted mill, which was situated a few miles from the place where he lived.

On his way he learnt that the schoolmaster had taken a holiday.

His wife he had already ascertained to have been absent since morning.

She had not expected him home till late next day, and he had baffled her.

Returned before she had anticipated.

Returned to discover his shame—her guilt !

"It is always dangerous to interfere between the bark and the tree, so the saying has it," muttered Nat, as he rose from his stooping position, and shook himself aright, to ascertain whether he was hurt.

He found that, beyond a black eye, whose painfulness he was yet to experience, a scar on the forehead, and a slight bruise at the back of his head, he was not in any ways injured.

"Never mind," he pursued, "I expected something of the kind, and do not regret it. Dick always had a temper of his own, and I might have got worse off if my good luck had not stood by me at the eleventh hour, as usual. Never mind, though; it strikes me forcibly that all this will end badly."

Thus soliloquizing, the "soi-disant" friend of Dick Spaldings seized hold of a huge blackthorn, which he ever carried with him, muttering, as he jogged along the the the path which led to his abode—

"A deuced good day's work, my boy ! Jenny will remember me for the future, I'll be bound, or my name aint Nat Smith."

CHAPTER III.

A DARK NIGHT—THE SWIFT ERRAND—THE FLYING LEAP ACROSS COUNTRY—THE ARRIVAL—THE VISIT TO THE HAUNTED MILL—JENNY'S PORTRAIT—THE HIDDEN WITNESS—THE GUILTY WIFE—SCENES OF LOVE—A FOUL DEED—A WOMAN'S WEAKNESS—A HUSBAND'S CURSE.

THE night was setting in.

The sun, which had long ago disappeared behind the tree-tops of the forest, and gone to rest until the forthcoming early morn, had heralded the rising of a strong easterly wind, which blew in fitful gusts in Dick Spaldings' face, who was, however, too pre-occupied to feel in any ways inconvenienced by the inclemency of the weather.

His long hair, through which swept the blast, hung in disorder upon his thick coat-collar, his eyes were fierce and bloodshot, his features stern, and covered with dust, and with a firm and feverish grasp he held the reins in his hands

He had to ride three miles more.

Three long miles, before he should reach his destination.

The spot which had been named to him.

The haunted mill !

Now, my friends, can you fancy his anxiety?

A husband in search of his wife.

Perhaps arrive too late !

Oh, the thought was bitter and excruciating.

Then his lip curled with a diabolical, fiendish smile.

Dick Spaldings drew breath.

Then he hurried on his horse.

The beast flew along rapidly.

Like lightning it glided onward.

It seemed to know its errand, for never had it assumed so swift a gallop.

Its heavy hoofs rattled upon the high road, and it sped along at a racing pace.

Its nostrils were dilated, its slanting shoulders bathed in foam, and it tore madly along.

Yet the farmer was not satisfied.

Cottagers ran out upon their thresholds to gaze upon the noble steed, and the burthen which it carried, and they wondered whither the rider was going, and returned to their abode to conjecture upon the strange sight.

But the farmer heeded them not.

His whole frame shook with rage and disappointment.

Maddened by despair, he lashed his horse with his heavy hunting whip.

"Go on, go on, you brute," he would exclaim; and he would dart his spurs in the animal's flanks until his boots would be soaked with the ruby which flowed from its flesh.

Up went the whip and down it came again.

Over ditch, fence, across the country rode Dick Spaldings.

There were no impediments in his way.

He would have cleared a stone wall of eight feet high and met his doom, sooner than to give up his mad course.

A hundred yards more, and then his journey would be ended.

In the distance the old mill, reputed to be haunted.

Dick Spaldings breathed satisfactorily.

"At length," he muttered, "I am safely arrived."

Now he halted.

Vaulted from his saddle and stepped upon the ground.

He reflected deeply.

What should he do?

Cautiousness was to be observed.

Too much impulsiveness would spoil his errand.

For if he were observed and his presence detected, what then?

His object would be defeated.

Again he mused.

Leading his horse by the rein, he walked on until he came within a few yards of the mill.

With pricked-up ears, the faithful animal was listening.

Perhaps its instinct caused it to understand its rider's sorrow.

Who knows?

Who could tell?

Dick Spaldings' feelings here gave way.

"Oh! good horse, my faithful friend," he said, stroking the swan-like shoulders of his mount. "You are an insensible brute, who cannot understand one's sorrow; and yet be a silent witness of what I am about to say. If my wife is innocent; if the report which I have heard is only a slander upon her fair fame, I will make that Nat wash his own words in blood; and I will fling myself at her knees, and ask her forgiveness, for having doubted her; whereas, if there is any foundation for the information I received—then, oh, then!"

Any one who could have seen Dick Spaldings, when he pronounced his last words, would have shrank from him as if from some dangerous fiend.

His features were of a ghastly white.

His eye kindled fire.

His hand trembled.

And his whole frame shook nervously; and he was a different man indeed from the one above we have seen so gay and so happy at the beginning of this thrilling narrative.

Presently, he fastened his horse's rein to the branch of a tree.

Next he wavered as to what he should do.

He feared to walk.

Feared to move a step.

Sad forebodings had come over his brain.

A secret voice was muttering to him:

"Go not further, if you do not wish to see your happiness for ever crushed! Advance not a yard, if you dread a broken heart—a blighted future!"

For he loved his wife.

He loved Jenny with the idolatry of an infatuated worshipper!"

At length, he took a resolve.

His steed was safely fastened, and he dreaded not its running away.

So he strode on.

Along a tortuous path, lined on both sides by thick hedges, which concealed his movements, quickly and impatiently did Dick Spaldings journey.

Then he came to a wooden gateway leading to an open field.

For some minutes he stood gazing before him, uncertain as to the line of conduct he should adopt in his critical position.

He retained sufficient coolness to halt and consider.

Was his wife there?

If so, she would notice him.

How fervently and how earnestly he prayed God to come to his help, and dispose of fate so as not to enable him to see she whom he sought. How anxiously he begged of Him to grant a miracle, so as to change Nat's words into dark, dire calumny.

But this was not to be.

Thus thinking, he heard steps approaching.

He saw two dark forms on his left.

They were coming towards him.

Voices also struck his ears.

Sounds that he had heard before!

One was bold, firm, emanating, doubtless, from male lips. The other he could not yet distinguish.

With staring eyes and dilated nostrils he listened.

Closer and closer the couple approached.

With a quick step, the farmer retreated backwards, and hid himself behind the base of a huge centenarian tree; whose luxuriant branches stretching in wild growth above his head sheltered his presence with its thick canopy.

And now, as if the angel of evil wished to favour the watching husband, the moon began to shed its rays upon the old mill, which for many years had not been used by its owner, owing to its dilapidated state; and, strange to say, since it had ceased to work very few ventured to approach the spot where it stood as they were those who had spread the report that it was haunted; and we all know how quickly similar statements are believed in some parts of the country.

There was, however, a large class of people who loved to linger in its vicinity, and admire the picturesque and gloomy appearance which it presented; whose minds were not filled with apprehension, a class of people, too, who rambled about the spot and preferred it to any other, since they knew well that their conversation was not likely to be interrupted by unwelcome eavesdroppers, and intruders of various descriptions.

They were lovers, and they are always many everywhere.

"Strange! strange! horrid! impossible!" murmured the unhappy husband, as soon as he had sufficiently collected his thoughts together, so as to be able to reflect quietly. "But, no," he continued, finding that the noise had subsided, "the idea is too terrible!"

And he shuddered.

And there was an oppression at his heart, a choking sensation at his throat, and he would have longed to appear before the couple who were now within a yard or two from him, but whose features he could not yet see, owing to the plentiful foliage which obstructed his view.

They were speaking in an under tone, and walking at a slow pace away from him.

Familiar voices again sounded in Dick Spaldings' ears.

Sounds that he had heard before, and at which he could not be mistaken, for they were wafted towards him by the breeze above the stilly night, and mingled not with any other.

Now he cautiously climbed up the tree, and nearly tore his fingers and nails to pieces in doing so; yet he relaxed not in his ascent, and glancing downwards, he saw on the sward beneath the two lovers, and distinctly recognised the features of the schoolmaster, and of Jenny, his wife.

Horror of horrors!

Curses of curses!

The handsome youth's hand was around Jenny's waist, her beautiful head rested upon his shoulder, and her eyes sparkled like two diamonds, brightened to their most dazzling brilliancy by the unusual satisfaction which she experienced at being caressed by him whom she loved.

Will Spanton, the young village schoolmaster, who officiated also as the church organist, was one of those youths who, under any garments, would have looked handsome and aristocratic.

He was of a faultless form, stout of limb, broad and full about the chest, and his erect posture, with his Raphaelite features, were suggestive of strong and unimpaired vigour.

Although he was rather heavily built, no objection could have been raised against his aquiline nose, his full, but well-shaped lips, and his regular lineaments to which the rich blood that coursed freely through the minutest veins gave a softening tone; taken all in all, highly calculated to produce an impression upon a weak and impulsive woman.

For Jenny was impulsive, and as we have not had yet an opportunity of sketching her portrait, and as she is to play rather a prominent part in the course of our story, we will now do so for the benefit of our myriad of intellectual readers.

She was small, delicately formed, but a perfect model of proportion; her figure was straight, her bust full and round, her limbs plump and of a waxy polish, and although only a farmer's wife, every movement and attitude of hers might have been a study for an artist, so perfect was each in natural ease and grace.

She was such a creature as Nature, in one of its freaks, takes pleasure in placing in the humble walks of life, to show that elegance and beauty can sometimes be found beneath the working man's cot.

Her features, too, were full of vivacious animation, with a Grecian nose, and a small, pouting mouth; while pearly teeth, dark, sparkling eyes, arching brows, and a smooth, polished forehead, from which her raven hair was combed back, and neatly arranged upon the crown and back portion of her head, completed the portrait of one upon whom Providence had not been miserly in bestowing some of her most precious gifts.

She was always modestly and elegantly dressed; and in the adornment of her person, she, in every respect, displayed that good taste and select refinement which are not only the attributes of birth, but are also to be occasionally traced in discerning women less fortunate.

The schoolmaster had seen her, and he had felt a deep love for her.

Can any one wonder at it?

How many of our male readers would there be, we will beg leave to ask, who could have gazed indifferently upon a picture so lovely?

Dick Spaldings had been a long time ere he could believe his sight.

But he was bound to credit what was before him.

Now, he plainly saw the figures of Will Spanton and of his companion.

And muttering endearing words, he observed them stealing round the edge which skirted the field upon which he stood, and which led to a shady nook, a secluded bower, called "The Lovers' nest."

In an instant, their intention flashed upon the husband.

"God help me!" he muttered. "For what misery am I reserved? My wife must not commit this crime, if I can prevent it."

And then his tongue became parched; and after having alighted from the tree, where he had first taken his ascent, he endeavoured to master sufficient strength to stagger along.

Bent firmly upon his purpose, he at length succeeded in creeping slowly behind the lovers.

Happily, they were so engaged—so full of love—that they never turned round to ascertain whether they had been followed.

Behind the thick foliage, Dick Spaldings at last halted.

Jenny and her lover had entered the bower.

"Oh, Jenny! sweet Jenny! dearest Jenny!" muttered the youth, clasping the lovely married woman close to his burning breast. "Oh, how hard that Fate should have given you to another! Does your husband treat you as he ought, Jenny?"

Bashfully did Jenny droop her eyebrows.

"Oh, he is good and kind to me, kinder than I deserve!" she sighed, in reply; "but, strange to say, I once thought I would love him for ever, but now—"

Dick Spaldings heard these words.

A heavy sigh escaped his lips, his teeth chattered, and he clung to an adjoining tree to maintain his footing.

"Hark! methinks I heard a rustle in the foliage!" exclaimed Jenny, rising.

But the youth's arm was soon around the affrighted woman's waist, and lovingly he passed his fingers through her wavy hair, and with heated cheeks, flashed eyes, and feverish brow, he imprinted upon her a fulsome shower of kisses.

"Oh, if I only had a knife! a glittering, shining blade!" muttered the farmer, "I would plunge it to the hilt in that youth's heart. Blood! blood! nothing but his blood will satisfy me now! Aye, aye, I feel thirsty!—I could drink it! I could satiate my parched tongue with it! Oh, Heaven! how can you permit such things? How can you allow a husband to be a witness to his shame—to his dishonour—to his wife's guilt?"

And he raised his hand to his forehead.

His brain was in a whirl.

And again he staggered like a drunken man.

Drunk! aye, he was intoxicated with rage and bitter disappointment!

And once more his sinewy hand clutched his garments in search of a weapon.

But it was useless.

"Oh, William, do not kiss me so!" Jenny now muttered. "Leave me, I beseech you!"

"What! dearest, is that you who speaks to me thus?" the youth inquired, his voice vibrating with a strange intonation. "You cannot be in earnest. You cannot ask me to leave you. Oh, Jenny, never could I consent to lose, perhaps, the last opportunity which is left me to tell you how much I love you! I will not see that face so sweet, those eyes so loving, snatched away from me while my heart beats. Like the miser, Jenny, for years I have gloated my eyes upon your charms, so voluptuous and so exhilirating! For months and weeks past have I dreamt of you, and now that fiction exists no longer; and that I clutch sweet reality at last, could you believe that I would even consent to lose so precious a treasure? No—a thousand times no, Jenny! While blood flows in my veins and my pulse throbs, it will be for you—and you only! And no one will ever, while I stand here, dare to rob you away from me, I swear!"

Gently did Jenny strive to get away from the youth's arms, which were wound around her soft neck; and, covering her eyes with her disengaged hands, she muttered, in a half audible voice:

"But my husband, Willy?"

"Curse, curse upon that word!" the youth replied. "You are my own, and will be my own darling for ever! To some distant country we will fly. I have saved money, not much, it is true, but yet enough for our passage. Once across the Atlantic, we can be happy; and with the sweat of my brow, I will work, Jenny, to give you bread."

"But this is a fatal love!"

"Pshaw! pshaw!"

"An adulterous love!"

And the sweet creature lowered the sound of her voice as she spoke.

"Yes, such a feeling as the one which you entertain for me cannot end well!" Jenny retorted, after a while.

"Nonsense! nonsense!" the lover replied, excitedly, and wilder in its expression grew the gleam in his dark eyes; and clasping Jenny's burning forehead with both his hands, he bathed the silken eyelashes, which fringed her brow, with a stream of voluptuary—with a shower of warm, feverish, and infatuated caresses.

"Oh, Willy, I beseech you once more do let me go! Mercy! mercy! for me! Do not compel me to sin! I feel giddy—"

And in an ecstacy of supplication, the girl flung herself upon her knees, and her fairy-like form throbbed and quivered with the agony of internal emotion.

Softly and gently did Will Spanton raised his sweetheart, and again she resumed her seat.

"Oh, Jenny, I love you! Do you love me?" he whispered.

"I cannot answer you, Willy!" the woman replied, quickly; and, with sudden impulse, she endeavoured to escape.

But her movement had been detected.

Stepping, with one bound, by her side, Will drew the wretched girl in the centre of the bower.

Despairingly, she clung to her lover, and made to him another appeal.

But it was in vain.

The youth was now excited beyond description.

Then Jenny attempted to shriek!

To call for help!

But her lover's hand was gently placed upon her mouth.

Again she attempted to resist.

She would not yield.

"Oh, tell me you love me, Jenny!" the youth inquired once more, and his sweet breath tinged the transparent skin of the fair listener; and like the summer zephyr, which refreshes the drooping flower, it produced upon her a mystic influence, which she no longer could withstand, and, at length, her strength gave way.

"Oh, God, help me!" she muttered.

And then her senses forsook her; and, under Love's magnetic spell, with dishevelled hair, streaming in long, wavy, tresses upon her nude, alabaster skin, with her eyelids closed, and her warm lips beseeching a husband's forgiveness, the exhausted creature sank upon the ground, and lost a woman's restraint.

With a gleam of triumph, the youth gazed upon his victim; and stooping over her long coveted form, he sealed with his burning caresses the accomplishment of many a dream, and satiated the burning passion which, for months past, had filled his whole being with desires, which no pen could adequately describe.

"Oh, no longer can I be deceived!" sighed Dick Spaldings, after he had witnessed the scene which we have related; and, after a moment of silence, he hissed, "*And now for my revenge!*"

Nat had spoken the truth.

His sickening words had come to pass, and the unfortunate husband's worst presentiments had, alas, been confirmed!

For an instant or two, he lingered a few yards from the spot, and then he halted.

"Hear me, Heaven and hell!" he hissed between his clenched teeth, pointing, at the same time, with his right hand towards the "Lovers' nest."

"Hear me, angels and demons, cherubs weep, fiends glory! for I take you this day as witnesses to an oath which I am about to administer to myself: 'From this hour do I swear to wipe the stain on my character with a vengeance which shall cause the honest man's blood to curdle, and Humanity itself to shudder at the deeds of its children! Steadily and secretly will I plod on until I have accomplished my aim! From no means, however degrading, will I shrink to carry out my fiendish work! Yes," he continued, with a yell of despair, "Heaven and earth, men and women, birds in the forests, wild beasts in the desert, thunder and lightning! hear me! And you, Jenny, no longer a wife, and you, Will Spanton, quail before my rage! The curse of an outraged husband shall never be recalled! It will haunt you night and day, sleeping or waking, and follow you wherever you go! Should I have to wait, willingly will I do so, until the hour shall come when I can hurl you both to an untimely grave—to an ignominious and shameful death, where you shall be left to die alone, without one kindred hand to wipe the cold dew from your brow, or one eye of affection to watch your last agony! Ah! then will I gloat upon my triumph, and rejoice upon your common fall, for there will be no voices of faith bidding you hope, or ask, with their prayers, a blessing upon your parting souls!"

He ceased; and, with quick steps, he sallied towards the direction which he had left but awhile ago, then a happy and contented man so far, for hope still buoyed his heart; but now a diabolical fiend thirsting only for two lives—for the blood of his wife, and that of the youth who had led her to ruin.

PRESENTED GRATIS with Nos. 1 and 2 of "THE DANCE OF DEATH; or, THE HANGMAN'S PLOT."

THE DEADLY AFFRAY ON THE HOUSETOPS.—"BOB O'LINK ON THE SPREE."

For a description of this Thrilling Scene, see an Early Number.

ONE PENNY WEEKLY.

"DOST THOU NOT HEAR THE BIRDS OF NIGHT MOCKING THEE IN DERISION?"

CHAPTER IV.

THE LADS OF THE NINETEENTH CENTURY—A STRANGE GROUP—A MIDNIGHT MASQUERADE—WHERE ARE THEY GOING?—BIG NED, THE SPEAKER—HIS CURIOUS COSTUME—BLACK KETTLE, THE NIGGER, IS TOLD OFF FOR DUTY—THE STREET ARABS HOLD A CONSULTATION —KOKORIKO, THE HUNCHBACK—CANNIBAL JACK THIRSTS FOR CLARET—BOB O'LINK, THE SWIPER— JOHNNY CRAPAUD, ALIAS, MONSIEUR ARMAND, THE FRENCH THIEF—HIS OBJECT FOR VISITING ENGLAND —A CONVERSATION BROUGHT TO A CLOSE—THE BOY BURGLARS AT WORK—BOB'S FIST COMES IN HANDY.

LONDON by night!

A night cold, dark, and grim.

Gloomy as the soul of a desolate and wronged man.

The lamps in the streets emit a foggy, glimmering light, scarce enough to show the line of demarcation between the side-walk and the pavement, known to the citizens as the gutter, a place peculiarly adapted in rainy weather, with bathing accommodation for hogs and inebriates.

There is no rain.

No wind.

But a murky cloud of vapour hangs like a dirty blanket between the earth and the sky.

Not a sound beyond the subdued rattle of some distant vehicle.

And nought disturbs the silence of night beyond the drunken snatches and bacchanal shouts of those who are patroling the streets in search of what they term fun.

Fun!

A word which implies the police-cell, disease, a frightful headache in the morning, often "hot coppers" for the day.

Where are the bobbies?

For they may be wanted; as the scene which we are about to describe occurred in the neighbourhood of the City-road, in one of those purlieus of London, where too strict a watch could not be kept.

Yes, where is the wandering blue?

Not far away from his beat, we dare say.

Down in the area with the cook, discussing the merits of a succulent rabbit-pie, of which the lawful owner hoped to regale himself with in the morning, not reckoning on a breakfast disappointment.

But why be too hard upon the worthy keepers of the public security?

The authority in blue, like every one else, has an eye to business, and he knows that there is more pleasure in sitting comfortably before a snug, cosy fire, enjoying the householder's larder at a very cheap rate, going in for fish, flesh, and fowl, and never forgetting "to have his mutton," which he gets on the same terms; than tramping up and down doubtful lanes, where such things as the contents of a very useful implement are often emptied by mistake upon his consequential helmet.

Doubtless, we will have, ere long, occasion to see this enlightened member of the force, who, on the evening in question, is good-humouredly basking himself in the smiles of the good-natured buxom cook of No. 17, whose waist (not a slim one) he is encircling in his loving grasp.

More congenial, indeed, it must be to his domesticated habits to earn thus gallantly the Queen's money, than to be witnessing the miseries of street life.

For is not the following a melancholy sight?

Here and there a wretched and unhappy girl, totters on, bending under the weight of misery and degradation.

Her steps quickening now and then, as she hears the stranger's tread approaching her.

Uncertain how to act.

Bold, yet fearful of a harsh reception.

For she knows by experience that it is late, indeed, to derive any profit from meeting new faces.

The green countryman or the drunken libertine is her only game, from others she dreads nothing but insult and abuse.

From night-vagabonds she shrinks.

But why should she?

For if from the beings to whom we are about to revert our attention, she could expect no present, she had no reason to fear their taunts or sneers.

They would be the last in the world to hurt or insult her.

For is there not a freemasonry between the London thief and the poor, forlorn creature?

Between shameless vice and prostrated misfortune.

Between he who has to live by robbery, and she who has to sell her smiles to insure the morrow's breakfast.

To smile through her tears, as the sun shines in a shower, when she would rather weep!

But enough.

Forget, we must, the blighted lily, to revert to other matters less painful.

Look!

Who are they—thus clearing the distance with quick, hurried steps.

Where are they going?

Sweeping quickly past her, and disappearing from her sad gaze.

Let us follow.

We have all our work to do, for they go fast, faster than we could, perhaps, keep up with them, were we not endowed with youthful limbs, like theirs.

Before a dilapidated, tumble-down, old house, at the end of a slimy, dark lane, upon whose muddy pavement a solitary jet is casting its fitful and yellow glare, they halt.

They are, indeed, a strange group!

A group composed of about twelve boys, averaging from the age of 13 to 17—all of them carrying a heavy life-preserver, which more than once they have used to protect their lives and their freedom from the myrmidons of the law, ever on their track!

No, there could be no mistake about it.

These were street arabs on a midnight excursion.

For what else could have brought them out at this late hour?

They were attired in strange, fantastic costumes; and, surrounding the tallest of the boys—evidently their leader and captain—they listened to the words he was uttering in a startled whisper.

This was Big Ned, the speaker.

Under the above name, we beg of our readers to know him for the remainder of this thrilling narrative, as he will play rather a conspicuous part in it.

His was a curious disguise!

Fancy a dark red cloak, a cartoon mask of a fleshy colour, hiding entirely his features; an indescribable mixture of showy feathers towering above his head; a long, dishevelled wig of oakum, and a false beard, which nearly reached his knees; and you have some idea of his costume.

He was a heavy built sort of a chap, and he looked hideous!

"Here Black Kettle!" he said, addressing a small nigger boy, whose woolly locks left no doubt as to the owner being a recent importation from the sugar cane country,—"Here, Kettle—sharp is the word!"

The boy thus addressed soon answered the call.

Submissively, he stood by the speaker's side.

"Vat do it be, Massa?" he asked, trembling from head to foot, for he feared to come into contact with one or two of Big Ned's caresses, which he invariably delivered with his heavy fist right from the shoulders,—"Vat Massa want me to do?"

The bully reflected for awhile.

He was evidently listening intently.

"Any one coming?" he asked, in an under tone.

The boys all looked towards the opening of the lane which led to the street.

"No, Massa, 'tis be right: me see no 'slops!'"

Again the bully mused.

"Oh, tis all right!" he renewed, after a moment of silence. "The coast is clear, I see. Mind you keep watch; and, if you hear the 'peeler's' step, know you the signal?"

The nigger scratched his head, for the want of something better to do.

"Quick! what is it?" Ned continued, and threateningly he raised his clenched fist upwards.

Black Kettle instantaneously retreated three steps backwards.

"Oh, Massa, do not harm de poor boy!" he muttered, plaintively.

"Well, what is the signal?"

Without any further bidding, Black Kettle placed his two fingers in his mouth, to show that he had not forgotten the part which he was expected to play on the night during which we introduce him to our readers.

"That will do, Kettle. Be off now, for I see you know your book!"

The nigger slunk away a few yards from the other boys.

Then he halted.

Big Ned could find no fault with him.

His instructions had been carried out to the letter.

He mused for awhile.

The lads were gathering around him.

Then Big Ned took another survey; and when he had satisfied himself beyond a doubt that Kettle was standing motionless and watchful in his post of observation, he wiped his nose in anything but an aristocratic fashion, dispensing, on the present occasion, with a very useful article to a man's wardrobe; and drawing from beneath his huge mask a quid of tobacco, which he had been chewing, he gave one or two subdued grunts, more like those of a pig than of a human being, and addressed his listeners in the following terms:

"Now, friends, to-night we have most important work to accomplish. Old Sally's husband's has given up the ghost — curse his old carcase! He was a receiver of our goods. He robbed us right and left, and yet he died in his own bed! You know that he was instrumental in forwarding the information which caused the 'Cadger' to swing for it last Friday!"

"Poor Cadger! he was not a bad'un, after all!" muttered several voices.

"Well, to come to the point, boys! This I maintain: although Martin was not of the right sort, I do not think that he would ever have acted as he did, but for the miserly greediness of the old Zezabel, to whom he, doubtless, left the hundred pounds' reward, which he got for having given the clue relative to the murder of the drunken sailor in the 'Ken,' in the Highway. Now, old Martin must have died rich!"

There was a moment of silence.

None ventured to speak.

"Now, boys!" the bully went on, "Martin was of a saving disposition, and he kept whatever gold he had in that house!"

As he finished his sentence, he pointed to the door before which he was standing.

"We are all hard up, aint we, lads?" he followed.

"We are! we are! Worse than that, even!" the boys replied.

It was true—some of them were famished!

"What shall we do?" Ned pursued. "Remain here gaping, or try to take the gold away?"

"Take the gold, by all means!" re-echoed the boys, with one unanimous voice.

"That's to say, if we can find it!" ejaculated a wrinkley, under-grown little fellow, who was called "Kokoriko, the Hunchback." "Not so very easy a job, perhaps, as you anticipate, my worthies!"

Here we wish that we could, on behalf of the object of our attention, say that his was an assumed deformity; but for the sake of our tale, as well as that of truth, we are bound to inform our readers that the tough and hard hump which he had on his back was, alas! genuine enough, he having been born with it sixteen years previously.

"Will there be any occasion to spill any claret?" another asked.

This was "Cannibal Jack," so denominated because in an affray which took place in Fullwoods' Rent between him and a man twice his size, he had made a bold spring at his nose, and bit off a large piece of flesh from it.

He was as thin as a ghost shadow, and as knock-kneed as a spavined horse.

His face was thin as a dried codfish, and much of the same complexion.

His nose was long, and of the rum'un order, being also set somewhat askew on his face, as if somebody had wrung it out, and forgotten, in a hurry, to replace it amidships, where it should have been.

His eyes, which were of a Scotch grey, "were looking two ways for Sunday," or some other purpose just as edifying.

Altogether, he was quite a duck—a perfect beauty! and, taken all in all, would have kindled the fancy of any girl, who, in addition to the attractions above described, would, for the sake of novelty, have got infatuated with heavy, overhanging brows, which, as far as we could compare them, resembled a clay-bank tumbling itself overboard.

"Silence! and hark to what the man has to say, otherwise he will be all night about it!" began another voice hitherto unfamiliar to us.

Permit us, therefore, to introduce no less a personage than the illustrious "Mr. Bob O'Link, the Swiper."

This appellation was not misplaced: for Bob had a strong liking for a white stuff, called gin. He was a good sort of a fellow, and every body liked him; that is to say when sober, which he seldom was; "for, oh, between us, didn't he get 'boosy'?"

He, too, had a mask upon his face, and a huge false jaw, and the white eyeballs, which protruded from their sham sockets, were enough to strike any one with fear.

We cannot devote much space to the descriptions of the various disguises of the band, suffice it to say, that one had on his back the skin of a wolf, with the ghastly head of a bear, while the others, who were attired in their every-day ragged and dirty garments, looked right well in it, and seemed to enjoy extremely the night's sport; their small features, upon which could be plainly traced the glowing hue of strength and health, which in their trials seldom forsook them, reminding one of the houseless wanderers who abound in all poverty stricken localities.

"Bob O'Link" feared no one, and he was always on for "a mill" when not using his legs and arms in another kind of mill (the tread-mill), of which he had a taste not long ago; thinking, and very wisely too, that there is some satisfaction in knocking down your adversary, while there is but little pleasure in an "everlasting staircase," where you are tramping up and down all day long without ever reaching the end of your journey.

This night Bob was as sober as the magistrate who had convicted him.

He knew there was coin to be made, and of course, without it, you can't get any "blue ruin," and he was too fond of "a peep at the ceiling" to lose a good opportunity like the present one.

Big Ned knew his own importance.

He was always pompous, and believed himself as great a man as the Lord Mayor, and no mistake?

He had now collected his thoughts, and was about to speak, when his attention was diverted from its proper channel by a voice on his left.

"Mille Tonnerres! (thousand thunders!)" dam it, whispered the speaker. "How long are ve goin to be abou de jobbe?"

"Yes, how long are you going to be about the job?" chimed Bob O'Link, who, let it be noticed here, was somewhat jealous of the sway which Big Nat held over his companions, and had often tried to obtain the command of the band, a piece of cheek on his part which, from time to time, led to serious encounters between him and Nat.

Now, we must tell our readers, that the first words emanated from a weazel-eyed young scamp with an emaciated appearance and a decided look of roguery. He was considerably under the middle height, with rounded shoulders and a shuffling and untidy gait. His hair was worn long and greasy, falling over his shoulders; and, albeit, he was very young, he could already boast of a thin light beard and a moustache, which he took no small pride in, twisting upwards in the dandified style of the Parisian loungers of the Boulevards.

This was a precocious young individual of seventeen years of age; a Frenchman by birth, who, having been sent to England "by his highly respectable parents," was doing his best to study the art of pick-pocketing on the approved English fashion, previous to his returning to Paris to practise upon his unsuspecting countrymen.

Hundreds come to England for the same purpose, but few return to their homes—if they have any, and that's a query—as quietly as they anticipated, for unless they are clever, very clever, before they become thorough experts in their lawless calling a considerate and benevolent administration from Scotland Yard gives them a very good chance of increasing their stock of English knowledge by providing them with board and lodging in convict prisons, at the Queen's expense.

This boy had picked up his English very quickly; and although his was a strange lingo, he, nevertheless, managed so as to make himself understood by his companions.

The boys were now at a stand-still.

But ere long, they would begin their work in earnest.

Again, Big Ned illustrated the saying about the sheep's head.

Being all jaw, he again began to talk.

"My friends!" he ejaculated, quickly, "do not flinch to-night! We must get the 'ready,' happen what may; but murder is the last thing out, unless—"

He did not finish his sentence.

It was useless.

The boys had understood him, and they shook their heads affirmatively.

Big Ned was now satisfied.

"Here, Johnny!" he said, calling the Frenchman. "You have eyes like a ferret. Get on my back, and try to look through the upper part of the door. There's an opening in it, I believe, and you might see within, and let us know what's going on."

The tiny Continental was accordingly hoisted to his dignified position by the help of several arms, which proved on the occasion more sinewy than many people would have thought.

Once upon Ned's shoulders, Mossieu Armand looked down with a broad grin; and but for his being threatened by his foot-hold to be sent head over heels in the event of his going on with his humbug—he most decidedly would have, as a preliminary to the information which he was about to convey—burst out with a most uncalled for fit of laughter.

"Drop your larks, will ye, you frog eater!" Cannibal Jack now said, addressing the little Frenchman, against whom he had a grudge: "and mind your own business!"

And thus speaking, he made a grimace at him.

Johnny, alias Mossieu Armand, was rather excitable.

He foamed.

"Frog eator!" he repeated. "Vat za you call me, sare?"

And he looked fiercely at the Cannibal.

"You are a canaille scoundrale! and by damn I shall—"

"Looker yer, old Parley Voo, you'd better sing small, or I'll give yer one just for a lesson."

These words restored order.

They came from Bob O'Link.

"Sing small!" the Frenchman still muttered "By dam! why do he calle moi a frog?"

But the last sentence was never heard, for, in a twinkling, Big Ned seized his burthen by the legs, and, with the dexterity of an acrobat, he allowed him to fall from his elevated position, and caught him by the shoulders just in time to save him from breaking his neck.

When safely landed, the Frenchman spoke.

In answer to queries, he replied that all was "dark, werry dark," and that he could see "notink—notink!"

The youthful boy-burglars, we must tell our readers, never sallied out without all the implements necessary for the "cracking of a crib;" and as they could not ascertain what was taking place within, they resolved not to remain out much longer ere they satisfied their curiosity.

The crowbar was then produced.

And a dark lantern was brought forth.

The operations now began in earnest.

But the door was stronger than they imagined.

It would not yield.

"What are you about, you Nincompoops!" a voice now exclaimed; and pushing every one before him, and thus clearing his way, Bob O'Link took a survey of the existing impediment.

First, he felt the panels of the door, and then he wrapped his hand in a silken "billy," which had once been a stock-broker's property; subsequently had been lifted out of his pocket by Mossieu Armand, and was now in the Swiper's possession, who had bought it for a trifle from its last unlawful owner.

"You are fine fellows, to be sure!" he muttered, sneeringly. "Why, that's the way to do it!"

And raising his bony and iron-like knuckles, he gave a strong knock against the door, which at once receded before the weight which had been brought to bear upon it.

Big Ned now cast a furtive glance towards the direction where Black Kettle had been, and was still standing.

"All smooth?" he asked, stepping towards the look-out.

The nigger shook his woolly covering in a most persuasive manner; and, within hearing distance, echoed the last speaker's query.

To delay would have been dangerous.

The boys knew that.

So, headed by Bob O'Link and Big Ned, they rushed headlong into the room.

And now, reader, if you please, we will take a stroll into another chapter, and a different scene, until we return to our young heroes, whom we will shortly see again.

CHAPTER V.

THE GORGEOUS MANSION—THE LADY MOUNTCARSDEN—THOUGHTS OF THE PAST—THE FLIRTATION—THE SECRET MARRIAGE—THE HONOURABLE HOUSEFIELD'S SUDDEN DEATH—THE ABDUCTION OF THE YOUNG HEIR—FLIGHT OF THE NURSE—HER LADYSHIP'S ILLNESS—HER RECOVERY—THE NEIGHBOURS' OPINION ABOUT THE CHILD.

Now, reader, it is necessary, for the comprehension of this tale, that we should pay a visit to a gorgeous-looking mansion, situated in one of London's most fashionable neighbourhoods.

It was, indeed, a splendid habitation, with its elaborately carved portico, its marble steps, its smooth, clean area, leading to the apartments where the bloated servants revelled; its broad windows, and heavy damask curtains, through which could be seen the dazzling rays of light, which, flowing brightly from the crystal chandeliers, shed a golden tint upon the handsomely furnished rooms.

The whole outward appearance, which truly well accorded with the extravagant display and costly splendour within the abode, betokened to the passer-by the unmistakeable signs of that gold without which life is a blank—a vale of tears !

How often the poor, half-starved wanderer, who slunk beneath the handsome balcony in search of his evening meal, moaned and sighed painfully as he raised his glazed, sunken eye, and glanced up on that temple of riches ; and how earnestly, also, the struggling milliner or needy clerk, on their way to their humble lodgings, longed for a little of the ease and comfort which to so many is denied, while to a fortunate few, " the upper ten thousand," as they are sometimes called, it is so freely and indiscriminately bestowed.

But think not, my readers, that the inmates of this mansion were happy.

Alas, frequently there is more joy and satisfaction to be traced upon the contented features of the thriving artizan than in the aristocratic physiognomy of the nobleman, whose time hangs heavily upon his hands, and whose craving for dissipation and pleasure undermines his constitution, and betimes sends his lawful heirs to the workhouse.

The Lady Mountcarden, at the time when we see her, was seated in an easy chair, and, although a book with opened leaves was beneath her soft and taper fingers, long ago it had dropped upon her lap, and its reading matter, its bold, clear type, were to her so many hieroglyphics, whose meaning her disturbed mind was unable to fathom.

She was plunged in deep reveries and silent musings.

For there was a mystery which shrouded the aristocratic brow of her ladyship.

There was a tale of woe connected with her proud escutcheon.

There was a skeleton in the house in which she lived.

And she was thoroughly unhappy.

For many years past she had become a gloomy and desponding creature.

Her ladyship had been twice married; first, to the Honourable Housefield, and then to the Earl of Mountcarsden, her present husband ; and although twice a mother, she had only seen her firstborn for a few days, it having been stolen shortly after its birth, as will be, hereafter, related.

What had become of it ?

She never knew; and, albeit, she had offered gold to ascertain its whereabouts, never yet had she succeeded in her endeavours.

" Yes, my child would have been nineteen today," she would mutter to herself, gazing listlessly around her ; " will I ever be fortunate enough to clasp it again to my own breast ere I die ?"

And mournfully she drooped her head.

Her ladyship was dressed with becoming elegance.

Upon her fingers shone diamonds of the finest water, her fine, glossy hair was combed in the most fashionable style of the period at which we write, and yet life had no attractions for her.

She had been the only child and heiress of one of the most ancient, as well as wealthy families in Yorkshire ; and having being spoiled and petted by those who had had the management of her fashionable education, who allowed her to gratify every whim which came into her head, the natural consequences had been that she was proud, head-strong, and capricious.

Still she had a woman's heart.

During one of those costly entertainments, which are given by the local and wealthy of the land to their equals, and the numerous parasites who hang upon the favour and hospitalities of their betters, Julia Norton had made the acquaintance of the Honourable Lucious Housefield, cornet in Her Majesty's regiment of Royal Horse Guards.

They were both young—they loved each other ; and a flirtation soon took place between the lovely Julia and the dashing and gallant officer.

Vows had been uttered.

Love letters exchanged.

An intimacy had followed, resulting in a secret marriage.

For the cornet was not of age yet.

Therefore, had not the power to act according to the impulses of his own heart.

But the marriage was doomed not to last long.

Their union was of a brief duration.

A son and heir was born.

Three days after it was ushered in the world his father died.

Only the day after he attained his majority !

The young wife was prostrated.

She tore her hair in despair, and wept over her husband's dead body.

Was distracted beyond description.

Ran about the house in a frenzy of gloomy disappointment and bitter despondency.

And strange to say, sad things were about to occur.

It was to be an eventful night !

Julia Norton, now the Honourable Mrs. Housefield, had left her child sleeping in its cradle, believing it to be safe under her nurse's guardianship.

But there were under-currents at work.

A deep plot was being wrought.

But ignorance is bliss, and she knew not what was about to take place.

The mother's mind was free from suspicion.

A terrible blow, however, was forthcoming.

A startling discovery in store for her !

For when she returned to the nursery, and walked towards the couch, where, but a few minutes ago, her child was sleeping soundly, and was about to imprint a motherly kiss upon its innocent forehead, her teeth chattered !

Her limbs trembled !

And she staggered back !

A cold sweat broke upon her brow.

Followed by a dizzy sensation invading her brain.

And an universal sickening feeling running throughout her whole frame.

Then she became pale as death.

Heavily her hands fell by her side ; and looking wildly around her — uselessly endeavouring to clutch a receding form in the darkness—she uttered a piercing, delirious shriek.

A shriek which brought the household upon the threshold of the nursery !

And now followed exclamations of horror and dismay.

The servants gasped with consternation when they heard the news, and the butler even was so thunderstruck by the intelligence that he allowed the lamp which he bore to drop heavily upon the floor.

The affrighted menials were soon around their mistress.

For they loved and respected her for her goodness.

But it was of no avail.

The unfortunate woman would break away from them, and, beating her forehead, exclaim loudly: "Oh, my child!—my child!"

For the news was heart-rending to realise.

The son and heir had been stolen!

The nurse had fled. The cradle was empty.

And the Honourable Mrs. Housefield was childless!

At length, exhausted by the blow which had so unexpectedly come over her, the proud Julia's eyes shone with a strange expression; her lips paled; her hand trembled; and she sank in a swoon upon the carpeted floor, from which place she was soon removed to her apartments.

For weeks the unfortunate woman lay upon a bed of sickness—between life and death—a prey to a raging fever; muttering incoherent speeches about her son—the child of her heart, her beloved boy—and raving about her deceased husband; and the family physician shook doubtfully his head, as if he feared a sadder conclusion than had hitherto been witnessed to the thrilling drama which had been enacted so unexpectedly, and within so short a period.

Julia, at length, grew better.

Gradually, she re-assumed her usual health.

But consciousness was worse than delirium.

She was now alone!

A widow—and a childless creature, pining for the loss of one who was the living picture of him she had so tenderly loved.

What had become of the nurse?

No one could say.

Detectives were hired, and paid handsomely, and sent through the length and breadth of the country.

A large reward was offered.

No less than a thousand pounds to him who should give a clue leading to the discovery of the nurse or the child.

But no one came to claim it.

It was a wonder to one and all.

What could have been the nurse's object?

Was she the hireling of the heir-at-law?

People thought so.

But the child's death must be authenticated.

One evening his clothes were found by the beach, apparently washed upon the shore by the waves.

Where was the body?

No one knew.

The stolen heir was reported to be dead.

The mother, however, would not believe it.

She would persuade herself that he still lived.

And what grounds had she for so concluding?

None, except a mother's affection; and knowing how fondly a doating parent clings to hope, the wise heads in the neighbourhood, like the family physician, shook their heads, and said there was nothing in it.

CHAPTER VI.

DICK SPALDING'S WANDERINGS—THE APPARITION BY THE BROOK—THE OLD GIPSY, THE WHITE WOMAN WITH THE BLACK MASK—A LONG STORY OF WOE—THE SILENT WALK ACROSS THE FOREST—THE LONELY PATH—THE DILAPIDATED HUT—THE DISAPPEARANCE OF THE VISION—THE PLOT DEEPENS—STILL MORE MYSTERY—THE BLOODY HAND ON THE WALL.

DOUBTLESS, it might have seemed strange to some of our readers that Dick Spaldings should have witnessed so quietly as he had done his wife's guilt; and many, we dare say, could be found who would persist in maintaining that his behaviour was impossible and improbable in the extreme.

But be indulgent, dear reader (dearest reader, I should say), if you are one of those frail creatures who, with all their faults, we do love still, and do not pass an opinion too quickly.

Many of those bright eyes who peruse me, know not, perhaps, what it is to be in love; but if they do, whether male or female, God help them!—we speak from experience—for they will find, sooner or later, that to meet with disappointment in love is enough to drive any one mad and frantic.

Unfortunately, it was so with Dick Spaldings.

At first, he had resolved to rush upon Will Spanton, but bodily strength had failed him; and when it did return, it was too late to prevent the foul deed ere it was accomplished; and reason dawning at last upon his lacerated brains, he then swore to carry out the frightful oath of revenge upon which we have dwelt in a previous chapter.

Had Dick Spaldings been a common mortal there never would have been any occasion to pen this tale; and it is sincerely hoped that it was fortunate that he was such as we will depict him, for it will give an opportunity to the writer to spend many pleasant hours in the company of those who cannot but take an interest in the events which are about to follow.

And now had Dick Spaldings followed at once the impulse of his feelings, and had he resolved upon taking a striking revenge upon his wife and her lover without any further delay, the probabilities are, that he would have gone in search of a weapon, and seized the first opportunity of destroying the lives of two beings, about whose guilt he could entertain no longer any doubt.

But when he left the neighbourhood of the "Lovers' Nest," so prostrate did he feel by the scene, of which he had been a spectator, that, for several minutes, he became plunged in a thoughtful mood bordering upon insanity.

He wandered anyhow, and soon strode away from the path, at the end of which he had fastened his horse; and not returning by the same way he had come, which was familiar to him, he took another road, which led more directly to the forest.

At times he was forced to bow his head, to prevent coming into contact with the drooping limbs of the great trees; but still he sped on, and it was only when he had entered the sombre solitude, and was left to more sober reflection, that he began to realise to himself the fact that he had lost his way.

He had walked several hundred yards, and now was descending an abrupt eminence, at the foot of which ran a shallow brook, when his attention was drawn to wild, delirious sounds, which emanated from a spot close at hand.

Dick Spaldings then stopped, and gazed carefully round.

The sound had ceased.

The farmer now felt thirsty; and, stooping over the brook, satiated his parched tongue with a few drops of water, which he was enabled to convey to his mouth by the means of his half-closed palms.

This refreshed him.

He was thus engaged when the same sounds again smote his ear.

The voice had now assumed a different intonation.

Before, it was harsh, and now, it sounded soft and sweet.

Sang a gentle lullaby, as if it were ushering some new-born child to sleep.

Dick Spaldings was lost in wonder.

What could all this mean?

Was he not alone in the forest?

Was it Jenny who had followed him?

Oh! if so, how could he have resisted the temptation of murdering her; how sweet her death would have been to him. But no, that would have been too quick a punishment—*it would not last long enough for him.*

Never would so paltry a retaliation compensate him for the hour which he had spent in the neighbourhood of the haunted mill—what he had suffered there no pen can ever tell.

Truly, this was a night of thrilling, stirring adventures.

The farmer looked up.

And staggered back!

Dressed in a long, white, floating robe, her dishevelled hair streaming upon her shoulders, and approaching him with a queenly gesture, behind a high rock that stood above him, he saw a woman.

She was about to sweep past him.

But his appearance struck her.

With starting eyeballs, and fearful looks he kept on gazing upon the strange vision, and beheld, with reeling brain and trembling limbs, her slightest movement.

A black mask covered the upper part of her features.

"Ah! ah! ah!" she shrieked, suddenly.

It was a wailing cry of anguish!

A cry that startled the farmer, and chilled his blood.

Then she stood still.

"Great Heaven," muttered the farmer, "what means this?"

And stricken with fear, motionless with awe, he stood like a statue in one spot, his feet rooted to the ground.

"Ah! ah! ah!" again repeated the woman, despairingly.

And then she raised her hand.

"Richard Spaldings is your name, aint it?" she inquired, slowly.

"Yes, it is," he replied, with a gasp.

"What brought you hither?" she asked, in a sepulchral tone.

"Why do you want to know, woman?"

"Will you answer my question?"

There was a moment of silence.

Again the woman with the black mask repeated her query.

"Tell me your reasons, for I know you not."

"Be it so, then," she replied, firmly, "you were happy *once*, Spaldings, were you not?"

What! could the woman know his secret already?

"Yes, once I was," he repeated slowly.

"Aye, once, I know; and how came you in the forest at the hour of midnight, for it is late, friend," she continued, firmly. "'Tis no time, surely, for happy husbands to leave their loving wives alone, exposed to—to temptation; ah! ah! ah!"

And the same mocking, derisive loud laugh echoed over hill and dale, near and afar, and mingled strangely with the breeze, and the ripple of the clear stream at the speaker's feet.

"Enough! enough, woman!" shrieked the farmer, aroused to anger by the stranger's allusion.

"Silence! silence! dost thou not hear the crow and the blackbirds of night mocking thee in derision?"

And the vision placed her long, bony, claw-like fingers upon her white, parched lips, as if to bid her listener to comply with her request.

The farmer was dumb.

"You were happy once, not so very long ago, either, Spaldings," she said, dejectedly.

"Evidently, she knows all," muttered the farmer.

"Know all!" repeated the woman, in a breath. "I do, Spaldings! There are few things that "Marian of the Glen" does not fathom. I once, too, was happy, Spaldings; but now I'm crazy, they say, and love only to brood over vice and crime!"

There was a pause.

Neither of the two beings who had so strangely been thrown together spoke for awhile.

At last, the woman with the black mask began:

"Can I be blamed for loathing the world, friend?" she asked, slowly. "You know not what tears I have shed; what sleepless nights I have passed! Once I was happy, too! Then life's stream ebbed on gently, and its clear, sparkling waters, day after day, brought me unalloyed happiness! Then I gloried in the name of a mother, and smiled with pleasure upon the charms of youth! Then I had a daughter in the morning of life—a sweet, lovely maiden, with soft, brown ringlets floating over shoulders by Venus unequalled; with a pair of bright eyes of heavenly blue, within whose lustrous depths might be read her pure soul's every emotion. But now the throbbings of the young heart have ceased to beat; nought of life's vivacity remains in the sunken, glazed eye; and Death's seal, for many years past, has left its impress upon its waxen, cold face: and I am left alone to pine, unable to visit upon the sons the sin of the father who hurled my child to disgrace and to ruin!"

Here the woman with the black mask ceased speaking; and, drawing the long folds of her white dress around her form, she remained motionless, listening intently.

"Your last words have brought sympathy to my ears, stranger!" the farmer now said. "Speak! can I in any way help you?"

"Perhaps you can!" slowly replied the vision; and, after a moment of silence, she continued: "But 'tis no spot to converse. Once I was happy; misfortune is now my lot! Once I smiled; now I weep! And this, too, will now be your lot, Spaldings! And thirst you not for revenge? If help me you will, follow me to my abode!"

The farmer reflected for an instant; and nodding, at length, his head in the affirmative, forgetful of the steed which he had left behind, he followed the steps of the mysterious woman, who majestically strode onwards towards a direction only known to herself.

Now, despite the feeling of awe which had crept over the mind of the farmer when he had first met the woman with the mask by the brook, he, nevertheless, resolved to ascertain, if he possibly could, to his own satisfaction, her real character.

With a steady step, he bore closely upon her track, not betraying any outward fear, or questioning her by any ill-timed queries, lest she should guess his inward thoughts, and discover that she had to deal with a coward.

But although silent, the farmer often wondered whither he was being led; for, having been born and bred in the country, he could not dismiss from his over-heated brain the train of superstitious musings which occasionally usurped it; and for being thus weak-minded, he was certainly entitled to some excuse, as the adventure which he had met with was extraordinary and uncommon in the extreme, to say the least of it, and highly calculated to excite the apprehension of a far more educated man than he was.

The vision led him to the bottom of a deep ravine, at the end of which was situated a small cottage, or, more properly speaking, a hut in a very dilapidated state indeed.

The only approach to it was by a narrow, winding foot-path, so over-grown with shrubs and tangled briar that they effectually concealed it from casual observers; and no wayfarer could, we feel certain, have found his way there, for the banks on either sides were shaded by stunted thorn and fir trees, which drew a scanty nourishment from the stony, gravelly soil.

When the woman with the black mask reached the outside of the entrance, she paused.

It was a low building, of brick and flint, with musty, green, old shutters, and half buried in the ivy, and parasitical plants, which grew in rank luxuriance around it.

Small as it was to all outward appearance, it was, however, large enough, we should say, for the occupant of it, who, being apparently single and unknown, was seldom troubled with visitors.

In short, it was one of those secluded retreats in which crime loves to brood, or solitary misanthropy retire from the world.

Whether it was devoted to either of these ends, or perhaps to both, the story will show as we proceed with our narrative.

Dick Spaldings wondered how old his mysterious guide could be.

It was dark when he had met her, and he had only been enabled to take a cursory glance of her, which had greatly frightened him, but now that the rays of the moon shone upon her through the interstices of the trees, and he could better see her, he began his survey in earnest.

Her step, though stealthy, had been firm, and her bearing queenly and erect, and from the quick pace which she assumed on nearing the abode, he could not but take her for a much younger woman than she really was.

The farmer thought she was, indeed, a strange looking creature.

Not an ounce of superfluous flesh could be traced upon her sinewy, iron frame, and through her black mask her eyes shone brightly, and with such a strange expression, that, notwithstanding the bold effort which he made to withstand her gaze, his eye cowed before its superior spell.

"None who ever entered this place before, Dick Spaldings, ever left it alive again," the woman began, after a moment's deep silence, having previously glanced around her, to see whether any one was in the vicinity, "but fear not to follow me, for no harm will be done to one who comes here under my protection."

And as a token of her promise, she stretched out her sinewy, bony, long hand.

The farmer seized it, and eagerly clutched it.

"'Tis sufficient, my friend!" she muttered. "And now you must in return promise never to divulge to any mortal soul that which you will see to-night!"

The farmer acquiesced to the woman's request.

Then she drew a small whistle from under her garments, and gave a signal.

She had been heard.

For another whistle answered her.

From whence did it come?

The farmer could not make it out.

He thought it proceeded from the bowels of the earth, and yet how could that be?

His curiosity increased tenfold.

And again he became more and more perplexed, for the door of the old house had ran upon its rusty hinges without any one touching it.

"Enter!" said the woman.

Interested beyond conception, the farmer delayed not in obeying his strange guide's request.

"Be not afraid of anything here, Richard Spaldings!" the woman began; "and, above all, be extremely cautious!"

The farmer nodded in the affirmative.

What was to be the end of an adventure so strangely began?

And he was about to turn round to ask the woman another question when he found that he was alone.

He rose to ascertain whether he could go out, but the door was hermetically closed, and he uselessly attempted to open it.

He was a prisoner!

His position was, indeed, an unenviable one.

That he was in the power of some strange being he could not but admit; and yet she had spoken so friendly to him that he could not believe that she meant to injure him in any way, or do him any bodily harm.

Still he felt uneasy.

All the tales of horror and blood which he had read in books came before him in rapid succession, and he remembered sundry incidents connected with ghosts and murderers which were far from cheering up his spirits.

There is always something terrible about a lone house!

The farmer, therefore, began to fret.

There are times in life when mental wanderings bring on more lassitude to the frame than any bodily exertions incurred, and it was so with the farmer.

He felt tired and exhausted, and was on the eve of drooping his weary eyelids, and to seek renewed vigour in comforting slumber, when suddenly he rose from the chair upon which he had sunk.

A sight had caught his eye.

A hideous sight!

A sight that startled him as much as the ghost of Banquo did King Macbeth!

Straight before him, on the damp, white wall, was the dark, clotted mark of five fingers, as if a bloody hand had been suddenly dashed against it.

There it was!

Glittering red!

Terrible and ghastly!

Horrible in the dying light of the fire!

That bleeding hand on the wall!

It seemed so like the realisation of his fears—so like a ghost risen from the dead to warn him—that he recoiled in horror from the grisly sight, and gazed upon it with bewilderment and fear.

All thoughts of going to sleep were now out of the question.

Approaching the door, he tried to listen.

But uselessly did he do so.

Quivering like an aspen leaf, again he listened; and he fancied he heard the subdued hum of several voices.

Men's voices, too!

What could it mean?

He was thus musing, when he felt an icy cold hand grasp his shoulder from behind with a grip of iron.

With a violent shudder, and a half-repressed ejaculation, he turned round to see who had thus unawares crept behind him.

"HURRAH! HURRAH, BOYS! UP SHE GOES WITH A SWING!"

"Hush! hush!" said a terrified voice, "don't make a noise, don't speak."

These were the words which were uttered in Dick Spalding's ears immediately after he had felt the strange grip, to which we have, ere now, alluded.

At first, a sickening feeling of awe had crept over the frame of the farmer, but now it gradually wore away.

For the speaker was not such as he had pictured to himself it would be.

She was a young girl, of about twelve years of age at the utmost, and, although you could not call her pretty, she was far from being ugly, and fantastic and strange was the appearance which she presented.

She was the most elfish mite of childhood he had ever beheld; with a small thin dark face, precocious beyond its years, and lit up by a pair of the most wonderful black, big, staring eyes that ever were seen.

Her dress was an odd affair; a short, red flannel shirt under a boy's jacket, and a boy's cap, crushed down on a tangled mass of short thick curls, from beneath which gleamed its odd, wild, cunning little face.

"Who are you, my little goblin, and what brings you hither?" the farmer immediately asked, in an astonished tone.

"My name is 'Griggles,' so they call me, and I have no mother beyond Marian, who loves me, so she says, although, when I laugh, she beats me, and very often makes my back very sore."

"And why does she do that?"

"Well, don't you see, she thinks I know too much, and she wants to close my tongue, and to make me see all and keep it to myself; but I can't do that."

The farmer was getting interested; he longed to hear more.

"Well, Griggles," he said, "and what do you know, then ?"

The young creature placed her finger upon her mouth, to enjoin silence.

"I cannot tell you now," she went on, "but do not stay here, that's all I got to say to you."

"Why so ?"

"Oh, come away from this place," she continued, without answering the farmer's question, "come away, I beseech you, if you value your life."

Thus speaking, she glued her ear to the key-hole, and listened intently. Then she rose.

"Don't make a noise," she muttered, "for if she sees you here, oh, then I pity you."

"If you wish, I will keep silent, but explain yourself." And the farmer gazed attentively upon the features of the young creature.

"Oh, I am glad you won't make a noise," she quickly retorted, and approvingly she held up her finger, and, for his compliance to her request, she gave him an approving nod.

"Don't you see, she thought I was asleep when you came here, but I am always on the watch, yes, that I am."

If a man was ever puzzled in his life, that man was Dick Spalding.

"And why are you always on the watch ?" he asked.

"To prevent dark deeds," she muttered, in a frightened whisper.

The farmer shuddered.

"And where do you sleep, my little preserver ?"

She bent her eyes downwards, and pointed to the ground at her feet.

"There, she said." And, before he had time to speak, she raised a trap beneath her, where could be seen a very tasty little bed-room, but small in size, as the space allotted to it was limited indeed.

"Am I not safe here, then ?" the farmer asked.

Griggle shook her head in the negative.

"What am I to do ?"

"Take to your heels, and run away."

"Easy to say, but difficult to accomplish."

"How so ?"

And the farmer looked towards the door. The girl understood him.

"Oh, I see," she said, "it is closed." And she stared knowingly.

"I am sorry I cannot conceal you in my room, they would soon find you, and we would both suffer then."

"Who do you mean by they ?"

"Old Till, and Kit, and Blage."

"Strange names, those."

"Very."

Then there was a moment of silence, which the farmer broke.

"Well, if they were to come up," he pursued, "what would they do ?"

This time Dick Spalding's voice shook with impatience, and he looked at the child with more curiosity than he had hitherto displayed.

"Why, they would put you down where they have put the others."

And the girl dwelt upon the last words.

"And where is that ?"

Here Griggle's large eyes dilated with horror.

"I cannot tell," she replied, "and do not ask me, I pray."

What could Griggles have to do with Marian ? What were the beings who dwelt in the Lone House ?

Such were the questions which the farmer placed to himself.

"I am a friend of Marian," he said, "so, young one, you need not fear, but I thank you all the same."

The eyes of the girl sparkled.

"You got no money, I suppose, that's the reason."

"Perhaps so. What if I had ?"

The creature was about to speak, when sounds were heard, close at hand.

"Farewell," she muttered, "she is coming."

Unwillingly did the farmer see her depart, he tried to stay her, but he could not do so.

For ere he could lay hold of her, the trap was raised. In an instant she had disappeared beneath it. Alone, now, was Spalding.

But his solitude was not so unbearable to him as it would have been had he remained in doubt as to the character of the place where he was.

When one is aware of danger, and ready to meet it, he is less prone to indulge in vague fears. To be wandering in the dark is terrible.

The farmer know, now, that the Lone Hut was a den of thieves, perhaps of murderers.

He was thus musing, when his attention was called to creaking sounds behind the wall.

But more about these, anon, and as the following chapter will contain revelations of a most extraordinary nature, we will now part company with Dick Spaldings, and revert our attention to the lads of the nineteenth century, whom we have left in no less a critical position.

CHAPTER VII.

A DISAPPOINTMENT TO BEGIN WITH—THE SECRETED DOOR—THE SLIDING PANEL—THE CAPTIVE MAIDEN—MOTHER MARTIN AT WORK—SCENES OF TORTURE—BOB O'LINK'S VOICE COMES IN STILL MORE USEFUL THAN HIS FIST—A TALK ABOUT BUSINESS—BLUE-EYED NANCY—THE TRIAL BY JURY.

SURELY the youthful band were not doomed to be baffled in their expedition !

From existing appearances, however, it would appear to be so.

The room where they had entered was empty—no one was to be seen, and, what was still more provoking, nothing to take away.

They listened intently.

"What can the meaning of this be ?" asked Koko-riko, in a disgusted tone. "That's a pretty go !"

And with his lamp he examined the room in which he stood, and gave way to a tremendous oath when he found that the furniture was coarse and worn-out, and that even the drawers contained nothing but women's clothes, which, to the best, were only stinking old rags, too worthless in their intrinsic value to be worthy of being bagged by the youthful thief.

But in his search he was soon disturbed.

Shrieks of pain now reached his ear, emanating from the lips of a woman in distress. She was close at hand !

Not twenty yards at the most from the boys.

Their curiosity kindled. They looked everywhere.

Felt up and down the walls, and yet could find no way of exit.

The mystery of their first adventure did not frighten them.

On the contrary, it only gave them renewed energy.

They should ascertain whether a dark night's work could not be prevented by them.

At all events they would not confess themselves beaten.

And it looked very much like as if something uncommon was taking place not far from the spot where they stood.

An instant or two elapsed, and then again wailing cries of pain were heard.

The same voice they had heard before, but this time more subdued.

At length Cannibal Jack gave way to an ejaculation of delight, and drew the attention of his companions to a low door evidently leading to an inward apartment.

It was a wonder that he found it out, for so much like the soiled and greasy paper was it that few, indeed, would have succeeded in discovering it.

They opened it. A damp and musty smell arose, and, stranger still, before them all was dark and silent.

"Be careful with the bull" (an abbreviation of "bulls-eye, we suppose), whispered Big Ned; "we must proceed cautiously, for who knows but that we may meet with greater resistance than we anticipated."

The boys clenched their life-preservers, and Cannibal Jack felt the edge of his poiniard, as sharp as that of a razor.

Big Ned's orders were at once complied with.

The low door evidently did lead somewhere, and feelings of the most intense curiosity usurped the souls of the boys, who were unable to account for the strange sounds which they had heard a few instants previously.

All bewilderment they waited.

But for a short while only.

Nought but the throbbings of their young hearts beating against their chests disturbed the silence which reigned.

Bob O'Link now gave the lead, immediately followed by Big Ned and all the gang.

Still more mystery!

They came to a concealed sliding panel.

At first they had some trouble to make it play.

But they were not to be frustrated in their design.

They were up to a move or two.

Soon, therefore, did they succeed in obtaining an entrance in a subterranean passage leading whither they knew not.

Ned stopped; and ere he proceeded he listened. "Silence," he enjoined.

Everything was now still.

Fearing not to be confronted by a superior force, he groped his way onward with cautious, stealthy steps.

Presently he arrived before a strong iron-studded door.

A survey convinced him of the madness of even trying to open it with the means which he had at his command.

He reflected.

There were, perhaps, living beings behind it! No doubt about it now!

Through the key-hole a light was perceptible.

He paused. Then he stooped. Suddenly a subdued exclamation escaped his lips.

Many would have started back, but he was too much accustomed to scenes of horror, crime, and cruelty, to be astonished or frightened at anything; thus, he only contented himself by muttering something inaudible.

What had he seen there?

"What is it?" the boys all asked in one startled whisper.

"Look!" he said.

One after the other his companions did so.

A cry of horror emanated from the lips of the youngest of those who were not yet so callous as to contemplate without a sickening feeling of repulsion, that which they saw.

But what could it be?

Laying supine upon her back, without one single garment to cover her form, was a young girl, dazzlingly handsome.

Fastened down by her arms and legs to a long, flat, black stone, writhed a beautiful creature, evidently a prey to the most intense sufferings.

Exquisitely formed was she.

Not above sixteen years of age could she have been, and although her features were not as regular as those which a Grecian sculptor would have chosen for a model, still they were sweet and expressive.

Her eyes were of a dark blue, but so heightened with sadness that they looked staring and inky.

Her neck was exquisitely modelled, her shoulders gracefully drooping, and soft and velvety was the white skin which covered her voluptuous breast, to which the plump solidity of youth had scarcely given place to the less exciting and more developed charms of womanhood.

Sweetly small was her hand, and symmetrical in its minutest lineaments were the thighs, and the luxuriant limbs, which seemed to wander in search of the prettiest foot that ever was seen.

To adorn a palace she would have been fit!

And like the humming-bird who delights his hearers in the nest of its choice, she was such as by her presence and her smiles would have rendered any home happy.

And yet, what was to be her lot?

The *bride of thieves*, perhaps!"

Sullied, contaminated by coarse jokes, the child of sin and lowdness, dragged against her will to a gaping chasm leading to ruin, left to die forgotten, like the flower robbed of its honey!

What?

Would you think that in a city containing over two millions of inhabitants such a girl could remain alone and friendless.

Is it possible that she is compelled to vegetate among beings of a class she abhors, if she does not wish to fling to the winds for a home of her own and a base existence that virtue which "the world" casts her off for not possessing.

Oh! good and charitable people, listen.

Add your voice to that of John Stuart Mill, M.P., the greatest thinker of the age; swell the ranks of our reformers, and see whether our monopolising manufacturers cannot be made to pay a better price for labour—whether the working man cannot get his own without "striking," and whether the last and more important point cannot be accomplished, namely, to give the white slave a better remuneration, and not, as it is the case now, just enough to starve, until she is forced to sin, and then because she sins to be driven off an outcast—"a nymph of the pave," who must die in the street or live in degredation.

Oh, wonder of wonders!

Was the poor girl, to whom we are about to introduce our readers, still pure and spotless?

Has she hitherto succeeded in preserving that innocence, for the loss of which our mother Eve forsook a kingdom of bliss.

And was that frame so fair—those charms so tempting, still uncontaminated by man's lustful and selfish embrace?

Poor girl, she suffers!

Here and there red marks are perceptible upon her faultless limbs, and just below the knee her skin is swelled by the over-strained pressure of the tight rope which keeps her fastened to the spot where she is stretched.

Her eyes shine wildly bright—bright with the delirium of pain.

For behold does not that dark curl which has got

astray and rests against her pallid marble cheek, and that black circle beneath the eyelids tells its tale of misery and of woe?

Who will deny, now, that there are people in the world who delight in cruelty?

Where are you, sceptical men, who talk a good deal and do but little to improve the welfare of suffering humanity?

Does not the following give you the lie?

Stooping over the poor creature, looking with demoniac fury upon those attractions which breathe love and youth, stands, with a birch in her clawy-like hand, an old woman whose career extends far beyond three score of years.

She is old and ugly, and loathsome in her whole appearance.

Her cheeks are parched and wrinkly; her eye hollow, false, and sunken.

Her hair of a dirty white, and she appeared indeed, like one of those female fiends, whose existence one would have believed could only have been confined to the records of some extraordinary improbable story.

"Ah, you refused to go out and earn money for me, you little vixen!" she was saying, "and now you will not tell me where my husband hid his gold."

Inert, and statue-like was the poor girl thus addressed. Her lips moved, but she spoke not.

The old hag considered for awhile.

She should now adopt a different plan. Where violence failed, kindness might be more successful.

"Do answer me, darling," she muttered, "you knew his secrets better than I did; tell me where he placed his money, and then I'll unfasten you, and I'll make a pretty girl of you, Nancy, and you will have it all your own way, and then you can buy yourself nice, tidy clothes, and look smart. Now, tell me, Nancy, and ——

She dreaded to speak for fear that the lie might choke her throat.

And, then, after awhile, she resumed, "Come, be a good girl, Nancy, then we will divide," she said, "come, come. Can I say anything fairer?"

She spoke those words in a quick, hurried manner, expecting, doubtless, a prompt reply.

She had read of the mysterious means adopted by the gaolers employed in the vaults of the Inquisition, and she felt sure of an answer.

She was not long in having it.

Nancy's breast heaved, and her white lips drew apart.

"Oh, do not torture me so!" she muttered, in a faint tone, "how can I tell you what I never knew, as Heaven hear me, I speak the truth?"

A smile, a satanical smile, played upon her listener's countenance. Her brow darkened.

"More of this," she muttered, "I will wring it out of you, I swear."

"Oh! for mercy's sake, spare me," the girl shrieked hoarsely, "spare me, spare me; I am dying."

The old hag, was, however, not to be moved.

Where suspicion exists, it is hard to shake it.

The gurgle in Nancy's throat seemed to be sweet music to her ears.

"By the Lord Harry!" Bob O'Link now exclaimed, looking in the room, through the key-hole, "I am fiddled, if the girl on her back ain't blue-eyed Nancy!"

"Mademoiselle, Mademoiselle Nancy," Monsieur Armaud muttered:

"Who is she? 'pon my honare, shentleman, she is a very pretty gal, or I ave make one grait mistake, Morbleu! Oui! she is bein belle."

And, with the two last French words, meaning very handsome, Mossieur Johnny twisted his moustache, and felt the brim of his turned-up hat, for, although a thief, Johnny adhered to fashion, and he had a great idea of the French style! (tile) excuse the pun.

"Nancy!" Kokoriko, the Hunchback echoed, and, making no allowance for the sad position in which the girl was placed, he opened his trap, and smacked his lips, with delight.

His was a low nature, and having seen the girl naked, his brutal passions were kindled, and he longed only for possession.

"I saw her in her shift one night!" Cannibal Jack followed, "and, oh, would n't have given a dollop for a big kiss? but the old man that used to look arter her, he was too watchful by halves, and if ——

"Hold your jaw, and be still, will ye?" Ned now asked, and giving a thundering good smack upon the cannibal's nose, he thus put a stop to a conversation, which, although very interesting, was anything but suited to the place where it was held.

The boys' attention now reverted to that which was going on inside. The poor girl's voice imploring for mercy was still heard.

But upon the stony heart of her torturer it produced no effect.

"Ah! is that the way you reward me for past kindness?" the old hag was saying, "There! there! Die, you little vixen, you little liar! Ah, you think that because you are young, and have a baby-like face, you can have your own way."

And the old woman dipped her birch in a jug full of vinegar which she had in the room, and began to inflict severe cuts upon the tenderest parts of the powerless creature.

"Oh, t'is does me good! Oh, t'is rejoices me!" the hag muttered, as she gazed with a fiendish smile upon the sanguinary fluid which began to ooze freely from the lacerated flesh. "Oh, where will your beauty be after a month of this treatment?"

Now let it be remarked here, that a murmur of rage and disgust escaped from the lips of the boys. And, had they not been afraid to rouse suspicion, and thus frustrate their plans, they would have given way to a bloodthirsty yell to relieve their outraged feelings.

But if the poor girl's prayers failed to succeed in moving her, an attempt from another quarter was more successful in its object.

It came from Bob O'Link.

Gently he gave one or two rat-tat-tat's upon the door.

Mrs. Martin's strength, which, while she was engaged in her fiendish work, had seemed to increase instead of diminishing, now forsook her as if by magic.

She glanced furtively towards the spot whence the noise had proceeded.

And immediately afterwards dropped her birch upon the ground.

Then she stood still.

Mute, breathless, unable to find a word.

At last she spoke.

"Who are you?" she asked.

No answer came from Bob O'Link.

"What want you, and how came you to find your way here?" she pursued, in a frightened tone.

At first, Bob O'Link knew not what to say.

But the "Swiper," when sober, was seldom at a loss for a word.

"I came here, and found my way *here* on business!" he said, rendering his voice as much like that of one of Mrs. Martin's female pals and neighbours as he possibly could.

"On business!" the old hag retorted. "Strange hour for business!"

"I am fully aware of that," Bob replied, "but it is upon most particular business. It is referring to your late husband's *business*."

Meanwhile, all the boys were laughing in their sleeves; the word business, which had been purposely brought in so often by Bob O'Link, adding considerably to their merriment.

"And what do you want with me?" Mrs. Martin asked once more.

"To speak to you, privately."

"But I can't."

"I am an old acquaintance."

"That matters not."

"Will you let me in?"

"Go back in the front room. I am astonished at you——"

She hesitated.

For she was about to say—

"At your impertinence to pry into a neighbour's affairs."

But as he came " on business," it was, doubtless, all right.

"I cannot go back," Bob continued, it is too cold there, and I have a good deal to say. And a little account to settle with you, besides," he continued, between his teeth; for we may as well here inform our readers that the Swiper had a grudge against Mother Martin.

One night he had got very tight, and created a great disturbance in the neighbourhood, and Mother Martin, assisted by "some highly respectable neighbours," had been the means of getting Bob a night's lodging gratis, which had ended in many more, for he having been identified by the worthy inspector who brought him before the magistrate for having been connected with a recent robbery, and given him the slip, he had been duly sentenced to six weeks' imprisonment, during which period he had often blessed the first cause of his incarceration.

Mother Martin was, however, still undecided.

"What is it about?" she asked again, previous to making up her mind to open her sanctum, where she by no means relished the idea of admitting a neighbour, who would naturally talk in the vicinity about her kindness of heart, and the treatment which she had inflicted upon the girl Nancy.

Bob was now getting rather impatient, and very disgusted at the delay, we need not add.

"Heavens above!" he whispered, still keeping up his voice, "how many times do you want me to repeat the same thing over. Are you deaf?"

The old hag reflected.

"It concerns your old man's gold," Bob now added, as a refresher, hoping thus to hurry on matters.

He so far succeeded.

Again Mrs. Martin mused.

She was too much excited to dream of anything unfair.

What should she do?

The boys were silent as the grave.

"The gold!" Mrs. Martin muttered to herself, "the gold! I may find it yet."

And she placed her hand in her pocket.

From it she withdrew a bunch of keys.

Then she looked at them.

"I hope you have closed the front door," she asked at last, in one breath.

"Of course I have; who ever heard of leaving street-doors open. Moreover, when there are so many thieves lurking about; of course I have, my dear Mrs. Martin.

The above conversation, which had taken place within the hearing of the boys, it may here be noticed, had the effect of illustrating a very old proverb; namely—

"It is an ill wind, that blows nobody any good."

For when Mrs. Martin had spoken, it reminded Big Ned that he had unfortunately dispensed with the precaution which she had suggested, and he had, accordingly, sent Kokoriko upon that very useful errand.

Just when he returned he heard a geering sound.

He was in time.

In time to enter the place.

The lock was rather rusty.

And it took a minute or two before the key settled in its proper place.

What pen could describe the anxiety of the street Arabs?

For let it be said to their credit, although they were at war with society, although they were compelled to keep themselves from starving by unlawful means; yet there were still among them feelings of generosity, which had kindled in their breasts a very natural rage against the old hag.

Nancy was well known in the neighbourhood, and a general favourite also.

Her birth was wrapped in mystery, and strange things were said about her; but, as other things now require to be described, we must attend to her in another part of our story.

The key rattled to and fro.

There was still a struggle going on in the old hag's breast.

Fear on one side.

Thirst for gold on the other.

Which would outweigh the scale?

The result was not doubtful.

For when, since the memory of man has there been a case when an old miser has been proof against recovering a long-hidden treasure?

The key settled at last.

The boys drew their breaths.

And now the heavy door ran upon its hinges.

But quicker than Mrs. Martin anticipated.

For down she went on a part of her body which we must leave our readers to imagine.

In the meantime poor Nancy had fainted.

There she lay, in a swoon, the very picture of death; her eyes closed, her lips pale and motionless, her white and pallid, yet handsome features, chilled by the gushing breeze which came in from the damp vault above alluded to.

Well, too, it was for her that she was insensible.

For the sense of being seen as she was, in all her nude voluptuousness, would have been more painful to her than all the cutting lashes which had so unmercifully been inflicted upon her.

Fate, you see, does all for the best.

And now let us return to old Mother Martin.

At first she had not known what to make of it.

She had thought of ghosts.

But Bob's voice, who soon threw off his disguise, left her no longer in doubt of the intentions of the promising specimens of humanity beneath her roof.

She tried to assume unconsciousness.

But although she was cute—very cute—(a very cute old lady was Mother Martin), she had to deal with sharp ones.

She kept her eyes shut; pleaded a pain in the back, and all that sort of thing.

But it would not do.

"This kite won't fly here, old gal," Cannibal Jack now said, "I see through you."

"As through a skeleton, for she is very short of one," continued another.

"Which means, that you are a very nasty old

hag altogether, and that you will be of very little use after your death, since it would be very difficult 'to bile you down for fat,' the price realised being barely enough to pay for the coals."

This coarse joke produced a general roar of laughter.

"Who talks of death?" Mrs. Martin asked, as if pricked by some concealed reptile, and, propped up by Kokoriko, she was soon on her "pins."

"Don't you like it? I do, and as Shakspeare says in his last work on kidneys?" Cannibal asked, with a brutal expression of cruelty darting from his greyish and cat-like eyes.

Mother Martin shuddered

She started back, and, raising her hands to the ceiling, shrieked for mercy.

Why ask for mercy?

What did she dread?

Had a forthcoming presentiment told her that her last hour had arrived?

Had a warning voice whispered ominous sounds in her ears?

And did she now think that a God and a merciful God, whose laws she had always discarded, whose sacred name she had, since her birth, outraged, was about to make her atone for her past life of vice and sin?

The boys were now surrounding the old woman.

"Blood for blood is our motto, old gal," Cannibal Jack now began, "you have been the ruin of many a poor girl, whom you entrapped into this crib and sold for gold. Your husband's made me what I am, and many more"——

And here Cannibal stopped.

There was a dead silence.

"She got me locked up, too."

"And when I brought two chains the other night she only paid me for one, and said the other was a bad un, and that was a lie, for I took it off a gent, and he was a gent, too, that carried all good about him, for he gave me a pound, instead of a bob, and he must have been a genuine one, or my name aint what it is."

"Now then, prisoner, what have you got to say in your defence."

This was spoken by a small boy, of about thirteen at the utmost, whom we have not yet described.

His name was "Dirty Dick," so called, because he had a very strong objection to linen, and a very great liking for eel-pies and cherry tarts, in the purchase of which he spent whatever money he could save from the clutches of those who employed him.

For the boys had their masters.

But let us dispose of one subject before diverting our attention to another.

Mother Martin was beginning to get very much out of sorts.

The boys, evidently, were not joking.

They looked like so many young cubs, thirsting for blood.

"May be we would have let you off easy," Bob O'Link now began, "and forgotten old sores, but this night's work has sealed your doom. To torture poor Nancy, as you have done, deserves punishment. Man despises you; Satan waits for you, and we, therefore, without a moment's delay, will become the executioners."

Not one voice broke the death-like silence which reigned around, and it was frightful to witness the staring, wild glare, which shot forth from the eyes of the youthful spectators of this appalling scene.

"Is this woman to die?" Big Ned now asked in a sepulchral tone, "this, boys, is her work."——

And with his finger he drew the attention of his companions to the senseless form of Nancy, from whose limbs the gore was slowly oozing:

"This would be murder!" a youthful voice now interrupted.

"Murder! murder is not the word here, boys; justice is what it can only be called."

"Once more, I ask you, my friends," Big Ned pursued, "to answer my question. This old hag has been the means of injuring us all, and many others besides."

"Sympathy for us poor forlorn outcasts, flung in the gutter to sin, she never had, and when she did ensnare thoughtless girls, it was to sell their smiles to the highest bidder. The black slave, ere now, has rebelled against the cruel owner who trampled him down, and galled him to madness. Are we white men to remain here indifferent."

"No! no! a thousand times no!" Loud and clear rose these words in the old hag's abode.

Mother Martin was now trembling.

Her sunken eyes were wild and dilating, her lips sprung white, and quivered apart, and her long lean, fingers sank in her parched flesh, her very breath suspended as if gasping for air.

There was something so solemn in that which we are relating that even the volatile Frenchman was serious now.

"Companions, we must bring this scene to a close. Think quickly and well over this woman's fate; form yourself in a jury, and if the majority of you bring in the accused guilty, I'll pronounce the sentence of death. The hand of the clock marks, now, ten minutes to one o'clock, when the hour strikes your foreman must bring in the verdict. And now silence."

Query, what was to be old Mother Martin's doom! Read on and see?

CHAPTER VIII.

THE HANGBOYS—A DISSENTING VOICE—THE VERDICT—PAT NOWLAN—THE HUNCHBACK HAS AN IDEA—BIG NED BUSY—AN OLD HAG'S RAGE AND DESPAIR—THE ROPE—THE SEARCH FOR PEN AND INK—AN ATTEMPT AT FLIGHT BAFFLED—WRITING FROM DICTATION—THE HOOK IN THE BEAM—THE EXECUTION—THE DEATH-AGONY—FINAL PRECAUTIONS—STOP THIEF! STOP THIEF!—THE BOYS TO THE RESCUE!

MANY years before we thought of writing, a great and illustrious French poet described with all the mastery and power of his fertile pen, the harrowing thoughts which are supposed to lacerate the brain of the convict who is about to be launched into eternity.

Read Victor Hugo's work called "Les deniers Jours d'un Condamné," condense all his phrases in a few words, change his days into minutes, and then only will you be able to imagine the feelings of Mother Martin, breathlessly waiting for the boys' verdict.

Life for many is a bitter lot!

Poverty is horrible, the sickening pangs of hunger are also terrible. To be penniless and friendless is an epoch in life that a good and merciful God never wished his image to go through—and yet how unwilling are all sufferers to die.

Let the cutting blast of adversity beat with unrelenting vigour against the houseless and the outcast, let the most excruciating pains distort the features of the patient on his bed of agony, and still death, dark, grim death, with its bony, long hand outstretched to clutch its victim, is a master from whose grasp humanity shrinks, and always endeavours to escape.

We have often been told, and remarked ourselves, that while engaged in pleasant pursuits, time flies with a rapidity which causes us to regret its consummation; but how long, also, on the other hand, do the seconds appear when threatened by some impending blow, which, we know, must strike us at a given time.

Fully conscious of the earnest and solemn character of the dark and real drama which the boys were performing, not a word escaped their youthful lips, and having, after two minutes' deliberation, resolved upon the step which they should take; with their eyes riveted upon the old clock, they were waiting for the metallic sounds which were to warn them them that the hour of execution had come.

At last the clock struck.

Bob O'Link now advanced in the centre of the room, and, with a ghastly voice, said :—

"Ned, we have made up our mind. We find Mrs. Martin guilty, with only one dissenting voice."

"And who's that?" the Bully asked.

"Pat Nowlan, sir."

The Bully turned round and gazed upon the boy, whose objection to the course which he was bent to carry out, seemed to excite his anger.

He was a youth of about fourteen, and was of Irish extraction, and he had been the only one who had mustered sufficient strength to give freely his opinion.

"And why, Pat, do you wish this woman to live?" he asked,

"Why, look here, Ned," said the boy, in a strong Irish brogue, "I know that the old hag is something like a fox, only a dale more cruel than that quadruped; I know, also, that there is'nt a dhrop of the thrue blood in the old spalpeen, and yet—"

"Enough, sir, 'tis no time for Irish romancing; the majority have found her deserving of the sentence, which we are about to carry out, and since you wish to kick against the bucket, you will be my assistant and I the executioner. If you object to fulfil my orders, here's the door, go, by all means, go—and you no longer belong to us."

Pat Nowlan reflected.

"Troth," he said, "I'll do as you wish me, by Gad. If there's a rale reason, as there must be, for her to be sent to the black gentleman, the devil a bit do I object to do the work.

There was a moment of silence.

The old hag was too thunderstruck to speak.

A storm was, however, gathering in her breast, and ere long it would burst.

Big Ned reflected.

He was thinking deeply.

"Prepare yourself to die, woman," he said, after a moment's forethought. "You have outraged this world, maybe you'd better think a bit about the next, now."

This sentence brought consciousness to the old hag.

Sounding loudly upon her ears, it caused her to remember the critical position in which she was placed.

Oh! how earnestly she hoped that some incident might happen by which she could save her old neck from the halter.

Suddenly she looked the speaker full in the face.

"Spare me! oh, spare me," she gasped, "and I'll give you all I got here; my wealth will be yours.

A loud laugh was the reply.

Then her shrieks became agonizing.

She felt that she could expect no mercy from her stern and heartless accusers.

And she burst out into a violent fit of impotent rage.

Her cries were appalling.

She cursed and swore.

Became fearfully violent.

Uttered the vilest of languages.

And shortly afterwards made a bolt towards the door.

But she was soon dragged back in the middle of the room, by the Cannibal, who, having guessed her intention, just stepped before her in time to hinder her flight.

Bob O'Link now came to the rescue, and holding her tightly in his grasp, he kept her as quiet as a child.

Exhausted by the vent which she had given to her feelings, she remained still. Stupidly and vacantly she gazed around her.

Big Ned, meanwhile, was ransacking the whole length and breadth of the room.

He was evidently in search of something.

"What are you looking for, Ned?" Bob now asked, seeing the minute inspection of his friend and chief.

Big Ned stopped.

"What am I looking for?" he asked, "A rope, of course."

"A rope!" ejaculated Kokoriko, the hunchback, echoing Ned's voice, "It strikes I have—"

"What?"

"An idea!"

And the hunchback placed knowingly his open palm upon his forehead, and his ugly face brightened with a vicious smile.

"An idea! demme, what do I want an idea for, you stupid?"

"I got an idea, mate, and an idea which will lead to the discovery of a rope. Whew! whew!"

This called Mother Martin's attention to the deformed, and, immediately afterwards, another of her shrieks rent the air.

Before every one else, she had guessed his intention.

"No, no, do not!" she muttered, "she, too, will rise against me, to accuse me."

But, heeding not the woman's cries, Kokoriko walked quickly towards the spot where Nancy was laying senseless.

Then, in a shorter time than we could describe it, he proceeded to untie the rope which had fastened the poor girl to the stone where she had been tortured.

Bob O'Link was soon behind him.

The girl Nancy opened her eyes.

A deep blush suffused her countenance.

Bob O'Link understood the meaning of it.

With praiseworthy conduct he took off a blanket which stood on an old bed in the room, and flung it over the girl's nude form.

A sigh of relief escaped Nancy's lips, and again she sank in a swoon.

"Hallelujah! Hallelujah!" exclaimed Kokoriko, "hallelujah with a vengeance. Who says that I aint a useful and enlightened member of society?"

Thus speaking he brought the rope to Ned, who eagerly clutched it.

It was wiry and slippery, it having been wetted in several places with poor Nancy's blood.

"Yes, that will do very nicely," he said, "how do you like the sight of this, old girl?"

The old hag placed her finger against her eyes, and, with a hideous growl, staggered back, with a shudder.

"Pen, and ink, and paper, is the next thing I want, Pat," Big Ned now said, carefully examining the rope as he spoke.

"Faith, and you'll get it, too, your honour!"

What did they want those implements of writing for?

This, we think, will be the question that many

of our readers will place to themselves, but let them not be too impatient for their curiosity will soon be satisfied.

Pat was not long in finding a bottle of penny ink.

Not so easily, however, did he manage to discover a pen.

At last he alighted upon a dirty old quill, which, judging from its general appearance, could not have been used more than once since it had been extracted from the featherly back of the useful bird to which it once belonged.

"Do you know how to write, old hag?" Big Ned now asked, turning round towards Mrs. Martin, who was at a loss to understand the object of her questioner.

"A little!" she replied faintly.

"Sit down, then."

Thus speaking, Big Ned, crammed down Mrs. Martin upon a rickety old chair, which creaked beneath the weight of its worthy occupant.

To Mother Martin these proceedings were a relief.

Hope began to buoy her heart with renewed freshness, for she, very wisely, thought that the longer they would be about carrying out their intention, the better the chance for her to see them frustrated by some untoward or unexpected incident.

A soiled piece of paper, at the back of which there was a voucher for three-quarters of a pound of "block ornaments," with which the good lady had regaled herself a few days previously, stewed with carrots, onions, and potatoes, and all the et ceteras, was next chosen and placed before the old sinner.

"Are you ready?" asked Ned.

The woman dipped her pen in the ink, and began to flourish it in a most ingenious manner, to show that she was waiting for further instructions.

There was something so ghastly-comic in the expression of the old girl's features, then sitting down, that were we endowed with the talent of a very rising young artist of our acquaintance, Mr. Edmund Hebblethwaite, we doubt not that it would have offered us a very good subject for the display of our pencil, and that we would have done far more justice to it with an illustration, than we could by attempting to describe it in tame English words.

"Write the following then," continued Ned.

Mother Martin took another survey of her quill, and then she wrote according to dictation.

"I do hereby pledge my oath to the following, and I beg to inform all those who will first enter this room, that no one is to be blamed for my—"

So intent upon her task was Mrs. Martin, that she jotted down the words as quickly as they were spoken, in a calligraphy of her own, which looked like as if a fly had been taken out of the ink and strayed anyhow upon the paper, to say nothing of the Queen's English, which read more like Hindoo, or any other Oriental language for which the reader may have a fancy.

"That no one is to be blamed for—" repeated Mother Martin, waiting for the next words.

"For my death," pursued Ned, "and that it is brought on by my own free will, being heartily sick of this world and every one connected with it, and more particularly the police officers, who, by their continual harassing, and watching of my conduct, have compelled me to have recourse to suicide."

Mother Martin had ceased writing when Ned had come to the word "death."

She, however, had waited until he had concluded his long sentence, and when he had, she tried to rise upon her legs.

But she found it hard to do so.

Guessing her intention, Bob O'Link's heavy grasp had been laid upon her shoulders, and had baffled her in her attempt.

"I'll never write that," she said, "I would rather die!"

"Well if it's all the same to you, you will have to do both, old stick-in-the-mud."

So saying, Kokoriko sprung by Mother Martin's side, and, being something of a scholar, notwithstanding her unwillingness, he compelled her by guiding her hand to write the whole of Ned's words, not forgetting to make her display, in bolder letters than the others, her worthy autograph at the bottom of the document.

As soon as the old woman had signed her name in full, not without having cursed him to her heart's content for his officious assistance, Kokoriko took up the piece of paper and examined it carefully.

"That'll do very nicely, mum," he said, with a grin. "The letters are rather crumbled, it is true, but, on the whole, it is a very creditable piece of writing; maybe you'd like to take a copy of it with you before you go?"

This facetious remark on the part of the deformed youth was the means of kindling, once more, the old hag's good temper, and should Kokoriko still be in the land of the living, he would up to this day have to thank Cannibal Jack for having prevented Mother Martin from flinging a huge jug at his head, which, at a moment when she was unobserved, she had seized hold of with the kind intention of knocking his brains out.

"Just be quiet, will yer? Cant you wish us your good-bye in a lady-like fashion; how can you expect civility from us after such a display of bad breeding?"

Thus speaking, Kokoriko kept on patting Mrs. Martin on the shoulders in a friendly manner, which, from the grimace which she occasionally made, would have led any one to believe, that now and then he was indulging in sundry good pinches, highly satisfactory to his revengeful mind.

Cannibal Jack, who for some time past had remained very silent, now spoke.

"Friends," he said, the streaks of morning are beginning to peep through the shutters, "let us not delay any longer, for if we do—something may turn up which may prevent us to give the devil his due. To delay much longer would be dangerous to say nothing of our safety. What think you?"

Jack's proposal was at once acceded to, and the wisdom of his remark having been felt by one and all, the boys proceeded to inspect the room.

After a while they succeeded in discovering several hooks which ran the whole width of the ceiling, and which, at some time or another had been used to hang old clothes to dry.

A gleam of satisfaction now lit up the features of Ned, and in earnest he began to grease the rope with a tallow candle, which lay upon the mantelpiece.

Through the strongest hook the rope was subsequently passed.

To dwell upon the abject supplication of Mother Martin, beseeching her pardon, would be useless, here; suffice it to say, that after a few minutes a running noose was placed around her neck.

When the hemp came in contact with her flesh she gave vent to a tremendous oath, and unable to harm any of the boys, she attempted to tear her clothes assunder, in the impotent fury of her fiendish rage.

Suddenly, the boys' attention was called to a distant noise.

It sounded like as if steps were approaching; they stayed their proceedings for awhile.

Big Ned started!

"HELP! HELP! HELP!"

But their forebodings were groundless.

The woman's attempts were frustrated.

We are only relating a scene which occurred some years ago, and for a description of which we could refer our readers to a file of obsolete papers, but as we do not wish to pander to the morbid taste of the age, we are compelled to proceed, quicker than we otherwise should, with the course of our story.

Perhaps some of those who read this have been present at an execution.

Let them fancy, then, what must have been the feelings of the boys who had constituted themselves judges and executioners.

We are bold and fearless—as novelists we understand our duty—but should an apology for what we are about to write be found necessary, will not the following true statement be a very good substitute?

How many convicts have there been who have had to pass through that evil, gloomy-looking, low door, which leads from Newgate Prison to the scaffold, who did not deserve their punishment half so much as the old woman to whom we are about to direct our attention.

Some of those branded felons, whose names have been ushered into oblivion, whose remains have been burnt with hot chloride of lime, and flung like dirt in the common burial vault, were guilty, doubtless, and atoned, with the loss of their life, for deeds prompted either by passion, jealousy, or blighted hopes; but we may well ask here, were they callous to all feelings, and had their lives been sifted through, would they not have unravelled here and there an act of charity, or a deed of kindness, perpetrated when the scaffold was but a name?

But was it so with Mother Martin, and was she entitled to forgiveness?

Let our readers form their opinion.

The executioner was on the look-out, and Bob O'Link's herculean strength was once more called into requisition.

With one lift, he propped Mrs. Martin upon the chair.

"Oh, do not, do not, my good young friends!" she muttered, "do not——"

But her cries were flung to the wind.

At last, finding that it was useless to supplicate any longer, her mouth foamed, and she tried to call out—

"Murder!"

But the word died in her throat.

The signal had been given.

With a movement quicker than thought, Bob kicked the chair from under her feet, and she was hoisted in the air.

"Hurrah! hurrah, boys! up she goes, with a swing!" yelled Kokoriko; and then there was a creaking sound—a subdued jerk—and with one pull, the old hag's neck was close to the ceiling.

There was something dreadful in the death-agony of that old woman, whose career had been one of continual wickedness, whose very name and deeds were so many blots upon humanity.

For a minute or two her eyes glared villanously, her toothless mouth screwed with hideous contortions, her hands crisped, her feet tore the vacant space asunder, and writhed with the last agonies of death.

But her earthly sufferings were not to last much longer; for presently there was a gurgle and a rattle in her throat, her hands hung heavily by her side, her limbs fell down, rigid and cold, and she hung motionless and still.

She was dead!

Ay, dead! after having died as she had lived; braving to the last hour, the ire of Him, before whose Supreme Tribunal she was about to appear, to give an account of her stewardship.

A mournful silence now reigned.

The horror of the crime which they had perpetrated, pressed upon the boys' minds, and many among them now repented having participated in the deed which had been committed.

Big Ned and Kokoriko, however, were not in any ways moved by the sight which they had witnessed; for, owing to the former's suggestion, Mrs. Martin's ugly corpse was lowered from its present position, and with the help of the boys, carried to another part of the room, where it was fastened by a strong handkerchief to a thick nail, which was stuck in the side of the wall.

An upturned chair was afterwards placed beneath her feet, to give currency to the document which was on the table, and everything was arranged in a manner which could leave no doubt as to her death being her own act, thus dispelling from the boys' shoulders, whatever suspicion might have been formed against them, for the murder of the old woman.

Satisfactorily did Big Ned gaze upon his handywork. Then he turned round to his youthful band.

"Boys," he said, "what's the matter with ye? Methinks I see some of ye chicken-hearted. What for? Is it because you have rid the metropolis of one of its most loathsome inmates, and thus performed an act of charity, for which the Society for Suppression of Vice ought to reward you handsomely. Nonsense! nonsense! cheer up, boys, and drive away dull care. Instead of standing there, uselessly, look out for number one, and see whether you cannot find some of the 'stiffun's' ready."

This speech produced the effect which it was meant to convey.

The boys fell to work with a zest and a zeal which deserved its reward.

Up flew the cupboard, and bang went the old locks of the drawers, and minutely, indeed, did they search everywhere.

Under the bed, in the mattrass, in every nook they pryed, but still uselessly.

That there was money somewhere, was a fact which could admit of no doubt, but where was it? that was the question.

And lo, behold! they were about to discover a heavy chest, which stood secreted in an out-of-the-way corner, and which, doubtless, contained valuables, when they were startled in their operations by the shrill sound of a whistle.

A peculiar whistle, to which the youthful band could not be mistaken.

Black Kettle's warning!

His signal of retreat!

"Away, away from here, boys," muttered Ned, in a startled whisper. "Away from this spot, if you wish to save your necks from Jack Ketch's clutches."

And he flew out of the room.

Followed by the band.

"What's up?" asked Kokoriko, as soon as he saw the nigger.

"Why, don't you hear?"

The boys listened.

Plain enough were the words.

Sounded distinct and clear.

Rose loudly above the hum of the crowd.

Always the same two words.

"Stop thief! stop thief!"

"The devil a bit will I stop him, if I sees him," Pat Nowlan mused, "sure its bad enough to be caught oneself, without helping to trap others."

"Stop thief! stop thief!"

"Go it, yer cripples," muttered the Hunchback.

"Stop thief! stop thief!" again broke the silence.

Big Ned was getting impatient.

He knew not what to do.

It was all very well to take it so coolly, but very shortly it might be the case with themselves.

But they did not fear the bobbies.

They were in force, and prepared to meet them.

"I say, boys," Bob O'Link now ejaculated, "our club is rather limited in number at present, and we want a reinforcement. Four of us were sent to the Reformatory, three days ago, and our grand master and chief is on his way to the Settlements, or, at least, taking a trip across the sea for the benefit of his health. What shall we do? Save the thief, if he be a boy, and make him one of us, or let him be flung in prison?"

"Save him, by St. Patrick, and all the saints in Paradise," exclaimed Nowlan, "I am on for a shindy; and although I aint a Fenian, I'll fight a peeler, any day. Yes, troth, I am on, and I'll not flinch when the hour comes, as Father O'Leary, the parish priest of Mullingar, used to say, when sitting before a quart bottle of old widow Lannigan's rale mountain dew."

"What say you, boys?" Bob pursued.

"Save him from the bobbies!"

"To the rescue, then!"

"To the rescue!" the boys replied, simultaneously; and away they went in a body towards the spot, where could be still heard the distant hum of voices, and the words—

"Stop thief! stop thief!" rising loudly above any other living sound.

"And what was to become of Nancy?" the reader may well ask—poor Nancy, whom we have left in company of her late torturer's hideous and ghastly old corpse.

CHAPTER IX.

A GLIMPSE INTO THE PAST—HARROWING THOUGHTS—THE GOOD LAWYER—AN INSIGHT INTO FAMILY AFFAIRS—AN INTERESTING INTERVIEW—THE APPEARANCE OF THE EARL OF MOUNTCARSDEN—HIS UNMANLY ACCUSATIONS—HIS TAUNTING SNEERS—MR. WARKIRK'S INDIGNATION—HIS ABRUPT DISMISSAL—HIS RESOLVE.

YEARS had now elapsed since the tragic scenes which we have related in the chapter dwelling upon lady Mountcarsden, and, yet, although time had traced its deep furrows upon her ladyship's brow, and many would have forgotten the existence of a child whom, in all probabilities, they would never see again, she, however, felt a lingering spark of hope which buoyed her heart with sanguine expectations.

The perusal of high-class literature, where the author, like ourselves, writing for the million, ever studies himself to interest and educate those whose morals he never loses an opportunity of improving, is always a very wholesome pastime; in which we would strongly recommend our hearers to indulge, but, unfortunately, the book which the patrician lady had been reading could not come under the above denomination, as it happened to be one of those sensational stories whose baneful influence can scarcely be exaggerated.

It was one of those trashy three-volume novels, got up in a very elaborate style, which had been through six editions of two hundred and fifty copies each, a capital dodge, lately tried with very little success, however, by a great humbug of a publisher, and it was written, as a matter of course, with a total disregard to Lindlay Murray's grammar, a very trifling point, considering the high sounding name of the author, hitherto a total stranger in the world of letters.

Worse than all, it was calculated to instil into less experienced minds than her ladyship's, very erroneous ideas of right and wrong, and had been altogether a very unprofitable speculation, notwithstanding the publisher's Scotch blarney.

This being said, our reason for alluding to it can easily be understood when we inform our readers that, strange to record, in this chapter, which her ladyship had just been perusing, she had become deeply interested in a fictitious episode incidental to the plot where was related an occurrence very similar to that in which she had herself played so very prominent a part in real life.

No wonder, then, that the past flashed vividly before the patrician's imagination, bringing forth a train of painful thoughts which had been the means of causing her to ponder over bygone events, and to feel anew the harrowing pain which she had experienced when she was, comparatively speaking, a maiden budding in sober womanhood.

The lady Mountcarsden was thinking of the past.

It is a fact, strange, yet true, but which deserves to be recorded here, namely, that we long far more ardently for the things which we do not possess than we feel pleasure in owning those that already belong to us, and so it was with her ladyship.

She had one daughter alive, and living with her. It was the offspring of her subsequent union with the Earl of Mountcarsden—whom she married a couple of years after her first husband's death, as we have previously stated—and yet she had a most unaccountable antipathy against Blanche.

The child, whose fate was unknown, as yet, to her, she felt she could love.

For her likings and dislikings no one can account.

The earl, on the contrary, was very partial to Blanche.

He was a rakish, dissipated, nobleman, without one spark of generous feeling beating within his heart.

Brought up in the lap of luxury, he knew not what want was, and when he used to see needy people in the street, he shrunk away from them as if they were beings whose contact was dangerous in the extreme, to such a high-bred, polished, and elegant individual as he considered himself to be.

He was madly fond of sporting. He kept a stud of horses, among which many a favourite had figured from time to time, but lately it was whispered in fashionable circles that the earl was very hard pushed, and doubts were entertained (should his luck continue to forsake him,) about his being able to meet his liabilities at Tattersals.

As much as a man of his stamp could love any one, the earl loved his daughter Blanche with a strange sort of feeling, such as he would have experienced for some favourite hunter, or some pet dog; and he would have been very offended had he been told that she was not the pattern of a father.

When we introduced our readers to Lady Mountcarsden, father and daughter were not at home. The family had received a general invitation for a select assembly given by a foreign ambassador to the Court of St. James, and it was expected that it should be a grand affair.

Her ladyship, however, had declined going, and preferred remaining alone.

"Oh, could I but find my lost son," she was muttering to herself. "He would be rich, for I have not yet signed his birth-right away, as they want me to. By his father's will he will be entitled to £10,000 a year, but if I give my authority to cancel the document, the fortune then becomes that of my husband, and my son is a beggar, but without me they can do nothing. This is so far satisfactory."

And her ladyship smiled with a sad smile.

"Oh! money, cursed money!" we may well exclaim here, 'enpassant,' "what harm had'st thou not done? Base, vile coin, what crimes have not been perpetrated to obtain thee? The ties of kindred are wrought asunder. The sweet joys of home are forgotten. The limpid stream of life is filled with mud, and its course uninterrupted where gold mingles with its waters."

Search, reader, the annals of Newgate Calendar, glance over the police reports of every day, become acquainted with the sad dramas of intimate life, and then, will you find that money has been the cause of many a sorrow never to be alleviated, of many a tear which has left its stamp upon the faded and worn-out cheeks of Mammon worshippers!

Again her ladyship reflected deeply.

She was thus thinking when she heard the tramp of footsteps moving along the carpeted floor which led to the room where she stood, and very shortly afterwards a powdered footman appeared upon the threshold of the apartment.

Lady Mountcarsden languidly raised her eyes.

"My lady," the steward began, "Mr. Warkirk wishes to see you; he has been told that your orders were not to admit anyone, as you were unwell, but he insists upon an interview."

Thus speaking, the menial presented to her mistress the metal salver, upon which lay the above named gentleman's pasteboard.

"Mr. Warkirk," retorted her ladyship, quickly glancing upon the name. "Show him up at once."

A few instants elapsed, and Mr. Warkirk made his appearance.

He was a man of about sixty years of age, and his features, which must have been handsome at one time, had considerably suffered from the progress of years, and from the many weary hours which he had spent in stooping over the numerous parchments and deeds which filled his office, for, let it be said here, the visitor was a lawyer, and although he was supposed to attend to the interests of the Mountcarsden's family, he was his ladyship's special adviser, and was, on that account, very much disliked by his lordship, who knew that the professional man studied far too much his better-half's welfare, to receive and carry out any instruction emanating from him, likely to be detrimental to the Lady Mountcarsden's private fortune, which she derived under settlements.

The man at law was one of those creatures who, knowing their own worth, and knowing, besides, that throughout life they have done their duty, and acted in a straightforward manner, which fears no rebuke, feel at home wherever they go.

For him the dazzling, gorgeous, pompous display had no attraction, and produced not any impression upon his penetrating, honest nature, and, albeit, he was not proof against the very excusable ambition of making money; he, nevertheless, allowed not his conduct to be swayed by any client, however powerful that client might be.

There is no doubt that had lawyer Warkirk been less susceptible, and, like the greater part of his colleagues, studied his own interest only, he would, by having adopted the latter course, have made a far more considerable fortune than he could boast of, but as he ever bore in mind, "That right is right, and wrong is wrong," and strictly adhered to this motto, he had obtained a good name in professional circles, of which he was so proud that we feel no reluctance to assert on his behalf that no amount of gold could, in his own opinion, have compensated for the loss of it.

Lawyer Warkirk knew the world thoroughly. Being daily accustomed to see calling at his office owners of some of the proudest families in the land, he was no novice, and, having besides, been engaged in several heavy law-suits involving inheritances to colossal fortunes, he had frequent opportunities of taxing mankind according to its fair value. Few men had seen more than he had, and in glancing upon the many iron safes which he had in his large, square, well-ventilated rooms, upon which shone in bold array high-sounding names, he could not but remember sundry dirty transactions of which certain big-wigs had been guilty of; and although he was such as could make allowance for the thirst of gold, so prevalent at all times, he often pondered upon the strange record of crimes and virtues, of blighted hopes and broken hearts, of ruffianly behaviour and of disinterested actions, which were contained within the four walls of his professional abode in Lincoln's Inn.

For an instant or two, her ladyship gazed upon the countenance of the lawyer, and after having, doubtless, made up her mind as to what she would say, she stretched out her hand towards that of her visitor to welcome him in her sanctum.

"How kind of you, Mr. Warkirk," she said, "to come here at this hour of night. I felt very lazy just now, and I assure you that your visit is very acceptable to me, as I need not tell you it always is."

The man-at-law bowed with a sober parliamentary bow.

"I feel very much flattered at your ladyship's high opinion," he replied, courteously, "but think not that I came here only to intrude upon your privacy."

"Intrude! intrude, Mr. Warkirk, you have proved too faithful, and too conscientious a keeper of my secrets, for such an idea to obtain currency in my mind; besides, you always have studied my interests too well for me to look upon you in any other light besides that of a friend."

"My lady, I only have acted like a man of honour, and a gentleman, and am not entitled to any praise for it; but now, allow me to tell you, that if I came here to-night, I had an object."

"An object, Mr. Warkirk?"

"Yes, my lady."

"And what is that, pray?" the patrician woman pursued, burning to hear the tidings which the man-at-law had brought her.

"It concerns the Fairfield property."

"Aye."

"And, of course, one who is dearest to your soul."

Lady Mountcarsden became thoughtful.

And she listened intently.

To whom could the news relate, except to her son?

Perhaps she was about to become acquainted with his fate.

Under that impression, she kept her eyes rivetted upon the lawyer, and knowing how systematic and slow Mr. Warkirk was in divulging whatever information he had to convey, and feeling convinced that many instants would not elapse, ere he would acquaint her with the duties which had prompted him to find his way to Belgrave-square, she resolved not to say a word which might have the effect of interrupting the thread of a communication, which from her manner, it was evident to perceive she took a deep interest in hearing.

"You know, my lady," the lawyer began, "what I have often told you before, as long as there is life there is hope."

The lady Mountcarsden nodded her head approvingly.

"There are few professions, you will agree with me, my lady," the lawyer pursued, "where better opportunities are daily offered to its practitioners to witness the accomplishment of the above saying."

Again her ladyship corroborated the statement.

"Day after day," the lawyer continued, "we are called upon to be spectators of most extraordinary occurrences; a client who has emigrated for a quarter of a century or more, on his return may hear of a large fortune left him by a relation about whom, he, perhaps, never dreamt, and in a very short time see the realization of dreams which years and hard toil abroad failed to accomplish. Another enters our office, as poor as Job, and leaves it rich as Crœsus. There are also cases where I could tell you of men who, with plenty, knew not how to take care of it, and died in want."

Lady Mountcarsden was well accustomed to the long preface of the lawyer, and, although she felt interested beyond measure, she dreaded to speak for fear of postponing for a few instants the real purport of his communication.

"I have not been speaking so many idle words for the sake of argument, my lady," the lawyer now resumed. "If I have ventured on one or two illustrations, it was to prepare you for one still more astonishing. Would it not be scarcely credible, my lady, if I were to tell you that, after considerable trouble, and no lack of expense, I have succeeded in tracing the spot, where five years ago, lived, in utter ignorance of the large fortune which was his own, a youth——"

"Oh, is he alive still?" her ladyship quickly inquired, for her heart told her that the good lawyer's words reverted to her long-lost son.

"He was at that period, my lady, but more I cannot tell."

This was good news for the bereaved mother.

To her it was like the healing of some bleeding wound.

It brought renewed freshness to her desponding heart.

Her breast heaved, and, unable to restrain the joy which the last words produced upon her soul, she rose from her seat, and walking with quick strides towards the lawyer, she took his hand and pressed it eagerly to her heart.

"Oh, thank you, Mr. Warkirk," she said, "thank you."

The lawyer was annoyed.

Although a good-hearted man, he was of that cool disposition which abhors anything like a demonstration.

He was, however, too refined in his habits to show by his manner the vexation which her ladyship's enthusiastic behaviour had produced upon him, and making allowances for a mother's feelings, he succeeded in summoning a smile upon his lips.

"Oh, dear Mr. Warkirk, will I ever be able to thank you enough?" her ladyship began afresh. "Friendship is too weak a word to express the feeling——"

She was about to add more, when the drawing-room door was flung open, and his lordship made his appearance.

As if she had been surprised in the perpetration of some deed of which she felt ashamed, thoughtlessly did her ladyship drop the lawyer's hand.

A dark scowl flitted across the nobleman's brow.

He was evidently playing his own deep game.

"I should rather think so, too, my lady," he began, "but it is rather awkward for the husband to suggest to his wife what she should best say under the circumstances."

Her ladyship rose indignantly.

The lawyer remained silent for awhile, as if stricken with palsy.

The truth had not yet flashed across his mind.

He was still dull of comprehension, and no wonder, either.

He was, however, about to speak, when his attention was drawn to his lordship.

"'Tis an ill wind that blows no one any good," the nobleman was saying, "and this night it has been so with me, for, after all—Blanche's indisposition, which was the means of causing me to return from the assembly earlier than I intended, has proved a blessing instead of otherwise. By the Lord Harry, I could not believe it! Still everything has been for the best, since it has enabled me to become the spectator of a very interesting interview meant seemingly for any one else besides the husband, I should fancy."

Lawyer Warkirk had hitherto failed to understand the purport of the Earl's words, but he could no longer remain blind to the insult which was so openly flung against her ladyship, and resenting it on her behalf, he at last gave way to his feelings of indignation, and advancing boldly towards the nobleman, he asked him what he meant by his strange conversation.

The Earl of Mountcarsden, however, was not to be hindered in his scheme.

"What next, Mr. Warkirk," he exclaimed, quickly retreating backwards, "what! would you dare to assault me, sir?-oh! 'tis plain enough you are in league with my wife to insult me in my own house." And he rang the bell to summon assistance.

"My lord, I assure you that you are mistaken," the lawyer resumed, in a more collected tone, which he knew was best suited to the critical position in which he was placed.

The nobleman smiled sarcastically,

"I beg of you to be silent, sir," he exclaimed at last.

"My lord, I cannot."

"You cannot?"

"I must and will speak!"

"It is useless; the loving position in which I found my wife—your attitude towards her—"

"My attitude!" the lawyer exclaimed, livid with rage."

"Yes, sir, your loving attitude. Would you deny it?"

"My lord!"

"It is perfectly unnecessary to prolong this interview—a mere waste of time, I assure you."

"My lord, we were speaking of a matter which concerned her ladyship solely."

"Ah, I doubt it not, Mr. Warkirk."

"My lord, for your name's sake, let me explain."

"An explanation is useless, I repeat."

"I insist upon clearing her ladyship from any suspicion."

"Which I might have formed against her," the nobleman retorted quickly. "I dare say you do. In your place, I would act precisely the same; but if I refuse to believe you?"

"To doubt my word?"

"Yes.—What then?" The earl asked, sneeringly.

The man at law could find no reply.

There are times when too much impudence strikes us dumb.

It was so with Mr. Warkirk.

Meanwhile, his rage was being kindled within his frame; and, had he not feared a "fracas," he would willingly have tried his strength with that nobleman, whose sarcasms had galled him beyond description, and roused his temper to a pitch, which, in any other place, would have led to violence.

Mute and silent her ladyship was listening.

"And, now, Mr. Warkirk," the nobleman pursued, "after what has passed to-night I must beg of you to leave my rooms at once, and never to allow your presence to darken the porch of my house."

"My lord, you will think otherwise when——"

"I shall have made up my mind to let you act as you please, then I shall—certainly not before. Now I understand the purpose of those long interviews which you had with her ladyship relating to that brat."

"A brat who stands between you and ten thousand a-year, my lord!" the lawyer now said, exultingly, delighted, at length, to find an opportunity of retaliating against the nobleman.

"And who was only a pretext to conceal a woman's unfaithfulness," the nobleman resumed, quickly. "Never mind, though; it is no use dwelling upon such matters. Very cleverly managed, Mr. Warkirk, but I saw through it at last, and spoilt your little game; a great pity, I grant, but very—very satisfactory, at all events, to the party injured."

The lawyer's mouth was foaming with rage.

He was not easily roused, but once so, his temper was frightful to witness.

"My lord," he gasped, "your conduct is truly in keeping with your tarnished character, for, think you I do not see that you are endeavouring

to trump up a fictitious charge against one whose
unsullied fame——"

"Go it, old fellah! Go it old fellah! a tribunal,
however, will soon decide whether the Lady
Mountcarsden is to be the mistress of a pettyfog-
ging lawyer, of an old libertine, or whether the
Earl of Mountcarsden is not to obtain a divorce."

"A divorce! I'll baffle you there, you blot upon
humanity!" the lawyer exclaimed, and impelled
by his justly outraged feeling, Mr. Warkirk made
a bold attempt to seize his lordship's throat, but
he was this time defeated, for, when he was about
to rush upon the earl, he felt a tight grip behind
his neck, and, turning quickly round, found himself face to face with the butler, accompanied by
two stalwart servants, who, at their master's request, led the visitor down stairs much quicker
than he had found his way up the steps about an
hour previously.

"You are witnesses to this man's assault," the
nobleman said, addressing the menials as they left
the room; "ere long, I dare say, you will be placed
upon your oath about it, and have occasion to nar-
rate this night's work."

With imprecations upon his lips, and bitter
inward curses, impelled by his rage, the lawyer,
meanwhile, was being dragged roughly down the
steps, and it was only when he found himself in
the street that he was enabled to gather his scattered thoughts.

"I must find out the youth, somehow," he muttered, "and, if possible, bring the husband to my
mercy, and comfort and happiness to her ladyship's
heart."

Thus speaking, the lawyer plodded his way home,
not, however, without giving a thought to her ladyship, whose fate he pitied from the bottom of his
heart, as the scene which he had just witnessed
confirmed him in the idea which he had previously
formed of the peer, namely, that he was one of
the lowest villains that ever trod the earth; a man
who would shrink before no crime, or no deed,
however dastardly, to carry out his schemes.

Now, it must be well borne in mind, that if the
lawyer resolved to begin the war, the Earl of
Mountcarsden, was not a man to allow the grass to
grow beneath his feet.

Their objects were different, indeed, and many of
our readers, doubtless, would like to know the result before-hand, but, unable to tell them so now,
we must beg of them to follow quietly the march of
events.

And now we will glide to another chapter.

CHAPTER X.

THE SEA-SHORE—THE PENSIVE YOUTH—THE STORM—
THE SIGNALS OF DISTRESS—THE VIVID FLASHES OF
LIGHTNING — THE DOOMED VESSEL — HELP! HELP!
HELP!—THE SHIP WRECKED—THE FLASK OF BRANDY
—THE DIALOGUE — STARTLING COMMUNICATION —
THE DAZZLING PROMISES — THE STOLEN HORSE—
AWAY ON THE ROAD.

WHERE the sight wanders over the broad expanse
of the waters, and can contemplate the fury of the
Ocean, heaving like a woman's breast in labour,
where the rocks are washed by the surging tide,
and the white crested wave dashes with a plaintive
sigh against the stony substance which hinders its
course, where many a broken spar of some doomed
ship, mastered by the storm, mingles with the foam
which bathes the pebbly shore, a youth was standing, with a thoughtful eye, and a palpitating heart,
gazing upon the sublime scene before him, and
dreaming of running away to sea, to place many
miles between him and the home where, but a few

hours ago, his mother had been insulted, and his
boyish respect and affection crushed in the bud!

The air was thick and heavy.

And, similar to the ominous calm which precedes some more than usually terrific outbreak,
there was a pause in nature, and the elements
seemed to have stopped their ordinary fluctuations
to summon sufficient strength for the gigantic
effort they were about to make.

"No; I will not return home!" was muttering
this youth, who was no other than our old acquaintance, Harry Spaldings, the farmer's son. "I'll
to sea. Had I deserved the treatment to which
father subjected me, willingly would I have sub-
mitted, but to be abused and spoken harshly as I
have been, and, moreover, when there was no reason for it, is a thing which I will and cannot forget!"

How many boys have, like the farmer's son, in a
fit of sulky despondency taken a rash step, of
which they cannot see the folly at the time, but
which they have often too much occasion to regret
having followed on the impulse of the moment—
when grown sedate and wise they conjure in after-
life visions of the past, and think how different
might their lot have been, had they refrained from
listening to an evil angel's voice, ever on the watch
to lead them astray.

A faint peal of thunder now comes from afar.

The dark, lowering sky is illumed with a blue
vivid flash, and reveals to the naked eye the ocean
in convulsions.

Like the signal fire which heralds the beginning
of the battle, it appears to awaken nature from its
lethargy, and one awful warning hurricane sweeps
over the country, and the waters swell terrifically
at the dreamer's feet.

Leaves are dashed from the boughs, the lightning
cleaves the air, the trees topple and fall, struck by
the blast. The biting, fitful gusts of the wind dash
the rain in the boy's face, and the storm rages in
its sublime fury.

Harry is unable to move.

There he stands, by the sea-shore.

His feet rooted to the ground.

What was that?

Lightning—an awful, vivid, terrifying flash—followed by a roaring peal of thunder, as if a hundred
mountains were rolling over on each other in the
sombre canopy of heaven.

The gale continues.

The power of the elements is at its height.

What a wild torrent of wind and rain!

Another flash!

A wild, blue, bewildering flash of lightning
streams across the bay, for an instant bringing out
every colour in it with terrible distinctness.

There is a lull in the wind.

Suddenly broken by the loud report of a gun.

Boom!

Another flash of lightning!

Boom! boom! boom!

And the gun keeps on firing.

Harry has seen it.

A ship in distress!

A vessel, dancing upon the waters with broken
masts.

It approaches the shore!

Oh, could the rain begin to fall in heavier torrents
and subdue with its weight the raging waves?

But the wind renews in strength, instead of
abating.

The dark, lowering clouds are still gathering.

Look out! Look out, for a continuation of the
hurricane!

Hark!

Cries of agony are heard in the distance.

By the bright glimmer of the lightning, Harry sees the crew on ship-board, hard at work—the passengers kneeling down in prayer.

But it is too late!

What can a frail piece of timber do against such might?

For it is a terrible night.

Again the blast shrieks and howls.

Thirsting for victims.

The gaping grave is opened!

It yawns ominously.

See! See!

A ship on its beam-ends.

How terrible!

Is it not a mournful sight?

Louder and louder are the supplications for help.

Evidently the crew are not willing to die.

But, what strength could hinder her fatal course?

With giant strides she approaches the shore.

Ah! what!

Her progress has been arrested.

What is that fearful crash?

That smashing of planks?

Is it the timber coming into contact with the sunken rocks.

Boom! boom! boom!

They are resolved to call for help.

Boom! boom! boom!

And another bright flash succeeded the reports of the gun.

She is still afloat.

How dreadfully she is tossed by the waves.

Up she goes!

Down again!

Up, up again!

Still she dances upon the waters.

A toy in the hands of the ocean!

Again she rises with a huge wave.

Not beaten yet!

But like a conquered foe, she swims but for an instant.

For there is another crash.

A creaking, hollow sound.

The pumps are going.

Then she fills.

Like a mere log, she swims round, a prey to the tornado.

Still the lightning sweeps across the dark waters.

The stern is already beneath the foam.

There is hope.

Aye! aye! hope still.

But, no!

Shrieks—voices of pain are wafted to the watcher by the sweeping gusts of the wind.

Where are the lights of the vessel?

The last beacon left to the mariner, who would venture out on such a night?

They have disappeared.

Oh, look at that gigantic wave.

Crash it goes against the ship's side.

This is too much.

This is the last blow.

For there is a bubbling of waters.

A whizzing sound.

It is all over.

She is gone for ever and evermore. . . . .

All is silent on the coast.

The ocean's thirst seem to have been gratified.

One victim this night is enough.

And the storm gradually subsides.

At last everything is still, still as the very grave, where the doomed vessel has foundered.

All hands lost, all foundered to the deep dark waters, doubtless, to become the food of the porpoise and the shark!

Who says so?

What's that?

Real, or delusion?

"A life to be saved!" mutters Harry.

In an instant he is on the sea-shore.

He has rushed to the rescue.

He is now on the beach.

The rocks towering above his head.

He waits.

Sees nought.

Oh, yes, there it appears again.

A wrecked man.

He is exhausted.

Can he yet be saved?

The receding tide will take him back again.

Happily Harry is there in time.

Help! help! help!" mutters again the drowning man.

And he stretches his cold hands from which life is gradually ebbing.

Harry waits for the tide.

Then it returns towards him, huge and gigantic. Yet he fears not.

His duty is that of a Christian, and God will not allow him to perish.

"Help! help! help!" gasps deliriously once more the drowning man.

Heedless of danger, Harry plunges in the roaring waves.

The boiling surf and the bounding spray submerge him.

But he rises victoriously.

Bent upon his praiseworthy work, Heaven gives him renewed strength.

And, in no way undaunted, he struggles against the waves.

Swimming, wading, scrambling, he dashes towards the spot whence the cries have been heard, and where a dark human form is to be seen appearing and disappearing from his gaze.

At last he succeeds.

He is satisfied.

For within his grasp he holds the hair of the drowning man.

With a superhuman effort he drags him out of the water.

They carries him to the beach.

And lest the returning wave from whose fury a life he has wrung, should rob him of his hard-won treasure, with a slow and staggering step, Harry winds his way towards the entrance of a cliff-worn cave, where only the roar of the sea is heard, and its strength powerless to harm.

The drowning man is now upon the sand.

He tries to rise upon his feet.

But 'tis useless.

With a groan, he sinks upon his bleeding knees.

And, with a convulsive shudder, lays prostrate upon his side.

The brave youth, however, is not disheartened.

Bending over him, he tries to bring him back to life and consciousness.

First he chafes him.

Then he bathes his child temples, and speaks to him in a soft, friendly voice.

The stranger languidly opens his eyes.

The soft, warm hand of the youth has recalled his answering spirits back from death.

And, beneath Harry's gentle touch and trembling care, the wrecked man gradually recovers.

Now his glance meets that of the youth.

A sigh escapes him, and he stares wildly around him to ascertain, doubtless, the fate of those whose livid corses will, doubtless, be hurled by the tide against the bleak shore.

Then he gives way to a curse.

A curse in such an hour, too.

When death was recently so near !

'Tis dreadful.

Harry tries to move.

He cannot.

Each limb of his seems weighed down by tons of lead.

And now, the moon, which had long been hidden by the clouds, begins to shine.

The yellow glare lights the sea, and slowly works through the interstices of the rocks, which are scattered over the upper part of the cavern, and form nature's canopy to the wild abode.

Harry now contemplates him whom he has saved.

He is a man of about forty, tall, heavy and muscular, his features are harsh and irregular, and a long, uncouth, unshaven beard covers the lower part of his countenance.

His hair is cut short.

Red and swollen are his wrists, and every appearance of having been lately pressed by manacles.

Harry notices not these things.

But we, as authors, who have the privilege of seeing all and knowing all, wish to inquire into these suspicious signs.

Who was the stranger ?

Could he have been an *escaped convict ?*

And would Providence have permitted one man, perhaps the worst of a cargo of three hundred souls, to live, when the others had been hurled into a watery grave at a moment's warning ?

Harry took off his coat, and placed it under the exhausted man's head.

"How do you like that pillow ?" he asked, slowly.

The man smiled, and his glance, which had a piercing and glassy expression, wandered upwards and rested upon the youth's features, with a steadfastness which could only have been compared to that of a physician minutely examining his patient.

"Any one saved besides myself ?" the stranger renewed, in a faint tone of voice.

Harry mournfully shook his head, and a deep-drawn sigh escaped his lips.

"I fear not," he muttered.

The ship-wrecked man remained silent for a while.

He had to deal with a boy !

He was old, if not in age, at least, in experience, and he knew how to play his cards.

"You must be cold, my friend," now said Harry, gazing upon the the shivering frame of his companion.

The man looked at him.

"I am," he said.

And it was no idle boast on his part, for his limbs trembled with a nervous chill, and his frame shook with inward pain.

"You want a fire," said Harry.

Again the man smiled, and not a word did he utter, to prevent the good-hearted boy to kindle a flame in the abode where Fate had thrown him.

Harry looked about him.

There were shrubs and pieces of wood about, doubtless, dried spars of some forlorn vessel, destroyed by the blast; the remains of some gallant bark who had left the docks able and strong, and who was fated never to return to the port where many a kindred heart was expecting her return.

Harry collected the materials around him in a very short time, and kindled a glowing flame.

The wholesome warmth soon brought the shipwrecked man to perfect consciousness.

He wavered.

What should he do ?

Tell that youth his own tale—his story of blighted hopes and misery—or deceive him ?

Harry was a good boy.

Youthful, handsome, beautiful, with a heart hitherto unsullied by contact with the world.

An outcast clings to new affections !

What should our new acquaintance do ?

Harry, with his big, blue eyes, with his soft, velvety hands, with his sympathysing soul, which was perceptible in its minutest look, rested upon the shipwrecked's features.

The man looked at him.

He passed his hand athwart his brow.

Then he mused.

"Who are you, lad ?" he asked, at length, "and how came you by the sea-shore, to save my life ? Destiny is wayward and strange. You are but a boy, and yet you have done what men would have failed to do; for you have preserved the existence of a fellow-creature."

Harry again gazed upon the speaker.

He was about to speak.

But the shipwrecked stopped him.

"The fire is burning brightly, lad," he said, "this cave is lonesome and quiet; we fear not to be interrupted by any new-comer, do we ?"

Harry made no answer, but, with a steady step, he walked towards the opening.

Then he scanned the broad expanse of the sea.

Before, tempestuous, swelling, and heaving with dark, inky, foaming waves, clashing asunder, now grey white, smooth, illuminated by the pale glare of the moon.

"No; we are alone," he said.

"And likely to remain so ?"

Harry nodded in the affirmative.

For he looked abroad and he saw no living being. The firmament was covered with bright, sparkling stars. The ocean heaved with a steady spell, and the waves came and beat against the shoals with a murmur, which, could they have spoken, would have said, we stop here because we can go no further.

The shipwrecked man, who was struggling against sleep and exhaustion, now felt his wet garments.

From his breast he withdrew a flask, filled with rum.

"Drink, lad," he said.

Harry took a long draught of the intoxicating liquid, and swallowed it as if it were water.

For his exertion had made him thirsty; and his parched tongue clung to his palate.

The man smiled for the third time.

"He will be drunk !" he muttered. "Once he is gone he is *my own.* Men forget all when they give themselves to an exhilerating power which knows no bounds; what will a youth do ?"

Harry gradually began to feel giddy.

He loathed the sight of the man, whose life he had snatched from the waves, and he longed to say so, but the drink, the cursed drink, as the ranting teetotaler preachers would say, was working its way, and his mind was getting filled with wayward enthusiastic thoughts, which unravelled the future before his inexperience, boyish age, in bright dazzling colours.

Who can adequately describe the bounds of a drunken man's imagination, leave alone that of a boy ?

"What's your name, lad ?" asked the shipwrecked, with a convulsive shudder.

"Harry ! father called me," replied the boy, drawing himself up to his full height, while a dark scowl flushed across his brow, a scowl which implied—What right have you got to cross-examine me so ?

"SACREBLEU! THIS IS A SMOOTH CARPET!"—[SEE NO. 6]

* The shipwrecked was no novice in the ways of the world; he knew, by experience, the real character of mankind.

Therefore, he felt, by the boy's demeanour, that he had gone too far.

"Excuse me," he said, in a drawling voice, which he endeavoured to render as weak and plaintive as he could, and a good comedian on the stage of life was he. "Excuse me," he continued, "if I have been too inquisitive, but you are my preserver, but for you, I should be dead now, and, of course, I wish to know to whom I must, one day, pay my debt of gratitude."

All Harry's dislikes vanished like shadows before so palpable a speech.

And leaning, once more, over the prostrate man's shoulder, he pressed his rough hand into his own.

The shipwrecked now turned his eyes towards the opening of the cave, and his glance rested, with a startled stare, upon the vacancy.

"Listen to me," he said.

The boy opened his ears wider than he had hitherto done, and prepared himself to hear what he foreboded, if his anticipations proved correct, would be a most startling communication. Attentively he gazed upon the speaker, who began the following:—

THE STRANGER'S STORY.

"The ship to which I belonged, and whose sad end you witnessed, was called the Black Wolf, and left Liverpool a week to-day.

"We experienced very rough weather, along thr coast. Our canvas was not once filled with a faic wind, and we kept "tacking aboutship" all day and night long.

"I have seen rough weather ere now, but I do not remember ever having passed such a week on ship-board, and were it not for the doom which awaited us in the end, I may truly say that I am not sorry to be once more safe on the shore.

"But 'tis useless to dwell any further, and as I can perceive by your glance that you are getting in-terested in my narrative, I will proceed with it without disguising any thing from you.

"About a month ago I was employed in a large warehouse in the city, where I acted as foreman, at a salary of three pounds a week.

"Although my position was such as many would have envied, still I was dissatisfied with it.

"An incident then occurred which I was far from expecting, and which, had I not been shipwrecked, would have led to the realisation of dreams into which I have long since taken a pleasure in indulg-ing.

"One morning my principal received a commu-nication from his correspondents in Sidney, inform-ing him that they were in want of a trustworthy, honest man, to whom they could confide their in-terests.

"While I remained in the service of my employer I always gave him general satisfaction, and, as he had often stated to me, that if a chance presented it-self, he would not lose an opportunity of forwarding my welfare; on receipt of the communication above alluded to, he at once came and asked me whether I would like to go abroad.

"He dwelt upon the sorrow which my departure would cause him, and the loss which he would feel at my absence, but still left it open to me to choose my own line of conduct.

"Since I can remember it, I never recollect hav-ing had parents to watch or take care of my steps in life; I am also unmarried, and thus having no ties to retain me at home, I soon made up my mind, and replied that he would find me ready at any time which he would deem fit to appoint.

"My principal then left me, and said he would very shortly prepare my testimonials and pay me my remaining wages, with a small present, which he would give me as a token of his high regard for my past services."

Harry was listening attentively.

The tale was a plausible one, and he took a keen interest in it, like many other boys, doubtless, would have done, moreover, emanating from the lips of one whose existence he had preserved.

"Now, for deciding to go abroad, I had two reasons," the man renewed.

"And what were they ?"

"Well, here is one to begin with, my boy: Eng-land is a very good place, a capital place, indeed, none better in fact, for those who have either in-terest, wealth, or patronage to back them; but for the hard-working man, who is ambitious, and wishes to rise above his sphere, and to make a fortune, re-lying upon his exertions only to carry out the same, it is the last spot in the world where, in my opinion, he can look forward to success.

"John Bull talks about his citizenship, his free-dom of speech, his independence, and uxultingly boasts of the name of Briton! And yet where's his freedom, his liberty, his independence ? They are mere words, empty sentences, absurd bravadoes. At home, he is taxed like no other in the world—a free and democratic citizen, he is made to support a court, from whose hollow pa-geantry, and gorgeous display he derives no earthly benefit—the ministry ruling the land—he is not admitted anywhere; and the Sunday, which is the

only day in the week left for recreation, is as dull as a deserted city, all places of amusement being strictly closed. All appointments with good salaries are filled by scions of the aristocracy, or their hangers-on; and with his earnings he has to pay rates and taxes, which, in the event of his failing to meet, causes him to be driven out of his holding, where a shivering and starving family gazes upon the cupboard, empty through the exorbitant price of food."

Harry was looking steadfastly at the speaker, endeavouring to fathom his inward nature, and although he could not have accounted to himself for the liking which he took in his speech, still, he was gradually getting more and more interested in his conversation.

"And have you got any cause to complain of society, then ?" he asked, with an earnest, and thoughtful tone of voice, "from your bitter man-ner it would appear so, friend."

An indescribable expression now swept over the man's countenance.

"No," he said, "I have not; but is not what I have stated true ? The market is overstocked. The supply exceeds the demand, and unless a man is fortunate—very fortunate, there is nothing left him but to starve."

We hope, sincerely, that our readers will not look upon the words which we have written, as sentences of Gospel, which must be implicitly be-lieved by one and all. In the stranger's speech, there was, doubtless, some truth; but as it is only one individual's opinion, the right from the wrong should be carefully extracted, and due allowance made for a freedom of language, which, in a novel, at least, is never denied.

"This is my first reason for wishing to leave England," the man renewed, after having brought the flask to his lips, and swallowed from it a draught of the cordial, to which, evidently, he was accus-tomed, for he passed the back of his hand across his mouth, and immediately continued—

"But there is another besides——"

"And that is——?" the boy went on.

The stranger here drew his breath, and remained silent for awhile, as if he were collecting his thoughts, and preparing an answer to the youth's query.

"Because I long to improve my condition, to become rich, as rich as a Crœsus, and in England I see no way of doing that. There is a land, though, that seems friendly and hospitable to the emigrant, and there I will go."

Harry's eyes sparkled.

Many a time, at school, he had fretted upon his stool, longing for the end of the lesson-hours; and many a time, in glancing over the sea, and following the track of some outward-bound vessel, whose white canvas spreading before the breeze, glittered in the glowing sun, he had formed an intention, which his father's behaviour had determined him upon taking.

"Australia, with its vast resources," the stranger resumed, noticing his listener's glance, which be-trayed the sanguine hopes which buoyed his heart, "with its endless tracks of uncultivated land, its rich mines its glowing vegetation, offers scope for talent and energy.

"There is room for the bold and the free in that far-off country.

"In the Land of the West a man is a man; an in-dependent spirit need never quail before the glance of the bloated aristocrat!

"No red tape routine, no conventional imbecili-ties in that rising territory!

"In the jungles, and in the wild prairie, the emigrant inhales satisfactorily the free air of his being, and knows that he is lord and master over that which surrounds him.

"The blue sky is above his head, the broad expanse before him, and if the remembrance of an ungrateful country is betimes wafted before him, when he enters a populated town he soon forgets his grievances, when he glances upon the proud banner which floats gloriously from the government house, reminding that if one of England's sons cannot thrive at home, her possessions are wide and distant, and that he is shielded by the first flag of the world, telling him in its mute, but thrilling language—

"'Here, there is a fair field and no favour, and like the mightiest peer of the realm, you can ascend the torturous road to honour and fortune!'"

Beyond a doubt this was a glowing speech, an enthusiastic speech, which would have kindled the hopes of many a less sanguine youth than the farmer's son. Thus our readers will have no occasion to wonder when we tell them that it was the means of exercising a strange spell upon Harry, and that he, there and then, resolved to link his fate with that of his sanguine companion.

"And when are you going to Australia?" he asked.

"Very shortly," replied the stranger. "But, firstly I must return to London to see my respected and kind employer, and ask him for a small advance, as all my goods have been lost in the doomed ship."

Harry's glance fell.

His youthful mind foreboded no delay, and he hoped to step on board of a vessel twenty-four hours after his conversation.

"Why do you want to know so particularly?" the stranger asked with a strange smile.

Harry was about to reply, when the word died in his throat.

When the lips of the speaker had drawn apart, he had noticed a toothless jaw, and his eye had sparkled with a fascinating, glassy expression, which had awed him.

The stranger, with a quick perception, noticed the boy's reluctance.

Guessing the cause which had provoked it, he worked his physiognomy to a friendly, kind aspect.

"What ails you, my boy?" he asked. "Are you afraid of me? Of course, I am not astonished at it. If I looked at myself in the glass I dare say that I would scarcely recognize myself. It was rough work on board, lad; no time for shaving, and my toggery which, I do not suppose, has been improved by the pickle process which it underwent, is not that of a howling swell—what think you?"

And the man laughed.

"Would you like to come with me, my boy?" he went on, "somehow or another I feel an affection for you; you saved my life, and if you do not object to the friendship of a hard-working man, there is my hand and shake it, and let us pledge our troth by a bumper of this here stuff."

So speaking, the man offered Harry the flask.

"No, thank you," he said, "I had rather not. I am not accustomed to spirits, and I fear to take more."

"Nonsense! nonsense, lad; drink away, it is A I., and it cannot hurt you. It is the best drop of rum I have ever tasted, and but for it I know not what I should have done."

Yielding to the solicitations of his companion, Harry took a long draught from the flask.

A cloud, darker than had hitherto obscured the man's countenance, now swept across his features, and a bright gleam of satisfaction shone forth from beneath his lowering, dark eye-brows.

"I've got an uncle in Australia, my lad," the man said, "and if what I heard is true, he is the richest man in Melbourne. He is not married, and I am, of course, his heir. If he likes, he can leave me all his wealth; and when it is my own, I know with whom I can divide it—with the bright-eyed, good-natured lad before me."

Harry heard no more.

Mechanically he allowed his hand to be grasped by the speaker.

The spirits were now working their effect upon his brain.

He felt mad—craving for more.

And he asked for the flask of rum.

He was now intoxicated.

The god Bacchus had inveigled him in his net, and he had lost all reasoning powers.

Occasionally, lucid thoughts came across his mind, and he would have wished to return home, to seek repose upon his tidy, little couch, to wish his mother good-night, and receive the parting kiss ere he slumbered for the night.

But it was too late now.

He glanced towards his companion.

Could he have been deceived?

Could the tale he had heard, and to which he had been so intently listening, have been a tissue of falsehoods to lead him to err.

He tried to speak. But the words would not flow.

There were incoherent speeches, without any purpose or meaning.

Then he placed his hand to his head, and passed it athwart his brow, where he felt a splitting headache.

The cavern was swimming around him.

The fire seemed filled with spectres advancing towards him, to seize him.

And he staggered towards his companion.

"I say, you seem queer, my boy. What's the matter, are you taken with the blue devils?"

And there followed a derisive, loud, wringing laugh.

Then the stranger rose.

And stood immediately before the cracking embers of the wooden fire.

Harry sank upon the ground and tried to sleep.

But he could not.

Then he heard the man muttering words to himself, and the following reached his ears:—

"Damme, if I aint as dry as an herring, and every bit as salt, I'll be bound. I likes a bloater with a drop of cooper; I wonder whether my friend the shark, would have thought me toothsome. A piece of fresh meat is good in its way, and, I dare say, that they would not have objected to it. But it matters not to them, whether I live or not for wont they have a glorious feed to-night? Only think three hundred souls all drowned, and I the only one saved out of the lot! By Jingo, I never could have thought it possible. But ah! I forget. I could not die. Hav'nt I wings to fly? Aint I called Wild Ralph, the gaol bird? Of course I am. But where's my wing, that useful little feather of mine, which if it does not enable to fly through the space—at least helps me to clear the path of any objectionable character who would wish to obstruct it. Yes, where is it?"

Thus speaking, the man's rough hand lost itself beneath the folds of his coarse garments, from which he soon withdrew a leathern scabbard, which could not have been above one foot in length and one inch and a half in breadth.

Harry now gazed upwards.

A nervous shudder now chilled his frame, his lips paled, and his eye remained riveted upon the man with a ghastly stare.

The stranger was minutely examining the shining blade of a tasty poniard, upon whose steel edge, the boy thought that he noticed *fresh stains of blood.*

Perhaps he had saved a murderer's life!

"Yes," the man muttered, "it is all right, not hurt by the water, good for future work, yet."

And with a cotton handkerchief, which he had dried before the fire, he wiped the stains off the stiletto, and carefully placed it in its scabbard, and consigned it once more to his pocket.

"And, now, lad, hurrah for the road!" he said, exultingly, advancing towards the youth, whom he tapped gently on the shoulder.

Harry, who had been lately plunged in a deep reverie, soon sprung to his feet, and his glance met that of the speaker.

With a supplicating gesture he asked him to allow him to leave the cavern, and return to his home.

"No, lad, I can't do that, you must come with me," the man began, "if you don't like the life, you can always leave it, but part with you I will not. Boy, I love you! I thought my heart was callous and ungrateful, but I was mistaken, I feel it now beating like it has never done before. I will reform for your sake if I can, and we will try the New World together. I want a friendly voice vibrating upon my ear, I want a kindred heart to sympathise with my fate. I have been lonely, a forlorn outcast long enough. Heaven has saved my life, given me a companion, there may, yet be a chance left for the felon and the haunted cur!"

Here a deep-drawn sigh escaped the shipwrecked man's lips.

What a sudden change, was it genuine?

Now, the sensations which Harry had experienced since he had left the paternal home, had been many, thrilling and extraordinary in the extreme.

They were such as would have made a deep impression upon a full-grown man, was it astonishing then that they were the means of plunging the boy's mind in a temporary vacancy.

What between the liquor he had drunk, the excitement by the sea-shore, the conversation with the stranger, and his hopes and disappointment, his brain gradually sunk in a fog of delirium, and he allowed himself to be led away by his mysterious companion.

And it seemed to him that a veil fell upon his eye.

And, mechanically, he trod on through a dark forest until he came to a halt, and fancied he heard the neighing of a horse and the clashing of hoofs against the ground.

Then he remembered no more.

He was alive, true, but his mind was gone.

And when he awoke once more from his lethargy, he found himself on horseback, fastened to a saddle, behind his companion.

He recognised his father's steed.

Tried to remonstrate.

Supplicated for a hearing.

But it was useless.

Away the horse went.

Away it dashed, with a bounding canter, and foaming nostrils.

Now along the soft bank.

Then upon the hard stoning of the high road.

Never slackening its pace, never relaxing its swift, rapid, hard trot.

Away! away! away towards London-town, **away** from the spot where Harry left those he still loved —away towards the metropolis, where he was to meet with a series of adventures which we will leave him to relate himself when we see him again —an event which we may as well inform our readers here, will not long be delayed by us, as we are confident that they feel as great an interest as we do, in the fortunes of the youth, whose generous nature, and kindness of heart, are sure to enlist the sympathy of those who have made his acquaintance in our company.

CHAPTER XI.

THE VAULTS OF DEATH—THE MYSTERIOUS APERTURE— THE LAMP—THE SLEDGE—THE SIGNAL—THE STRANGE CONCERT—THE DARK CELL—THE FUNERAL PILE— THE MYSTIC CHAIR — THE HYENAS — THE BLACK BRETHREN OF THE CRYSTAL DAGGER.

HAVING left the farmer in a very critical position in a previous chapter, it makes it incumbent upon us to tell our readers that, when alone with his thoughts, his first act was to strain his eyes to pierce the darkness, and to open his ears to try to discern any sound which might disturb the silence which prevailed around him.

Prepared for the worst, he stood still, and gazing steadfastly before him, he listened.

Well, too, was it for him that he did so, for presently he heard a noise before him, and he thought that he saw the wall giving way.

Surely this was enough to astonish him, and to cause him to ponder over the strangeness of the sights which he had witnessed since he had left the haunted mill, where had been enacted the scene which was to exercise so great an influence upon his future conduct in life.

So far as we have written, the farmer's hearing had not deceived him, and his sight had not confused visions of a diseased brain, for he had not waited above five minutes, at the utmost, when he saw plainly before him an aperture in the wall.

Wider and wider it grew, until the vacant space, which it formed, gave admittance to a form which he had seen before.

The vision with the black mask. The woman whose real character was still a mystery to him!

Dick Spaldings at times was a man of a few words, often he was morose and silent.

And on the present occasion he did not belie the character which he bore for knowing how to keep his mind to himself.

But, there are periods when to remain dumb is an impossibility, as will be shown by the following.

That the vision was a woman, who had flesh and bones like himself, he could not for a moment doubt—and had he felt inclined to range her in the category of goblins and ghosts, who only exist in the minds of old nurses wishing to wile children to sleep—the words which she had uttered had been so plainly spoken that any lingering illusions of his could not have withstood the ordeal of her speech.

"Richard Spaldings," she said, "do you wish to leave the place or to remain here."

"Remain," he replied, in a firm and manly voice, where no signs of the fears he had once experienced could have been traced.

"You are not afraid of me?" she asked.

"No," replied the farmer.

"Follow in my track, then," the woman retorted, "and ask no idle questions."

The farmer bowed his head in the affirmative.

There is but one step between love and hate.

That step had been taken by Dick Spaldings.

How many would have preferred the control of their conduct to the loss of it, and how many would have feared, while there was yet time, to sell themselves, body and soul, to a woman whose strange ways were wrapped in mystery.

But the farmer could not withstand the magnetic spell which the woman exercised upon him, and without a word he followed her steps.

Besides, he had something to carry out.

A vengeance to accomplish.

And within his brain had risen a ghastly, hideous plot, which he meant to perform, and which, as our readers, doubtless, can perceive, will occupy no inferior part in the course of our narrative.

For let it well be understood here, the words which he had uttered were not futile ones, and he firmly resolved to fulfil the ghastly meaning which they conveyed.

Then, without a syllable escaping his lips, he abided by the woman's request.

And now, when he had crossed the aperture, which led to a darkness that made him shudder, and found himself landing upon what seemed to him to be a vault, he could not refrain the curiosity which he experienced, and turning quickly round, he cast one last look upon the room where Griggles had appeared to him.

Perhaps, by the flickering light which came from the dying embers of the fire, he hoped to see that strange little girl.

Hoped to meet her wild, bright glance, which, extraordinary and indescribable, contained a fascination for which he could not account.

But if such had been his anticipations, they were doomed to be disappointed.

For he saw nought.

By an inexplicable and unaccountable magic, the wall had closed behind him.

The woman now descended a staircase.

Staggering rather than walking, he followed.

What was he about to see?

The atmosphere, where he groped his way, was damp and cold.

Slimy to his touch were the walls, as they receded before his touch, and he vainly clung to them for support.

And more than once he was on the point of slipping upon the muddy ground upon which he trod with an uncertain step.

But his guide was, doubtless, accustomed to the vaults, along which she glided like a shadow.

So fast, indeed, that it was as much as he could do to keep up with her swift pace.

The farmer was nearly out of breath.

Still he made no complaints.

Too far had he now gone to think of retreating.

Thus, to place a bold face upon the matter, and to feign courage, was the only step left to him.

The woman had been walking for a good while now.

A hundred yards more or so she cleared, and then she came to a winding, next she halted.

Evidently, it was no difficult matter to lose oneself in the intricate labyrinth along which she had been moving.

"At last," muttered the farmer, "my journey is ended."

But it was not as he thought.

The woman had stopped her course for one reason.

To light the lamp which she had been carrying.

It was a wonder to Spalding she had not done so before.

But neither the time nor place were suitable for musings.

The woman was now before what seemed to the farmer to be a solid front of rocks.

Blocking up her progress.

She mused.

Listened.

And then looked about her.

A sledge-hammer lay upon the ground.

She stooped.

Picked it up.

And after having carefully examined it, she gave three peculiar knocks, which vibrated with a shrill, hollow sound throughout the mysterious vault.

Both waited for a few seconds.

The woman was fearless and still.

The same, however, could not be said of the farmer.

In breathless suspense he paused, and eagerly waited for what might follow, while the perspiration stood in heavy beads upon his broad and expansive brow.

Shortly afterwards the sound was re-echoed from within.

Again the woman with the black mask struck another blow.

She knew that her signal had been heard.

The next thing was to see it obeyed, which was soon done.

For, behold! the apparent huge rock slid aside, disclosing a narrow opening just wide enough for one person to pass at the time.

Stooping slightly beneath the aperture the woman strode on.

The farmer bore upon her footsteps.

And now strange sounds smote his ear.

A mystic concert.

No, never before had he heard such sounds.

Such as they were, too, in the dead silence of the lonesome night, contrasting so strangely with that which he expected to hear.

Soft, low, and inexpressibly sweet was the music.

Now dying away in a faint wailing cry like the voice of pain, now rising plaintively as an angel's prayer, occasionally, too, swelling out high and grand, and sublime like the notes of a triumphal march, till the listener's heart bounded in his breast and every pulse leaped as if he had been some forlorn emigrant in the wilds of the desert listening to "Home, sweet home," uttered in some kindred voice, or a French Republican in the bloody times of '93, listening to the Marseillaise Hymn.

Still he heard it.

Now high.

Now low.

Now wild.

Now agonised.

Now soft, plaintive, and sweet, vibrating high and beautifully clear, with one vast thundering crash, and again dying away in a low sobbing sound, as if of a strong heart in its last agony.

Oh! never was earthly music so sweet at times, so terrifying at others.

Now entranced, enraptured, he listened.

Then frightened, dimly wondering from whence these strange sounds proceeded, he followed his strange guide.

Suddenly it ceased.

The two beings were now in a large circular cavern, lit only by a single lamp, which was suspended from the ceiling by an old and rusty iron chain.

Around the cavern were iron-studded doors, with thick heavy bars, leading to dark cells, where, doubtless, many a prisoner had been starved to death, without a friendly voice being nigh to soften the bitter pangs of his forlorn state.

The guide walked on, followed by the farmer.

And now another sight met his eye.

One upon which we are loath to dwell.

Repulsive and ghastly as it was, in a large, gloomy, lonesome cell, which stood on his right, and of which the door was opened.

Here and there were large, strong tubs, filled with a thick, black substance, which looked heavy and clotted.

What could they contain?   Could it be true?

And yet, what was that sickening smell which arose, and made him fancy that he was in a slaughter house?

Truly these were, indeed, the vaults of death!

He could no longer doubt.

Truth, dark, stubborn truth, now stared the farmer in the face.

Availing himself of an opportunity which presented itself, and profiting of a moment when he was unobserved, he dipped his hand into one of the tubs.

Quickly he withdrew it.

A ghastly palor covered his features.

His eyes sunk.

His limbs trembled.

Like so many shadows, all lingering doubts vanished.

The loathsome smell of the lukewarm fluid.

The clammy, sticking touch.

All confirmed a suspicion which he fain would have been to entertain at any other time, or under any other circumstances.

For everything tended to show him that it was—

Yes, what was it?

Human blood!!

Like a madman the farmer staggered along.

But was soon stopped in his course by something which yielded to the pressure of his feet.

He looked downwards.

And then, by the faint and doubtful glimmer which the lamp cast, the farmer saw, lying in a heap by his side, the headless trunks of human bodies, so carelessly wrapped up in their shrouds that he had no difficulty in discovering what we have described.

Men and women, doubtless, who had been lured away and murdered in the dead of night, without their shrieks having succeeded to summon to their assistance the help which they so much needed.

The farmer's heart sank within his breast.

He felt a giddy whirl in his head.

And would have fainted but for his attention being called to his guide.

"Stand back," she said, harshly.   There was something so commanding and so peremptory in the woman's tone, that no one could have refused to comply with her request.

Willingly, therefore, did the farmer retreat a few steps backwards.

Immediately afterwards a large chair, of a most peculiar construction—and somewhat resembling a sedan chair, with the difference that it had accommodation for two instead of one—was lowered from the vaults above by a strong twisted wire rope, which looked very much like a telegraphic cable.

With a metallic sound the chair rested upon the ground at their feet.

Springing quickly into it, the woman bid the farmer take a seat by her side.

No sooner had he done so, than a spring was touched by the woman, and both were raised steadily in the air through space, nearly as large as the cave below, until they were hauled up at least two hundred yards.

And, strange to say, just as they were leaving the ground the howling of wild beasts reached their ears.

The farmer could not clearly distinguish the sound.

Still, nevertheless, he thought that the noise which he had heard must have been caused by hyenas.

Hyenas! Those carnivorous animals who subsist upon dead bodies, and who, it is said, issue from their lairs in the dead of night, and rob the graves of their fresh corpses to satiate their morbid hunger and that of their young cubs for human flesh.

A thought, a bitter, excruciating thought, entered the farmer's mind.

The bodies he had seen.

The hyenas.

He reconciled these two things together.

And he was about to question his guide, to ask her whether there were some of those loathsome animals confined in cages in the vaults which he had just visited, and with whose mysteries he was yet but partially acquainted with, when the chair rested itself upon a heavy piece of stone.

There was something so strange, so terrible, so mystic in the scenes which the farmer had witnessed that more than once he believed that his mind was only the toy of some fanciful dream.

But reality was there.

He could not be mistaken, however inclined to be so he might have been.

For if his sight belied him, how about his hearing?

The woman now landed upon a stairway, leading to a door, which was covered with a black drapery, upon which were written in white silver letters the following—

"The Black Brethren of the Crystal Dagger,"

or,

The Knights of Satan."

The farmer shuddered.

But no alternative was left him but to proceed.

The chair had been lowered.

And bending slightly forward, he saw an abyss of darkness, a gaping chasm which led to the vaults below.

"Choose between becoming one of us and death," muttered the woman, pointing with her long, lean finger towards her feet.

The farmer flinched not.

"I am willing to proceed," he replied in a manly voice.

Thus speaking he glanced towards the strange inscription which stood in bold and gloomy array before his bewildered gaze.

CHAPTER XII.

THE CONCLUSION OF THE BANQUET—THE SECRET MEETING — THE ANTIQUE CHAMBER—THE WELCOME—THE PORTRAIT—THE MAGNETIC SPELL—THE PLAINTIVE GUITAR—THE WEDDING SONG—THE MOCKING CHORUS —THE MARQUIS OF AGUADO—THE ORDEAL—THE POISONED RING—THE OATH.

THE woman now ascended the steps.

Reaching the landing, she pushed the door, which receded softly before the touch, giving her admittance to an antique chamber filled with men, sitting down and drinking sparkling wine from golden goblets.

The tables are profusely laid with viands of the most sumptuous description, and everything that wealth can give is there.

As she stepped in the room, there was a dead silence.

And immediately on seeing her, the whole band rose.

They wore black masks, and long white cloaks

were flung in the Spanish fashion, around their shoulders.

The farmer gazed around him.

Curious and quaint carvings adorn the floor, which is of polished oak.

The ceiling is high, and not a window to be seen, the air penetrating through small interstices scattered here and there in the roof.

Curious paintings adorn the wall—and with symmetrical and artistic precision glittering daggers and swords of all descriptions, besides guns and pistols with burnished steel, which reflect brightly in the light of the crystal chandeliers—cover the sides of the room, making it look like an armoury of days gone by.

There is, however, one portrait in that room which we must here describe.

It is that of a man of about thirty-five years of age, with a deathlike paleness, a receding brow, a small compressed mouth, and tightly compressed lips, and a pair of wild, dark, glaring eyes, with a strange expression upon which no one would have cared to look twice.

Around the gilded frame are heavy silken and damask furnishing, and a small coffin which lays in the background of the picure, gives it a funeral aspect, and a sad gloom to the brightness which otherwise should exist.

The woman advanced with the farmer in the centre of the room, and in a slow, steady voice, said—

"Knights of Satan, Black Brethren of the Crystal Dagger, I bring hither as a guest, one whom I trust shall be shortly enrolled among you. He has been sadly handled by the hand of fate, and he has sworn revenge against those who have blighted his happiness."

"Welcome!" came like a deep echo from every part of the room. Welcome are all those who come here under the auspices of Marian of the Glen."

The farmer gazed vacantly around him, and his eyes rested upon the portrait which we have described.

It was only a painting!

And yet he saw a fiendish smile on those tightly compressed lips, and he kept on staring at the mocking glance which he thought it gave him.

The spell of a serpent could not have produced a greater effect upon him than did the fixed glare of those awful, sunken, metallic-looking eyes, which from the canvas seemed bent upon his face.

"Spaldings," Marian said, "have I not, ere now, read your inward thoughts?"

"It is strange, yet it is true, and I must admit you have."

"And are you ready to take the oath?" she asked.

The farmer reflected.

"A word," he interposed, "whose likeness is that?"

"Take the oath, and then you'll know; not before."

And Marian bid one of the brethren to bring her guest a goblet of the liquid which was on the table.

He bowed in acknowledgment.

"Stay, Spaldings," now pursued Marian, "I do not wish to press you; and weigh my words well in your mind."

There was a pause.

After a while Marian continued.

"Remember, Spaldings," she went on, "that from the hour you become one of "The Black Brethren of the Crystal Dagger, or the Knights of Satan, as we are called, you wage war against society, and forget all ties of kindred, and begin the work of vengeance which has induced you to join this Lodge. The men you see here

have already done so. They are all either robbers, murderers, or have chosen the life of their own free will. Some have brought misfortune and shame upon themselves by their own vices and misconduct; others have been so unjustly treated by the hand of Fate, that they have resolved to work their bitterness and disappointment by seeking to become connected with any deed aiming to harm humanity."

Here there were several sounds of discontent issuing from the lips of those who, knowing the truth of Marian's words, and feeling its cutting meaning, wished not to let her thus freely express her opinion, without displaying their disapprobation.

But she took no notice of their dissatisfaction.

Her glance swept round the room.

All eyes cowed before it.

Then she renewed—

"What's life when once happiness is blighted, and what is sweeter than revenge?"

The farmer was still undecided.

He placed his goblet to his lips.

And slowly drained off its contents.

Never before had he tasted so sweet a nectar.

At last he sank upon a chair.

Then the strange music which he had heard before, began afresh, and a soft, silvery voice sang the following:—

"Our wedding-day was bright, love,
    No cloud upon its sky;
Our hearts were gay and light, love,
    And joy was in each eye!"

The farmer's face grew pale.

Surely, this was a mockery.

A delusion!

A snare!

Immediately after the voice had ceased, sweet notes reached him.

It was that of a guitar.

And the same voice sung derisively—

"Hah! hah! hah! hah!
Hah! hah! hah! hah!"

And the whole band joined in the mocking laugh.

"You breathed, as I, the vow, love,
    To be for ever true;
I vowed, e'en as thou, love,
    To live and die with you!"

And again the derisive laugh followed, and the mocking chorus, encored by the band, resounded loud and clear in the huge room.

"Enough," sighed Spaldings.

"Thank God, we have not changed, love,
    As oft the heartless do:
For hearts were ne'er estranged love,
    If linked by love so true.

Hah! hah! hah! hah!
Hah! hah! hah! hah!"

A derisive smile was now on Marian's lips.

"Only one verse more," she said, "you like that song much, do you not, my friend? I did not wish to press as I before stated, as I felt that it always requires time for one to make up his mind."

And, again, after a soft prelude on the guitar, the voice renewed.

"Then, up the goblet fill, love,
    With rich and sparkling wine;
We'll drain the marriage cup love,
    To bliss thine and mine,

Hah! hah! hah! hah!
Hah! hah! hah! hah!"

The farmer waited to hear the chorus re-echoed, and then he rose.

"What's the oath?" he asked in a voice, trembling with rage and emotion, "I am ready to take it."

The guitar then played a melancholy tune.

And a sweet voice sang a gentle lullaby, and slowly and gradually the sounds died away, and silence once more subsided in the room where the Black Brethren of the Crystal Dagger were about to enrol another member to their dreaded and mysterious order.

But the stillness which had followed the farmer's words did not last long.

For, presently, a subdued murmur escaped the lips of the Black Brethren of the Crystal Dagger, and similar to Indians who bend their knees before the Brahma priest who perform the rites of their gods, the whole band bowed their heads low before the painting, which now seemed to recede beneath a pressure which came from behind it.

Gradually and slowly it rose towards the ceiling, leaving a space where stood, pale and motionless, the man whose features on the canvass had produced such a deep and lasting impression upon the farmer's mind.

The apparition was dressed in a black suit of velvet, of the most expensive description; a splendid dagger with a crystal handle, inlaid with pearls and rubies, hung from his belt; and upon his head he wore a dark sombrero, with costly feathers; while upon his fingers shone costly diamonds, glittering with a dazzling brilliancy, which could only have been compared to that projecting from his dark, piercing, hawkish, eye.

The man advanced slowly towards the farmer, and, raising his hand upwards, pointed to the coffin in the picture.

This was evidently a signal.

For the whole band drew their swords from their scabbards and surrounded the farmer.

"Remember!" said the unknown, in a sepulchral voice, "Remember!"

"Remember!" echoed the band, and loud and clear sounded the voices in the antique chamber.

"Are you ready to take the oath?" the unknown asked.

The farmer nodded in the affirmative.

"Hear me, then," he said, "I am thy chief, and bow before the Marquis of Aguado, the supreme commander of the Black Brethren of the Crystal Dagger."

"And now for the ordeal!" broke in the voice of Marian of the Glen.

"Are you prepared?" asked the Marquis Aguado.

"The strong are ready to undergo anything."

One man then stepped forward.

He raised his sword.

The blade glistened, reflecting the light of the chandeliers like a flash of lightening.

But Spaldings betrayed no fear.

"This ordeal is sufficient," said the Marquis of Aguado. "This man is fearless and brave, enrol him among us."

A large book, with a heavy steel binding, and whose broad pages were filled with strange characters, was now taken from an hidden recess in the wall. Marian, having read the contents first, Spaldings was made to repeat after her the following words—

"In the name of Satan, I swear that I shall never reveal the secret signs, touches, words, doctrines, and usages of the Black Brethren of the Crystal Dagger.

"I pledge my lips to the above, and should I prove false, and break the silence enjoined, I hope that my brethren will show me no mercy, and that I shall undergo the punishment of a traitor."

Here Marian ran over the leaves of the mysterious book, and having at last alighted upon a page written in red, crimson letters, she read—

"That my lips may be burned with red-hot iron, my hand severed, my tongue cut out of my throat, and my body suspended in Lodge during the time that a new brother is being admitted, in order that my guilt may be branded, and my example serve as a warning to others. That my corpse be deprived of a burial ceremony, and flung by torchlight in a dunghill; there to rot away, and mingle with the loathsome worms, so that the memory of a traitor may utterly perish, and his name be wrapped in oblivion."

"Amen!" said the farmer.

"Amen!" echoed the band.

"I am satisfied with thee!" now resumed the Marquis of Aguado, "as a token of the truth of my words, here I present thee with this ring. Beneath the stone, there is a deadly poison. The diamond is valuable, but part with it you must not. And now, farewell, until the next meeting, which will be held in Paris, and of which you will hear."

"Farewell!" said the farmer, and he saw his chief depart, followed by Marian.

Then he was led back by one of the Brethren, to the entrance of the hut, where he had stopped into but a few hours ago, and where he little then expected to see what he had seen.

On his way through the dark, mysterious vaults, he more than once tried to find out from his guide the meaning of the strange sounds he had heard—sought for an explanation of the bleeding hand on the wall, but uselessly, for, from his companion he could obtain no reply.

At last, he reached the open air, and when he did so, a sigh of content escaped his lips, and rapidly he walked towards the spot where he had left his horse.

It was gone!

"Doubtless, its instinct caused it to return to its stable," muttered Dick Spaldings; and thus thinking, he wound his way with quick, nervous, brisk steps, in the direction of the farm, where Jenny was anxiously expecting the return of her son, for whose long absence from home she was unable to account.

CHAPTER XIII.

THE CROWD—THE CHARGE—THE LAW FRUSTRATED—THE BEGINNING OF THE MILL—THE FIGHT BETWEEN THE PEELERS AND THE LADS—"TEN TO ONE ON THE BOYS" —THE WANDERING BLUE CUTS A CAPER—MONSIEUR ARMAND'S "GRAND PAS" ON A SOFT CARPET—A NEW RECRUIT—THE HALLELUJAH CLUB—THEIR ABODE— "THE SWELL THIEF."

AFTER divesting themselves of their night costumes, which they entrusted to the care of Black Kettle, to carry safely to the crib where they lived, and where, in due time, we will pay them a visit; howling, shrieking, yelling, bawling, running, the boys directed their steps towards the spot where the cries of "stop thief!" resounded loud and clear.

In the distance they saw a thick crowd, and Bob O'Link having informed his comrades that "something was up," the boys slackened their wild speed, and cautiously mingled with the assemblage of people—among which Monsieur Armand quickly worked his way, and his hands, too! for profiting of the grand occasion offered, you may rest assured, that he began to make the most of it by plying in earnest his profitable, albeit, unlawful calling.

"MERCY ON US! ARE THEY BOTH DEAD?"

Who has not mingled, during his rambles in the metropolis, with a gathering, suddenly collected by some unexpected street incident?

How quickly, to be sure, the people flock together!

The pavement, as it were, seems to vomit swarms of human beings, who come from—God knows where!

From every lane and corner rush men, women, boys, and girls, with a strong scent about them, which is, certainly, not one of Rimmel's best, and linen that once was white—to say nothing of the comical appearance of that good woman who lives just close at hand, in the alley, and who will keep on taking out her darling child in her arms, whenever there is anything going on, sure to attract the proverbial curiosity of her sex.

Old ladies with red noses, suggestive of anything but too much abstinence—fat, sleepy errand-boys, munching pennyworths of pudding, and reading the last tale of highwaymen, in penny numbers— young clerks, out on office business—and all the paraphernalia of street traffic, halt, to see what is taking place, and even cabby, who cares not a jot for anybody but for his fare (if it be a fair one), reins in his spavined, old horse, and alternately gazes upon the scene before him, and the "pub," at the corner, where, ere long, he will just do "three of rum, hot."

But what's all this about, reader?

You want to know, don't you?—so do I.

What is the meaning of all these exclamations?

"Oh, so young! aint it a pity? Look him up? sarve the young vagabond right! What has he done!

"What's the row? I say, Jim, what is it?"

Now, if you please, we will ascertain for our-selves.

Come, let us push our way through the motley crowd—let us poke that old fellow in the ribs, and secure a good view among all these busy people standing looking on with gaping mouths and dilated nostrils.

Yes, what's all this hubbub about?

What has caused all this commotion?

Here we are at last; and have a front row, too!

The curtain rises.

Now for a description of the play!

Behold a man of about six feet high, and as strong as a bull, holding by the neck, as hard as he can, in his iron grip, a boy of fourteen, at the utmost.

"Let him off for this time," says a voice.

"No, I shan't."

"Just show him mercy!" asks another in the crowd.

"Not if I knows it."

"You are a bad-hearted man!" exclaims a sym-pathysing old lady.

"I don't care."

"You have no Christianly feeling."

"What! for a young thief?"

The man who has just finished the last words looks about him.

He, evidently, is expecting the arrival of some enlightened member of the force.

At last, the authority in blue appears.

They muster strong on the occasion.

One Inspector, and four worthies.

"What is it, governor?" asks the Inspector, in a cool, collected manner.

"What's the matter, sir?"

"Yes, what is it?"

"Now, look here——"

"I don't want you to say 'look here;' I want you to let that young boy go, or to let me know what he has done—don't you see that you are creating quite a disturbance?"

The tall man rubbed his head, and then he be-gan—

"Why, Mr. Inspector," he said, "I was sitting in my shop a reading last evening paper—running down some publications for offering prizes, and not giving credit to others, for being genuine, when—"

The man had to stop.

The Inspector had interrupted him.

"Go on," he had said, "I don't care about the paper and so forth, I want you to look sharp."

"All right, governor. Well, I was a reading the paper, when this 'ere lad rushes in my shop, and bang he clutches off a loaf, and mizzles with it."

"Without paying for it?"

"Of course."

"And what did you do?"

"Ran away after him."

"And have you caught the thief?"

"Why, this is him, Mr. Inspector."

Thus speaking, the man, who was evidently a baker if his trade could be guessed from his speech, tightened his prisoner's neck with such a pressure that it caused the tears to start from the poor boy's eyes.

"And where's the loaf?" the Inspector asked.

"He dropped it."

"Are you sure that he is the party?"

"He!"

"Yes."

"He? Of course he is; do you think I am blind?"

"Be civil," the Inspector said.

The baker collapsed.

Meanwhile the "bobbies" made themselves busy,

and some of them were telling the crowd "to move on."

"Move on," that objectionable phrase, which geers so strongly upon your hearing, and which is so freely lavished by the enlightened member of the force at the West End, on the young hopeful who will remain knocking about the Haymarket after one o'clock, a.m.

"And are you sure this is the boy who stole your loaf?" the Inspector asked again, wishing to give immense importance to the incident.

The crowd was gathering fast around him.

He was a pompous sort of a chap, and he liked to display his authority.

"Yes, perfectly," replied the baker.

"And do you give him in charge, then?"

"I do."

"You got no right to do that," said a voice.

"Who says that I got no right?"

The Inspector pricked his ears.

He re-echoed the baker's query.

"I do," replied the same voice.

It was Bob O'Link who had spoken.

"Why so?" asked the baker.

"Because you have no proofs that he has done it."

"I'll charge him, though."

The Inspector here interposed.

"There, don't make yourself busy," he said to Bob, gruffly, "or I'll lock you up too."

Caution was to be observed.

Bob looked around him.

The boys were close at hand.

So for a minute or two he remained silent.

The baker then proceeded to give all necessary particulars to the Inspector, who duly entered the same in his book.

This was soon concluded.

"Take that young vagabond to the station," he said to the policemen who had accompanied him.

One of them seized hold of Harry—for it was the farmer's son whom we are now meeting again—and proceeded to drag him along.

"Did you say you would lock me up, Mr. Inspec-tor," Bob O'link now said, advancing towards the striped blue bottle.

"I did."

"Because I told you that you were exceeding your duty?"

"Now, if you don't make yourself scarce I'll lock you up, and I won't be long about it, that's all."

"Will yo?"

"Yes."

"No you won't."

"Won't I?"

"Do you defy me?"

Bob retreated backwards.

"Whew, whew?" he geered in a loud voice, and so speaking, he placed his five fingers to his nose, and made them play in a manner anything but calculated to give the spectators a great idea of the fear which he had concerning the threat which had been made to him.

The crowd burst into universal laughter.

The Inspector was exasperated.

He foamed.

He advanced towards Bob O'Link.

And he was about to seize him, when the swiper, relying upon his right, delivered a fister from the shoulder that sent him reeling to the ground.

"Egad, there's 'the wandering blue,'" exclaimed Pat Nowlan.

He was alluding to a policeman who, having seen his inspector's plight, was about to inflict a severe blow with his baton on the the head of the aggressor.

But it was suddenly snatched from behind by the Cannibal.

"You'd better go home at No. 17, where you spend most of your time, and coax the old lady, and drink her bottled stout, you old vagabond, you ought to be ashamed of yourself! Do you remember me, old boy?"

These and several other sundry remarks, emanating from the boys, who had an object in view, namely, that of rescuing Harry from the clutches of the law, had the effect which they wanted to accomplish.

Gradually the policemen, seeing that their Inspector was getting the worst of it, became more and more quarrelsome.

And now there began quite a spirited mill between the slops and the boys.

The scene which we are now relating occurred in the neighbourhood of London, where there are many thieves, and where the force did not happen to be general favourites with the people.

Thus, the crowd howled.

The boys shrieked.

The women screamed.

And the boys were cheered on, and their assailants hissed.

And there was such a row.

Such a lark!

No, never had there been such an exibition!

Big Ned came to the rescue.

"Holloa! Is that you, my worthy," he said, addressing a policeman, who, doubtless, he had met before.

This was No. 10,000, of the R division, who was always very courageous when surrounded by others, but remarkably quiet when by himself.

"Yes," he said surly, "what ails you."

"Are you going to take him to the station."

He meant Harry.

"Yes."

"No you shant."

"I shant?"

"No!"

"Who will prevent me?"

"I will."

"You will?"

"Yes!"

"How?"

"This way."

Thus speaking, Big Ned rushed upon the policeman.

Kokoriko, meanwhile, was looking for some weapon with which he could humiliate the constable.

At first he was at a loss to find one.

But suddenly a cry of joy escaped his lips.

There was a crossing sweeper close at hand.

"Lend us your broom," he said.

"What for?"

But before the lad had time to speak the broom had been wrenched from his grasp.

The Inspector was now cowed, and the wandering blue was also on the broad of his back.

He had been mastered by the boys, who, assisted by Patrick Nowlan and Cannibal Jack, who had dealt a blow behind the bobby's head, had had no difficulty in preventing him from carrying out his threat of locking Bob up.

The crowd, meanwhile, were looking on.

It was capital fun.

To be spectators of a scene which does not occur every day, was, indeed, a treat for many.

Besides some of the female spectators—whose calling was not exactly in accordance with the acknowledged laws of society, which the force is bound to protect—felt a universal delight in witnessing their downfall.

Kokoriko now came to do his part.

He was armed.

A strange weapon was his!

He was unable to reach far with his arm, so he had carefully rushing to the rescue, with a broom.

Another bobby was just arriving on the spot.

To give help to his comrade.

But the Hunchback was too much for him.

Up went the broom.

And up he pushed it in the face of the worthy.

It had been used to clean rather a doubtful corner in the lane, that morning, and a muddy spot, which was very similar to—but never mind—came in contact with the nose of the policeman.

Sooner than to remain thus longer exposed to the broom, the worthy retreated.

The Inspector of the three policemen, up to the present, had had the worst of it.

The boys were in high glee.

Harry was not free yet.

A bobby still held him tightly in his grasp.

"We must look sharp, and rescue the lad."

"Of course we must."

"The other chap is gone for a reinforcement."

"Is he?"

"Yes."

"Ten to one on the boys."

"What did you say?"

"Ten to one on the boys!"

This conversation was being held between a betting gentleman, who, of course, had seen better days, and, it is to be hoped, a better coat, too, for his garments were ragged and soiled, and shone with grease and wear, and an aristocratic inspector of public buildings, who was feeling his pocket to see whether he had fourpence to pay for a pot of beer, in the event of his losing the bet, which consisted of the valuable beverage above alluded to.

"Put your book in your pocket, and let us know what you mean," he said, finding that his money was right.

The betting-man reflected.

"I tell you what—the boys will succeed in releasing that youth.

"Will they?"

"Yes."

"I say, look here."

"What?"

The betting man and his friend's attention, who after all did not bet, were now attracted to a new incident.

This was Monsieur Armaud, the Frenchman, who was among the crowd.

Twisting his moustache, he was dancing a grand pas on the wandering blue's body, whose heels were uselessly endeavouring to hit a certain part of the Frenchman's coat, which hid a portion of his anatomy, to which we won't dream of alluding any further.

"Sacrebleu! This is a smooth carpet!" he was saying.

And then he kept on dancing upon the stomach of the worthy peeler, meanwhile, flourishing his life preserver in a most impressive manner.

What between his strong French accent, and his whole demeanour, never before did the people laugh so much.

Let us hope that the same hilarity will be produced upon our readers when they bring to their minds the talented cut which embellished our last week's number.

Cannibal Jack now climbed up a lamp-post with the swiftness of a monkey.

He wished, like the look-out sailor on the fore-castle, to see how the land lay.

"Keeping watch, eh?"

"Yes."

"Any bobbies in the distance?"

"Quick! try to free the boy."

"Why?"

"They are coming."

And there was no mistake.

In the distance could be seen a batch.

Headed by the baker.

This tall fellow had been too much of a coward to face the boys, and he had gone to the station to acquaint the force with that which was taking place.

In a twinkling the boys were all together.

Cannibal was soon at his feet.

He took out his poniard.

And when the bobby, who retained Harry in his grasp, saw the shining blade, he soon relinquished his hold.

Harry was now free!

Better, however, had he been taken and locked up.

For what awaited him now?

Among such companions as those that fate had thrown in his path.

The cry of Cannibal Jack, warning the boys that the bobbies were rapidly advancing towards them, for a few instants more was lost upon their hearing.

"Give it up lads," he said, "they are coming."

Still the boys took no heed.

They had a capital opportunity.

A fair chance of revenging old sores.

And they were making the most of it.

Their fists were falling heavily upon the features of the slops, who were now crying for mercy.

They had had enough.

Still the fight continued.

Now the Inspector rose.

And again he was flung down by the boys, whose aggregate strength far exceeded that of a single man.

But as the best of friends sometimes must part, so must, also, the worst of enemies.

Moreover, when there is danger.

Big Ned, therefore, warned his band that it would be madness to remain any longer on the battle-field.

Never did assailants leave their antagonists more reluctantly than the boys did, and it cannot be wondered at either, for let it be confessed they had behaved nobly.

Seldom had more determined courage been displayed on both sides.

The force was at a discount on the present occasion.

But it would be a great pity if they were to meet every day with similar reverses.

For where would we all be, then?

Vice and rapine would sway the land, and we would not be safe in our own homes.

That memorable fight, followed by the victory, is chronicled among the annals of the wandering tribe which we are pourtraying.

Up to this day, young thieves listen, with no small amount of glee, to the story when their pre-decessors had the best of the authority in blue.

The facts, as we have written them, are told by the old hands to the young ones, who are always sure to take a deep interest in those by-gone exploits.

For their victories are not many on record.

Like angels' visits, they are few and far between.

Generally, the policeman has the best.

What he says is law.

For have we not had lately a case at the Crystal Palace—severely commented upon by the public press, when a member of the P division far exceeded his duty, and was liable of the grossest breach of the liberty of the subject on record, and what's still worse, refused to apologize to the party injured, after having been requested to do so.

But we are not able to digress.

This would take too much space, and we must proceed quickly with our narrative, as more thrilling adventures than we have hitherto described, remain to be told.

At last, it was deemed expedient for the boys to "cut."

With cat-like agility, they did so.

Harry found himself dragged away.

He offered no resistance.

Allowed himself to be led onwards.

For were not his guides, his preservers?

Madly did the boys run off.

Harry had no time to speak.

I see my reader's features.

He wants, doubtless, to know how the farmer's son came to steal a loaf, and to be arrested for it.

He must wait.

Everything will be explained in due course.

The boys were not slow in reaching their abode.

The crib where they lived.

Harry was a stranger in London.

The big town bewildered him.

The bustle, and crowds which he saw, were so different from the peaceable, jog-along style which he had been accustomed to witness, in his native place, that he was perfectly *flabagasted*.

He crossed a bridge.

Old Blackfriars.

Then his guides wound their way towards the Mint.

A nice place, that is, too!

They skirted slimy lanes, thickly populated with doubtful customers.

Still the boys sped on; all the while followed by a hideous, snarling cur, barking at them with all his might.

And being warned, as they passed by certain houses, whether the peelers were in the vicinity or not, they knew how to proceed.

At last, they halted before a chandler's shop, situated at the end of a small street, on the left of which stood a thoroughfare where few would have ventured after dark.

Big Ned looked about him.

The crew were all right.

No one missing.

That was satisfactory.

Black Kettle now appeared upon the threshold of the shop.

"The governor and missis are waiting inside," he said, to the boys. "Any plunder?"

"No."

"What?"

"How can I tell?"

"Perhaps Johnny Crapaud."

"Of course he has," here interposed the Frenchman, and he withdrew from his pocket, several soiled, old purses, which he had lifted out of the garments of those who being so bent upon the sight which we have, ere now, described, had not felt the sleight of hand practised upon them by the subtle foreigner.

Harry had become thoughtful.

He knew not what to make out.

He was not an ignorant, foolish lad, and yet he was lost in wonder.

And we cannot be astonished at it.

For how many boys would have been unable, at first, to make out the real character of such companions.

The boys entered the shop.

There was a musty smell of tallow, and a stale perfume of third-rate groceries.

A hideous looking girl was behind the counter.

That was cocked-eyed Sally.

She was thin and ugly.

Harry did not like her appearance much.

He was not very anxious to make her acquaintance

And longingly he turned round and looked towards the entrance.

He wished he could be off.

Would have preferred the company of the bobbies to that of the boys.

But Big Ned soon guessed his intention.

"Go on," he said harshly.

Thus speaking, he pushed Harry before him.

The farmer's son was now at the foot of the staircase.

Could it have been called so?

The steps were old and dirty.

A rope served as a bannister.

"Walk up, young one," said Bob O'Link.

Harry laid hold of the rope.

Then he ascended the steps.

Occasionally his foot would become entangled in some hole beneath him.

It was a tumbled down old house and no mistake.

The boys soon came upon the landing.

On the left there was a door.

Bob knocked.

"Come in," said a voice.

The boys then stepped in.

What a sight awaited Harry's eye.

It was a dingy old room. Dingy curtains hung from the windows, and it had a dingy, dismal appearance, altogether.

There was a bed in that room, an old cupboard, and several chairs.

Oh, yes; there was something else.

About half a dozen mattresses scattered here and there, upon which the boys slept; that is to say, when they did not prefer to pay 2d. a night for their shelter in a model lodging-house.

There are two beings in the room when we enter it.

One is an old man of about seventy years of age.

Vice and dissipation have left their seal upon his parchment-looking flesh; his cheeks are hollow and cadaverous, his hands look unusually large and emaciated, for his wrists are withered and bony.

He is gazing upon the fire; his frame occasionally shivering with a spasmodic shudder.

Remembering, doubtless, some dark deed perpetrated when life for him has attractions, he sits ill at ease upon his three-legged stool.

That's the governor.

He presents truly a loathsome sight, calculated to inspire one with feelings of abhorrence, if not of pity.

That man is dying!

For who could be mistaken at the dull spark which, from time to time, shines from his ghastly eye-balls, like the last flicker of a candle whose tallow is rapidly burning out.

His name is Marks.

Not much longer will he bear it, though, if appearances prove true in his case.

There is some one besides him.

The old woman with whom he has been cohabiting for many years past.

She is seated in front of the fire.

A bright specimen of humanity she is, too.

Her retreating forehead is low and wrinkly, the left side of her nose has been eaten away by some terrible disease, and in her old jaw stands a stumpy black pipe.

She is rocking herself to-and-fro.

Meanwhile, vigorously puffing at her short stump, which she has managed to colour a great deal better than could have done the most inveterate smoker that ever trod a ship's deck.

She ceases her intellectual occupation.

She has heard the noise behind the door.

She turns her head round, and sees the boys flocking into the room.

"How are you, my little duckies?" she asked, coaxingly.

"As right as nine-pins."

"Sit down."

"Going to have any supper?"

"Rather."

The old man now raised his eyes.

"Who have you there?" he ejaculated, noticing Harry.

"A fresh importation."

"Where did you pick him up?"

Big Ned related the circumstances which we have already detailed.

The old man shakes his head.

"Another thief," he muttered in a faint voice.

And he stretched his hands before the fire to warm them, and, perhaps, to recal the circulation of blood in the fingers, which are gradually getting chilled by the freezing atmosphere of death.

"How do you like the crib?" asked Bob O'Link of Harry.

Harry shakes his head.

Big Ned is looking threateningly at him.

"Very well!" he mutters, at a loss for a reply.

"Have you had anything to eat?" asked the old woman, addressing Harry.

The boy replied in the negative.

"I say, you would not require another feed, had you stuck to the loaf, would you, old boy?"

This is the Cannibal's remark.

"He stole it, did he?" the man faintly mutters.

"A precious big one, it must have been, for the man whom he took it from made noise enough about it, God knows!" says the Hunchback, not wishing to remain silent.

"You are hungry, aint you, boy?"

"Yes."

"Come on, then."

Thus speaking, Bob O'Link pushed a door before him, and initiated Harry into another room, comprising the suite of apartments of the thieves' den.

"This is our reception-room," said Bob.

Harry looked round.

Dressed dummies hung from the ceiling.

In the pocket of one is a silken handkerchief, in the waistcoat of another a watch-guard, and in the cravat of a third a pin.

The dummies are literally covered with small bells, and the great idea is to withdraw the contents of the garments, without causing them to sound.

What we state here is perfectly true, as we have ourselves seen the bells, which are very like those which are sometimes attached to a dogs' collar.

This had been the target upon which Monsieur Arnaud had practised.

He had successfully done so; and he was now an adept in his business.

Several trunks fill the room.

Besides any amount of stolen property—coats, trowsers, soiled handkerchiefs, knives, forks, boots—being among the sundry articles which attract Harry's attention.

The jewellery is carefully locked up.

"To whom does that belong?" asks Harry.

"To the club."

"The club?"

"Yes."

"What club ?"

"The Hallelujah Club, of course, of which you are now one of the members."

"Indeed !"

"Yes."

"What's your name ?"

"Harry."

"Gentlemen, listen."

Thus speaking, Bob addressed the boys.

"What is it ?" they asked.

"Allow me to introduce to you Velvet Harry."

"Why Velvet ?"

"Don't you see his skin ?"

"We aint blind ?"

"Aint it soft ?"

"Like a woman's," says Kokoriko, patting the boy's cheek.

"Is that a good name, my friends ?"

"Very."

"Shall we decide upon it ?"

"By all means."

"'Velvet Harry' will it be ?"

"Yes."

"Is that concluded ?"

"Settled !"

"Perfectly !"

"Shall we call him Harry, or Velvet, for short ?"

"Velvet."

"That's the idea."

"Do you object, Harry ?"

"No, sir."

"Well, Mr. Velvet, come on and have some prog. Where are the victuals ?"

Black Kettle now bustles about.

He officiated as steward to the boys.

Rapidly he darted across the room.

And with a key, which he drew from his pocket, opened a cupboard, which stood immediately above one of the trunks which we have noticed.

Harry's glance followed the nigger's steps.

His eyes sparkled.

He was hungry.

And the run for liberty, which he had had in the morning, had kindled his appetite.

"Where's the table ?"

A big board was now fetched from the room where the old woman was smoking her pipe.

The boys dragged the trunks in a circle.

Placed the board upon their knees.

And then waited to be served.

Their voracious appetites were great.

They howled for food like wild beasts.

Black Kettle then raised his arms, and withdrew a large wooden plate, upon which stood a fine turkey, stuffed with chestnuts.

Big Ned operated as soon as the dish was before him.

He served everybody.

Then he tried to cut himself a leg.

But, unable to do so with the knife, he seized hold of the carcase of the bird, and wrung it asunder, and dispensing with any fork, he began to peg away in great style.

"Black Kettle !"

"Sir !"

"Where is the beer ?"

"Right, sir !"

There was a large bucket in the room.

This was the boys' "jug."

He soon rattled down the staircase, and up he came again in a few minutes, with it filled to the brim.

The foam of the porter looks right.

"Capital stuff !" muttered Bob O'Link, taking a long draught from the bucket, whose contents fell over his waistcoat, and soaked him nearly through and through.

Harry called for a glass.

Black Kettle went in the next room.

And returned with one in his hand.

Then Harry drank.

But "Velvet" is his name—why not call him so, for the future ?

We will do so.

"Velvet, what do you think of the 'swipes' ?"

"Good."

"Any more turkey ?"

"Please."

"Any more chestnuts ?"

"I don't mind."

Velvet now smiled—he was beginning to think that, after all, a thief's life was not so bad as people were trying to make out.

He devoured his turkey.

But without chestnuts this time, for they were all gone.

Still, he relished his meal very well.

"Now, look here, Velvet, tell us how you came to London town," Bob O'Link now began. "You look like a young man from the country."

"I am."

"I thought so."

"Why ?"

"Because you would have stolen something better than fourpenny-worth, if you had been in town long. As the old proverb says—'Who steals a pin will steal a bull.' A deuced fool is he who does not carry it out, if he can get rid of the latter as easily as he can the former."

There was a general laugh.

"Well, if you want to know my story," Velvet now said, "I'll tell you."

"Do," exclaimed the boys.

And anxiously did their youthful glances rest upon the recruit's lips.

"First, I must inform you, that I was stolen from home."

A derisive laughter emanating from Big Ned now interrupted Velvet.

The blood rose to Harry's cheeks.

"Do you mean to say, sir, that I'm a liar ?" he asked.

And he clenched his fist.

Now, although Big Ned was not a coward, he did not wish to incur the hatred of the lad who had joined them.

Not that he would have done him a good turn if he could ; but knowing the growing antipathy of the boys against him, and feeling convinced that his reigning supremacy was gradually dwindling down, he wished, like a crafty politician, to keep in the opposite camp, if not a friend, at least one who would not prove a foe in the hour of emergency.

"No," he said, after a while, "I do not say you are telling us a falsehood, it may be a white lie, you know, and there is no harm in that; however, go on, and it strikes me forcibly that if any one smoked you for a fool he would get very wise ashes."

"Would he ? And don't you believe what I stated ?"

"Believe it ?"

"Yes."

"I can't say I do."

"Explain yourself."

"I will."

"The day is passed off, my boy, for all that kind of thing, don't you see ? Stolen children, old gypsies, and all that sort of humbug is overdone.

I don't believe in it. But let me not interfere with ye, for all that."

"Drop it, Ned."

"Now Bob, that'll do."

"Yes, why can't you let Velvet tell his story without a contradicting him?"

"Since I find the voice of all is against me, I must apologise—Velvet, I meant no harm."

"All right," good humouredly replied the farmer's son.

"Now for the story."

"Well," once more began Harry.

The boys were attentively listening.

But neither they nor our readers will have their curiosity satisfied this time, for an unexpected incident intervened, which postponed the forthcoming communication.

On the threshold of the room a new character had appeared.

"Who have you got there?" said the new comer, spotting Velvet at once, and wishing to ascertain how a stranger happened to be sitting among the members of the club.

Big Ned soon acquainted the speaker with the details already known to our readers.

The new comer smiled,

"There was a mill, eh?" he asked, "something a la Tom Sayers and Heenan, eh? By Jove, I wish I had been there. Any betting going on; many fellah's books on, eh? Very provoking, very provoking, very! Had I been in the way, I would have laid odds—deuced provoking, expect when you go in for next drawing of claret let me know, eh?"

Velvet gazed with astonishment upon the new comer.

"Who's that?" he asked, leaning against Bob O'Link's shoulder.

"Who do you mean?"

"The person who has just entered, and who is standing talking to Big Ned."

"That fellow?"

"Yes."

"That is his lordship, my boy, Lord Fitzboodle, alias Twisers, alias Captain Fortescue—in fact he is one of us. That is one of the cleverest dodgers in London, we call him—"

"Yes, what?"

"Wild Will, the Swell Thief!"

CHAPTER XIV.

A SKETCH OF A RISING YOUTH—HIS ANTECEDENTS—HIS CHARACTER AND APPEARANCE MINUTELY DESCRIBED —A THOUSAND POUNDS FOR A SET OF TEETH—THE PROPOSAL—HIS LORDSHIP DOES A WEED—PAGE OR SECRETARY: WHICH?—FASHIONABLE TALK.

VELVET minutely examined the appearance of Wild Will, the swell thief, as the latter had been called by Bob O'Link.

"London," muttered the farmer's son to himself, "is, indeed, a strange place! I had read a good deal about it, and yet I could never have believed that such things as I have witnessed, could ever have come to pass."

His lordship was too busy talking to Big Ned to notice the glance of the new addition to the Hallelujah club, and as an opportunity presents itself to say a few words about him, we will not delay in describing his character and costume to our readers.

And so while he is conversing with Big Ned, let us proceed at once.

Wild Will was a youth of about nineteen or twenty years at the utmost, and it was known by the boys that, four years ago, he had held a rising appointment as junior clerk in a London Bank.

But there are some beings, who, let them be trained as you will, will prove vitiated and corrupt. He was so.

Not satisfied with the salary which he derived, and notwithstanding the junior post which he filled, Will had, nevertheless, managed to forge the signature of the head partner of the firm, and, having cashed it for a thousand pounds, with the proceeds of the robbery he had gone off on a trip to the continent with a dark-eyed beauty—a girl of the name of Rosa Waters—whose attractions had fascinated him to ruin.

Those who have spent a fortune can easily fancy the rapidity with which money does fly, nay, even those who have no occasion to do so, need not be told that gold melts too easily with all of us for them to believe the truth of our statement.

Thus Wild Will's thousand pounds had dwindled down to shillings, and from shillings to pence, and two months after he had left London, he had found himself penniless.

Rosa Waters then advised her young friend to return to London, and to make it all square with his father, and get him to pay the banker—a very good and advisable step, indeed, could it have been safely carried out, and could the ends of justice have been frustrated, as is too often the case with young scamps, who have friends and affluence to back them.

But Will's father was dead—his mother had disappeared from the Capital—and the youthful forger was apprehended on a warrant, and sent to the reformatory; from which he came out much worse—and as cute a gaol-bird as ever defied the watchful eye of the police.

What was he to do?

He had no money—no friends—and had no inclination to work. Thus he sought bad companions, which he soon found, and became what he was now—a thief.

We must give the devil his due!

There was a great style about Wild Will!

He looked a gentleman—every inch of him, and he wore costly clothes, which he bought from the most fashionable tailors in the town, with an ease and an elegance which did him great credit.

His features, which were handsome in the extreme, would have deceived many, but they were only a mask, lent him by Satan, to conceal the depravity and utter immorality which actuated every deed, prompted by the callous, and prematurely old heart which beat within his breast.

As we will have occasion to follow this promising young gentleman in some of his midnight adventures, we hope that our readers will excuse us for dwelling at some length upon his aristocratic self.

Besides, we describe ugly characters when we meet them; why then, should we not adhere to the same rule when relating to a handsome youth—although that youth be a thief?

His lordship had a great opinion of No. 1, and when he went "on the spree," he always got himself up regardless of expense.

But you should bear in mind that Wild Will combined business with pleasure.

But more of that anon.

And now for the would-be nobleman's portrait and costume.

Symmetrical and faultless was the cast of Wild Will's countenance. His large, almond-shaped eyes were shadowed by a broad forehead, and lashes which were so smooth, and so black, that at first sight, they would appear to have been pencilled by some expert hand. His nose was rather thin, but regular; his small lips, rosy and pouting; and when he smiled (which the fop never missed doing, at least, a thousand times a day), he displayed such a row of faultless teeth, that a " well-know fast lady " had offered him one thousand pounds for his set—her mouth not being open to too close an inspection.

But Wild Will had made a grimace—and had answered—

" No dear! not if I know it. Don't see the fun of the biceps extracting my pretty little teeth," and he had become very coaxing.

Now for his outward man.

A shiny, polished hat, such as you would get at Delarue, in Coventry Street, for 18, or at Lincoln and Bennett's for 25 shillings.

A snowy linen shirt, with a Shakesperian collar; a dark satin scarf, with pearl pin attached; a blue frock coat; a pair of tight inexpressibles, fitting so closely that he might, indeed, have dispensed with them altogether; patent leather boots, with yellow cloth uppers; the *tout ensemble* relieved by a pair of soft kid gloves, which he got direct from Paris to make sure of the best quality.

Now reader, what think you of him?

Would you like to turn out such a swell?

Methinks I would! I cannot afford it! Can you?

Well, never mind, it is better, my friend, to dress plainly, and act honourably and well, than it is to be like Wild Will.

For it is not all gold that glitters, and you must follow his fortunes with us, and, perhaps, then you will not envy him.

Not him, I mean his nice tidy clothes.

Wild Will had concluded speaking.

His glance now met that of Velvet.

" That's exactly the boy I want," said he to Big Ned. " He looks smart, and he will make a deuced nice page. There is something frank and open about the lad, and, demme, he is exactly the cut for me."

Thus speaking, he advanced towards Velvet.

" Would you like, ah! to come with me, young fellah?" he said, " I'll give you a pound a-week, ah! and any amount of perquisites."

The farmer's son's eye sparkled.

He looked towards Bob O'Link.

The swiper smiled good-humouredly.

" Shall I go?" he would have said, but he feared to speak.

Bob moved his head in the affirmative.

Velvet made up his mind.

Inwardly he wished to leave the Hallelujah Club, for if he did so he might have a better chance of running away from one man, than from many masters.

His lordship was standing by his side.

Puffing, meanwhile, at a sixpenny segar, and leisurely blowing the blue clouds through his nostrils,

" What will I do if I go with you, sir," he asked.

" My lord, if you please!"

And the swell thief settled his coat, and the tip of his finger parted the white ashes from the butt of his havanah.

" Well, my lord, then," smiled Velvet.

" Why, confound it, ah, you know, ah, you will act either as my page or my secretary—clean my boots when I am hard up, ah, and examine my cheque book when I am up—want a smart lad, a kind of jack-of-all-trades, anything from pitch-and-toss to manslaughter, you understand, you ' Savez, cher ami,' as the French Countess said the other day, when dancing a varsoviana with me at the French Ambassador's ball."

Here Velvet burst out in a violent fit of laughter, in which the boys joined him.

His lordship curled his lip.

He evidently did not like the hilarity of the youth before him.

But his game was to be conciliating.

Thus he did not seem to notice the laughter which was going the rounds.

CHAPTER XV.

BIG NED HAS AN EYE TO BUSINESS—A BOY'S SERVICES AT A PREMIUM—SALE OF HUMAN FLESH—TWENTY POUNDS BID—THE UNEXPECTED BORROWING—IS THERE ANY HONOUR AMONG THIEVES?

THEN there was a pause.

" It is all very well to ask him to go with you, Big Ned now resumed, after a moment's silence, advancing towards the swell thief, " but that boy's services belong to us!"

" Yes, they do," all the others echoed.

His lordship mused.

" I see your object," he began after a while, " you want to bleed me.

" You have guessed right."

" And how much do you want."

" I want ten pounds," said Bob O'Link.

" And I want another," said Ned.

" Go it."

" So do I," exclaimed Kokoriko.

" How many more wants are there?" now proudly asked his lordship, drawing himself to his full height, and assuming the theatrical gait of Charles Kean in one of his favourite characters.

So saying a dark scowl knitted his brow.

We know of nothing more calculated to ruffle a man's temper than to ask him for cash.

A friend is a friend, perhaps! but ask him to put his hand in his breeches pocket to lend or give you money, and then you find him out.

Wild Will was no exception to the rule.

Still Velvet was worth purchasing.

" How much do you want, Ned, for the boy?" he asked.

Ned reflected.

" Name your price, and then you can divide it among the lot," the swell thief pursued quickly.

" All right."

Here Ned whispered a few words in the swell thief's ear.

" I don't mind," he said.

" How much?" the boys inquired.

" Twenty pounds."

" Will that do?" asked his lordship.

" Yes," the lads exclaimed.

" To-night, then, I'll be here," said Mr. Tomkins, *alias* Captain Fortescue, and I'll bring you the money."

" Agreed."

" No flimsies, if you please."

" All gold."

" I'll try it."

" None of your coiner's manufacture."

" Honour among thieves."

" Good Proverb."

" Not always adhered to, though."

These were some of the exclamations which followed each other in rapid succession.

" It is decided, then, that this young gentleman comes with me," said his lordship, waving his hand in an aristocratic manner to the boys.

" What o'clock."

" Twelve."

" Without fail."

" Punctuality is the soul of business."

" *Au revoir*, my friends," once more said the swell thief, and with these words he paced quickly across the room.

But he was not going to be let off so easily.

Bob O'Link had followed him.

" I say, Tomkins."

"DUPLESSIS GASPED, AND HE PLACED HIS HAND ACROSS HIS EYES, TO HIDE FROM HIS GAZE A HIDEOUS, LOATHSOME SIGHT."

The swell thief turned round.

"Well, what's the matter?" he asked.

"You are a nice boy."

"A gentleman, sir!"

"I aint going to let you off like that."

"What for?"

"How much am I to get?"

"Twenty pounds among the lot."

"And do you range me among the lot, then?"

"Of course."

"It aint of course."

"I must be off."

"Well, before you go, just let us have a couple of quids, or so."

"Nonsense, man."

"Do you think I did not see through that whispering you had with Big Ned?"

"What about?"

"You promised him something for himself, I know."

"What if I did?"

"I must have the same."

"Will one pound do?"

"For the present, yes. Slip us the other to-night."

The swell thief nodded.

"I'll give them both to you by-and-bye," he said.

"No, nothing like the present, if you please. 'A bird in the hand is worth two in the bush.'"

"Bob, you are a bore."

"Granted, my lord."

The swell thief smiled.

"Here," he said.

Thus speaking, he gave Bob a sovereign.

With these words, he departed.

And so did Bob; for bang he went into the first "public," and "lushed himself up," as low clerks, out at night, would say.

Velvet had remained in the room, where the boys were now sitting upon the various trunks, expatiating upon the narrow escape which they had had during the day.

CHAPTER XVI.

A SHRIEK!—MOTHER KONKLESS—THE CHAMBER OF DEATH—A DROP OF BRANDY—SOOTHING A MAN'S DYING MOMENTS — THE PARCHMENT—INCOHERENT SENTENCES—GOD IS GOOD—THE LAST GASP—THE DRUNKEN VIRAGO—THE SWOON.

SUDDENLY, there rose a loud shriek!

The boys suddenly darted to their feet.

What could it mean?

They stared at each other.

And in a body, rushed towards the inner door.

It was locked.

"I say, boys, keep quiet!" now said a voice; harsh, strident, and rough.

It was that of the old woman who had been sitting before the fire.

Instinctively the boys retreated and resumed their seats.

"Mother Konkless seems to be out of sorts," said Kokoriko.

Konkless was the appellation by which the boys had nicknamed their old female keeper.

The name under which she went by was Mrs. Marks.

Velvet had alone remained close to the door.

Wishing for help, Mrs. Marks opened it.

"Come here," she whispered, and she dragged Velvet close to her.

And with a rapid move, again she closed the door, and locked the members of the Hallelujah Club in what they facetiously termed their reception-room.

"Give us a song, Pat," asked the Cannibal.

"What's the use of singing now," the Irishman replied. "I'll tell you what's going on, or I am greatly mistaken; old Marks is kicking the bucket."

The boys listened.

It was too true!

"Lend us a hand to carry him on the bed," was saying the virago to Velvet; "he is sinking fast."

"Not yet! not yet!" was muttering the old sinner, "not yet."

He had heard the last word.

His death-knell!

Old Marks was now placed upon the bed.

His hand shivered—his limbs trembled—and his eye shone with an unearthly glare.

"Mother," said the sick man, "one last favour ere I die!"

"What is it, Marks?"

"Give us a drop of brandy."

"I got none."

"Fetch it."

"Oh! do, do!"

His voice was supplicating.

Konkless' heart, for the first time in her life, was moved.

"I'll get it for you," she whispered.

Then she left the room.

Mumbling, as she went down the steps—

"I'll just do a drop for myself—it is of no earthly use keeping life in him, for he can't last much longer."

And she sallied on her errand.

The dying man listened.

"Is she gone," he asked from the boy.

"Yes," he replied.

The old sinner now tried to rise upon his couch.

But he had no strength to do so.

"I am afraid to die!" he gasped.

And hideously repulsive became his features.

"Come here," said the man.

"I am a great sinner," he muttered.

Velvet grasped his hand.

"God is good," he said, pointing with his left hand towards the ceiling. "If you repent, he will forgive you."

"Forgive me? Hah! hah! No!"

"Yes, my friend; his mercy knows no bounds."

These words seemed to bring a smile upon the old man's lips.

A passing ray of satisfaction flitted across his features.

"Thank you," he mumbled.

Then he looked round.

"Any one in the room?"

"No," whispered Velvet, bending over the old man.

"Hark, then."

The man's voice was every instant getting hoarser.

"Take this," he said.

Then from beneath his garment he drew a piece of parchment.

The boy clutched the paper.

"It is worth thousands and thousands," the man continued.

"Speak lower."

So said Velvet, for he feared that the others, in the adjacent room, should hear.

Marks nodded.

The boy consigned the paper to his innermost pocket.

Sounds on the stairs were now heard.

The old wood was creaking beneath the pressure of feet.

"Is she coming back?"

"I think so."

The dying man now raised his lean arm, and drew Velvet towards him

"Nancy——old Martin——Aguado——not dead ——aha!——wealth!"

And he strove to speak plainly.

But he could not.

The above words were the only incoherent sentences which reached the boy's hearing.

"Repent; God is good!" once more muttered Velvet.

And mechanically old Marks tried to repeat the sentence.

But his power of speech had nearly forsaken him.

"Oh, God!" he muttered; and with this heavenly name in his mouth, he relaxed his hold, and fell heavily upon his pillow.

Then his eyes closed.

Again they opened.

And his limbs stiffened; and his hands, which Velvet had been chafing in his own, became icy cold.

"He is gone! May God have mercy upon his soul!" muttered the boy, when he found that the being at whose death-bed he stood had ceased to breathe.

And then, with a friendly touch, the poor boy drew the clammy lids over the dead man's eyes, hitherto staring at him from their sunken, hollow sockets with a glassy, fearful expression; and taking his kerchief from beneath his garments, he placed it over the rigid features, which even in death appeared more repulsive than when lit up with the glow of life.

Konkless now entered the room.

She was humming some old song.

Seeing the corpse, her eyes stared vacantly.

A drunken hiccup escaped her lips, and she nearly dropped a black bottle which she was carrying in her arms.

Velvet gazed upon the old virago, and from her his glance reverted to her defunct partner.

He saw life on one side.

Death on the other.

Life still more repulsive than grim death!

The thin, ugly, emaciated form on the bed—the bony, lean arm hanging stiffly upon the blanket—the colourless lips—the gaping mouth—were sights, indeed, for a boy!

And the old woman's drunken, ringing laugh to pile on the hideousness and ghastly terror of this terrible scene, would have awed many a full-grown thinker.

And could a lad of fourteen summers have been expected to see what we have described, without suffering from the baneful effects of a contaminated atmosphere?

Hot and sickly had grown the room; filled with the reeking aroma of a foul black pipe, and the corrupt gas issuing from a dead body, fast decomposing.

To withstand it would have been an impossibility.

Velvet tried to reach a chair.

But his limbs refused their office.

And with a prayer on his lips—a prayer that he might be able to preserve the document entrusted to him, Velvet staggered and fell, and the poor boy's head came into contact with the slimy floor with a hollow, painful sound.

Konkless saw the boy's strength forsaking him.

Did she rush to his rescue?

No, this would have been too much trouble.

So she contented herself to puff away at her old pipe, and to gaze upon the boy's pale features with a look of idiotic contempt.

Then she reeled by the fireside, and squatted in a crouching attitude upon her three-legged stool, coaxing with her long, lean fingers, the bottle—the child of her adoption!

And then silent and still became the chamber of death.

Gradually the old woman's chin rested upon her knees, and vacantly she gazed upon the hearth.

And the embers of the fire creaked with a plaintive, melancholy sigh.

And there he lay, the poor boy!

His soft, pale face shadowed by the wavy curls of his luxuriant hair, whose dark hue contrasted so painfully with the livid features, that had a stranger entered the room, he would have believed that he, so hopeful and so handsome, had been doomed to die in his prime—to be consigned, in youth's golden period, to that dark, mysterious bourne from whence no traveller returns.

CHAPTER XVII.

A COUNTRY SCENE—THE HORSEMAN—THE THOUGHTFUL MOOD—THE POACHER—THE PISTOL—A CONVERSATION ON THE HIGH ROAD—A STRANGE CHARACTER—THE GOOD-HEARTED BROTHER—THE ARRIVAL.

THE moon had climbed high in the heavens.

Bright and clear shone the yellow stars, and cold and dry was the atmosphere on the winter's evening when our chapter begins.

Period—about sixteen years before the accomplishment of any of the events which we have related in the course of our story.

Time—night.

Country—France.

Hark!

See the pheasant in yonder field disturbed in its rest, rising with a lazy flutter of his wings, and settling himself down far away from the high road—where resounds the clatter of a horse's hoof, every instant becoming plainer and plainer.

Who is this cavalier, mounted on a dark chesnut steed?

He reins in his horse. Handsome is the mount.

It yields to its master's bidding, and relaxes its swift, bounding canter.

The traveller gazes near and far.

Around him is as fair a picture as a lover of Nature could have wished for. On one side the deep waters of a river ran slowly in their channel—on the other the land stretched away in bright meadows and luxuriant vineyards.

Our traveller, however, remarked not or gazed but with indifference over the landscape, and from the expression of his eye, which turned in a thoughtful mood to his saddle-bow—or seemed to follow listlessly the white road before him, it was evident that he was pre-occupied and anxious—perhaps unhappy.

Doubtless, his reverie would have lasted far beyond the period when we introduce him to our readers, had not an incident, which for a moment startled his horse, caused him to forsake for awhile the dream-land in which he was indulging.

This incident was the sudden appearance of a peasant, clad in the coarse brown-cloth which is generally worn by the labouring classes of the country to which we allude.

The peasant appeared suddenly on the crest of a ditch, which separated the road from the field, and bestowed on the horseman a stare, in which a naturally morose disposition, or perhaps a dislike for the traveller, was by no means carefully disguised.

The traveller noticed the man's look.

The calm and lovely moonlight threw its silver beams over the features of the peasant, and the traveller's hand mechanically wandered to his saddle-bow, where, for precaution's sake, he kept a pair of pistols, which more than once had proved useful in the hour of need.

The peasant, who, to any one practised with country habits, appeared to be a poacher, retreated a few steps from the horseman.

"Methinks, he said, "that you give me credit for being what I am not, sir."

There was something very haughty and very commanding in the man's voice.

The horseman smiled.

"You are poaching, my friend; to me that's clear, for your bag is full, and as I believe that wisdom is the best part of valour—I am ever on my guard."

And the horseman withdrew a pistol and cocked it significantly.

"You are a stranger in these parts, sir; my life to you would be but of little use, and, perhaps, my tongue may serve you—want you any information?—freely will I give it."

The horseman consigned his pistol back in the saddle, from which place he had withdrawn it.

"After all, my friend," he said, "I may have been mistaken; kill away the game, if you like, and tell me how far I am from the chateau of Monsieur Duplessis."

"Monsieur Duplessis' chateau?" The man repeated, with a tone of derision vibrating in his voice—"why it has changed owners—Monsieur Duplessis was sold out but five weeks ago, and he lives in that house at the bottom of the hill."

As he spoke the man pointed with his right finger to a small thatched cottage a few hundred yards distant from the place were he stood.

"And how came he to lose his fortune?"

The voice of the speaker was friendly, soft, and low as he uttered the above words.

"If you had shot me, you see, it would have been a mistake on your part. Are you anxious to know?"

The horseman nodded.

"Well, I'll tell you."

And the poacher mused.

The traveller guessed his thoughts.

"Here," he said—

And he flung him a purse full of glittering coins. The man picked it up.

"Why, don't you see, Monsieur Duplessis gambled his fortune away, for what between his dice and women, and that kind of thing, you know, money does not last long."

"Well," the horseman answered gravely.

"Well," repeated the informant, "the creditors thought that they should, if possible, have a little of their due, and so they turned him out."

"And how did he withstand his misfortune?"

"Oh! right well."

"Is he at home now?"

"I should advise you to go and see for yourself."

With these words the man slunk away.

"Strange being that!" The horseman muttered, and a feeling of pity invaded his heart, as he gazed upon the poacher, who, with one bound, cleared the ditch, and soon disappeared behind the thick hedge which divided the field from the high road.

The horseman then spurred his steed. A few seconds brought him to the spot which had been pointed out to him.

"Oh! my brother!" He soliloquised, as he alighted from his saddle, "in what state will I find you after many years' absence?"

Thus thinking, he fastened the bridle of his horse to a stray branch of a tree, which sheltered the small house where he was about to enter.

This done, he knocked.

From the inside a voice answered, "Push the door before you, and it will yield to your touch."

"Yes, that's poor Jule's voice," the traveller once more muttered, and with a heart beating with brotherly affection, he stepped in the abode.

But as many things require to be told, we will, if permitted, begin a fresh chapter to that effect.

CHAPTER XVIII.

A FEW WORDS ABOUT A FRENCH CUSTOM—THE ABODE OF POVERTY—THE LOOK OF ENVY—THE LONG TALK—THE CONFIDENCE—THE MILLIONAIRE—THE WILL——THE DAUGHTER MATHILDE—CROSS EXAMINATION—THE TEMPTATION—SATAN'S WHISPERING VOICE AT WORK.

IN France, and in several other continental countries, it is the habit for men to kiss each other.

With regard to ourselves we do not approve of the fashion.

We think that affection needs no display, and that deeds and not outward caresses ought to be the best test of one being's regard for another.

Thus we consider the French "modus operandi" rather ridiculous.

Besides, God has left us animals of the male species too pleasant an alternative for wise men to question its propriety.

For are there not always many of the weaker sex ready to be kissed?

They do not object to the entertainment.

Indeed, some rather like it!

Why, then, interfere with the prerogative of the fairest of the fair?

We consider the above remarks necessary, for without our timely prologue many of our readers would have been at a loss to understand our writing.

And now to resume.

When the traveller entered the room, a man who had been sitting down before a rough deal table, rose to welcome him; and flung his arms around his neck.

"Ah! Jules," said the horseman, "how altered you are!"

The brother shook despondingly his head.

"I am ruined," he said with a sigh.

The traveller smiled sadly.

"Speak not so quickly, you may still be rich," he began.

And thus speaking he divested himself of a wide cloak, which he had been wearing, and carelessly flung himself upon one of the ricketty stools in the abode.

Duplessis, senior, was gazing upon his brother.

A glance of envy was dashing from his eye, as he contemplated the glittering diamond which shone upon his younger relative's fingers.

"See my abode," he muttered after awhile, "how different from the georgeous Castle of Duplessis, whose proud towers and battlements for many centuries past had sheltered the old family who bore the name."

The younger brother looked around him.

It was indeed a strange looking place!

The room was tolerably spacious, with a low ceiling.

A few hurdles suspended from the rafters, blackened by the smoke, contained one row of rancid cheese, whilst, at the other end, the sunken ceiling exposed, through the thick cobwebs, the hay which filled the loft.

During the day-time the light could only find its way in through the upper panel of the door—a sliding panel, but without a glass.

The walls, uncreviced here and there, were plastered with moist patching of brown soil, and the rough, uneven floor—entirely consisting of trodden earth—let up the water in several places.

On one side of this chamber stood a high chimney, if chimney it could be called, what was really but a wide brick pipe, four or five feet from the ground, jutting from the wall, and over a hearth made of a large stone, on which the fire was kindled, as in the hovel of a savage, so that the least blast of wind blew back the smoke into that room, already so unwholesome.

That evening, at the time when we pay a visit to the abode, in order to abate in some degree the damp piercing cold of winter which invaded the place, the broken down gentleman (he that had lived in a chateau) had laid upon the hearth crossways over each other, two dead saplings of fir tree, whose earthy roots extending half through the room, omitted a sharp black smoke.

Not far from the chimney stood a worm-eaten bread-bin and above it, on a mouldy shelf, a few articles of broken crockery, opposite to these things a cupboard of walnut wood.

Finally, in the back part of the room stood a bed of enormous height, consisting of a straw mattrass three feet thick, and a thin one of uncombed wool.

The remainder of the furniture was scanty and poor in the extreme, consisting of three ricketty old stools.

A deep drawn sigh escaped the lips of the traveller when he had concluded the survey.

"How came you in such a place, Jules?" he asked, after a while.

"I had no choice, the fields or this shelter. Bad as this last is, it was preferable to the former."

"And what brought you to this?"

"Speak not."

The brother held out his hand.

"Be candid with me," he said, "I am not come here to reprimand you."

"Well, Le Jeu! cette passion terrible!"

As he spoke, the brother's eye rested once more upon the jewellry which the traveller wore.

"Yes, such is my abode," he went on bitterly, "what think you of it?"

The brother made no reply.

"And this is my crystal chandelier."

Derisively he uttered the above words, as he pointed to the single lamp stuck in an old grated lantern, which lit up the cheerless, comfortless room where the interview was taking place.

After the gambler had spoken, there had followed a moment of silence.

When many years have elapsed since we have spoken with those whom we love, we are often at a loss to find a word to begin our conversation.

The heart of the traveller was too full to enable him to renew the dialogue at once.

For there are times in life when to think is bliss.

After a while, however, the traveller began.

Laying gently his hand upon his brother's shoulders, he awoke him from the revery in which he had sank.

"Jules," he said.

"Brother."

"It is a long time since we met."

"Many years."

"When I sailed from Marseilles, little did I think that I would have found you on my return in the sad condition in which you now are."

"The freaks of fortune are strange and wayward."

"It would seem so."

"Since we said farewell to each other many things have occurred."

"Oh, many."

Here there was a deep pause.

After awhile the traveller resumed—

"I sailed for a new land."

"And I remained in Europe."

"Life for you was full of attractions, for me, dark and drear, and yet —"

"I have spent a fortune."

"And I Jules — ?"

"Have made one."

"I risked thousands on the dice —"

"And lost them."

Here the gambler sighed, and a strange expression shone forth from his dark eye.

The younger brother resumed—

"Jules, why be so desponding, so long as there is wealth in the family you know well that you need not fear the pangs of poverty."

"Why so?"

"I can and will help you."

The gambler's eyes brightened.

"But you may have enough for one," he observed, "and not for two, for I am extravagant."

"I know that—but your experience ought to be of some service to you."

The gambler shook his head.

"I fear not," he muttered.

"Jules."

"What?"

"I am rich now."

"Rich!"

"More, I am contented with my lot."

"And tell me, brother, where did you remain hidden so long? For never did a line of yours reach me during your absence."

"I know that."

"You never wrote."

The brother smiled,

"I was in the land of the East, in a remote territory, where postal communications did not exist."

"And there?"

"I offered my services to an Indian prince, and amassed thousands."

"You did?"

"Yes, and now I am a *millionaire*."

"I cannot believe it!"

"I have the proofs of my words with me!"

"You have?"

"Yes."

"Where are they?"

"Look!"

"What is that?"

"My will."

"It is dated three years ago."

"I made it in India."

"Let me see it, read it."

"There."

The gambler quickly grasped the paper, and eagerly perused it.

Nay, he swallowed the contents.

Thousands after thousands figured in bold array upon the paper.

"I see my name, ah! you forgot my ingratitude?"

"I did, Jules."

"And in this you make me your heir?"

"In the event of my death."

"Or that"—

"Of Mathilde."

"Who is Mathilde?"

"My daughter."

"Where is the darling, oh! I could love her for your sake?"

"In Paris."

"What street?"

"Rue Vivenne."

"And number?"

"Twenty-five."

"We will go and see her."

"Would you love her?"

"Like as if she were my own child,—and I see brother"—Jules continued, still glancing on the will, "that your property is all in India?"

"Every farthing."

"Mathilde will be very rich?"

"The wealthiest girl in Paris, should she live."

"And if she were to meet with *death*," mused the brother, I would *inherit*."

Never had the traveller thought how dangerous and imprudent it was on his part to place bread before a hungrey man—gold before a gambler!

"Brother, I see no mention here of the mother of Mathilde."

"Of my wife!"

"Yes."

"No, Jules."

"How is that?"

There was no immediate reply but two warm tears coursed each other down the cheeks of the millionaire.

Jules understood the meaning of them—

"Oh! I feel for you," he said hypocritically."

And he pressed his brother's hand.

Judas could not have played his *role* better.

Nay, Cain would have gloried in a villian of this cast.

"You are in deep mourning," Jules remarked after awhile?

"For her."

"She is gone."

"For ever in this world, at least!"

"I loved her, Jules!"

Here the brother's voice trembled—

"I need a relative's affection," he said with a melancholy sigh.

There was a pause.

"Bitter and terrible was the blow; you cannot realize my grief; you never were married, were you?"

Jules replied in the negative.

"I was not," he mused slowly.

"'Twas painful to lose her, Jules; to lose her, too, in the hour of prosperity! While I worked she worked —with her kind heart she cheered me on. The path along which I trod was not always smooth. Sickness in India is frequent. Many a time she soothed my pillow when I feared death's warning. Still I struggled on; aided by her advices I speculated successfully, and when I did reach the end of my journey to find the old companion gone, to miss the well-known voice, the sweet, kindred smile; oh! 'twas hard, hard to bear."

And the wanderer's voice shook with emotion as he spoke.

"But you have a daughter."

"Mathilde!"

"The living likeness of her kind, dear mother."

"She is very young, though!"

"Not above five years, is she?"

"A daughter an obstacle to my inheriting that fortune which he has amassed for me!" Now mused the elder brother, and the same thoughts which entered Cain's brains racked the broken-down gentleman's imagination, and filled it with demoniac, satanic, fiendish plans which he resolved to carry out.

CHAPTER XIX.

THE NUMEROUS QUESTIONS — THE SLUMBER — THE HATCHET—A DEED OF HORROR—THE SUDDEN APPEARANCE OF AN OLD ACQUAINTANCE—THE BOND OF DEATH.

THE variety of our incidents might puzzle many of our readers who would carelessly glance over the contents of our story, so, ere we proceed, we would most respectfully beg of them to peruse very attentively our narrative, for, although, at first sight, fresh personages introduced by us might be deemed characters unappertaining to the tale, yet it must be well borne in mind that they are all, more or less, connected with the plot, which we are doing our best to render attractive and interesting.

Having thought it necessary to say the above, which we hope will be abided by, we will return to the two brothers whom we have left in the previous chapter.

Now, had any one entered the poverty-stricken room where the dialogue was taking place, and had that one been an individual well acquainted with the expression of mankind's physiognomy, and been able to read in a man's eyes his inward feelings, he would have been struck with the difference which existed in Jule's look and in that of his brother.

The traveller's gaze was soft, friendly, and open, —that of his brother, false, grasping, and terrible.

And strange to say this change had only succeeded the communication which the younger individual had made to Jules.

Had the gambler seen his brother poor and ragged, he might have felt disposed to welcome him in a heartfelt manner, which would have as much inwardly genuine as it was outwardly so, but to meet him after years of absence, rich, when he was poor, considerate and respected, doubtless, when he was despised, and as low as he could have been in the estimation of the world, was galling and bitter to a nature like his own, vitiated and depraved.

When the younger brother had concluded speaking, Jules rose and walked towards the door, which had remained ajar.

"What are you doing?" the traveller asked.

"Making ourselves snug, friend; the night is chilly and cold, and of little use would be the hearth were we to allow the warmth to issue from our abode."

There could be no objection to such a request, and so the young brother remained silent.

"Whose horse is that?" asked Jules, coming towards his brother after he had fastened the door.

"My own, and a right good beast too, it flies like lightning, and seldom requires the whip to make it answer my call."

The two brothers were now sitting down—Jules was pre-occupied, and a dark frown knitted his brow.

He had seen in the distance the proud building where, but a few weeks ago, he had lived lord and master, and he longed to buy the noble mansion from its present owner.

How could he do that?

But one obstacle in his way

One Life!

That out of his path, he could again revel in all the luxuries of life—satiate his passion for gambling — gratify his feverish desires for the reigning beauties of the day, dazzle once more the Parisian society with the display of his wealth.

And, on the other hand, should the dark shadows of suspicion looming in the distance, hinder him in his purpose, should he fear the voice "what hast thou done with thy brother's life," he had a reply ready.

The world knew that fortune sometimes had favoured him—that on the green baize he had clutched with a miser's greediness the earnings of a lucky throw of the dice, that he had been reported to break the bank more than once with his luck; if he were again wealthy who would dare to doubt a tale with some appearance of truth?

"Brother," he said, after a moment's silence, during which he had been thinking over that which we have written, and planned in his own brain a dark deed of horror, "Brother!"

The traveller, thus addressed, looked up.

"Jules you are thoughtful," he said.

"I think over bygone times, and, then, I curse myself for my past foolishness."

"Even so—forget."

Then Jules resumed—

"How long is it," he asked, apparently in a careless manner, "since you left Paris?"

"Only four days."

"You were not long travelling."

"No, I longed to meet you."

"Thanks."

There was a moment of silence.

"Did any one know you were coming to see me."

"No, Jules."

"And why did you keep your visit a secret?"

"A freak!"

"A strange one."

"I wanted to confine my joy to myself."

"Doubtless you expected to find me at the chateau?"

"I did."

"Any one see you on the road?"

The traveller made no reply.

"Why such questions Jules?" He asked after a moment's respite.

"Oh!" he muttered, "I mearly wished to know."

As he spoke he looked about him.

Jules now rose.

"I suppose you will have some supper?"

"A crust of bread and a piece of cheese will do for me, and as I could not sleep here, I'll go to the nearest village and get a bed there, and to-morrow you can come and join me."

"How kind."

The horseman, however, had been travelling for many days past, as our readers are aware, and as horse conveyance is very far different from railway accommodation, he was heartily tired, and after having said he should be ready in a few moments for supper—his eyelids dropped and he fell in a deep slumber.

Jules had risen with the intention of bringing down one of the cheese, which we have alluded to, and as he raised his arm to take one from the row above his head, his hand came in contact with a rusty hatchet which had been used to cut wood.

The younger brother was now in a deep sleep.

At that instant Jules' glance rested upon his brother.

Upon his jewellery.

Upon the *will* which lay upon the table!

What impelled him?

Was it a natural cruelty?

Was it his passion for gambling?

Was it the whisperings of a fiend in his ear?

No one knows yet.

But he seized hold of the hatchet!

With creeping footsteps he stole behind his brother.

Raised the heavy weapon!

And now who could describe the unearthly demoniac glance of the libertine gambler, as he sold his soul to Satan?

It was terrible!

Fascinating!

Repulsive.

His arm was raised.

Will he be a murderer?

A fratricide?

The will is there staring at him.

The temptation is too great.

One blow—

One death blow—

One sure aim—

And he is a *millionaire*.

The sleeper now moves.

A word escapes his lips, but the sentence began is never ended.

The base-hearted watcher has raised his weapon.

And down he dashes it with all his might upon the bare, defenceless head of the sleeping relative before him.

There is a dull crushing sound as the frail bones are shivered by the angular points of the hatchet.

A smothered groan.

A convulsive quiver of the body.

A sickening dabble of blood and brains.

A shrill cry of horror.

Followed by a dull, heavy fall.

*   *   *   *

The fratricide flings the murderous weapon aside.

Then he gazed upon the body.

"I will be a millionaire," he whispers, hoarsely. "Mathilde is in the way—curse her! Can I not get rid of the daughter? There are many wh——"

"If you make it worth their while we will do the job for you," now echoes a voice, issuing, as it were, from the bowels of the earth.

"Who speaks?" gasps the murderer.

And with agonised looks, he stares in the direction where the voice had been heard.

The door is flung open.

And upon the threshold appears suddenly an old acquaintance, the poacher, whose strange behaviour had so astonished the traveller on the high road.

The two men shake hands.

Mutter to each other, words meant not to be heard by the silent night itself.

They enter into a contract of infamy; and, in agonised whispers, sealed the bond of death.

"And, now, Mr. Duplessis," says the poacher, "what about the body?"

"Ah!"

"Let us destroy all traces of the murder."

"Agreed."

And the two men set to work.

The poacher rifles the body—Jules has become silent.

He thinks.

And mutters between his clenched teeth "The cursed gold! I will be rich—but *blood*—my *brother's blood* is upon my hands.

CHAPTER XX.

A GRIM, COLD NIGHT—THE FRATRICIDE AND HIS PAL—DISSECTING IN THE OPEN AIR—REMOVING TRACES OF THE MURDER—THE SLAUGHTERED HORSE—THE RIVER.

DARK, gloomy, grim, and cold had become the night!

The wind shrieked and howled!

And the fury of the blast tore despairingly the branches of the trees.

Inky and threatening were the lowering clouds.

No longer did the stars shine.

And lurid and feeble was the parting glare of the receding moon, ever and anon piercing the pitchy darkness.

It was cold.

Bitter—bitter cold!

And it would seem as if the old oaks groaned with impotent rage, when two men were seen cautiously issuing from a low-thatched house, at the bottom of a steep hill.

Who are they?

And what is that heavy load which the tallest of the two is carrying upon his shoulders?

Our two acquaintances.

Monsieur Duplessis and his companion.

The fratricide and his accomplice.

The brethren of blood.

And their burthen? the body of the horseman.

Let us follow them.

As they walk on the leaves sigh.

And nature—silent witness of a dark deed of night, moans plaintively as the murderer and his companion—now walking at full height—then bending down, shading along through the reeds—direct their steps towards that deserted, desolate spot.

They halt.

The poacher digs the earth.

The body is placed upon the turf.

And there he stands, the fratricide—with his hand athwart his clammy brow—anxiously awaiting the moment when he can consign a friends' remains—a relative whom he has murdered in cold blood—to a forlorn and unknown, solitary grave!

Terrible and ghastly is the dead man's face.

"Quick, quick, Mercedes!" mutters Duplessis, "the sight of him causes my heart to sink in my breast!"

And he points to the body at his feet.

The man who had been called Mercedes looked up.

"'Tis hard work to dig, worthy master," he said, "I am getting tired."

"I'll reward you handsomely."

Tres bien, mon ami.

And the poacher renews his task without another word.

Deep and gaping was now the grave.

"Do you want me to help you, Mercedes?"

"Not yet."

"Oh, this is terrible! If we were surprised?"

"No fear of that."

"How can you tell?"

"Why who would venture out on such a night?"

"Few, truly!"

"Oh! this wind is refreshing," muttered the fratricide. "I am nearly suffocated."

The poacher smiled.

"You look queer," he said, "for Mille Tonnerres, you are a picture, master."

As he spoke Mercedes gazed upon his companion, who presented, indeed, the picture of a murderer.

His eye shone piercingly—heavy beads of perspiration streamed from his pale forehead—and the wind rushed wildly among the stiffened locks of his dark hair.

Hideous, indeed, was he!

And he appeared, indeed, like one who would have been allowed by his Plutonic Majesty to roam about for awhile on the earth, to commit havoc among the children of men

There he remained, pale and motionless.

Statue-like—his feet rooted to the cold ground.

Now he noticed one of Mercedes' movements.

"What are you about to do?" he asked; seeing his companion withdrawing a long knife from his belt.

The poacher remained silent.

The fratricide repeated his query.

"You do not doubt but what you [have settled him already, do you?"

The gambler nodded.

"And yet," he pursued, quickly, "what's the meaning of bringing out this sharp blade?"

"Is it to make sure that life is extinct?"

"Nonsense."

"What then?"

"You see this?"

As he spoke, Mercedes raised his knife.

"I do but speak."

"Precaution, you know."

"How can——"

"Silence."

"I am going to bury the body here."

"Do it, then."

"Do not be in so great a hurry, Messire."

"I insist, for I am at a loss to understand you."

"Dull of comprehension?"

"By ——, explain yourself."

"The poacher whispered a few words in his companion's ears.

He shuddered.

"Is that right," asked Mercedes.

"Stay."

"Am I to proceed?"

"Yes—yes. I give you 'carte blanche.'"

Duplessis gasped quickly, and he placed his hand across his eye—to hide from his gaze a hideous, loathsome sight.

Mercedes now began his work in earnest.

Rapidly and quickly he severed the still and rigid head from the body.

With the fratricide's help the corpse was then allowed to fall in the earth.

The poacher wiped his blood-stained blade.

And the two men tramped over the newly-dugged ground.

And the dead? the reader may well ask.

Was carried to a pond a few yards distant, and flung into the stagnant waters.

The waters bubbled.

And it was all over!

Swiftly the accomplices walked away.

But had they stayed they would have heard a croaking, and they would have seen small beads rising on the surface of the waters.

Wherefrom these sounds and signs? and could they have been provoked by the slimy frogs, stinking rats, and slippery worms, beginning their loathsome and hideous feast?

*   *   *   *

"And now, what about the horse?" asked Mercedes, as he stood outside the cottage. "May he not be in our way."

The gambler mused.

"What think you about it?"

"Get rid of him."

"How can you manage that?"

"Was my last cleverly done?"

"Superior."

"And my next will be as talented."

"Must I assist you?"

"*Sans doute.*"

Neither Mercedes or the fratricide spoke.

But why dwell upon a scene which we are loth to describe?

Why pander still more to the morbid and the fiendish?

Why not hurry on with our narrative at once, tell our readers that the horse was led to the water-side by Mercedes.

The fratricide meanwhile following gloomily.

At last the two pals halted

They had reached their destination.

The night was still dark and gloomy—and beyond the shrill cry of the owl, not a sound disturbed the death-like silence which reigned.

Mercedes was careful.

He reflected.

Looked around him.

Again mused deeply.

At last he made up his mind; for when he felt certain that not one eye was watching him, he plunged his steel to the hilt in the poor horse's chest.

The animal bled profusely, and then sank down lifeless.

Mercedes gazed upon the dying quadruped, and then he fastened three heavy stones round its stiffened limbs; and when he believed that the weight was sure to make it go straight to the bottom, he dragged the carcase to the river's edge, and allowed it to fall with a heavy splash in the dark, eddying waters—whose silent stream could perhaps have told many a tale of darkness, blood, and sin.

And what was the fate of Mathilde, the poor child robbed of her inheritance?

Did Duplessis become a millionaire, and did his wealth last long?

And what about Mercedes?

Was innocence to be thus crushed?

Guilt to triumph?

And was the dark and blood-thirsty murder so well contrived as to remain undetected?

Willingly would we answer these questions, reader, but you would not like us to encroach; so, with your permission, we will pay another visit to the Hallelujah Club, and see how the worthy members are getting on.

"WILL I DO NOW?" ASKED THE SWELL THIEF.

CHAPTER XXI.

THE BOYS TOGETHER INQUIRE FOR BOB—A TRUE TALE—
THE RETURN OF THE "SWIPER"—GAMBLING—THE
FRENCHMAN PROVES GENEROUS.

READER, I fancy I see your features, and as you
are perusing my work, I can perceive, by the steadfast glance of your eyes, that you have taken a
great interest in my narrative.

Many things you want to know—poor Jenny's
fate.

And Harry's lot.

Of course you must follow them.

You *do* like interest in Harry—don't you?

For he is only a boy—finding himself thrown
'mong thieves before he could help it.

And will he manage to get rid of them? If he
does?—which is a query.

We have left him in a very unenviable position.

In a deep swoon—with Mother Konkless for a
companion.

Bright watcher she is.

That handsome boy—with his handsome looks—
what is to become of him?

For he is not to be blamed.

His good heart was his only fault.

He acted on the impulse of the moment.

Like a great many, he did good, and evil was his
blessing.

A strange mis-appropriation of words—is it not?

A strong abuse of English grammar—freely
written, to be freely catechized by educated men

(should there be any), and by low journeymen and engravers' apprentices.

After Velvet had fainted, indeed, long before—the boys had been so much engrossed with their own conversation that they never thought of—or ever guessed the nature of the sad incidents which were taking place but a yard, at the utmost, from them.

With the exception of Bob, who had gone to get drunk, as we have seen, the boys were all together.

Poor boys—pity them !

In a moral point of view, only.

Otherwise, they are all right.

Reading a very clever book the other day, written by Miss Carpenter, on our "Convicts," we gathered in its pages a true statement, which we already knew to be correct.

And what were the contents ?

That a pickpocket, in a few years, managed to earn money to the amount of thousands.

And that is no exaggeration.

See Wild Will's career.

Read his strange adventures.

No confounded statements.   No absurd figures. You will have the facts, and these given to you in a language made readable.

"I say, where's Bob gone," the Cannibal now asked, from Ned.

"How am I to know."

"Had he any money."

"A little."

"No, I don't think he had."

"And what about his adventure at Bow Street the other night."

"What was that ?"

"Don't you know ?"

"No."

"Did he not tell you ?"

"Not he; so let us have it."

"All right."

The boys were all listening.

"Now for it."

"Look sharp about the tale."

"Is it a good one ?"

"A good one ?"

"Yes."

"I am sure I can say."

"Well, what was it ?"

"Silence, if you please."

The boys all gazed attentively at the speaker. He began.

"He was down the market."

"Where all the flash women go ?"

"Just so.

"Bob was hard up.

"Looking for Wild Will !"

"Could he find him ?"

"Where did he go ?"

"To a place called The Yellow Grapes."

"What, the Yellow Grapes ?"

"You mean the Public ?"

"Yes, and a nice place that is.

"Talk about our girls, and call us thieves ! why, a man is robbed there right and left, and the police allow that den of infamy to remain open."

"Why, that is the lowest place in London."

"I say, gently."

"Can you maintain what you say ?"

"Yes !"

"Well, he was not there."

"What did he do ?"

"He waited his opportunity.

"Sunday is a bad day.

"Unless you go outside a church, when the faithful come out.

"Rare opportunities then.

"Capital."

"Well, after all, you talk a good deal, Ned, and yet tell us but little."

"Friday last Bob was away."

"He was."

"For twenty-four hours."

"Over that,"

"What occurred to him ?"

"I'll tell you.

"Well he was a-looking for Wild Will—"

"Where ?"

"Down the Haymarket, I tell you once more."

"Wanted ' the rag ?' "

"Exactly."

"Did he get it ?"

"I think not."

"And where did he stop all night ?"

"All in time."

This was the interesting conversation which was taking place among the boys.

Big Ned was the speaker.

The querists were many.

Every one wished to put in a spoke.

Ned answered all.

He did not mind.   To speak is cheap.   It costs nothing.

"But where was Bob ?"

"All right."

"How long are you going to be with your talk ?"

"Well, I am going to begin.

"Well, Bob looked about."

"Did he ?"

"Yes."

"He had a couple of pence."

"Yes."

"Went into a public."

"Raffled some one."

"Only a woman."

"How much did he get ?"

"A purse."

"Any coin ?"

"Two shillings."

"And what did Bob do ?"

"Spend it !"

"And what became of him ?"

"Got locked up for drunkenness."

"And in the morning ?"

"Yes."

"Could not find half-a-crown to pay the magistrate."

"Could he not ?"

"He did !"

"How so ?"

"Was locked up."

"Yes."

"With a gentleman ?"

"Yes."

"Drunk like himself."

"I suppose so.

"But Bob soon gets sober."

"Wonderful fellow that way."

He looked about him.

"Just like what he would do."

"Saw a swell."

"Sleeping hard by his side."

"Placed his hand in his pocket."

"And took his money."

"How much ?"

"Eight half crowns."

"But !"

"What ?"

"The swell awoke."

"A natural consequence.'

"Calls for a bobby."

"Did he come."

"Of course he did."

"Well, Mr. Policeman," says the drunken gentleman, "I had some money in my pocket."

"Had you?"

"Yes."

"And it is gone."

"Who has got it?"

"This man."

"Bob was then placed upon his oath—or rather, upon a close examination."

"Had he the money?"

"And when they searched him?"

"Did they find it?"

Such were some of the questions which were rapidly put to the narrator, for, like ourselves, the boys were getting interested in the yarn, and wished to know what became of the half-crowns.

Big Ned remained silent for a while, and assuming that knowing smile which is often perceivable upon the features of those who are placing to another party a puzzle for solution, he at length said—

"Well, you are all very clever, ain't you? Now Cannibal, what would you have done had you been in Bob's place."

"I would have made the most of a bad job, and given them up."

"Would you?"

"Beyond a doubt."

"Well Bob did not."

Pat Nowlan was growing impatient.

"Och hone!" he exclaimed, "it is you that are a bore, Ned. To the divil with the sowl of ye, can't ye be afther telling us the story without any further patter?"

Big Ned smiled.

"Well," he went on, "the bobbies did not find the coin."

"Did they search Bob?"

"Of course they did."

"And it was not in his pockets?"

"No."

"Or in the cell."

"No."

"I give it up, then."

"So do we," exclaimed all the members of the club.

"Bob stuck to the half-crowns, though, and when he went before the beak he made a very good tale of it, spoke about his innocence, and so forth, and was discharged."

"And what about the swell's half-crowns?"

"Bob found them next morning, but, of course, they were very black."

"Eight half-crown, eh!"

"I thought they would have choked him."

"They did not, you see."

The conversation was now interrupted by the sound of a well-known voice.

"Hurrah! hurrah!" exclaimed Bob, and without taking any heed of poor Velvet he walked straight before the door of the room where the boys were assembled, and flung himself upon the first chair which was vacant.

The boys flocked around him.

Bob was very far gone, and when he was so he was always jolly, and on for any amount of larks.

"I got the tin, aha! aha!" he began, "who will toss me?

"I will," said Ned.

And the two worthies began their gambling.

Now our readers may, perhaps, not be aware that no two classes of society are more addicted to gambling than costermongers and thieves.

As they indulge in that very innocent pastime in open defiance to the law, they are always compelled to choose for the amusement either some low pot-house, where the landlord allows them to do as they please, their own cribs, or some by-lane or corner where they are sure to remain undisturbed.

Often, in his rambles in the metropolis, the author has seen young thieves and costermongers playing together for sums which sometimes reach to pounds, and he has besides noticed that there exists between the gambling fraternity a freemasonry which would perhaps astonish many.

For instance, if the coster looses his money he seldom grumbles at his bad luck, and what is a still more remarkable feature, cheating, on either side, is very seldom attempted.

Bob O'Link and Ned played a long time together.

At last, Bob won about one pound from the worthy chief of the band.

"I am d——d, now!" ejaculated Ned, "if I aint the unluckiest fellow out. Every time I cried a head it was a tail—and every time I cried a tail it was a head."

"Never mind, Ned—don't show the cur. Money freely won should be freely spent—and I'll do so; Kettle, here is the 'ready,' and get the jug filled with sherry."

"How many bottles shall I get, sir?"

"What money have I given you?"

"One pound, sir."

"Spend the pound then. Since I was not 'done for a rump' lately, I may as well be generous."

Black Kettle was about to mizzle.

"Not so fast, my worthy," said Bob, "where's Johnny?"

The Frenchman was then in the act of counting the money which he had robbed during the day.

"Johnny."

"Oui, Bob—que veux tu?"

Every time the Frenchman came out with his French there was a general laughter.

The boys liked his occasional sprinkling of "parley vous," as they termed it.

The words which he had spoken would be, in a literal translation:—Oui—yes; que veux tu—what do you want?"

"Why, look here, Johnny—you ought to place a few shillings towards the treat. I noticed you very close to an old gentleman, with blue spectacles, and I am sure you 'trisked his cly' (emptied his pocket)."

"I did," said Johnny, "and if you had not been in such a confounded hurry 'with that cant over the kisser,' (a blow over the mouth) which you gave the Inspector, and thus spoilt my little game before I had quite done—I would have made a very good day's work. However, as you ask me to 'part,' I'll do so. How much did you give towards the 'lush'?"

"An Irish, long-tailed one?"

"What's that?" inquired the Frenchman—who was not yet thoroughly acquainted with the thieves' lingo.

"One-pound-note—from Pat's country."

"Eh! bien!" Johnny went on. "I'll fork out another."

I do not know whether any of my reader friends have ever made the acquaintance of foreigners in this country.

If they have—will they not agree with me in admitting that every student of our language always takes a delight in learning the most objectionable terms in our vocabulary—a failing to which Johnny was not proof—as we can easily perceive.

"That will be two pounds to the good, then, boys," Bob retorted. "Champagne is the word, now, Kettle, rouse up."

The nigger scratched his head—looked attentively upon the speaker—greatly puzzled as to his being joking or not.

It is impossible, however, to tell how long he would have remained in his contemplation, had he not seen Big Ned making a move to advance towards him—noticing which, the "child of the sun" bolted down the stairs with the alacrity of a hunted rabbit.

Perhaps it may seem extraordinary to my readers that young thieves should indulge in the luxuries above alluded to.

Let them not be mistaken.

"Buzzers," a slang word for grown-up pickpockets; and "buznappers," another for the juveniles of the same calling—"bludgers," manly thieves, and house-breakers, seldom want food, or even the more expensive commodities of life.

Of course, there are times when their star will not shine—as it was the case at the period when our perusers first made the acquaintance of the members of the Hallelujah Club; but, generally speaking, they and their "doxies" (female thieves) can truly be said to enjoy the best of a life—which would be one of continual pleasure, were it not rendered irksome to Christianly and good natures, by its very sinfulness, and the constant anxiety in which everyone at war with society must be, at being apprehended at any time for past misdeeds.

To some of those who read us, our characters may appear over-drawn—but if they will believe us, in good faith, they will rely upon every word we say—for, in addition to our testimony, is there not that of an immortal poet—who many centuries ago, proclaimed that— "Truth is stranger than Fiction "—a fact which, during the whole of our experience, never once have we heard contradicted.

CHAPTER XXII.

THE WOULD-BE AUTHOR—BOB O'LINK'S SONG—THE CHAMPAGNE—WILD WILL ONCE MORE AMONG THE THIEVES—VELVET IS TAKEN GOOD CARE OF.

"WELL Bob, what have you been up to since you left us?" asked the Cannibal, "you look like if you had been drinking."

"Drinking," repeated the worthy Bob O'Link, "my dear boy, you are making a mistake, I am a teetotaler."

There was a general laugh.

The fellow's words contradicted so much with his general appearance that we cannot wonder at the hilarity of the youthful band.

"Wait a bit, my worthies," now resumed Bob, after he had leaned his head upon his crossed arms, as if in deep thought, "wait until the 'cham' comes up and I'll sing you a song."

"What."

"An original song, sir."

"What," Big Ned exclaimed, "How do you take it out, eh? In monthly or weekly numbers. We ain't going to believe in that."

Bob O'Link seemed disgusted.

"Do you think, then, that I could not compose a song my own self, without any one helping me."

"I do."

"Wait for the ' swipes,' and then I'll soon show you."

The boys waited attentively for the "cham" as to hear Bob sing a song of his own composition, would certainly add to the treat in store for them, and ever and anon they glanced towards the door but uselessly.

Black Kettle did not return.

He was a long time away, this time.

And although the lads could not account for his procrastination, maybe, we can, and if we were to say that, perhaps, the publican was manufacturing the fashionable beverage in his cellar, not wishing to lose a chance to make a few shillings, by the boys whom he knew well, we might not be far from the truth.

Now there was a dead silence.

Which was soon, however, broken by the Hunchback.

"Do you know, boys," he said, "I have often thought of writing a tale."

There was a derisive laugh.

"Where would you take your story from," asked the Cannibal.

"Never mind."

"From his hump," grinned another.

"Let the man speak," said Bob O'Link.

The Hunchback grew bold.

"Well," he said, "if I got a hump I got no two wriggle eyes, like the Cannibal; look at them now."

Everybody turned and gazed upon the Cannibal.

At that time, if ever, his eyes were "looking two ways for Sunday," they were then, for he was squinting in a most dreadful manner, and his glance anything but prepossessing.

"And what would you call your book," asked Ned.

"The *Confessions of a Sharper*, or, in and out of Newgate!"

"Not a bad title,"

"And how would you publish them?"

"In weekly penny numbers."

"I see!"

"And you would have a beautiful presentation plate, would'nt you?"

"And suppose you got no readers?"

"Why, I would go about the streets myself and sell them: I would give the buyers a good penny-worth, a nice illuminated wrapper, and lots of blood and murder in every chapter, and then that, backed by what I have seen, would make a devilish good tale."

"You'd better try."

"I will."

"You will try the numbers and I the songs," said Ned; "and now, since the ' cham ' aint come, boys, be all attention, and listen to my song."

Bob passed his hand across his mouth and coughed.

"And what would be the tune?" asked Big Ned, wishing to annoy the boy composer.

"' Slap bang! here we are again!' would be as good as any, but have the words first, and, if you think it good, I will send the copy to Meyerbeer for him to set to music, in his next *Hopera*.

Bob O'Link waited a few instants longer.

Now and then he cast a sheep's eye towards the door.

But Black Kettle did not turn up.

"I see it's no use waiting, gentlemen," he said, "so I should beg of you to remember the chorus well, and to join me with your harmony."

"Egad," exclaimed Pat Nowlan, "that's the ticket; we wanted a frae and aisy in this place. We have now a composer; I will be the tenor, and troth when the stuff comes up I'll consider myself as happy as if I was at a wake or a weddin' in auld Ireland, and as free from arrest as if I had a book of St. Patrick's confessions in my buzzum."

This last remark, followed by others from the boys, soon exhausted their stock of fun—or would-be fun, which?—and Bob O'Link, having taken another survey of those around him, began in a stentorian voice to sing the following:—

"The spree boys of London are we,
　Who always are game for a lark,
We're ready to go on the spree,
　Any moment from morning till dark.

Street Arabs we are called by the swells,
But, call us whatever they may,
We'll bet them, or any one else,
That we are as jolly as they !''

Chorus :—

"Then drink, boys, drink!
The devil take care and grief;
There are no joys on the earth, my boys,
Like those of a London thief!''

"It is all very well to say drink boys drink,
where the devil is the —''
"Here it is, gentlemen,'' said Black Kettle,
coming in with the champagne.
Up flew the corks, and round went the bottles,
the youths dispensing on the present occasion with
a glass.
"Go on, go on, Bob, with the next verse,'' now
ejaculated the Hunchback, it opens devilish well,
and, as far as it has gone, it beats my penny number hollow.''
Bob O'Link laughed, and took a long swig.
"Gentlemen,'' he said, "please not to drink
when I tell you to do so in the song, but wait until
I have repeated the chorus.''
"Which will give me a very good opportunity to
swipe away while they will be harmonising,''
thought the worthy speaker, and then he went on.
"Verse the second, gentlemen.''

"For bobbies we care not a jot,
They're sharp, but they find us as deep,
We slip frm their grasp like a shot,
And shout 'Catch a weasel asleep!'

"With our girls on our arms every night,
Oh! who are so happy as we?
We show whether sober or tight,
That we know how to go on the spree.''

"Now then gentlemen for the chorus.''

"Then, drink, boys drink!
The devil take care and grief;
There are no joys on the earth my boys,
Like that of a London thief.''

And while they sung Bob fulfilled the meaning
of the chorus in a gallant style.
"And now for the last verse.''

"The days of Jack Sheppard's brave gang,
And Turpin's are gone, we regret;
But we Arabs, whom no one can hang,
Are happy and flourishing yet!

Then, boys, never mind what you're at;
The worst we can fear's the stone jug,*
And for rations and rest, and all that,
No crib in the world is more snug.''

"Then drink, boys drink!
The devil take care and grief;
There are no joys on earth, my boys,
Like those of Mighty Bob O'Link!''

"Hurrah! hurrah!''
"Good, good.''
"Well done.''
"Bob, you deserve to be the Poet Laureate; did
you send a copy to her Majesty?''
Bob O'Link had suddenly become thoughtful.
"Where's Velvet,'' he quickly asked, "where's
the boy? a nice selfish sort of a chap I am,

drinking champagne, and not getting the lad to
have some.''
"Yes, where's Velvet?'' re-echoed all the boys.
It was only now they were missing him.
Here Black Kettle spoke.
"He is in the next room,'' he said.
"How came he there?''
The Cannibal explained.
"Is he making love to Konkless?'' Big Ned now
asked, wishing to be funny.
"He was asleep when I passed by, just now.''
"And why did he leave you, boys?''
"Konkless called him away.''
"And has he not returned here since?''
"No.''
Bob waited not for further particulars.
Up he rose from his chair, and was about to bound
into the next room—when he was prevented from
so doing, by the appearance of Wild Will—who
confronted him.
The swell thief carried a parcel in his arm—
which, if its appearance was not deceitful, would
have led one to believe that it contained clothes.
Wild Will was rather excited.
His eyes flashed brilliantly— and he spoke in a
reasonable voice this time, and occasionally he
would place his hand to his breast-pocket, to ascertain whether some object which he had concealed
there, was still beneath his touch.
"I say, Pat,'' he began. "That's a nice state of
things. I can't make it out, Mother Konkless snoring
like an old hog—Marks dead, and cold as marble
—and Velvet lying senseless upon the floor. I have
unfastened his waistcoat, and he seems still to remain unconscious? What has taken place since
this morning?''
"My dear fellow, what you tell me is the first
news—I went out immediately after you, and returned about an hour ago. I was so busy with my
own affairs, that really, I did not notice the things
you speak about. But now,'' continued Bob O'Link,
going in the room. "I see that there can be no
mistake about what you say. The next task, then,
is to see whether the boy is beyond recovery—
which I strongly doubt.''
"Unless he has been poisoned,'' suggested the
swell thief, for want of something to say.
"Poisoned be blowed, who wants to poison a boy
who does no harm to anyone?''
The boys had heard the above conversation, and,
noticing Bob O'Link and the swell thief stepping
in the next room, they followed.
Then, when they saw the ghastly tableau which
the book of every-day life offered them, they resolved to help, at once, the poor boy.
And so—one having got a pillow, the other a
mattrass, and the third a blanket—the remainder
carefully carried Velvet in their reception-room;
where they made him as snug a bed as he could
have wished for had he been at home instead of at
the thieves' den; where, strangely enough, Fate
had thrown him.

CHAPTER XXIII.

THE SWELL THIEF AND BOB—VELVET GRADUALLY RE-
COVERS—HAS THE DEED BEEN TAKEN AWAY FROM
HIM?—HE HEARS THAT HE IS SHORTLY TO APPEAR
IN A NEW GUISE—THE SUIT OF CLOTHES.

"DID you ever, in all your life, see such an old ugly
corpse?'' asked Cannibal Jack, pinching the nose
of the defunct Marks, lying stiff on the bed. "He
must be as dead as mutton; or wouldn't he already
have made a dash at me?''

* Stone jug—Newgate.

Bob O'Link, who was the party thus addressed, made no reply, but walked towards the fire, shrugging his shoulders in a manner which was anything but approbatory of the Cannibal's low remarks.

The swell thief, meanwhile, was biting his lips with annoyance, and listlessly playing with the tortoiseshell handle of a very expensive Malacca stick, which he happened to have at the time, we see him for the second time.

Wild Will had a great idea of aristocratic life, and all that sort of thing, you know, and it was a great bore to gaze upon dead bodies, drunken old women, fainting boys, and all the other drawbacks inherent to criminal life in England.

What was the use of his staying in that room, unless by so doing he accomplished some good for himself? Such was the query which he placed to himself.

In the meantime he had laid upon the chair the parcel which he had brought with him.

He thought it right, therefore, to make a move either one way or another.

"Ned," he asked from his companion, "where's my boy?"

"Where's the money?" asked the low thief, in a breath.

"I got it all right."

"You are a brick, Wild Will. Velvet has been taken in the other room, and the boys are trying to resuscitate him."

"Deuced provoking thing, if he can't come with me."

"Why?"

"I want him."

"What for?"

"That's my business."

"A bit of burglary on, eh, Will? Look out, old boy, you have been allowed to run free a long time, you know, and you may be at last 'done for a rump.'"

"Convicted, oh, no!"

"Yes."

"Don't talk nonsense."

"How would you like bread and water, and a few ounces of meat once a week?"

"'Sufficient for the day is the evil thereof.' Ned, you will oblige me if, once for all, you would mind your own business."

The swell thief had had the best of it.

Notwithstanding the cross-examination to which he had been subjected by his pal, he had not told him why he wanted Velvet, and what were his motives for offering twenty pounds for his purchase.

The Cannibal and Ned now looked at each other.

The swell thief had taken his segar-case from his pocket, and was lighting a weed with the tallow candle.

He would have preferred to ignite a piece of paper in the fire, but Mother Konkless was there before it, and her old, lean legs were stretched so asunder, that it would have been an impossibility to do so without waking her.

And for many reasons Wild Will did not like talking to the old lady.

She spoke so ungramatically—she stung so fearfully—she was so objectionable altogether, that he hated the sight of her, and if he could have done so he would willingly have choked her, but in this world you cannot do as you like, and if you take another's life the chances are you have to 'swing' for it in exchange.

Sundry grunts now escaped from Konkless' lips, she was hard asleep, and was not likely to shake off for some time at least, the drowsy slumber which succeeds heavy drinking.

Candidly the Hallelujah Club, and its members,

votaries, inmates, &c., were types which should be transmitted to posterity.

Wild Will was smoking.

Like all idle men the youth indulged a good deal too much in the narcotic.

Ned and the Cannibal were speaking to each other.

And how long this state of things would have lasted it is impossible to say, had not cries of joy diverted the attention of these three individuals from their highly useful, and satisfactory occupation.

A few seconds elapsed, and Bob O'Link rushed in the room.

"Velvet is gradually recovering," he said. "In half-an-hour, or so, he will be himself; but he complains of having lost something. What can he mean?"

Wild Will made no reply.

Speech is silver, but silence is gold!

"Do you know what he has lost," continued he, addressing the Cannibal and Ned.

They replied negatively.

They knew nothing about it, maybe, though, there was some one who did.

"I hope," began Wild Will, after a moment of silence, "that no one has robbed the lad—what could he have about him? Demme, it would be demmed hard lines, if, previous to delivering the colt, you should rifle him of his harness, after having agreed to sell him for a certain sum—soul, body, toggery and all included."

"His clothes are right enough, but he says that he has been robbed of something, but what that something is, he won't tell."

Wild Will thought it advisable to change the current of the conversation.

"How is the boy getting on?" he asked carelessly.

"First class."

"Do you think Velvet will be able to come with me to-night."

"And what do you want him for."

"A matter of the utmost importance."

Pat Nowlan now appeared in the room.

"Velvet is as right as a trivet," he said, "and he is sitting down in the room, talking to the others, as if nothing had occurred."

The swell thief withdrew his scented kerchief from his pocket, and in a most studied manner, wiped his lips.

"He is rather shaken—you understand, old boy; but, as Johnny says, 'the *tout ensemble* is up to what might be expected.'"

One last look to the chamber of death did the swell thief give—and, laying hold of the parcel, he boldly sauntered in the reception-room.

"His lordship!"

"A man of his rank and smell carrying a parcel!"

"West-end life at a discount!"

Wild Will listened to all these remarks.

Like a clever politician—a knowing shot—a subtle crocodile, which he was—he noticed not—or, at least, did not seem to notice the jeers around him.

He walked straight up to Velvet.

The farmer's son was cool and collected.

But his features were pallid—and upon his lips, could not be traced the ruby of youth, this great characteristic of healthy boyhood.

"I am up to time, sir," he said, addressing Velvet. "I should say, from what you have seen here (although it might have seen worse), that you have not altered your mind—that you are still ready to come with me."

Velvet muttered a faint—

"Yes."

"Feeling confident of your willingness to sail with me across the tempestuous ocean of life," Wild Will went on, "I have brought with me your toggery. You must wear it for appearance's sake, my boy —and you will find that your share of the profits will far exceed the salary which I promised to you this morning.

Very—very unwell—very much so, indeed, Velvet felt now.

He was weak—and an indescribable giddiness, which had crept over him with the death of old Marks, had not left him—yet he did not like to confess his inability to follow the swell thief.

Thus it was, with a feeling and an expression of countenance very similar to those which the martyrs of old must have possessed in dying for a cause which they understood but partly—that the farmer's son rose and solicited the order of Wild Will.

The swell thief opened the parcel.

"This is bran new toggery," he said. "Once in those clothes, my boy, you should remember that you are the confidential servant of Captain De Vere —the name under which I will for the future be known in fashionable circles.

But we must now leave Harry and the swell thief together, to pay a visit to Bournemouth, to see how his mother supported the loss of her son.

CHAPTER XXIV.

JENNY'S SORROW—RETURN OF DICK SPALDINGS—HIS ALTERED MANNER—TALK IN THE VILLAGE—AN UN-ACCOUNTABLE FRIENDSHIP—THREE PALS ALWAYS TOGETHER—A WOMAN'S RESOLVE—WHAT IS TO BE-COME OF THEM ALL.

SHE sat, awaiting his return, in the room of that pretty cottage, in Bournemouth, where we first introduced our readers.

But she could not remain still.

Now and then she would rise from her chair, relinquish her work, and pace up and down the room with throbbing pulse and palpitating heart.

At length, she could no longer contain her feelings.

With an unsteady step she staggered towards the threshold of her door, and her lingering glance swept the country near and far.

But uselessly did she do so.

Then fretful, broken-hearted, her mind filled with sad forebodings, which, alas, were doomed to be confirmed, the poor creature's eyes became filled with tears, and a warm stream of sorrow bathed her pallid cheek.

"Where's Harry? What has become of the poor boy?" She would mutter, and she would clasp her feverish brow with her heated palm, and her thoughts would lose themselves in wild conjectures.

Poor Jenny! thou hads't sinned, and although the Lord was merciful upon thy poor fallen sister, but little pity will the world bestow upon thy dishonoured state, and bitterly, aye, bitterly, indeed, will thou have to atone for the erring step which thou heedlessly took.

"What will his father say, when he finds his boy gone?" again soliloquized the farmer's wife—the treasure of his heart—the idol of his thoughts, will not be there to welcome him home.

As she spoke, Jenny directed her steps towards the bedroom where her son was wont to rest, and as she gazed upon the empty couch she shook mournfully her pretty head.

"Oh, he may return yet, before his father comes back from the fair," she would mutter, and so thinking, she flung herself upon a chair, and tried to sleep.

But this was a difficult task to accomplish, although the night, or at least, the morning, was already very far advanced, she could not rest.

How long the night appear, reader, when you remain tossing upon your bed, without being enabled to close your weary eyelids.

To Jenny it was a martyrdom of pain, which no pen could fully and adequately describe.

She wished to forget, and yet she could not.

Her body was tired, her mind pre-occupied and anxious, and her heart sunk within her breast as she realized to herself the bitter truth that her son had disappeared from her home, for reasons for which she could not account.

The minutes passed, and time hung heavily upon her, and she could hear the belfry of the old cathedral chiming the hours of night with a loud and monotonous sound.

Morning dawned!

And yet no one came, and she remained alone—alone with her thoughts—looking upon Harry's disappearance as one of the many blows sent to her by destiny to make her atone for her crime.

＊　　＊　　＊　　＊　　＊

And then the heavy-loaded cars on their way to the next town, rattled over the high road—and as the streaks of morn peeped slowly through the interstices of the closed shutters, louder than ever rose the concert of the birds in their nests, mocking the faithless wife in her grief!"

Suddenly she heard a sound close at hand.

Yes—she could not be mistaken:

It was the well-known footsteps of her husband.

Rapidly she darted towards the looking-glass, and passing her handkerchief across her eyes, she wiped away the tears that would still linger there.

Her toilet was nearly concluded, and she was just about to pass the comb in a hasty manner through her luxuriant hair, when nearer and nearer came the footsteps.

With one bound, she confronted Dick Spaldings.

He seemed reckless, and a strong scent of spirits escaped his breath.

"Richard," she said, flinging her arm, on the impulse of the moment, around her husband's neck, "you have been drinking!"

"What's that to you," he asked, roughly, "aint I at liberty to accept the offer of a treat when I can get one."

"Oh, Heavens!" muttered Jenny, "what a change. And who," she asked, in a penetrating tone of voice, "induced you to pay a visit at the 'Rose and Crown.'"

"Oh! no one particular. Nat Smith, our old friend."

The farmer placed a strong intonation upon the last words.

Jenny became deadly pale.

She knew that she had no friend in Nat Smith.

"Strange enough, Jenny," the husband continued, with seeming carelessness, "I saw at the inn one whom I was far from expecting to meet in such a place."

"Indeed," echoed Jenny, "and who was that?"

"William Spanton, the schoolmaster!"

And, having spoken, the farmer sank upon a seat, and began to light his pipe.

Not a word had yet been said about Harry; not a remark did Jenny make concerning the schoolmaster.

Of course Dick Spaldings thought that his son was in bed, and had he been in the house he would not have inquired after him, until his wife would have told him all the news which he longed to get acquainted with.

"Richard," Jenny began after a moment of silence

and the words which she was about to pronounce died in her throat. "Richard!"

The farmer gazed stupidly upon her.

"What's the matter?" he asked; "Jenny, are you taken unwell? Speak?"

The wife could find no reply.

She approached her husband, and leaned over him.

"Richard," she repeated, in a soft voice, "know you where our boy is?"

"In his bed, I s'pose!" growled Dick.

No, Jenny could not make it out.

Could her husband know the truth? she asked herself, and at once dismissed the idea from her mind.

"He is not asleep, Richard," she pursued, slowly. "In the course of the day he went out, and he has not returned."

"And were you here then?" he asked, carelessly.

"Yes," Jenny replied, unflinchingly, and her features became of a crimson hue.

The husband rose.

"Oh, I'll see after him to-day," he quickly retorted. "He is, perhaps, gone on the high road to meet me, and he sank asleep; doubtless he will return, for I do not know what could have otherwise become of him."

Cooly, indeed, did her husband take the information, and sullen and quarrelsome he grew suddenly—finding fault with Jenny at every movement she did to prepare the morning meal.

But the day passed off, and Harry did not return; and Jenny wept, and the husband inwardly cursed his wife for having been the cause of his boy's departure—the boy whom Spaldings loved with a father's deep affection.

Not a word did he mention to his wife about the day's occurrence, not a syllable did he utter concerning the harsh manner with which he had spoken to his son—a manner which had been the means of hurrying the thrilling event which we are about to describe.

Now, it is a well-known fact, that there are some natures which, from being generous and affectionate, can become selfish and cruel, and lose all noble feeling once their hopes are blighted.

Such was the farmer's.

But, although his speech was rough, his manner altered—yet he possessed sufficient command over himself not to let Jenny guess the reason which had wrought the difference in him.

"Richard," said Jenny, in the evening, "there was a time—not so very long ago—when you used to make me your confidante, share your joys, and weep over your sorrows; now you seem quite changed. What have I done?"

So genuine was Jenny's speech, and so loving was the glance of her bright orbs, that many would have treated with supreme contempt any report damaging her fair fame. But it should be here remembered that the farmer had not relied upon hearsay only, but, alas! ascertained beyond a doubt the truth of the information which Nat Smith had given him.

"What have you done?" he asked; and penetrating and deep was his searching look—a look before which Jenny's gaze quailed. "Oh! nothing, my dear Jenny—nothing, that I am aware of."

The glance and the words were so contradictory to each other, that Jenny was lost in bewilderment, and feared to open once more her lips to question her husband.

Dick Spaldings noticed the inward commotion which was taking place within Jenny's breast—and wishing not to let her know what he felt, he thought it a wise policy to remove all doubts on her part, and to make her believe that he was over the same towards her.

There are many who might think that such a vile character as Dick Spaldings proved himself to be, could only find its conception in the brain of the novelist—but erroneous, indeed, would that impression be.

For without retrograding very far, perhaps many of our readers may remember having read a very clever story by the pen of Mr. Smith, which appeared in *The London Journal*, under the title of "Woman and her Master"—where Ned Cantor there plays a hideous *rôle*, indeed!

To say that the character was overdrawn, would be but a poor excuse, for was not the immense popularity which the work obtained—being read by over 500,000 people—a sure guarantee that the type of the man existed, and that it was delineated in a graphic style, which had won the sanction of half a million of readers.

"What would you wish me to tell you, Jenny?" the farmer now asked, after a moment of silence—during which he had become plunged in thoughts which no one could unravel. "Say, and I'll speak. I have no good tidings to give you. I had a very bad week's work; and, to make things still more pleasant, my poor 'Bonny' fell under me, and I had to sell him to the knacker, as he injured himself in a manner which rendered him perfectly useless to me."

These words, which we know to be but a tissue of falsehoods, were spoken in reply to a query which Jenny had made relating to the horse, which, during the day, she had ascertained to be absent.

The farmer, meanwhile, had tried to recover his stolen property, but as they were many strolling vagabonds in the country, he had consoled himself with the unpleasant reflection, that, if the beast had not returned to the farm it had become the property of some thief who had ridden on his back to some distant path, from which he was not likely to return to Bournemouth.

Everything, in a small village, is very soon known, and many hours had not elapsed ere the neighbours spoke about the heavy blow which had fallen upon the hitherto happy couple, and many pitied the afflicted parent, while a greater number still heard with joy the news which was likely to cast a funeral pall over two beings whose felicity they had more than once envied from the bottom of their heart.

For our own part, we can also, without fear of being contradicted, name a certain party who enjoyed and chuckled very much over the discovery, and smiled with a ghastly grim smile as he bandaged of an evening the scar which Dick Spaldings had left upon his old face, scars, which we beg to inform our readers, were but slowly healing.

Many attempts were, however, made by Jenny to recover her son, but meeting with but little success in her endeavours, she ill reconciled herself to her fate, and tried to win back to her heart the affections of her husband, who, a few days after his return from the fair, was fond of the public-house, and took to drinking with a madness which led many to say that it would not last for ever, and that ere long the brokers would pay a visit to Dick Spalding's abode.

The wise-heads in the village used to say that poor Spalding had been so broken down by the loss of his son that he had recourse to drink to forget his sorrow, and people generally believe it—but what they could not make out was this:—

How did it come to pass that Dick Spalding was so friendly with Nat Smith and Will Spanton, the young schoolmaster, who had lately lost his appointment, and that the trio were never to be found, except in the skittle-ground or the tap-room, where they treated everybody with good sterling money, which came from some source which no one had yet succeeded in discovering?

"GENTLY, MY BOY! OR I'LL MAKE THESE BARK!"

CHAPTER XXV.

VELVET IN HIS NEW GUISE—CAPTAIN DE VERE DOES THE HEAVY—CABBY, HERE!—THE LONE HOUSE——THE OLD MAN—THE SUICIDE.

IT would be useless for us to dwell upon the toilet of Velvet, as it would only be encroaching upon our space, when more important matters than the ones alluded to are to be related—thus, not to keep our readers a minute longer than we possibly can help, we will inform them that it did not take long for the boy to cast aside his countrified costume, and to assume that of a gentleman's page.

The boys gazed with feelings of curiosity, mingled with a certain reluctance at parting with their new acquaintance—upon Velvet in his new guise—and heartfelt and affectionate was the farewell which sounded upon his hearing as he respectfully followed the steps of the swell thief, who lost no time in paying off Big Ned for his living merchandise, and with quick steps glided down the rickety old stairs which led to the door of the thieves' den.

"You look slap-up, Velvet," said Wild Will, as soon as he found himself in the open street; "and in my company you will see town life; and although you are very young, you will, I doubt not, confess that it has its charms."

Velvet listened to Wild Will

"Town life," he muttered to himself. "What can it mean? Truly, if it is of the same description as that which I have already witnessed, little, indeed, do I care to see more of it, for some time, at least."

And he became thoughtful, and he followed silently his new master.

Now, to tell the truth, Velvet had more reasons than one to be fretful.

In the first instance, he regretted his home, and he longed to return to Bournemouth, a difficult thing, indeed, for him to do—for in the days of which we write, the modes of conveyance were not so rapid as they are now-a-days, and it took you nearly as long to go from London to the place where his family lived, as it does now to cross the Channel, or, more properly speaking, to reach St. Petersburg, or any other far distant Continental country—and in the second instance, he felt very much annoyed, nay, grieved, at having lost, or having been robbed (the latter most likely) of the deed which had been entrusted to him, and which, if old Martin's words contained any truth, were of great value.

Somehow or another, he believed that Wild Will had stolen the paper—for although he could not have sworn to the fact, yet he thought that certain features which had appeared to him when in his half-consciousness, were very similar, indeed, to those of his companion.

This was, however, a most ticklish point, which he could not solve at once, and as he knew that too much talk would be very likely to excite suspicion, he inwardly resolved to say no more upon the subject, and to keep a sharp look-out upon his companion's movements, as he doubted not that ere long a good opportunity to satisfy his own curiosity would be forthcoming.

Wild Will was, meanwhile, walking briskly by his side, speaking but seldom to his recruit, and evidently planning in his head some scheme where the boy's help would come in useful.

"What do you think of Captain De Vere, Velvet?" the swell thief at length asked, wishing to draw his young companion into conversation, thus to enable his discerning nature to take stock of the boy's mental resources. "Do you like it? Does it sound aristocratic?"

"Captain De Vere!" Velvet repeated.

"Yes, Captain De Vere, ah!" Wild Will continued, strongly accentuating the last sentence. "Something striking about it; is there not?"

Velvet did not quite see it, you know—but as he was performing the rôle of "buttons" he thought that it would be as wise on his part if he were to carry it out to the letter, and abide by the rule laid down for menials, so he re-echoed Wild Will's sentiments.

The two individuals had now arrived in the neighbourhood of Piccadilly—a part of London-town which Velvet had never visited, and which, as it is well known, is a most fashionable part of the metropolis.

"Where are we going, Captain?" Velvet now asked. "We have been walking a good while, now, and I am getting rather tired."

Wild Will reflected.

"What a confounded ass I am," he said. "I should have taken a 'hansom,' long before now, and saved my legs and yours; but since Charles Reade says that 'It is never too late to mend,' we will call a cab, and step into it without any further delay."

And without another word, Wild Will remained at a standstill.

"Cabby! cabby! cabby here, ah?" he would keep on saying, but all the vehicles which he hailed being occupied, he had to wait some time; at last, a smart looking Hansom drove up, and Wild Will and Velvet jumped in.

Velvet liked the drive immensely. He squatted upon the back cushion of the conveyance with a freedom which was too natural not to be genuine, and would, doubtless, have fallen asleep had not Wild Will's hand rested rather heavily upon his shoulder.

"Now, young cockolorum," he said, "just look up abit. I'll want your assistance very shortly, for we will soon be at our destination."

"And where are we darting off at this rate?" he asked in reply; "this seems to me as if it were the country,"

And so it was the country—for the Hansom was rattling over a solitary road situate in the neighbourhood of Hampstead Heath.

To Velvet's question the swell thief had made no reply.

Still the vehicle rattled onwards.

At length, the driver opened the little trap-door above the heads of the occupants of his conveyance, and asked them how far the place was where they wished to be taken to.

Wild Will, in answer, told him to stop.

The coachman did so.

Then Wild Will and Velvet alighted from the vehicle, and the latter, having waited five minutes, during which the swell thief and the cabman had been quarrelling together about the fare, he was at length joined by his worthy and illustrious governor.

Wild Will, however, did not walk on at once.

He first waited until the retreating sounds of the Hansom had told him that the cab was far away —and then he briskly cleared the space before him.

"Where are we going?" once more asked Velvet, who was getting very impatient, and very curious to know what motive could bring his master in such an out-of-the-way place.

"Buttons, hold yer tongue."

And with this gentlemanly remonstrance, the captain pursued a narrow path, at the end of which could be seen a small cottage, whose dimly-lighted windows were partly concealed by the shrubs and branches of trees which grew around it.

Velvet followed.

The swell thief at length reached the outside of a door, and with his stick gave a most peculiar knock against it.

"Who's there?" asked a voice.

"Willy Rack," replied the swell thief.

"Right," pursued the voice.

And the door opened.

The swell thief then entered the abode, and shook hands with the inhabitant of the place.

But here it is necessary that we should describe the same.

He was an old man, of about eighty years of age —his features were parched and wrinkly, and his eyes, which were sunk in their hollow sockets to a frightful degree, glittered like those of a ferret.

The glance which he cast upon Velvet when he entered the room, was anything but calculated to impress him with the lawfulness of his intentions towards him.

"Who's that?" he asked, eyeing the boy still more minutely than he had hitherto done.

"That's my valet," replied the swell thief; "but he is all right, so speak away."

The old man reflected.

"Well," he began after a moment's silence, "What news?"

Wild Will mused.

"I have none," he said slowly. "I came here to obtain some clue relating to the—

"I know."

Here the two worthies whispered a few words in an undertone.

Velvet had sat down before the fire.

But although he seemed to be engrossed in the contemplation of the earth, he was not without lending an attentive ear to the conversation which was being held.

He learnt a few things that night.

For the old man having at one instant forgotten the presence of another being besides Wild Will, spoke in a louder key than he had hitherto done.

"And what will he give to do the job?" the old man asked.

"He promised me a hundred pounds."

"Not so bad if he stumps up to time."

"I think he will do that; but, a minute, is he not a foreigner?"

"Yes."

"What do you call him?"

"The Marquis of Aguado."

"And she—"

Evidently the conversation relates to some woman, thought Velvet. Let us hear still more if we can.

And he listened still more intently.

"He has seen her somewhere, I believe," pursued Wild Will, "and he has taken a great liking for her."

"A brutal passion, you mean," related the old man, "and he wants to gratify the same. We know all about that."

And the old man smiled with a demonic smile.

The swell thief, meanwhile, was silent.

"I say, old boy," he began, after a moment's deep thought, "who is to bring her here?"

The old man mused.

"I don't know," he replied, slowly.

Wild Will now clasped his brow, and his eye brightened.

"I have it," he said, suddenly. "Ralph the Gaol-bird wont object. He must be hard up, you know, for he escaped from the convict-ship—and he will cling at any chance to make a few pounds."

"To whom could the words refer?" mused Velvet. "Could they be speaking of the man whose life he had saved by the sea-shore?"

Oh! how he longed to ask Wild Will who he was—but to do so would be unwise—so he thought it right to remain silent.

"Ralph!" the old man repeated derisively; "not he."

"Why?" quickly asked Wild Will.

Here the mysterious old man laughed loudly.

"Because——" he said.

"Because——" pursued the swell thief, in a breath.

"He had a fit of drunkenness on this morning, and he betook himself downstairs, and did not return—I went to look after him about half-an-hour ago, and where do you think I found him?"

The swell thief looked puzzled.

"How am I to know?" he quickly asked.

Again the old man mused.

"Why," he said, "I found him stretched on the broad of his back, bleeding like a pig—and dead—for he had taken it into his head to cut his throat with a razor."

Coolly, indeed, did the old man give his information.

A shudder broke over Velvet's frame.

But Wild Will did not seem in the slightest degree moved.

"It is provoking," he said; "is he down-stairs?"

"Yes; would you like to look at him?"

The swell thief nodded.

"Velvet," he said, as he followed his informant, "did you ever see a suicide?"

The boy replied in the negative.

The old man again laughed loudly.

"No, I did not," boldly went on Velvet—wishing to show, by his manner, that he was not awed by the old man's impertinence.

"He'd better have a look at him, then."

"I will," said Velvet.

So firmly had he spoken, that not a word was uttered in reply by his two listeners.

The old man led the way.

The swell thief followed—and Velvet bore closely upon his track.

CHAPTER XXVI.

THE DARK VAULT—THE BLEEDING CORPSE—VELVET'S HORROR—THE GORGEOUS ROOM OF INFAMY—THE MISER—THE DEPARTURE.

Many of those who read this strange book will be somewhat startled at the communication which it will contain, so let them fancy what was Velvet's astonishment when, after passing through a dark vault, he descended a staircase leading to a door which gave him admittance to a low-roofed cellar; where, in the corner, stood several barrels of brandy—while in the other, scattered anyhow, could have been seen the skeletons of at least fifty individuals.

Immediately beneath a barrel lay a fully-stretched corpse.

A sickening feeling of intense uneasiness broke over the boy's frame.

For he had recognised in the corpse the features of Ralph, the man whom he had saved from a watery grave, and who had brought him to London.

The dead man presented, truly, a ghastly sight.

His clothes, the same which he had worn when Velvet had left him—under what circumstances it is not our purpose here to tell, as they will be related by him at a future period of this story, were literally saturated with the gore which had flowed from his neck, which was frightfully mutilated—his lips were white and distorted—and his cheeks clammy, and lividly repulsive.

The old man and Wild Will gazed upon the senseless body.

"He has done for himself, at all events," muttered the old man. "Do you know, Will, that he was quite altered when he came here this morning."

"Explain yourself."

"Why, he spoke about some lad whom he decoyed away from home, and all that sort of thing—that God would never forgive him—God, fancy! ah! ah!—and he was in the blue devils, I guess, when he severed his whistle."

Wild Will examined the cellar.

"I see you have removed that big black stone," he said; "when do you intend to bury him?"

The old man looked up.

"Not just yet, Will," he said. "This place is cold, and he will keep here; and don't you know if she is to be buried also it will save time, and I'll kill two shots with one bird."

"You mean the other way, my worthy," Wild Will retorted, noticing the graphic expression of his companion; "but it is all right—I understand you all the same."

Velvet had now become sad and gloomy.

And it may well be asked here—could he have been otherwise?

"She," he kept on muttering. "Who can she be? Doubtless, there is a murder about to be perpetrated, but if I can help it—Heavens. know that I will not be wanting."

"A penny for your thoughts, Buttons," Wild Will now said, noticing Velvet's silence. "What has come over you? Are you afraid of the dead one?"

Little did the swell thief know the nature of the resolutions which the boy was now passing in his own mind.

And then, after he had spoken, Will suggested the propriety of returning up-stairs.

His advice was abided by—and the old man and Wild Will and Velvet retraced their steps towards the entrance of the cellar.

The old man now took a ponderous key from his pocket, and placed it in the lock of the door.

"Nothing like locking him up," he said; "he might take it into his head to pay me a visit, and I hate ghosts."

With this idiotic remark the old man moved on.

But ere he wound his steps towards the small room which faced upon the lane, he halted.

"Did you see my new furniture, sirree?" he asked, questioning Wild Will.

The swell thief shook his head in the negative.

"Well then, come on, and I'll initiate you to my new apartments."

Not being told to go away—Velvet followed his master.

The three individuals now stepped into a tolerably large-sized room, furnished in a style which would baffle description.

All that wealth could give was in this place.

The floor, which was lined with a soft, smooth carpet, groaned under the weight of the heavy, massive furniture, which had been selected regardless of expense. Here, the most critical upholsterer could not have found fault with the make of the Turkish bed-sofas which relieved the monotony of the less comfortable chairs—while the walls, covered with a paper of a tasty pattern, were ornamented with cleverly executed pictures of the Hogarth style—representing subjects which, if they would have caused the eyes of a maiden to quail before its revolting selection, were calculated to gratify the morbid and satiated taste of the coarse libertine who gazed upon them.

"This is very clever!" muttered Wild Will, noticing an engraving, entitled— "The Lord of the Manor among his preserved"—the meaning of which was obvious, when the likeness of a certain Irish marquis was brought to mind, and the artist's idea conveyed by the drooping eyes and deep blush suffusing the cheeks of a pretty colleen, fearful to withstand the gaze of her master's lustrous glance.

Although Velvet was very young, he was not long in guessing the purpose to which the room in which he was standing was placed.

And instinctively a reflection dawned upon his mind. He shuddered.

"And has this room been used yet?" asked Will.

The old man smiled.

"Not since the improvements," he continued.

"And when will it be, governor?"

This was a most important question, and Velvet firmly resolved not to let it escape him.

Thus he became very attentive.

For who knows but what he might be the means of preventing a dark deed of night.

Of saving a timid gazelle from the fangs of the tiger.

Of snatching some budding flower from the atmosphere of corrupt filthiness, and pestilential miasma?

The old man now led the way out of the room.

"The furniture must have cost you something," now began the swell thief, giving one last glance

upon the room; "but it has more than repaid you a thousand times over."

"It has; but there's one part which I do not like. No, I do not——"

The old man pursued, as if he were greatly offended .

"It is being obliged to——"

Here the words which followed were spoken in an undertone whisper.

"And what does he want?"

The remaining sentence between Wild Will and the old man but partly reached Velvet, yet he believed that he had heard that on a certain date, three days after the evening when we write, a woman was to be decoyed to the lone house, and murdered.

Whether a boy like Velvet, with no resources at his command, and, we may say, entirely under the power of his master, would succeed in accomplishing successfully that which could escape the laws of a well-established force, is a point which we will hope to solve before long, for the benefit of the curious.

"And who is that man we have just left?" asked Velvet, as soon as he crossed the threshold of the lone cottage, and found himself treading along a path, in company with Wild Will.

"It would be of little use to you to know his name," replied the swell thief. "Besides, you are too fresh with us yet to hear everything—only this I can tell you—that man has a ruling passion, and to gratify it he will do anything—its nature."

"I think I know," said Velvet.

The swell thief smiled.

"What's it?" he asked.

"He worships gold, does he not—and he's a miser?"

"You are a 'cute boy, my worthy—you have guessed right; and now let us be somewhat brisk in our march, for I must be home shortly."

"Is it far from here?"

"Don't fear, as soon as we get away from the house we will ride."

And truly spoke Will, for he soon hailed another cab, and once more Velvet came in for a drive—and once more he wondered whither he was going.

CHAPTER XXVII.

THE END OF A DRIVE—VELVET'S ASTONISHMENT—THE BATCH OF FLUNKEYS—THE ATTENTIVE HOUSEKEEPER.

THE scene which Velvet had witnessed, and the interview which he had had with the old man in the lone house, had produced such a strong impression upon his mind, that as soon as he found himself in the cab, sitting by the side of the swell thief, he became plunged in a mood which foreboded him no good.

Still the cab rattled on, and the boy wondered whither he was going.

"I say, Captain de Vere," he asked from his companion, "where are we off now."

The swell thief smiled.

"Do not be impatient," he said, "we will soon reach our destination;" and he looked around.

The vehicle had now arrived in Bond street.

Here the cabman lifted the trap above the heads of the occupants of his vehicle, and asked the swell thief whether he was to stop.

"Dam you, fellah !" replied the captain. "Nice fellah you are to drive about town, don't you know yet where Long's hotel is."

"Beg your pardon, sir," replied the cabman, and he reined in his spavined old horse, and halted before a gorgeous looking mansion.

This was Long's hotel.

Velvet was getting still more and more puzzled.

"Surely," he said to his companion in a half-whisper, "you are not stopping here?"

The swell thief enjoined silence; Velvet became quiet.

In a twinkling the boy alighted.

The swell thief followed him.

"How much is your fare, ah! old fellah!" the captain asked, eyeing the worthy driver.

"Three-and-sixpence, sir."

The swell thief felt his pockets.

He knew the request to be exhorbitant, and would doubtless have objected to pay it, but he could ill do so now.

A consequential flunkey had appeared upon the steps.

Flunkeys, in general, are a cute set of people, a man who stops at Long's hotel should not grumble about the fare.

"Give me change of a sovereign," he asked, handing a golden piece to the driver.

The coachman fumbled in his pocket, and drew sixteen-and-sixpence.

The swell thief took the change, and without ever reckoning it, walked towards the door.

The flunkey was still there.

"I say," Captain de Vere began, addressing the servant, in a cool, collected manner, "did you prepare a suit of apartments for me?"

"For me!"

These two last words had been pronounced in a manner which required an immediate reply.

The servant did not know what to answer.

"Who could the gentleman be? he wondered, and he scratched his head, he had said for me, of course he must have been somebody, perhaps some nobleman, Heaven knows! besides, had he not a servant with him, a servant with a livery that was tasty and expensive."

Thus, he resolved not to delay.

"We are rather full at present, sir," he said, "but I doubt not that we can accommodate you and your suite."

The swell thief reflected.

"You must have received my note," he said, just tell Mr. Long that I would like to see him, I wrote to him from my place in Staffordshire two days ago, giving him full instructions to have a landing ready for me."

The servant bowed.

"What name shall I say, sir?"

Velvet was very much amused, and he was grinning like a monkey.

Of course, the hilarity on his part was all the better for Captain de Vere, for the boy's cheek only tended to confirm the idea that the servant had formed respecting his master.

"Captain de Vere is my name," said the swell thief.

The flunkey now disappeared.

The swell thief and Velvet were now in the hall.

Such fine furniture! such handsome glasses, such a soft velvet carpet! no, never had Velvet seen such things before.

A minute elapsed.

Then another individual appeared.

Evidently he was the head waiter.

He was dressed to the ninety-nines—any amount of a white choker—a glossy tail coat—tight fitting trousers—and everything about him regardless of expense.

"Who's that," mused Velvet.

The man walked straight to the swell thief.

"Captain de Vere, I believe!" he said, bowing before the swell thief.

"Yes, I wrote to Mr. Long about retaining some apartments, have you got them ready."

The head flunkey mused.

"The letter must have miscarried," he said, "for no such communication reached us, but I dare say we can find room for you, although we are very full at present, for but an hour ago his Serene Highness the Prince of Carabouliski, and the Count of Peelordinotitafiram arrived here with their suite, quite unexpectedly.

"What does he say?" mused Velvet, who had been unable to refrain a smile when he had heard the fashionable names above alluded to.

"Yes," said Captain de Vere, "I suppose that I must rest satisfied with what accommodation you have to provide me with. But I have no doubt that I will have no occasion to complain."

"I hope not, captain; at least, we will do our best to make you comfortable."

Captain de Vere smiled.

"My friend, Lord Fitzboodle, says, this is the best house in town—and he ought to know."

"A friend of Lord Fitzboodle," mused the head flunkey, and he led the way.

Captain de Vere had played his part well.

He knew the ways of the world, and he knew, also, that servants are a class of people to be conciliated.

Velvet, meanwhile, was lost in conjectures.

What a life his had been since his arrival in London.

What scenes he had witnessed!

What a short career—and yet how full of stirring incidents!

Robbed from home by a convict, whose clammy corpse he had gazed upon with feelings of horror. The guest of thieves—now the valet of a sham captain—what was he to see or to do next?

We have seen, ere now, that he was doomed to play some strange rôle in London, for had Fate destined that it should be otherwise, he would have been taken to the station, and subsequently been brought before the magistrate.

His story would have been listened to—and if the magistrate by whom he would have been tried had caused inquiries to be made into the truth of his statement, which he most likely would have done, the probabilities are that he would have been sent back to Bournemouth to his family, and that the theft which he had perpetrated would have benefited him instead of otherwise.

But evidently it was not to be so.

While we have been engaged in writing, the head butler had transferred the swell thief and Velvet to the care of a buxom housemaid, who was to usher the two new-comers into the apartments which they were to occupy during their stay in the hotel.

With that ease and coolness which is only acquired by a long apprenticeship in the ways of West End life, Captain De Vere followed his guide without speaking a word.

At last they reached a landing.

"It is deuced provoking, madam," the swell thief now said, when he found that the housekeeper was about to open a door before her, "that my letter never reached Mr. Long. I am rather short winded, and I hate walking up a staircase."

The old lady mumbled an apology.

And while we are reverting to the white slaves of England—servants to wit—we may as well inform our readers here, that the swell thief produced quite an impression upon the lady—an impression which was greatly enhanced by the appearance of Mr. Velvet, whose good-looking face was not thrown away upon the matronly dame.

That evening, while the swell thief was sitting

in his bed-room; busy, indeed, became the group down stairs, and every one in the servants' pantry, who had seen the captain and his servant—fully agreed that he was a thorough gentleman—quite a young swell, every inch of him.

But let us remain in the captain's company.

The old lady had now opened a door which stood before her, and with a queenly bow had ushered the captain and his servant in a large, well-furnished single bed-room.

"Captain de Vere," she asked, "will this room do for you?"

"Oh, yaas—yaas, very nicely, indeed; but, of course, I want accommodation for my *valet*."

Velvet smiled again.

"Oh, he is not very big," said the good lady, casting a meaning glance upon the small boy. "I dare say that we will manage things all right with him."

The captain nodded.

The housekeeper then ignited two candles, and after having ascertained whether the gentleman was all right—being told by him that his *luggage*, a most important item to think of, would be sent up next morning by the railway officials, who had detained it through some mistake—she bowed once more and withdrew.

The captain sat down, and bid Velvet to follow his example.

Then he listened intently.

He wanted to make sure of his not being spied upon, for although that he should be so was most unlikely, still he knew that prudence is a great point in a swell mobsman's tactics.

The retreating footsteps of the old lady was now dying away in the distance.

Then the swell thief rose.

"How will I do now," he asked from Velvet, dressing and undressing, to while away the time—meanwhile glancing at himself in a looking-glass just before him.

Velvet knew not what reply to make.

"You are a wonderful master, sir," he said after awhile. "A wonderful individual altogether."

"Oh, you know but little yet, my boy. Just pull the bell."

"What for?" asked Velvet.

Without condescending to waste another word, Captain de Vere flung himself in an easy chair, and pointed with his finger towards the bell-rope.

Velvet rose.

"And, now, young man, just bear this in mind," the swell thief now began, "you see everything, hear everything, and make no absurd answers, for if you do, you will get, not only myself, but yourself, too, in the hole."

Velvet clearly saw the wisdom of the remark.

He nodded affirmatively.

And he summoned a servant.

In fashionable, expensive hotels, generally speaking, but little fault can be found with the attendance; thus, five minutes at the utmost elapsed, and a servant appeared.

It was all a wonder to Velvet how they were to see any different faces.

The new individual, of course, wished to know the gentleman's pleasure.

"What's your name," asked Captain de Vere.

"John, sir."

"John."

"Yes, sir."

"Well then, John, bring me a bottle of brandy, and some hot water.

The brandy was soon brought up, and the captain

poured himself a very fair allowance, smacked his lips, and said that the cognac was very fair.

The servant was about to withdraw, when the Captain bid him to come up in about a quarter of an hour, and to get his servant's room ready.

When Velvet and the swell thief were free and together, the former spoke.

"This is a very nice place, Captain," he said, "did you ever come here before?"

"No, my boy, but I intend to, please God; that's to say, if I do not find it too hot," he continued, between his teeth, fearing that his words should be overheard.

"Now Velvet, my lad," he resumed after awhile, "you are my servant; I have not given you any wages yet, but since I have engaged you, and you do not object to my company, here's something to bind you."

Thus speaking, the Captain handed a sovereign to Velvet.

The farmer's son feared to take it, and he longed to say that he objected to a gratification, but after consideration he did what all boys, nay, not only boys, but men, women, and girls would have done, namely, stuck to the coin.

It was a twenty-shilling piece, and Velvet was not proof against the temptation of gold.

True, he knew it was money unfairly won.

Perhaps it was the proceeds of some burglary.

May be the price paid for some dark deed of night!

Yet after all money has no colour, and like dead men, in many instances, it tells no tales, so Yelvet thought that there was no great harm in consigning the gift to his innermost pocket.

With the half of it he might run away from his master, and return to his home.

Whether he will do so, or not, is a conclusion which, not being able to see in the clouds of the future, we are unable here to divulge.

At length the hours passed, and Velvet, was shown to a snug little bed-room, very near to that of the housekeeper.

Whether he was like Joseph, pounced upon in the middle of the night, and preserved his innocence for the sake of his garments, or whether he yielded in the dark to the modern puephar's advance, is a query which we will not attempt to solve, as we know too well that we could not be treading upon so ticklish a ground without offending the morals of some of our female readers, and God forbid that we should do that.

But as we are now going to conclude the chapter we may as well inform our friends that whatever did happen—and that must remain for ever in the dark—Velvet rose fresh and hearty in the morning —felt very hungry—and did ample justice to a breakfast of bacon and eggs, which the worthy housekeeper had given orders to have prepared for him.

CHAPTER XXVIII.

THE SWELL THIEF DOES HIS WINE—VELVET AMONG THE SERVANTS—THE CAPTAIN MAKES A MISTAKE—WHICH TURNS OUT TO BE A PROFITABLE ONE—THE DISCOVERY—"ROBBER! ROBBER!"

WHEN Velvet had left the swell thief, to return to his virtuous couch, Captain De Vere had sat thinking in his easy chair, pondering over the incidents of the day, and revolving in his mind the best means to adopt to get his value out of his page.

"I had great difficulty," said the Captain, "in getting a few pounds to-day, and cursed Big Ned and the others! They would never have parted with the boy had I not paid them their price. Now I am very nearly cleaned out, what am I to do?"

So soliloquizing, the Captain emptied his waist-coat pocket, and discovered that he had about four pounds altogether.

That was little enough!

Moreover, when he had boxes, clothes, &c. to get out of the same, for we must tell you that the Captain had lately been hard up, and that he was now trying to make a good haul.

The life of man, at best, is one of constant vexations, contrarities, and disappointments—what must be that of a swell thief?

"I know," the Captain went on, "that the foreigner will pay; but, damn it all, I do not like to shed a girl's blood, if I can help it," and very appropriately the gallant captain stroked his chin, and his hand coming into contact with his neck, such a name as Jack Ketch flitted across his mind, and made him feel rather uncomfortable.

The swell thief's soliloquy, as our perusers need not be told, reverted to the long conversation which he had with the miser.

Velvet had also heard it, and had resolved to prevent the accomplishment of some nefarious plot.

We hope sincerely that he will succeed, and that it will be our pleasing duty to record the events in these columns.

"No," once more repeated the swell thief, "I do not like to be concerned in a murder—at all events, let us see what's to be done."

Then he reflected.

"Oh, I see!" he muttered, striking his forehead with his hand. "Good idea, that."

And he smiled knowingly.

Again he helped himself to the cordial on the table, and when he had drank sufficient to make half-a-dozen men the worse off for the imbibing process which he had undergone—he rose, and paced up and down the room.

But this soon tired him, and hoping that the next day would bring something forth, he went to bed, and was soon lost in a wholesome slumber.

Indeed, had any one entered the room, and heard him snoring as he did, he would have fancied that he had a clear conscience, for his was, indeed, the sleep of the just, Godly, and righteous, could the grunting noise which he made be looked upon as a criterion.

Now if there is one thing which we are more or less fond of, it is a good sleep.

I know men that would sleep themselves to death.

Although the Captain was not one of the above, he was, nevertheless, very lazy, and it was eleven o'clock ere he awoke.

Velvet had thought of going up to his master, but as the servants told him that he should wait until his bell should ring, he abided by the wholesome advice.

We forgot to mention that before Velvet had parted company with his master, he had been fully instructed by him as to what he should say in the event of his being questioned by any one.

But as it mostly happens, when we are prepared to meet an impending blow, we are seldom called upon to do so, and, as Velvet had been well tutored he had not any occasion to abide by the lessons which he had received.

Now a word ere we proceed.

There are many who would make Velvet a most wonderful boy, endowed with the most wonderful virtues, thinking, that by so doing, the greater would be the interest felt in his career.

We have not done so, because we feel confident that had we adopted that course, we might have,

for the sake of the narrative, represented human nature in a false light.

He had his good qualities and his failings, for is there any one perfect, be he the hero of a romance!

Thus he remained in the servant's area, very quietly, not at all anxious for his master's bell to sound.

But while there, he could not help his mind to wander, and gradually, from a temporary wandering, it began to settle upon the things which he had witnessed, and in vivid colours the scene in the lone house appeared before him.

The remembrance, also, of the convict, dead and ghastly livid, was a terrible sight, which he could not dismiss; and he wondered whether he would pay another visit to the den of crime, where such dark deeds as he had heard of were perpetrated.

Also the loss of the parchment which old Marks had given him, was a source of bitter disappointment to him, for firmly he believed that a great importance was attached to the document.

He was thus musing, when a sound attracted his attention.

"Captain de Vere's bell," said a voice. "Now, youngster, you had better go up, and see what he wants."

Velvet would have suggested the propriety of remaining where he was, but feeling somewhat anxious to see his master after the night, he rose, and, without a word, he glided upstairs.

He found the captain standing up in his bed, rubbing his eyes in a most lazy manner.

"Well, Velvet," he said, as soon as he recognised the youth, "how do you like the hotel—are they taking care of you down stairs?"

The boy related to the captain the incidents which had taken place since the previous evening.

The swell thief jumped out of bed.

"Any suspicion afloat?" he asked, walking quickly towards the boy.

Velvet said that he believed not.

"Were they cross-examining you down stairs?" the captain went on.

The answer that Velvet gave this time was also satisfactory.

"We'll do them. Velvet, you go down stairs, and say that I want some breakfast, and ask whether my luggage has arrived. If they tell you that it has not—and I don't see how they can do otherwise—appear very disgusted—blackguard the railway officials, and in a quiet sort of way expatiate upon the annoyance which the delay is sure to give me. Do you understand?"

"Perfectly."

Velvet having remained a few instants longer then departed, and he was not long ere he performed the part which the Captain had made him rehearse in his company.

But while Velvet is downstairs, let us see what the swell thief is doing.

He is fast dressing.

A servant enters.

"I see," says the swell, glancing on the morning papers, "that several fashionable arrivals are chronicled in this morning's post. I suppose you send in your list every morning.

Perhaps by the above, our readers may not understand our meaning.

We will explain ourselves.

There are some hotels in London, at the West End, patronized, of course, by the *elite* of the fashionable world, and the names of every guest to the place is duly entered in a book, and forwarded to the morning papers.

" We have not sent it yet," replied the waiter, " do you wish your name to appear, sir ?'

" Oh, certainly ! Not that I like that sort of thing, you know. I hate display—but one has friends in town, and, unless they hear of you through the medium of the press, why one half must remain in ignorance of your whereabouts.

The waiter said that he should lose no time in forwarding the list, and he soon came up with a book, when the swell thief was asked to enter his name.

Then he wrote Captain de Vere beneath the Prince of Carabouliski and the Count of Peelordinotitafiram, and he had a very good opportunity of seeing the numbers of the rooms where lived the Big Whigs, that resided beneath the same roof as himself.

His object had been one of business, he wanted to know exactly where were quartered the foreign noblemen, whose high sounding names had so kindled Velvets' curiosity.

Once satisfied upon that point he determined to make the most of his information.

How will he do that ?

We will soon tell you.

The swell thief was once more alone.

He peeped his head outside the bed-room door.

Before him all was still.

Not the sound of one footstep smote his ear.

His game was a critical, dangerous one, yet the swell thief feared not the accomplishment of it.

He listened intently.

" No one about," he soliloquized, " that's clear.

Then with a cautious, stealthy step he walked along the smooth carpet which lined the flooring of his landing.

Quickly he descended one flight of stairs.

Then he found himself upon the first landing.

Before him a door.

Quickly he cast a look around him, then he opened the door before him.

That was the bed-room of the Baron Comtes.

Unfortunately, he was awake.

" What do you want, sir ?" asked the foreigner, with a strong accent.

The swell thief expected as much.

" I beg your pardon, sir," he said; " I made a mistake."

The Baron made a reply—

" Oh, don't mention it," and he turned round and went to sleep again.

" Let us try the Prince now," soliloquized the swell thief, and he walked on about eight yards farther.

Gently he opened the door.

The old gentleman—the Prince Peelordinotitafiram was hard asleep, and snoring like Old Harry.

To delay would be madness.

The swell thief knew that.

So again with cautious, stealthy steps he walked towards the bed, and drew the bed-curtains together, so as to prevent his presence being noticed.

So subtle and so experienced was the movement of his hands, that he did that which we have described in a quicker manner than any one else could.

Then the swell thief remained for an instant or so on his tip-toes.

He held his breath.

Across the room, and just by the window-sill stood a splendid dressing-case.

It was opened, and within its silver casement showed a gold watch of a fabulous value.

What we state is not uncommon in the slightest degree, for it is a well-known fact. These foreign noblemen are exceedingly fond of display, and are great lovers of fine jewellery.

The Prince of Carabouliski was hard asleep.

With a cautious, stealthy step the captain glided across the apartment.

Then he halted before the dressing-case.

There was a rustle coming from the bed.

Captain de Vere was evidently in a pickle.

Should his Serene Highness awake, what was he to do ?

Doubtless he would shriek, and call for help, and the worthy captain would be marched to the station-house.

Rather an unpleasant state of affairs for one with his aristocratic ideas.

Fancy Captain de Vere between a batch of bobbies, and Velvet grinning at him.

Then it would be a case, and no mistake, and then it would be the time to inquire—

" How will I do now ?"

The captain considered all these things.

But no, it was not to be.

At least, he hoped not.

There was a splendid gold watch on the table before him, as we have already said.

It was a Geneva—but of the best make, and the swell thief knew that should he be short *his uncle* would at any time accommodate him with twenty pounds upon it.

Decidedly, this was too good a chance for him to lose it.

Then the swell acted on the impulse of the moment.

With a sleight of hand which Professor Anderson would have envied, he consigned the gold watch to his pocket.

Another rustle in the bed.

Yet the Captain did not like to move.

" Here it goes," he muttered ; and he collared all the jewellery before him.

Then, with his pocket heavily laden with the stolen goods, he tried to retreat towards the door.

But he was doomed to be in for it this time.

The old gentleman had jumped out of bed, and was standing in his night shirt, upon the carpet.

The swell thief had reached the door.

The Prince of Carabouliski was a strange looking individual.

He had a nose like a radish in an apoplectic fit, his face was pimply and rubicund, and altogether he was a very queer specimen of a foreign nobleman.

" Holloa ! Mosseir," he said, " Vat do ye ve do here."

The swell thief bowed.

" My Lord, I beg your pardon," he replied, " I was looking for the ——,"

" Oh, I compreney, If you'll allow me I'll show you ——."

Then his Serene Highness, the Prince of Carabouliski, who had been flattered by the appellation of the Captain, led the last named gentleman to a certain place, which we hope our readers will understand without any further explanation.

" Thank you, my lord." the captain continued, standing before Mrs. Jones' abode. " My name is Captain de Vere, and although I have not had the pleasure of an introduction to you, I hope you will excuse me for soliciting the honour of cultivating your friendship."

" In the British army, I suppose, captain ?" continued his Serene Highness, who was, perhaps, looking in his pocket to oblige the captain with one of those things which one would require in his osition.

"LOOK OUT FOR THE GRAVY!"

The captain smiled, and drew a soiled letter from his pocket, and rubbed it in a most impressive manner.

"Yeas," he said, "I am in the British Army, my lord."

His Serene Highness was getting cold.

Standing in a hall without a coat was no joke, and so he thought he would return to his room.

"I hope," he said, ere he went, "that you will find the place comfortable."

With those words his Serene Highness betook himself away.

The swell thief gazed upon the nobleman, and then he quickly went up stairs.

"This is a pretty go," he said, "the chap in sure to miss his toggery, and he will raise an alarm. What a muff I was, not to take away that fur coat of his."

And surely, it was plain enough ——.

"Robber! robber! I am robbed!" came in loud tones, from his Serene Highness's apartments.

Wild Will hears the alarm which is being raised, and he wonders as to the line of conduct which he shall adopt.

Critical, indeed, has become his position!

For ere long he must be discovered.

How can he manage to baffle the pursuits of one and all, and save himself from the station-house?

There is, however, no time for reflection.

The seconds are centuries to him, and his liberty hangs upon a thread!

With the rapidity of one racing for his freedom he darted upstairs.

Once more the swell thief is in his room.

He thinks—and resolves to lock himself up—but although practicable, such a proceeding on his part would only make matters worse.

At length, to do so he deems unwise.

Presently the servants suspicions against him will be kindled, and they will guess the truth.

"Robber! robber! I am robbed!" are the only sentences which reach the swell thief's hearing.

He cannot be mistaken at the voice.

It is that of his Serene Highness, the Prince Carabouliski.

And then the bells ring—and then follows a general uproar.

Also the startled hum of several voices is plainly perceptible.

"A daring robbery has been committed."

"Who can it be?"

"Perhaps the gentleman in No. 16."

Such are some of the exclamations which sound loud and clear.

The flunkeyed paraphernalia is busy.

Wild Will cautiously opens his door.

He listens.

He looks outside.

No. 16. is upon his door.

"Ere long, they will come up stairs," he mutters, and he becomes restless and uneasy.

Of course, the events which we are describing are occurring quicker than any pen could write them.

"I am trapped," he said, "what am I to do?"

Then he smiles.

An idea has come over him—an idea which he intends to carry out.

He puts on his hat, and feels in his pockets to ascertain whether he has his life preserver.

He is satisfied—for he finds that he is not without means to defend himself.

Swiftly he glides.

Down stairs.

He is upon the first landing.

Louder grows the sound of voices, and then there is a pause.

The prince is speaking—relating his interviews with Captain de Vere.

"He must have been the robber," he says, "for what could have brought him here—go up to his bed-room and upon my shoulders will I take the responsibility of giving him in the custody of the police."

The prince's speech is eagerly listened to.

There are voices of dissent.

"Dangerous is the suggestion," says one of the servants, "for if the Captain is innocent, he will leave the hotel, and ruin the character of the house."

And then confusion follows.

Meanwhile, the time passes away, and a good opportunity presents itself to Wild Will to escape.

"Yes, I will search him myself," mutters the head butler.

"Not if I know it," soliloquises the swell thief, and he pauses. "What am I to do?" he asks himself once more.

For, doubtless, the entrance of the hotel is blocked up.

"Send for the police," mutters a voice.

Then there is a tramping of footsteps—and the heads of many are seen emerging from the prince's apartment.

Wild Will becomes bold.

He must not be detected.

"Has he been discovered?" he wonders, and takes a resolution.

He is not long in carrying it out.

Swiftly he clears the last flight of steps.

He is now in the hall.

A pompous porter sits in the chair.

Will he brush by him and run in the streets?

Hark! There is a voice outside the hotel.

The crowd is fast gathering.

He thinks that he can detect the uniforms of the force forcing their way towards the entrance.

To meet them would be sheer madness.

He winds his way to the kitchen.

It is full of servants.

On his left the pantry, and upon a large dish a splendid plum-pudding attracts his gaze.

Oh, this is a piece of good luck!

Besides, he has seen the garments of a male cook.

There is the white frock and the white apron.

Wild Will casts his clothes aside.

Quicker than we could write does he do so.

Then he seizes the toggery.

Half a minute has sufficed him.

His disguise is complete.

He listens.

There are ominous sounds everywhere.

Above him—around him.

He hears the voice of the head butler speaking to some persons above his head.

Then his costume is described, and his features accurately pourtrayed.

Wild Will can no longer doubt.

He listens intently, and he shrinks as he recognises the well-known voice of a clever detective of the G division.

Will he face him, or remain where he is?

The door on his left opens.

There is a shriek!

It is that of an old woman, and he sees a strange face.

She, too, raises a cry.

There are cries everywhere.

"And now for a bold attempt!" mutters Wild Will, and he lays hold of the dish upon which the plum-pudding is.

Then he walks up-stairs.

He is in the hall, and before him the public dining-room.

His forebodings are confirmed.

He has to encounter the gaze of two policemen, and a detective—the very man whom he fears most.

He bowed his head.

"Look out! look out!" says a policeman.

The swell thief grows courageous.

Now the detective retreats before the cook.

For no one likes to have his clothes soiled, and rich and fat is the gravy which surrounds the pudding.

Encouraged by the success of his scheme, Wild Will walks on.

He is about to step in the dining-room, when he sees the hall-door—a clear path before him—no one guarding the entrance.

He gives vent to a mocking laugh, a derisive, loud fit of glee, and he drops the plate at his feet.

This incident has saved him, for there are exclamations of surprise, and all eyes are turned towards the smoking dish.

The crockery has been smashed by the fall.

The policemen are puzzled, and even the detective knows not how to proceed.

Wild Will sees one last chance.

Profiting of the disturbance which reigns, he makes a dash towards the door.

Swift and rapid has been his flight.

But the detective has recognized Will.

He follows quickly his steps.

Wild Will, however, knows that it is now a race for freedom.

He has reached the door.

He is about to clear the threshold, when the detective seizes him by the shoulder.

Then there follows a fierce struggle.

The whole attention is directed towards the detective.

And the thief—and so confident do the policemen feel about Wild Will's capture, that they make no attempts to rush to the rescue.

Shortly afterwards, however, they begin to think that the force will shortly be in danger, for they have perceived a life preserver in Wild Will's hand.

Then they determine to lend a hand to the detective.

But it is too late now.

Wild Will has escaped—in his cook's clothes, leaving a keepsake to the detective in the shape of a heavy blow upon his head, which sends him reeling to the ground.

And then there are yells of disapointment, for Captain de Vere is nowhere to be seen, and has baffled the myrmidons of the law, carrying away with him the Prince of Carabouliski's jewellery.

CHAPTER XXIX.

THE BAGNE OF TOULON—THE GUILLOTINE—THE DEATH KNELL—THE CHIEF OF THE BRETHREN OF THE CRYSTAL DAGGER—THE PRIEST.

WE must now return to Paris, and from Paris we must bring our readers to the Bagne of Toulon.

"What is that place," many may ask?

As we are aware of the importance of enlightening one and all upon matters with which they may be unacquainted, we will do so.

The Bagne of Toulon, in France, is the same as Spike Island, in this country.

To the Bagne are sent convicts.

Some remain there all their lives, others for a few years only, while others are confined for a certain period, until they are bundled off to a penal settlement.

It is a strange place.

We will describe it.

All the men wear a costume of coarse brown cloth, and caps upon their heads.

It is a peculiar cap, reminding one very much of a nightcap, with the difference that it is red, instead of being white.

They are watched by guards, who are called *garde chiourme*.

We would entreat those of our young friends who have hitherto followed us, not to be frightened at the French words.

There is no literal translations for *garde chiourme*, otherwise we should give it.

The Bagne of Toulon is alive that morning.

No longer do the convicts droop their heads, and gaze upon the ground in a listless manner.

Something is to take place at twelve o'clock.

An execution!

An execution upon the *guillotine*.

The blood-stained guillotine, which was invented many years ago, and which was used during the Revolution of 1793, to behead two-thirds of the French nobility.

It is a peculiar instrument.

It is a large knife, and the blade falls upon the neck of the culprit, and severs it from his body.

We would not enter into a minute description of this terrible instrument, for if we did we would only be engrossing our readers' attention upon technical and mechanical matters only.

Thus, to have a good idea, fancy a man laying upon a wooden plank, above him is a sharp blade, a rope is pulled and the blade gives way.

In a future number we intend to give a plate representing the subject which we are describing.

Therefore, it is perfectly useless for us to dwell upon it, as the artist's talent will be a very good substitute for a lengthy description.

But what is the matter?

In one row, at least nine hundred men are assembled.

They are silent.

Their eyes are directed towards a low-roofed door.

That is the chamber of death.

The Chamber of Death! so it is called.

There the convict spend the last hours he has to live in this world.

A mournful silence reigns.

Why so?

No man can laugh or smile when his brother is going to be executed.

For such scenes come to London only.

Go to Newgate.

There only will you see nature's hideousness.

We have assisted at executions, and seen men hanged.

Oh, Heavens! what sight!

What do I say? What sight?

Which do I mean?

That of the convicts or of the lookers on?

The latter.

Besotted, drunken prostitutes, thieves of all description are there, your pocket it not safe—when the condemned man expires — when the death rattle shakes his throat with the quivering spasmodic convulsion of inward pain, then the flatch kennured vagabonds begin their work.

For there, the sight of a man about to do die is nothing.

But in the Bagne of Toulon, on the morning when we bring our readers there, it is not so.

The man who has acted wrong through life, and who suffers his punishment at the hands of the law thinks.

Thinks that if he is atoning in this world he will have mercy in the next.

But there is a doubt.

Is there another world?

Ah! let sceptics laugh—let imbeciles doubt—but, who made the Heavens? but, who made the stars? who made creation?

A supernatural being, of course.

But, who is to die, to be executed in the morning?

An acquaintance of ours.

The clock strikes.

It is ten.

The first sound has been heard.

The *garde chiourme* are on the *qui vive*.

They are attention, for they fear an outbreak—an outbreak which occasions something.

They fear that the forcats—or convicts—may try to snatch the convict from the scaffold.

There is a stillness.

The stillness of death

The drum beats.

Here he comes.

Hear.

That is the Marquis of Aguado!

Yes; those features are the same; yes, that is the chief of the Brethren of the Crystal Dagger—yes, that is the captain of the knights of Satan.

And is he to die?

And where is the help which one should think his secret order would not fail to find.

The priest walks by his side.

He is a grey-haired old man, and he carries in his hand the cross.

That symbol of mercy!

The Marquis of Aguado is deathly pale.

He has been sent to the Bagne.

There he could not remain long without having a quarrel with another.

It came to words, and then to blows.

The Marquis lost his temper.

Seized a stone, and threw it at his companion.

The shot told.

The man reeled—and fell dead.

He had been hit upon the temple.

The Marquis was a murderer!

In the Bagne, trial is unnecessary.

He who kills is to be killed.

The governor has ordered that the Marquis is to be guillotined.

And the signal has been given.

He is doomed to die!

CHAPTER XXX.

THE MARQUIS OF AGUADO—A TERRIBLE DRAMA—THE EXECUTION IS POSTPONED—SAVED—THE CONDEMNED CELL—THE DAZZLING WOMAN OF MYSTERY.

SLOWLY he advances towards the scaffold.

There it stands.

Hideous and ghastly!

The executioner is at his post.

A smile curls the Marquis's lips.

There is hope still.

He ascends the steps.

Then he is fastened to the plank.

A death-like silence reigns.

They are waiting for the half-an-hour to chime.

At last it does come.

The clock strikes.

The knife falls.

At that instant all the convicts bow their heads.

Some of them even close their eyes.

It was a drama.

A terrible drama—which was enacted in the tenth of a second—a drama like no one ever saw on the stage—a drama which it would take too long to describe—the knife had fallen—and yet——

The head of the convict was still upon his shoulders!

The knife had fallen—and yet——

There was no headless body.

The instrument of death had stopped in its march at half a foot above the head of the condemned man.

How so?

But one being could have answered that question.

And who was it?

There was a shudder which went round the convicts.

Even the guards were unable to repress their feelings.

A mob composed of curious would have given way to ejaculations.

Shrieks, sighs would have been heard!

Cries of disgust!

The Marquis howled.

He shook his shoulders.

And tried to get free of the rope which bound him to the plank.

But the knife did not fall.

Again the executioner seized the rope.

Pulled and pulled it over and over again.

But there was something wrong.

Again the knife fell.

But never reached the patient's neck.

Then the crowd gave way to a long yell—which drowned the Marquis's loud breathing.

Happily, the commissionaire came forward.

That was the foreman of the prison—the foreman whose duty it was to superintend the execution.

"Unfasten that man," he said, "and take him to his cell."

By this request, the governor was not only actuated by a sentiment of humanity, but was also preventing a mutiny.

"I have lived a hundred years in one minute!" murmured the Marquis Aguado.

That is the name under which our readers know him.

But his appellation in the Bagne was "No. 557."

The governor's words were attended to.

557 was unfastened.

When he rose, and that his glance swept around him, and he saw all the convicts looking at him, he breathed satisfactorily.

"I am alive still!" he muttered.

And who had placed in the guillotine some impediment?

Who had come to his rescue?

He was unable to know.

For he thought that when free he was without friends.

Once condemned to death, he must have been worse still.

Then he descended the steps.

"Let not this occurrence make you hope still," said the priest, as he led 557 to his cell; "your doom is only postponed."

557 smiled.

Something told him that a man is not saved so miraculously as he had been without being linked, as it were, with some strange decrees of Fatality.

And then the minutes followed, and the time came when the convicts were locked back in their cells, and the condemned was placed in a dark vault.

People then conjectured.

The governor could not make it out.

The convict man mused.

And the forcats were puzzled.

The two arms of the guillotine, those red things between which the knife runs, had been misplaced, and it was necessary to take the instrument to pieces before it could be mended.

Free workmen were called.

But they refused to do the job asked.

And then it was deemed a case of necessity to call forth the industry of the forcats.

A carpenter, who was a convict, and who had been condemned to twenty years penal servitude for having murdered his wife and his two children, declared that it would take at least twenty hours to mend the guillotine.

This was agreed to.

To order a guillotine from Paris would take too long.

To make one would entail a greater loss of time.

"The Red bonnet will not be executed to-day," said one convict to the other.

"A lucky dog that!" muttered another.

"557 is a wonderful fellow," put in a third.

"To-morrow is Sunday," pursued a fourth.

"Sunday! what is Sunday to us? a day of rest, a day of thanksgiving, ah! So it is, it is nothing but a few hours, which are irksome, because then we are not so over-worked, and if our body is not employed our minds are taxed."

He was right.

Taxed! aye, the minds of convicts must be taxed when they think.

And a few do, only a few, but those few deserve a kind word.

Meanwhile 557 had been led to a vault.

In the Bagne, at Toulon, the vault of the men condemned to death is situate thirty feet beneath the ground.

It is necessary to go down two flights to reach it.

It is a small, low, cell, which is so constructed as to baffle any attempt to escape.

557 was placed in that dark gaol, to await the moment when the instrument of death would be ready.

Since the days of Charles the First, the Martyr King, who died on the scaffold, and who, it is said, regretted life; up to the present period, the feelings of mankind are ever the same.

One does not wish to die.

No one does.

But when one has seen the glittering blade above his head, when he has felt the kiss of grim death on his lips, when he has escaped it he longs to remain in the land of the living.

Fancy, then, the feelings of 557.

The unfortunate, when in his cell, began to laugh.

Loudly and derisively.

Mocking justice.

Then he wept.

And took pleasure in so doing.

He had heard one of the gaolers saying he had got but a few hours to live.

A few hours.

A few hours more.

In a state bordering now upon prostration, then upon delirium, the condemned man mumbled incoherent words without any meaning, and was brushing the walls with his body to convince himself that he was not still in a dream.

He waited.

He knew not what the carpenter had said.

The Marquis of Aguado confined in a cell!

The chief of the Black Brethren of the Crystal Dagger. The Captain of the Knights of Satan, in prison.

He reflected.

"I have been here over seven hours," he muttered, after awhile; "Heavens, how long the time appears."

And so it does where pitchy darkness is around us.

Solitary confinement is a disgrace to humanity!

Solitary confinement is more than death!

Solitary confinement is a blot upon civilization!

Let them who read me try it!

Deprived of friends, of companions, of the powers of speaking, and exchanging your thoughts with another, what may be more terrible!

Now fear crept over the frame of 557.

The least noise made him shudder.

At every instant he thought he heard the footsteps of the guards.

Coming to drag him away from his cell.

And then night came!

Night!

It was night!

For the faint glimmer which had hitherto peered through the interstices of his cell was no longer brightening his forlorn position.

The condemned man realized to himself his critical state.

Night had come!

Life all night.

And then death—sure—certain—in the morning.

And then he slept.

And the gaoler brought him something to eat.

But he could not eat.

Night passed.

Then morning came, and with it morning's streaks.

The condemned man again shuddered.

His teeth chattered.

The gaoler who had first spoken to him had received strict orders to remain dumb.

An hour elapsed.

Presently 557 heard the sounds of footsteps in the corridor.

Then, like a beast of prey surprised in its lair, the culprit slunk in the darkest corner of his cell.

They came to fetch him, doubtless.

The iron door ran slowly upon its hinges.

A man entered.

It was the gaoler.

He was a plain spoken loutish sort of a man.

He fulfilled his duties, and that he did to the letter.

Never a word of sympathy escaped his lips.

Indeed, it would seem as if he took pleasure in gloating over the martyrdoms of reckless humanity.

But 557's fears were without foundation.

The gaoler came on his usual business.

He brought victuals.

"When am I to be executed?" asked 557.

The gaoler looked at him with a stupid, ignorant, derisive sort of a look.

Yet he made no reply.

Again 557 repeated his question.

The gaoler heeded him not.

"Am I to live, then?" he asked.

The gaoler mysteriously nodded his head.

A yell of joy escaped the lips of 557.

"Not yet, not yet," he pursued, and then he rose and danced about in his cell.

"You'd better dance while you have time, a pleasant amusement!" growled the gaoler, and he quickly went out, and closed the door.

Happy for him did he do so.

For 557 would have tried to murder that man who came to insult him in his agony.

Alone once more was 557.

"Strange," he said, "very strange."

And then Nature, once more, resumed her sway upon that man.

He began to eat.

The governor had told the gaolers to free the convict from his manacles, and to provide him with some wine.

He ate now and drank with avidity.

Like a a famished wolf.

A hungry bloodhound!

And when he had satisfied the cravings of hunger, he flung himself upon the bunch of straw which served him as a bed and tried to sleep.

He was now in a fever.

The gaoler had remained outside.

Curiosity had caused him to halt instead of pacing up and down.

557 was deemed a strange character.

Besides, all knew that he had received a first-rate education—an education, which his gentlemanly manners tended to corroborate.

The gaoler heard 557 growling ominously.

Hitting the door with his fist.

"If that lasts much longer," he said, quietly to himself, "that fellow will be mad ere he dies."

Again the day passed.

The gaoler was right.

For the behaviour of 557 only confirmed his idea.

He was a prey to a wild delirium and pronounced incoherent sentences.

Suddenly, towards the middle of the night, 557 was awaken.

He had sunk in a deep lethargy, and yet he had heard sounds which withdrew in front.

He listened intently.

The noise was still going on; nay, it was every moment increasing.

Where could it come from?

Above or beneath him?

He studied the laws of instinct.

And rose from the straw.

Then again he strained his eyes all round him, and tried to pierce the darkness.

Monotonous were the sounds.

They had lasted for about two hours.

He thought that there was some one digging the earth.

It was on his right.

Distinct and more distinct the sounds became.

Yes; there could be no mistake.

And, yet, how could he escape?

Folly to think so.

Around him, beneath him, above him, the granite was hard.

Under his feet there were large, even slabs of stone.

With his heels he tramped upon them.

But no echo came—still the sounds continued.

Hark!

Louder and plainer are the knocks.

Suddenly the stone on his right, where he was leaning, gives way.

He looks round.

He clutches at the stone.

Tries to speak.

Cannot do so.

His hand grasps the wall.

It recedes.

Is he mad?

He clasped his brow.

Then a sweet perfume tinges his brow.

His passions are kindled.

For many weeks he has been deprived of womankind.

Is it his saviour?

If so, she must love him.

Then if she comes, what shall he do?

Throw himself upon his knees, and cover her feet, her hands, her limbs, with a stream of kisses, with a stream of voluptuous gratefulness, for could a divinity expect more idolatry than he is ready to bestow upon her?

At length a large aperture becomes plain.

A light is seen.

And the features of a woman are perceptible.

557 is in ecstacy.

"Are you dead or alive?" he exclaimed.

"Alive, friend!" muttered a voice.

And it sounds sweet to him, like the strains of a delicious harp, played by some angels' exhilirating touch.

"Follow me," says the voice.

"No, I will die! I must die!" exclaimed the Marquis of Aguado, and then he strained to his breast the new comer.

She has appeared at last.

Poets, I defy you! Romanists, I say that no one can describe her!

Oh, what eyes.

For such as they are, seen by the bright glimmer of the lamp which she carries, are almond-shaped, and there is a volume of love contained in them. Her skin is as white as the driven snow, and soft and smooth, like the most expensive velvet which ever was manufactured—her finger-nails are rosy and well trimmed—her bust is voluptuous and beautifully formed—her feet encased in a pair of silken sandals, would have been worthy of Juno!

and her whole appearance would lead you to compare her to an angel, flying from Heaven to satiate mankinds' most extravagant desires.

"Come! come! Aguado," she says, "and do not press me so tightly."

He refuses to comply with her wish.

She asked him once more.

557 yielded.

And then he followed her through a large subterranean vault.

She glides on swiftly.

"Where am I going?" mutters 557, and he follows with quick hurried steps, unable to say a word for the alteration which he has experienced are too much for him, and for a while, at least, he has become drunk.

CHAPTER XXXI.

VELVET AND THE HOUSEKEEPER—A GOOD ADVICE—THE NEW LODGINGS.

THERE was one individual, among the many characters of this tale, who requires our attention.

He is the youngest of those among whom chance has thrown us, and to him we must revert.

That is Master Velvet.

Where had Wild Will gone? This we cannot answer yet.

We must also describe Velvets' feelings.

While the events which we have related in a previous chapter, were occurring, Velvet was in the kitchen.

Everybody was awake.

And he!—was asleep.

Then he knew nothing whatever of that which was taking place.

The old housekeeper, however, was thinking.

She knew that Velvet was a handsome boy.

Handsome boys are not at a discount in this enlightened nineteenth century. Should they be, old ladies would not think so.

Then she came down to the kitchen, and saw Velvet asleep.

Gently she shook him.

The boy opened his eyes.

"What's the matter," he asked.

The old lady placed her hand over his mouth to enjoin silence.

Velvet looked puzzled.

"My boy," she said, "who's your master?"

Velvet looked at her.

"My master," he said, "my master is Captain de Vere."

"How long have you been in his service?"

Velvet mused.

"Not very long," he said; "but he is a very nice fellow, and I hope I will always have such."

Velvet remembered his tutoring.

The words which the swell thief had spoken had not been thrown away upon him.

He did his part well.

The old lady glanced upon him.

"Your master is gone," she said, "has run away."

Velvet rose to his feet.

"Ha——" he asked.

"Yes.

"Why?"

The housekeeper, availing herself of the opportunity which presented itself, took the boy's hand in her own.

Velvet made no objection.

It was a case of a woman seducing a boy.

"They say up-stairs that he is a swell-mobsman;

and a detective, who had been sent for, declares that he is one of the greatest rogues out."

"I know nothing about that," replied Velvet; "but there may be some truth in it."

The housekeeper was all attention.

"Listen to me, my child," she said; "when did you meet Captain de Vere?"

Harry—or at least, Velvet—was a 'cute chap.

He reflected.

What should he say?

Declare the truth to the housekeeper?

He was young.

Again he considered.

"Speak," said the good lady, "and don't delay over it, for there is no time to lose."

Velvet was puzzled.

A few minutes elapsed, during which the housekeeper told the boy all that had occurred.

"I see," said Velvet.

Then he related to the housekeeper his adventures since he had come to London.

"Oh, Lor!" muttered the good lady, "is that true? Why, I could never have believed that such things took place in London; and what are you to do," she continued.

Velvet felt his pockets.

He had a sovereign.

The one which his master had given him.

He showed it to the housekeeper.

"Keep that," she said, "and where do your friends live?"

"Bournemouth," said Velvet.

"Where's that?"

Velvet told her.

"Well, look here, they will lock you up if you do not decamp.

"Lock me up," said Velvet.

"Yes, lock you up!"

Then he remembered his adventure with the thieves, the loaf he had stolen—the words which the woman said struck him as if they were not deprived of some truth.

"What am I to do, then?" he asked.

"Have you got any friends, my child?"

Velvet thought he would make a clean breast of it.

"I have not," he said.

"What do you suppose to do, then?"

"I don't know."

"Well, my boy, if I introduce you to a lady friend of mine, will you remain with her until we see what can be done with you."

"Am I not to remain here, then?"

"Remain here?"

"Yes."

"No."

Then the good lady explained to the boy—who being an intelligent lad, soon saw the wisdom of her words—the propriety of his going away from the hotel.

In the meantime, reader, you may well ask what were all the servants doing?

The answer is simple.

They were all gossiping.

All talking together.

The theft was quite an incident.

It is not every day that a swell thief finds his way in a fashionable hotel—and robs a serene highness' jewellery.

The business of the hotel was at a stand still.

The Prince of Carabouliski was very much annoyed.

The late Emperor of Russia, King Nicholas, had made him a present of one of the rings which had been stolen.

To get it back he would give three times its value.

And he was swearing, and he was damning all the saints in paradise, and saying that such a thing had never occurred to him in the whole course of his life.

And the flunkeys were all in the room of his serene highness.

This is how it was that the old housekeeper had it all her own way.

And now return we must to Velvet.

"I'll go where you wish me to," he said, "for I am alone in London."

It was then decided that Velvet should go into the housekeeper's room and wait until the evening; when she would take him to his friends.

But more of that anon.

CHAPTER XXXI.

VELVET IN THE LONE HOUSE—HOW HE GOT RID OF THE MISER—THE DARK DEED OF NIGHT—THE NECESSARY WOUND—WHO'S THE GIRL?

IT may be necessary here to tell our young friends that Velvet having seen the wisdom of the housekeeper's words, resolved to abide by them.

With her help he contrived to escape the vigilance of the police, and when they looked for him they found that he had gone.

There were cries of disgust on everybody's part and everybody swore that the captain and his valet were in league, and that had they remained in the house much longer they would have acted much worse than they did.

Velvet, meanwhile, was sleeping in the housekeeper's room.

It was a snug place, and he felt very much at home.

She locked the door after her.

Then Velvet remained by himself.

Should a stranger be in a strange room, what would he do?

Why, his first step would be to look about him.

This Velvet did.

Then he felt tired, and he flung himself upon the bed, and tried to sleep.

At first he could not do so, but at last he succeeded.

The evening came.

"Come on with me," said the housekeeper; "this evening is my day out."

Velvet was not long in getting ready.

He kept his costume.

Then it required no small amount of dodging to go down-stairs.

The housekeeper saw to that.

She managed all things.

The path was soon clear.

And then the lady and Velvet thought of moving.

The old party who was to take care of Velvet, was a person, who, in her day, had been housekeeper in a nobleman's family.

She had saved a few pounds, and with it she had bought some furniture, and let lodgings at the West End.

She happened to have a room vacant, which she said she would have no objection to let to Velvet for five shillings a-week.

The price paid by swells was double that amount.

The housekeeper who had brought Velvet offered to clear the preliminary expenses.

She had said that she had met the boy somewhere or another, and that she had taken quite an interest in him.

The woman who let lodgings believed everything.

Velvet was now in a respectable way of living.

He wished good-bye to the housekeeper, and went to his bed-room.

Nothing very extraordinary occurred.

There was a pause.

Velvet pondered.

What has become of Wild Will? he often asked.

At last the time, when he had heard that the murder was to take place, arrived, he lost no time in finding his way to the lone house.

This was occurring three days after he was in his new lodgings.

He walked along the path which led to the den cf infamy.

This was all very well, but should he meet resistance, what then?

The house looked bleak and dreary.

But one light was to be seen, and Velvet did not like to let any one know that he was coming.

He proceeded cautiously.

Then he listens.

There were shrieks proceeding from the house.

A female voice.

Velvet had brought a pair of pistols with him.

He trimmed them.

Then he knocked at the door.

The old miser answered the call.

"Good-evening, sir," said Velvet, "my master—"

"Yes."

"Sent me here to ask you whether he did not leave a valuable stick the last time he came here."

"A stick," repeated the miser.

"Yes," re-echoed Velvet.

"I have not seen one."

This was a very good trumped up excuse on the part of Velvet.

The miser eyed him.

"Your master," he said, "cannot require your services very much if he sends you out on such a goose errand."

Velvet felt very much inclined to punch the speaker's head, but, after consideration, he refrained.

So he said nothing.

Again the cries of the woman reach his ears.

Doubtless, the dark deed which he had heard mentioned, is being perpetrated.

"I say, sir," he began, submissively, "would you allow me to look about, I think I know where the captain left his stick."

Again the miser eyed him.

"You are welcome," he replied, "do as you please."

Velvet required no further bidding.

He saw that the old man closed the door.

Once within the abode he felt more at home.

The miser was still in the room.

"Young man," he said, addressing Velvet, "you must not stop here very long, for I am expecting company."

Rough and harsh were the words as they were pronounced by the old man.

Velvet knit his brows.

Still he said nothing.

And now, in agonised tones, the voice of a woman in distress reached Velvet's ear.

He longed to rush to the rescue.

Yet he knew, with his strength as a boy, he would never be able to compete against that of the miser.

He watched his opportunity.

He saw the miser winding his way downstairs.

"I will wish you good bye, sir," he said to the old man, "as, by the time you come up again, I will be gone."

The old man looked at him.

Distrustingly he held out his hand.

Velvet clutched it.

Then he stood on the threshold of the door.

Providence was favouring Velvet.

Something came over the old man's mind, and he slunk away.

Velvet waited.

And then as soon as he had gone he closed the door behind him, and locked him in.

There were no impediments now in his way.

The cries of the woman had now diminished.

It seemed as if, like some conquered victim, she was giving way before superior strength.

Owing to the knowledge which Velvet had of the place he walked towards the gorgeous room of infamy.

He lent an attentive ear to that which was taking place inside.

There were two voices.

One of a man.

The other of a woman.

"For Heaven's sake!" mutters the last one, "oh, spare me! oh, spare me!"

*   *   *   *

These words had an ominous signification to Velvet.

He determined not to wait much longer.

Then with a rapid, quick movement he withdrew the pistols from his pockets.

He cocked them.

And with a nervous hand he opened the door of the room.

It receded before his touch.

Then the following met his gaze.

A woman on her knees, beseeching mercy!

A man above her head, holding a knife in his hand ready to strike her.

The knife is uplifted.

But one second later, and the deed would have been done.

The sudden appearance of Velvet postponed events.

Postponed the dark deed.

Frustrated the accomplishment of some terrible drama in that lone house.

The individual about to accomplish a murder gazes upon Velvet.

The brave, bold boy is not cowed.

"Gently, my boy, or I'll make these bark!" he exclaimed, as he pointed the barrels of his two cocked pistols at the head of the man about to murder the woman.

"Who are you?" exclaims the unknown.

Ah! could these features have been the same as those of the *forcat*, who ten years previously had escaped so mysteriously from the guillotine?

Can it be the Marquis of Aguado whom we are meeting again?

"Who are you?" asks the unknown.

"Let that girl go, or I'll blow your brains out!" roughly replies Velvet.

The man refuses to unfasten his hold.

Velvet fires.

The shot has told.

For the man reels upon the floor as if mortally wounded.

"Come with me," exclaims Velvet, "come with me."

The girl has heard the words.

She gazes upon the wounded man.

But for one instant only.

Then she darts towards the door.

Velvet's arm is around her waist.

She is dazzlingly pretty, and voluptuously attracting.

THE
DANCE OF DEATH;
OR,
𝕿𝖍𝖊 𝕳𝖆𝖓𝖌𝖒𝖆𝖓'𝖘 𝕻𝖑𝖔𝖙.
A THRILLING ROMANCE OF TWO CITIES.

No. 11.   SATURDAY, JANUARY 13, 1866.   ONE PENNY.

THE LONELY MEETING.

CHAPTER XXXII.
THE GIRL AND THE HANDSOME BOY.

THE girl, to whom Velvet had spoken, hears his words.

Under any other circumstances she would have objected to his help.

But there was but little time to keep things in suspense.

Velvet takes the girl's hand in his own, and brings it close to his heart.

There is a pressure about that boy's touch which speaks volumes.

She makes no objection.

And with tottering steps she allows herself to be led.

Oh, who could describe Velvet's feelings?

He had saved a girl from death, from moral destruction.

Who was she? he knew not.

Without a word escaping her lips she followed him.

They walked on for hours and hours together.

Something—what was that something? had come over them *both*.

It was like the poison which enervates—or the perfume which exhilarates.

Strange meeting!

The girl was getting tired, and Velvet also felt his limbs stiffening.

To walk a long distance is but a common-place feat. When you are hearty and healthy—when you know that you are doing so for pleasure only—but to walk through spots which are unknown to you—to walk without any fixed destination is a task which is tiresome in the extreme.

The two beings had been tramping for some time when they came in the neighbourhood of St. John's Wood.

What road they had taken no one knew—not even themselves.

The streets were cleared—the alleys were passed—the squares skirted—and yet they walked on.

They still proceeded onwards.

Willingly would Velvet have spoken—told the girl to come home with him.

But although he was a maiden boy—a boy who had never known womankind—so as to get *disgusted* with it before he should do so—yet he felt that to ask a girl, a perfect stranger, to come home with him—was a thing he was reluctant to carry out.

Perhaps also the girl had produced an impression upon him.

Perhaps he loved her!

Nonsense, nonsense, will exclaim some sceptical readers, a boy to fall in love with a girl.

Absurd, ridiculous!

Why a lad of Velvet's age would never think of such a thing!

Stop, then, the progress of nature — prevent warm imaginations to dream—hinder the growth of the flower—fling a wet blanket upon youth's young dream—nip in the bud the rose about to bloom—destroy the march of thoughtful conception—implant hoary looks upon luxuriant wavy hair—damp and extinguish the spark of the rising fire——render tottering and sedate the sanguine and wild hopes—cover with wrinkles the smooth forehead—put decayed and rotten teeth in the pearly row—and say human nature I do not understand you, you are but a myth.

Velvet had reached a spot, which, from its loneliness, suited him.

Dark arches, besides sundry building materials were about.

The place was deserted and still.

Nothing was heard beyond the subdued rattle of the vehicles in the distance—that suggestive and yet slow and monotonous hum of the big town about to sleep—wafted to Velvet's ear as if to say to him —not far away from thee there is life and yet *thou art alone.*

Then he clung to the girl he had saved.

And gazed upon her.

And his bright, big, blue, eye lightened—and his heart beat within his breast with strange and hitherto, unknown palpitations.

A revulsion of feelings was taking place in that boys' being.

He could have left the girl—have said to her good-bye—and returned to the landlady where he had a snug lodging, for some time at least.

Instinctively he felt his pockets.

He had some money.

Half-a-crown, altogether.

That was not much, still it was something—he had bought a new coat with Wild Will's sovereign. Not that he cared for clothes, but he loathed the livery which he had been told to wear, and he had left it off at the first opportunity.

That opportunity had not been wanting. His landlady's son had died. She had several suits of his, and, for a few shillings, she had accommodated him with his left-off garments.

Velvet had accepted the offer.

And no bad bargain did he make—for really he looked a young *swell*.

There could be no mistake about that.

His coat fitted him to a T, and the waistcoat, although somewhat loose, was tasty, and nicely finished.

Now that we have spent some time in reverting to Velvet, we may as well here attend to his companion.

Perhaps it is likely that our readers have seen her before.

She was very pretty.

It was not the garments in which she was attired which attracted notice—although somewhere or another we have heard it stated that "fine feathers make fine birds"—it was her make, her personal appearance.

She was dressed humbly, but not without taste.

And then the languid, velvety eyes dazzled brilliantly beneath the silken fringes—and then the nostrils inhaled the fresh air at times with quite a resolute manner—and then the small mouth curled with a very coquettish smile—and the bust heaved in a fashion which meant something.

We do not wish to be too plain.

Readers, do you know that we have been told that we are too true in our description.

We remember reading our old friend, *Charley Wag*, and the parsons, and we think that we could not have written more plainly.

Velvet was, meanwhile, pondering.

At last he turned towards the girl.

"Come and sit down for awhile," he said, "for I am getting tired."

"Where?" she asked.

Had Velvet been in Wild Will's place he would have said that it was a damned bore that people did not provide seats for people, and cursed the want of accommodation—but, as it happened, Velvet kept his tongue to himself.

"There!" he said.

As he spoke, the boy pointed to a stone—a large big one, it was, too—and intimated to the girl the wisdom of her sitting down upon it.

She looked at him.

There was no light but that of the moon, and although it did not shine quite as bright as the day, yet it was every bit as useful.

She saw the boy.

Then, without another word, she bent upon his track, and when she had reached the stone, she sat down.

CHAPTER XXXIII.

THE LONELY MEETING.

"It is very strange," said Velvet, as soon as the

girl had sat down, "that I should have overheard a few days ago, a certain conversation."

"A conversation?" asked the girl.

"Yes," replied Velvet, "by which I gleaned that some girl was——"

Here he stopped.

"Did you go in that house before, then?" asked the girl, looking wildly around her.

"What house?" asked Velvet.

"Where you rescued me, to-night," quickly retorted the girl.

Then there was a pause.

After awhile, however, Velvet spoke.

He related to the young creature his adventures since he had arrived in London.

Again the girl looked at him.

It was a night during which two forlorn beings thrown together were to speak together—were to tell each other what they had done, what they had seen, were to seek consolation, repose, and momentary happiness in the exchange of a few mutual words.

"Who and what are you?" at length asked the girl, after a pause.

Velvet mused.

There was no one listening to him—that is to say, as far as he could see—the evening, or more properly speaking, the morning was mild and bright—and a conversation for him—perhaps for her, had its charm.

The boy made no reply.

"You are asking me questions already," he said in a *naïve* manner, "I like you very much—but, pray, who and what are you yourself?"

The girl nodded her head.

Velvet stood mute and silent, at a loss to say a word.

So sweetly and so softly had the girl spoken, that it sent him headlong in a dream.

Now you should remember, whoever you are —and not much account, I fear—although, when you call for your prizes we will have some occasion to look at you well—that Velvet was a boy, who had been taken away from his home, and who, having been spoilt by his parents, felt the forlornness of his position, much more than many less favoured boys would have done.

For poor Jenny! sweet Jenny, as she had been called in the village, had loved him, and spoilt him, and he regretted his home.

"You asked me just now who I was," said the girl, after a moment's thought, "Not much, perhaps."

"What's your name?" asked Velvet, quickly, his lips pouting.

"Nancy."

"Nancy!" repeated the boy, "Nancy, a very pretty name, I have heard it before, though."

"Have you?" asked the girl.

"Yes," replied Velvet.

"Where?" she continued.

And evident signs of curiosity were perceptible upon her handsome features, and her eye rested itself upon the boy with steadfast flattering expression.

"Among thieves!" replied Velvet, slowly.

"Among thieves!" the girl repeated to herself in a melancholy manner.

"Among thieves!" she soliloquised over and over again.

Could the handsome, bright boy, who stood before her, have been one of those outcasts who live by outraging the laws of man and defying heaven's ire.

She would not, could not believe it.

And yet it was plain enough!

And are you a *thief*, then?" Nancy exclaimed, suddenly, rising from her stooping position, and eagerly clutching the boy's hand.

Velvet smiled.

"No," he replied, with a sweet intonation of voice.

"How, then, could you have fallen in such hands? how could you have met thieves?" she asked.

Velvet liked to prolong the girl's anxiety.

"Have you had any breakfast?" he asked, quickly, "and are you hungry?"

Nancy was puzzled.

There was something so wild, so incoherent in the boy's manner, that she could not make it out.

"Yes, I am hungry," she replied.

"Got any money?" asked Velvet.

The girl blushed.

"No," she said, "and yet I—"

Here she stopped abruptly.

"Speak," said Velvet.

"And yet," she resumed, "I might have had one hundred pounds.

"How?" asked Velvet.

The girl blushed deeply.

Velvet understood.

"Ah!" he muttered softly, "who says that among the poor, destitute classes there is no honour, no shame? Who says that gold will buy everything—it has not bought *her*.

Then he mused.

"Come and have some breakfast with me," he said, and he withdrew his last half-crown from his pocket.

They walked on till they came to a coffee shop.

It was a low-sort of an establishment, and there were many people assembled in the room.

It was a strange gathering of faces, a queer mixture of humanity!

Here, in one corner mopping up a pint of coffee in a most listless manner, was a woman whose vocation needs no description. Her eyes were weak and bloodshot—her hands emaciated and quivering—her forehead was furrowed by premature wrinkles brought on by days of hunger, nights without shelter. She seemed to be dead to this life at least, for her glance was mournful, idiotic, and sullen, and her whole appearance was such as to inspire disgust from heartless beings—sympathy from Christains, Christains only—from those who can make allowance for the fall of humanity, and who let the poor outcast, (whoever she may be,) know that she deserves to be helped because she brings back to your mind the picture of one sublime and great one who was the mother of Christ.

There were also stupid, loutish, night cabmen having their breakfast—men with a lot of low cunning, but without intelligence.

Velvet and the girl sat down.

They waited.

At length the attendant came up.

She was a girl of about thirteen; being very young, she was employed by the proprietor.

She knew not her price.

She was pretty—and dirtily dressed—her feet were encased in slipshod boots—her dress was soiled and common, and her hair was uncombed and rough.

She walked straight up to Velvet.

"What will you have, sir?" she asked.

Velvet looked at Nancy.

"I don't know," said Nancy.

"Coffee or tea?" asked the assistant.

"A cup of coffee for me," said Velvet resolutely.

"I'll have the same."

The assistant mizzled.

She shortly returned.

She brought two pints of coffee.

"How much ?" asked Velvet.

"Three-pence, sir, if you please."

Velvet boldly took out his half-crown out of his pocket.

"Only three-pence !" he soliloquized to himself.

He paid for what he had, and placed his change in his pocket.

Then he gazed upon Nancy.

The two beings drank.

Then they had something to eat.

Slices of bread-and-butter, only a half-penny a slice—that's all!

Velvet, for himself and his girl, paid sixpence.

Good value for the money.

"Tell me your story," now began Nancy, approaching the boy.

She had sat down upon the same bench as himself.

Velvet then related his story.

Began from Bournemouth.

"Yes," said Nancy, "after you had saved him from being drowned, what did you do ?"

"Listen !" said Velvet.

Nancy opened her eyes wide.

The boy took up a slice of bread-and-butter, and began to eat it, and did not proceed with his narrative.

"Listen !" he repeated.

It is needless here to say that a similar request was perfectly unnecessary.

Fancy, my dear reader, yourself in the same position as Velvet or Nancy.

Fancy yourself alone in London, and meeting a friend.

You would then like to know the inns and outs.

On both sides, therefore, there was not anxiety, but curiosity.

He related what we know already.

To repeat it would be useless.

And then he went on with that which we are unacquainted.

"Yes," said Nancy.

"What then ?"

"We rode away," said Velvet, "for miles and miles."

Nancy was listening.

"Miles and miles," continued Velvet.

Nancy's big blue eyes opened wider than they had hitherto done.

CHAPTER XXXIV.

A LONG STORY.

WALK in a thickly-wooded forest—stray amidst solitary paths—beneath the oak tree rest—sit upon a mossy bench—let your glance sweep near and far—halt in your wanderings—and then think and consider.

*   *   *   *

You will find, if you try to do so, two flowers linked together.

Violets without perfume!

But yet full of beauty and of growth.

Things that will attract a pedestrian's notice.

The violets are explained, they are Velvet and Nancy.

Poor forlorn creatures, flung in the world by the mistake of providence, poor forlorn creatures which ought to be, one in wealth, the other in comfort.

Nancy is the one, the other is Velvet.

It is but a poor excuse for one to say, that a novelist's business is to overdraw.

Whatever we relate is true.

Nay, not only is it true, but it is *under done*, not *over done.*

"What, then ?" asked Nancy, reverting to the subject, which Velvet had began.

Velvet, we must let you know, had been telling Nancy all his adventures by the sea shore.

They could have been resumed in a nut-shell.

We are aware of them already.

"Away we went," said Velvet, on horseback, I think."

"Yes,"

"Then we halted."

"Go on," said Nancy.

"My mind had been wandering, but the fresh air did me good."

Nancy, the girl who had been rescued by the thieves, was attentviely listening.

Take them in every station of life—take who ?—why everybody—and tell them something interesting, and they like it.

"Well, we stopped before a house," pursued Velvet, resuming his narrative, "and the man halted."

The girl was getting interested.

"What did you do then ?" she asked.

"The man alighted from the horse, and so did I.

"I was reeling.

"I remember it now, Nancy," pursued the boy, "because I am relating it to you, but otherwise I should have forgotten the whole thing."

Nancy was getting impatient.

"I say, I say," she went on, "I asked you how you came among *thieves*, and you won't tell me."

Now it struck Velvet that he could have told her his story in five words, and he had been keeping her over five and twenty minutes

The people in the coffee shop, meanwhile, had been looking at the couple.

No one tried to listen to what they said, because there was no money to be made by them—yet their appearance was such as to attract attention.

Nancy was one whom we have already described, (read all early numbers of ours, and you will see her portrait there)—Velvet is another, upon whom it would be useless to spend more time.

I do not think that on Velvet's part any fault could have been found.

By rights, you know, he should tell his story.

As it is he did not.

At length he went on.

"We entered the house," he pursued, relating to his subject, "and then, Nancy, I saw that I had fallen in the hands of one whom I despised. To try to run away from him would have been an impossibility. I said nothing but waited.

"We went in.

"Everybody eyed us.

"This was ten, aye, twenty miles, from Bournemouth."

This conversation, much shorter in words than we describe it in lines, was taking place in a low coffee shop.

"Well," asked Nancy.

She wished to know how it came to pass that the boy had been thrown among theives.

"In the room which we visited," Velvet went on, "there were few people, and all men—some drovers, others, men connected with country work—I could not make them out—they had an appearance which I liked—how I longed to rush away from my keeper, and tell the first one whom I saw my tale—but it was but a chance, and I feared to risk it—fear, not fear of being harmed—but somehow, I cannot account for it."

It is a very pleasant thing, *entre nous*, to be

speaking to another being—boys, men, like to hear themselves talking—that itself is pleasant enough, even if strangers are listening—but when you are engrossing a girl's attention, and that girl is very nice, why, it is better still.

"Why did you not run away from the man who stole you from your home?" asked Nancy, "any kind hearted being would have felt for you, and seen that you were not wronged."

What the girl was saying was perfectly correct, and Velvet seeing the wisdom of it corroborated her words.

"I suppose," said Velvet, after a few moments' silence, "that it was not to be, and that Fate had decided that I should undergo what I did."

"And what was that?" asked Nancy.

To delay in his narrative was a point which Velvet considered unwise, as he felt that however interesting his adventures on the road would be to a stranger, they would lose a great deal of their attraction were he to postpone them much longer.

For an instant he mused, gathering, as it were, his thoughts together, and when he had conceived in his mind the most stirring events which had been witnessed by him, he bid Nancy not to interrupt him.

A similar request was perfectly unnecessary, yet Nancy nodded her head in a manner which left no doubt to Velvet that he would have it all his own way, and he shortly afterwards began in the following manner:—

"Nothing of much importance occurred to us while staying at the inn," Velvet resumed, "Ralph remained in the coffee-room drinking, and I sat by his side watching him minutely.

"He spoke so slowly, and his whole manner was so outwardly frank; he seemed so plausible in the stories he told, that more than once I began to ask myself whether he could have been the low creature which I believed he was.

"All the drovers were looking at him also, and, although many of them allowed a smile of incredulity to play upon their lips on hearing some extraordinary tale of Ralph—yet none of them were bold enough to contradict him.

"A few hours passed; and then, one by one, the company retired to bed.

"After awhile, Ralph, who had sunk in a reverie, rose suddenly; and turning abruptly towards me, he bid me follow him.

"He had made a bargain with the landlady, and she had approved of it—and I felt certain that there was no fear of our being locked out, and that we were certain of a night's shelter, for I had seen money passing between them.

"Here there is an incident which I must relate," pursued Velvet, looking stedfastly at Nancy, "and that is the strange manner of the landlady.

"'How much,' demanded Ralph, 'will you charge me for a room where myself and the boy can sleep to night?'

The landlady looked at him.

"'I will do my best for you,' she said, 'but I am always paid in advance.'

"'I've got no objection to that if your terms be moderate.'

"The landlady mentioned one-and-sixpence each, and said that she would give a very good breakfast in the bargain for the same.

"Wild Ralph smiled.

"Then withdrew a crown-piece from his pocket.

"The landlady seized it.

"'You had some beer besides,' she said, 'and the reckoning will come to four shillings exactly.'

"'Pay yourself then, marm,' replied Ralph, 'and let us have the change.'

"The landlady seized the money, and as I thought would have gone to ascertain whether it was a good one, but she did not leave us for that purpose.

"Seizing the coin, she placed it in her mouth and bit it.

"'It is a good 'un,' she said, 'and I wish I had a hundred thousands of them.'

"There, Nancy," Velvet went on, "what do you think she did? she spat down upon it. and when I asked her what that was for, she said for luck."

The girl could not refrain from giving way to a smile.

"Then we were shown to our room. It had nothing particular about it, and it resembled very much those of the Tregonwell Arms at Bournemouth, where once I went with father to see a farmer on business, so I will not dwell upon it, but merely inform you that it was a very large one, with two beds, one of which I chose for my own, after having satisfied myself that I was not interfering with the selection of my companion.

"There was nothing up to the present period very remarkable about my journey," Velvet resumed, "but I was called upon to see other things afterwards which I little expected."

The coffee-room where Nancy and Velvet were seated, was now getting deserted, and beyond a drunken ostler, who, with his head laying upon the table, was snoring heavily, there was no one to overhear their conversation.

"We left the inn right enough," said Velvet, "and then we rode on.

"At last the horse became disabled, and although Ralph did all he could to get it upon its legs, the poor creature had sunk exhausted to rise no more.

"'This is provoking,' growled Ralph, as he gazed upon the carcase of the poor brute (who had turned out to be my father's horse). 'I would have sold him, and made a very good thing out of my visit to Hampshire.'

"I stayed," pursued Velvet, "and patted the poor animal's shoulders, hoping to soften its last hours in this world, but poor Bonnie had become perfectly senseless.

"Once, and once only, it opened its eyes, and then it glanced sadly upon me, and it was all over,

"'The brute is dead,' now said Ralph, dragging me away by the shoulder; 'it is no use stopping here, young gentleman, so come on.'

"Now, I liked poor Bonnie," Velvet pursued, "and its death grieved me a great deal more than perhaps it would have done under any other circumstances. It was a link which connected me with home, and loth, indeed, was I to leave it.

"But Ralph was not the man to be trifled with, and as his voice was rough and determined, I made no objection to his request, and at once abided by it.

"'How do you propose, to go to London, sir?' I asked of Ralph after a moment of silence, during which we had been tramping quickly over a smooth path which skirted the high road. 'Will we walk or ride?'

"'Young hopeful,' he said, turning his head towards me, 'that will depend entirely upon circumstances.'

"We walked on for several miles together, until we came to a small town.

"As we approached the houses and skirted several small farm-houses, which stood on the side of the road, Ralph gradually ceased speaking and became morose and sullen.

"At last Ralph halted.

"'Youngster,' he said, eyeing me cutely, 'this is the whole of my fortune,' and he held a shilling between his fingers.

"'A shilling,' I muttered, 'that's little enough.'

"'Moreover,' continued Ralph, 'when it has to go towards keeping two for some days to come—as we cannot dream of being in London before the end of the week.'

"'And what will you do without money,' I queried, 'is it a difficult thing to earn a pound or so?'

"'A difficult thing to earn money—rather, young man—don't you remember the story I told you at the sea shore?'

"I pondered, and over and over again wondered what was to befal us.

"We were now within six or seven hundred yards of the town hall—which could be seen in the distance.

"It was getting cold—a thin, drizzly, rain was beginning to fall from the clouds above—and the shades of night were slowly issuing from the starless firmament.

CHAPTER XXXV.

THE GAOL-BIRD AND HIS COMPANION.

"'I am a bird—a gaol bird—my boy,' Ralph now went on, 'and my nature loves darkness and crime; thus, when night—dark, pitchy night—comes, I am myself once more, and I fly boldly in search of food.'"

There was a sinister tone in Ralph's words, as he slowly uttered them, and Velvet shuddered as he realized to himself the meaning of the last part of his speech.

"'Are you on for some prog, my boy?' suddenly asked Ralph.

"'Yes,' said I, 'that I am, but if you spend our last shilling, what will you do?'

"Ralph laughed meaningly.

"'I am never at a loss for some scheme or other,' he said, 'but if I was I would not allow myself to go without food.

"'Yonder,' he continued, 'is a house which I know well, although I have never lodged in the house before myself, and there we will stay. I will order a first-class supper, any amount of swipes, and then, when it gets late, we will see about getting some money!'

"'Getting some money?' I asked, 'I hope it will be by fair means.'

"'By fair means, if it can be obtained that way, by unfair means if it cannot be worked otherwise,' he sullenly replied.

"Ralph boldly walked up to a flight of steps which led to the door.

"I followed him without saying a word.

"'Good evening to you, landlord,' Ralph began, as soon as he stood face to face with a rubicund, fat, jolly, monkish-looking individual, who appeared to be the master of the place. "I and my nephew want a night's lodging beneath the roof of the "Red Lion."'

"The landlord was one of those easy-going individuals, who are never once in their lives troubled with an idea—be it good or bad—and he never suspected people.

"'If a top room will do for you, mate,' the landlord replied, "I can let you have it for two shillings, and that, of course, will include your young companion.'

"'A smart young fellow, he is, too—my nephew, that is, landlord,' Ralph went on, 'and he is a very clever gentleman for his age, having been highly edikated by his late father—as good a man as ever breathed the breath of life, while beadle to the Wandsworth Union.'

"The landlord listened to the speaker—and although from his manner I should fancy that he thought that Ralph's appearance was anything but that which he would have expected from a beadle's brother, he nevertheless felt for me, and said that he would give me as nice a supper as ever I sat down before.

"This somewhat cheered me on, and revived my drooping spirits.

"I thought that a man that would give you a supper out of his own pocket would not be very hard upon you in the event of his bill not being discharged, and I knew it could not be unless Ralph had some unknown ways of *raising the wind*; a graphic phrase of his, which he had made use of in alluding to the subject.

"Shortly afterwards the landlord called me to him and introduced me to his wife and daughter, and they were all very kind to me, and sent me back to my uncle at about eleven o'clock at night.

"'Where is my uncle gone?' I asked, finding that he was not to be seen in the taproom, 'he was here just now?'

"Oh, I longed for an answer, I flattered myself that perhaps he had taken it into his head to go away without me—and I was fully determined this time not to lose an opportunity to escape.

"But I was doomed to be disappointed, my wild and bright hopes were soon crushed and my heart which had beaten within my breast with a throb of sanguine expectation sunk within me.

"For the individual, to whom I had spoken, replied to me that he had gone to his bed-room in a very bad humour, and had often inquired for me during my protracted absence.

"From one of the servants in the place I learnt exactly where the room was situated; and glided upstairs.

"Fearing to enter abruptly in the room where Ralph was, I previously knocked gently against the door.

"'Come in,' growled a voice.

"It was that of Ralph.

"'Were have you been, you young scamp?' he asked, roughly, meanwhile, clenching his fist at me, 'you deserve a dam good thrashing, and I have a great mind to——'

"Thus speaking, he advanced towards me with a resolute manner, which greatly awed me.

"I slunk away in one of the corners of the room, and sought forgiveness.

"'On *one condition* only,' replied Ralph, hastily.

"'And what is the condition?' I re-echoed, growing somewhat bold after the danger had disappeared.

"'That you must come with me to night and help me to do a——'

"Here he stopped abruptly, and gazed attentively around him.

"Catechising and fixed was the searching glance of that man as he scrutinised the panels of the door, examined the length and breath of the walls, and listened intently to hear any sounds which would warn him of the approach of some eavesdropper.

"In his search, whether it proceeded from the eyes or the ears, he was satisfied, for after a few minutes he convinced himself that he could speak freely, and without fear of his speech being overheard.

"'That condition is,' Ralph renewed, 'that you will give me your help in the cracking of a crib, upon which I have fixed my eyes.'

"'*The cracking of a crib!*' I said, 'what's the meaning of that.'

"Ralph explained.

"It meant nothing more or less, than to give him my co-operation in a case of burglary which he was premeditating.

"I shuddered.

"'Oh! Mr. Ralph,' I said, 'I hope you are not in earnest, and that you are only joking.'

"'Joking, ah! ah!' and he showed me the shilling-piece, 'joking, I wish I was; but something must be done, for if I do not pay my reckoning here the landlord can take it into his head to have me prosecuted as a vagrant, and then my previous character is looked into, and I find myself snugly lodged, at the Queen's expense, in some philanthropic establishment kept on purpose for good men like me.'

"There was a cynical, low meaning in Ralph's words.'

"'I thought,' I said, 'that you was going to reform, you told me as much.'

"The convict mused sadly.

"'Reform!' he exclaimed, in a hoarse, subdued whisper, 'reform, when an outcast has one shilling in his pocket and the world to face. Reform! when the bitterest foe he has is man! Oh, yes! it looks very pretty in print, sounds very pretty, also—go and tell that to the Horse Marines. And did you believe it, eh?'

"I looked at Ralph, and feared to speak.

"We were now both sitting down before a fire, which Ralph had given orders to light in his room, and he was gazing in the embers before him, while I was thinking over his words to me, and hoping sincerely that they would never come to pass.

"He had been silent for some time, when he suddenly rose from his chair with a startled shudder.

"'I thought,' he muttered, 'that I heard footsteps outside.'

"I wished to conciliate Ralph, so I walked towards the door, and cautiously unloosend it.

"On tiptoe I stood on the landing before me, and listened.

"I returned to the room, and informed him that his fears were groundless, for not one sound could be heard beyond the squeaking of the mice, gambolling about in the interstices of the wall.

"'That will do, then,' said Ralph. 'Get yourself ready.'

"'Ready?'

"'Yes.'

"'Why, I am already ready,' I repeated; 'I have nothing to get ready with.'

"Ralph looked strangely at me.

"'This is what I mean,' he said.

"Thus speaking, he was taking off his boots from his feet.

"In a stentorian voice, while, however it was subdued, was nevertheless threatening, he bid me to do the same thing.

"'I, accordingly, without a word of reply, took to taking off my boots; a task which lasted much longer than I thought—my boots happening to be laced ones.

"Ralph, meanwhile, was getting ready—as he had just said.

"A few instants was all that we required to take off our clodhoppers, and once that Ralph's feet were bare, he enjoined me to be silent, and not to speak to him on the stair-case, if I valued my life.

"To some people, a similar request would have been laughed at; but, however, to me it was not suggestive of much merriment, as the knife which Ralph held in his hand had an ominous signification, which no one could for a moment have mistaken.

CHAPTER XXXVI.
THE EXCURSION.

"To prepare ourselves for the excursion in which I was reluctantly compelled to join, was about the easiest thing to accomplish—but to walk out of the 'Red Lion' unnoticed, to conquer the difficulties with which Ralph's project was fraught, was one of those tasks which few would have had the boldness to undertake, or if they had it, would, doubtless, be wanting in the needful craft and subtlety.

"To carry out Ralph's plan seemed to be an impossibility.

"I wished he had remained in his bed-room, and faced the landlord in the morning, instead of sallying upon the criminal errand at stake.

"But, as I knew that to try to shake his resolution would be a useless speech on my part, I made the best of my position and followed him.

"We were now at the top of the staircase.

"Above us the skylight windows, through which from time to time the yellow glare of the moon shone faintly, beneath two flight of steps.

"'Walk as smoothly as you can,' said Ralph, to me ere we started, 'for, if you do not, you will attract notice and may be discovered.'

"I replied in the affirmative.

"And, Nancy," the boy went on, "you may rest assured that I did my best not to lay myself open to blame, for what I knew of Ralph (and I had seen but little of him, but that little is quite enough for me,) I felt convinced that if surprised, in a moment of panic he would use the instrument which he carried.

"The knife.

"The bloodstained blade which I had seen by the sea shore.

"Then I prayed fervently heaven to come to my rescue, and to make me much lighter than I was, for, if any one awoke, there might be a murder, and I guess I would be the cause of it.

"The word was enough to chill my blood.

"Murder! aye, yes, murder.

"Now, whether Ralph guessed my thoughts or not I am unable to tell, but, as we reached the landing he whispered in my ear not to be afraid—and to follow him wherever he went.

"We had so far overcome a few of the difficulties in our way. No one had discovered us on the staircase, but the worse part was still to come.

"How were we to get out in the country?

"We had been in hopes that we should have managed to get out of the house by the back-way, but in that we were disappointed, for every door was hermetically closed.

"We remained at a stand still.

"Who could ever realize to himself the feeling which crept over me when I stood in that landing, fearing every instant to be discovered by some of the inmates of the house.

"But this was not to last long.

"For withdrawing a skeleton key from his pocket, Ralph placed it in the lock of a huge door which led to the yard.

"But we had reckoned without our host, as the saying has it, for no sooner were we outside the house, than two dogs before us, who were happily fastened to their kennels, began to bark and to yell in a manner which, we doubted not, would attract notice, and, perhaps, bring the landlord upon us.

"It had been raining all the earlier part of the evening, and now the ground was wet and slippery, and the moon, which shone through the clouds, cast its fitful light upon the country before us.

"'I say, let us not delay longer than we can help,' said Ralph, 'this yard once crossed, we are free.'

"And suiting the action to his word, he boldly crossed the yard.

"It was now very dark.

"A murky cloud had obscured the moon in the Heavens—and not a star could have been traced in the dark vault of Heaven.

"Nancy," the boy went on, "it was indeed a terrible night, and few would have ventured out on the errand which compelled us to leave our warm beds in search of plunder."

The girl had not spoken for a considerable time—the manner with which Velvet was telling his story was so simple, that unwillingly she took a great delight in listening to it.

"What did you do when you left the house," now inquired Nancy—her mouth kissing the ear of the boy.

"You have not forgotten, Nancy," the boy pursued, "that which I have previously told you, namely, that Ralph had fixed his eye upon a certain house which stood in the distance."

"No," replied Nancy.

"Well then, towards it we walked, and tedious and weary was our march, although it did not extend over three hundred yards at the utmost.

"Ralph had made inquiries in the course of the evening, and he had ascertained that the inhabitants of the house were an old lady, with two female servants, and a male servant, who had been in the service for many years past, and who fulfilled all duties, namely, those of coachman and butler.

"The name he had been unable to ascertain.

"You know, doubtless, Nancy, what the country is in wet weather; fancy, then, myself tramping across a turnip-field, which had been recently ploughed.

"Many a time my foot slipped, and more than once I was knee-deep in mud.

"Ralph, however, did not seem to fear the mud, or to take the slightest heed of a thin, drizzling rain which was beginning to fall, and which wafted in our faces by sundry gusts of wind, was anything but pleasant under the circumstances.

CHAPTER XXXVII.
VELVET STILL RELATES HIS ADVENTURE.

"THE house towards which we were directing our footsteps, could now be seen more plainly than before.

"It was a tasty-looking building, with out-houses attached to it—a carriage-shed, stables and a small garden stretching away before the portch.

"There was a gate to cross to obtain admittance in the garden, but as it was only a wooden one this impediment was not likely to hinder Ralph's project.

"With a quick and nervous movement he broke it open.

"The noise which he made in so doing geered strongly upon my hearing, for I feared that the inmates of a small house on my right would be attracted by it.

"But such was not the case, the porter remained in his lodge, thinking, perhaps, that prudence is the best part of valour, and we were allowed to proceed unmolested.

"'Velvet,' Ralph began, when we were about twenty yards from the house, 'listen to me.'

"'What?' I asked.

"Ralph mused, and taking a broad survey of the surrounding scenery, he thus began—

"'You must stay there,' he said, pointing with his right finger to an artificial bower with a wooden bench and table in its centre, 'not five steps distant from me.'

"'Very good, sir,' I replied, 'and what do you require of me?'

"'I'll soon let you know.'

"Of course, Nancy, I was anxious to hear more.

"'Go where I told you,' said Ralph, 'until I 'reconnoitre' the dangers in our way, and see whether our chances of success balance them.'

"Shivering, with my clothes soaking wet—with my boots sticking to my feet, and a sickening feeling of apprehensive awe chilling my mind, as well as my body, I nodded my head, and told Ralph that I would act as he wished me to.

"And I was about to direct my steps towards the bower, when Ralph called me back towards him.

"'Remain in that bower,' he said, 'and stand upon the table—then you will be able to see and not be seen, as the branches and the trees conceal you from observation—keep a sharp look-out, and if you detect any one coming give the signal, and we can then lose no time in effecting our escape.'

"I replied to Ralph that I would do my best, and having taken up my post of observation in the bower I strained my eyes to discover any one hostile to us.

"Ralph, after having given me the signal, which consisted of a peculiar shrill whistle, had crept noiselessly and stealthily towards the house.

"'What success will await him?' I muttered to myself, in dread suspense, every instant expecting to see some one coming, and to drag me away with him.

"Nancy, I think that it would be an impossibility to describe adequately the feelings which I experienced when I stood in that bower, watching the house, and ready to warn Ralph should any signs betokening the approach of enemies be forthcoming.

"I could not but admit to myself that I was Ralph's accomplice, and I longed to see the end of this thrilling adventure.

"A few minutes ago, the moon had shone but for a short time only, and now once more it had disappeared, and total darkness reigned.

"Suddenly, I thought I could hear the sound of glass breaking, and a quick tramping of footsteps.

"Then I saw a light moving in the upper apartments of the house.

"The perspiration trickled in thick, heavy beads upon my chilled forehead; my teeth chattered, my limbs trembled, and although I tried to speak I could find no voice to do so.

"My powers of speech had, as it were, forsaken me, and I grew faint, and had I not clutched quickly at the branches before me for support, I should have fallen from the table where I was standing.

"But a voice attracted my attention.

"Quickly I turned round.

"I listened intently.

"I thought I recognised the well-known tread of Wild Ralph.

"I was not mistaken.

"It was he.

"'What's up,' I asked, in a breath.

"'Silence,' he replied.

"It was an agonised whisper—a whisper as would emanate from the lips of a man whose life would hang upon a thread.

"'Jump down,' he said to me.

"I did so.

"I was now on the ground.

"Nancy, can you conceive my anxiety? My heart was beating with rapid pulsations! Oh, that moment, will I ever forget it?

THE DANCE OF DEATH;

OR,

THE HANGMAN'S PLOT.

A THRILLING ROMANCE OF TWO CITIES.

No. 12.]　　　　　SATURDAY, JANUARY 20, 1866.　　　　　[ONE PENNY.

THE DEATH STRUGGLE.

CHAPTER XXXVII.—CONTINUED.

Nancy was looking at that boy who was telling her all his trials in London.

Nancy was gazing upon that handsome youth who had been so much injured.

And instinctively she loved him.

Men, whoever you are, I defy you to run down womankind.

For what is a woman?

A woman, young and true? why, a jewel.

It is purer than gold.

"And how," said Nancy, after a moment's silence, "did you manage to find your way in the house?"

"Silence—silence," once more said Velvet.

Here the big blue eyes of Nancy became filled with the softness of love—the love of innocence—and, without uttering another syllable, she remained mute.

Then her glance rested upon Velvet.

She could drink his words.

Yes ; she could have swallowed his speech.

"What?" she asked.

"We went in the house," said Velvet.

"How?"

"Well, look here, Nancy ; of a short incident I do not wish to make a long story. I told you that I heard steps coming. That was Wild Ralph's tread."

"Yes," said Nancy.

"'Come here, young gentleman,' he said to me, 'and I will pass you through one of the windows, and you can find your way.'

"'What am I to do?' I asked.

"'Follow me,' he replied.

"I did so.

"And then, before I could say Jack Robinson, he pushed me through the broken pane of a window. The distance was not very great, so bang I tumbled down foremost upon my arms."

"Yes."

"The next thing was to open the door."

Nancy nodded her head, like a girl who understood it all.

She did not.

Poor thing !

Poor flower !

Womankind—girlkind—is a magnificent era in the annals of civilisation.

Nancy was a girl who, through poverty, through misery, had preserved her innocence.

Her innocence !

What is that ?

A girl's innocence ?

Why, it is like refined gold ; like the perfumed flower ; like the bright stream which meanders through forests and prairies ; like the white snow, which, driven away from the canopy of heaven, reaches the ground to be contaminated by common footsteps.

Reader, forgive us for thus expatiating.

"Well, Nancy," Velvet resumed, "I found myself in the hall."

"Fortunately I succeeded in opening the door."

"All was still when Wild Ralph and myself entered the house."

CHAPTER XXXVIII.

WHERE VELVET RELATES THE ASSASSINATION OF A GIRL IN A MOST POSITIVE MANNER.

"Ere we ascended the staircase Wild Ralph laid his hands upon my shoulders.

"'Listen,' he said.

"I waited.

"'Let us move a step forward.'

"I could ill do so, my feet were cramped.

"'Let us listen once more,' observed Ralph. 'There may be some one walking in the house.'

"Now I would have liked to have made an objection or two to Ralph ; but after what I had seen I could not.

"We both lent an attentive ear, but nothing attracted us.

"'Luck favours us, my boy !' Wild Ralph now said.

"And we trod on.

"Nancy, I wish I could in a few minutes relate to you what I experienced then ; but it is an impossibility for me."

The girl drank her coffee and listened to the boy.

"'By George !' said Ralph to me ; 'there is no doubt about it. This is a swell house.'

"Still there was a gloom about the place which induced me to indulge in the most wayward thoughts.

"I could not make out how a place like it was—so isolated from the world—should be so well furnished.

"Ralph was an old stager : at least, I think so now.

"Would you think, Nancy, that he had brought with him slippers, which, being worn over the boot, prevented footsteps from being heard.

"A short time after Ralph had spoken I was ready.

"Having informed him that I was awaiting his orders, he led the way, and I followed in his track.

"If I had been walking to a certain doom, my hand could not have trembled more, nor could my heart have beaten quicker.

"In the house there was a light.

"How it was there I know not, unless the servants of the house wished to be well on the qui vive.

"But now I was not in the slightest degree frightened, nor was my companion.

"Had it been darkness I would have been afraid.

"But where there was light I was bold.

"The hall was paved with diamond slabs of black and white marble ; and it was polished as a smooth piece of glass.

"Then Wild Ralph walked on, still leading the way.

"We soon reached a banister.

"Ralph warned me of the step, and not to make too much noise.

"So softly did we glide upstairs that it would have been impossible for any of the inmates to awake through us.

"Nancy," the boy went on, "who could picture the diversity of thoughts which invaded our minds.

"The crisis had now come.

"I had not yet rendered myself liable to any punishment, but I knew that if I persisted in blindly obeying my guide, something terrible must happen."

Again Nancy's big blue eyes opened.

"Transportation for life.

"Nay, the scaffold if I soiled my hand with blood.

"Oh, listen Nancy.

"Now could be heard the slumbering whispers of some creature doubtless asleep in the room before which we were standing.

"What if she were to awake and give the alarm !

"From what Wild Ralph had told me I fancied that in the house there was but an old woman with a large retinue of servants.

"As I strained my ears I heard sounds which were those of a young girl.

"'Ralph,' I said, in a startled whisper, 'there is a young woman asleep.'

"'Yes,' replied Ralph, in a breath.

"A woman !

"This was a word which rang in my ears. That I, Nancy, should be compelled to take the life of one whose frailty I was bound to protect.

"But, Nancy, the time had arrived.

"I felt that any objection on my part to comply with Ralph's injunction would have been met with contempt.

"'And now let us enter the room,' said Wild Ralph, and take your post by the side of the bed."

"So peremptorily had Ralph spoken that I could not hesitate.

"'You must remain there watching the woman,' he said, 'and when I will have done my part of the work I will give the signal.'

"No further colloquy ensued.

"With noiseless steps I crept forward.

"'I can rely upon you now,' said Wild Ralph; 'to your post, old fellow.'

"Now I was under the impression, from what Wild Ralph had said, that there was but one woman in that house, and that woman was the mistress of the same.

"But I felt—at least my instinct as a boy made me so feel—that there was some one else besides.

"We went in the room.

"I was not mistaken.

"In it there was a girl.

"She was handsome.

"She was sleeping in a state of blissful ignorance.

"As she reclined voluptuously upon her back, encircling her short little neck with her soft hands, she might indeed have been compared to the unconscious traveller, who, having reposed his weary limbs in one of the most inviting spots in his wanderings, prepares himself to go to sleep, heeding not the serpent awaiting to coil its folds around his frame, and pierce his heart with its venomed sting.

"Now, Nancy, my heart beat.

"'Yes, there was a girl asleep.'

"Should she awake!

"Doubtless, had the poor thing known by whom she was surrounded she would not have reposed and lounged so carelessly.

"She would have hid her small head under the bedclothes instead of beginning to play listlessly in her slumber with the golden tresses of her wavy hair, losing her taper fingers amidst the forest of her silken fringes which fell in abundant clusters upon a bare bosom of alabaster hue, and of so faultless a shape in all its minutest lineaments that many a Venus might have envied it."

Nancy was listening to that poor boy who was talking to her.

"Now, Nancy, we had expected to find everything fair and square,

"We were mistaken.

"Who could have dreamt of finding a young girl in that house?

"As soon as the bull's-eye glare of Wild Ralph rested upon the fair sleeper he began to wonder.

"He had anticipated meeting an old woman.

"However, he could not retreat.

"When a man—be he what he may—whether a nobleman, an officer, a sailor, a clerk, wants a shilling, he is not the person to step backwards.

"We had no money.

"On we went.

"Suddenly there rose a shriek!

"A terrible shriek!

"A shriek which went through the house.

"I had no weapons.

"Wild Ralph, however, had

"THE KNIFE!

"There was no time for reflection.

"The alarm had been given!

"Then there came a sudden panic upon Wild Ralph.

"Hence, no sooner had the cry for help been uttered than a whirl of dizzy sensations overpowered his whole being; and the fear of being detected adding considerably to the blow given to his imagination, he rushed forward.

"Then, in the dead of night, ere he could stop the progress of his arm, Wild Ralph thrust his knife heavily downwards.

"And, alas! it found a sheath in the white luxuriant breast of the voluptuous maiden.

"The blood spurted!

*   *   *   *

"The ruby flowed from the snowy skin!

*   *   *   *

"'Heavens! Heavens! Heavens!' I heard Wild Ralph saying to me; 'I am punished at last!'

"'What mean you?' I asked.

"With all the incoherent expressions of a sorrowful heart, Wild Ralph then told me, in a few hurried, agonised whispers, a long story of woe.

"He had murdered one who was dear to him.

"One who was a companion to the lady whose house he had entered.

"One whom he had not seen for years.

"HIS DAUGHTER!

*   *   *   *

"'Come on! come on!' said Wild Ralph. 'Away! boy; away!'"

*   *   *   *

On hearing the startling revelations of Velvet Nancy was unable to refrain a sigh of astonishment and disgust.

"What!" she exclaimed. "Do you maintain that that which I have heard is true?"

Velvet shook his head.

"And I was an accomplice to the murder, Nancy."

"An unwilling accomplice, friend."

"What followed?" the girl renewed, after a moment's silence.

"The alarm had been raised. In an instant the whole house was up. There was tramping of footsteps everywhere. It is impossible to say what might have occurred had not Ralph and myself taken to flight.

"Onward we ran, never once turning round to ascertain whether our pursuers were on our track.

"The worst was," the boy continued, "that Ralph seemed to have lost all energy. 'I have murdered my daughter. Oh! Heaven will never forgive me.'

"I asked Ralph whether we would return to the Blue Lion.

"A hollow, bitter, Satanical laugh was his only reply.

"'No! a thousand times No!' he replied; 'the fresh air for me. In a room I would die of suffocation.'

"Although Ralph was a man of the lowest stamp—although, from his own account, he deserved not to be pitied—yet I felt for him.

"It appeared, Nancy, that ten years ago his daughter had been taken away, and placed in a respectable school, by a charitably disposed man. Since then he had not heard anything else about her.

"That she was well cared for he had not a doubt; but to find her in the manner in which he did was excruciating to his feelings, however depraved and corrupt they might have been.

"We rested beneath the foliage of an oak tree.

"Then the convict told me that he knew that he would not live long."

Velvet then related to Nancy the sad sight which he had witnessed in the Lone House—the den of infamy from which he had rescued her.

"And what did you subsequently do?" asked Nancy.

"Away to London town we went.

"Ralph had become gloomy and silent.

"At length, when we saw the houses of London town in the distance, Ralph turned abruptly towards me.

"' Boy,' he said, ' I am no companion for you. Leave me. You are young and healthy, and in London a man can always live. My society would harm you. I can do you no good. Forgive me for having taken you from your home.'

"Then I saw a tear glistening in the convict's eye.

"Fain would I have spoken; but I could not.

"I remained at a standstill, unable to say a word.

"Then Ralph held out his hand, and wished me good bye.

"I shook it, and was about to tell him to hope, when I was prevented from doing so by his absence.

"For he had suddenly glided away; and so astonished had I been by all which I had seen and experienced that I never tried to run after him."

Here followed Velvet's adventures—his rescue by the police from the thieves—his acquaintance with Wild Will, the swell thief—his stay at Long's Hotel—and every other incident with which our readers are already acquainted.

"Never mind," said Nancy, after a while; "we are both young and hearty. Ralph told you that you were already so. I have no money—no friends; have you?"

Velvet was about to say that he had a father and a mother in Bournemouth, and that he could return to them if he wished; but somehow he did not like to abandon the girl to her fate.

"I have not," he said, " I am as forlorn and as destitute as you are. What do you purpose to do?"

"Face the world," said Nancy. "and see whether with God's help, we can succeed in London, if not to make a fortune, at least an honest independence."

"I fear not the numerous difficulties in the way. If you will try, Nancy, I will also."

The girl nodded her head.

Then the boy drew Nancy's forehead towards his lips, and imprinted upon it a kiss in which was contained an immensity of affection. The affection of one who was noble, true, and kind, and trusted in his own energy.

Was he to be one of the many victims of hope?

Was Nancy to fail in her bold plans?

These questions will be answered in a future portion of this story, but for the present we must part company with Velvet and Nancy.

CHAPTER XXXIX.

THE FARMER PLOTS.

There was one man alone in the room of the cottage at Bournemouth, where we have already paid a few visits.

That was Dick Spaldings.

Care had traced deep furrows upon his forehead—his clothes were ragged and dirty—his eyes were bloodshot and fierce—and his hands trembled with a nervous feverish twitch.

Difficult indeed would it have been for a stranger to recognise in the small room where Spaldings sat the appearance of comfort which once existed in it.

Beyond a bundle of straw carelessly flung in the corner there was no furniture whatever.

" Sold out! sold out! " he was muttering: " the bailiffs have done their worst. The villagers have had a good laugh at my expense, and Jenny, curse her, has run away with Will Sparton; and where is my revenge, and of what avail is it to me to have entered into a secret compact with the Black Brethren of the Crystal Dagger?"

And then he glanced uneasily around him—and the cold sweat of disappointment trickled down his furrowed forehead.

" *But I will be revenged yet.* . . .

" Will I though?" he continued, with a Satanical smile, "but slowly am I accomplishing my work. I have proved to the vicar William Spanton's dishonesty. He has lost his situation, that's true—but then? what? why he has run away with my wife."

Here a low demoniacal smile issued from the man's lips, and his eye glared with a villanous fiendish expression of bitter hate.

"What had Jenny to complain against me? That I got drunk? aye, I did, but I had a deep game on hand. That I beat her?—why she richly deserved it. That I brought misery upon our home?—aye, home—our home. What a prostitution of a word which means happiness, content, the sweet joys of mutual affection.

As he was thus musing Dick Spaldings' attention was attracted by the sounds of footsteps. Quickly he turned round.

Standing upon the threshold was our old acquaintance, Carrotty Nat.

Uncertain how to proceed, he awaited the moment when the farmer would speak.

Dick Spaldings gazed at the new comer.

" Come in," he said, " and sit yourself down upon this stool."

Thus speaking, Dick Spaldings pointed to the solid trunk of a tree which was used as a chair in the poverty-stricken abode.

With a ruffianly swagger Carrotty Nat advanced.

" I have got news for you, Dick," he said; "I have ascertained from a little girl called Griggles, who occasionally comes to the village, the whereabouts of your wife."

" You have!" asked the farmer.

Carrotty Nat shook his head in a most persuasive manner.

" And how did you manage that," he quickly retorted, " which I have been unable to do? Your means of discovery must be much more extensive than mine."

" I know how to go to work," was the brief reply.

Dick Spaldings thought it unwise to cross-examine any further his old acquaintance.

" And where is she?" he asked quickly.

" In London, living with Will Spanton in the Ratcliffe Highway."

" Ratcliffe Highway!" repeated the husband; " low neighbourhood that."

" Very," mused Nat.

" And what does Will Spanton do for a living?"

" He has gone to the bad."

" Ah!"

Then there followed a long conversation between the two men, which ended in putting Dick Spaldings in a violent fit of rage; and they both parted, Carrotty Nat chuckling in his sleeves, Dick Spaldings resolving to start for London, and to lose no time in laying plans for his revenge.

CHAPTER XL.

WHO WAS SHE?

Through a dark vault, along a subterranean passage, was the convict whom we have left at the Bagne of Toulon, led by his mysterious saviour.

At last, gliding with the swiftness of two phantoms, the convict and the woman who had rescued the Marquis of Aguado from a certain doom came to an opening through which a lonely path could be seen.

Never had 557 seen the spot before.

" Where are we?" he asked from the woman.

She made no reply at first.

With a steadfast, slow movement she allowed her glance to sweep near and far.

"In the outskirts of Toulon, about a mile from that spot where the blood-stained guillotine raises its ghastly head, and awaits the moment when it will smile at your death agony."

557 shuddered.

"I am saved," he murmured; "and by whom?"

The woman smiled.

"You will soon know," she replied, in the measured tones of a voice which vibrated musical and clear.

There was something so voluptuous about the firm, white bust; there was something so attractive about the snowy skin; there was something so gorgeously expressive about the dark eyes; besides, there was such loving smoothness about the rosy, clear white nails, that the Marquis of Aguado stood transfixed.

The morning was now bright and warm; the birds sang merrily in the branches of the trees; a bright stream meandered gently at the woman's feet; and the golden sun cast its dazzling beams upon the convict's saviour.

"I do not remember ever having seen your features before," the Marquis of Aguado began. "I believed that if *certain friends* failed to succeed in saving my neck from the guillotine, a weak, frail woman would have been unable to accomplish the task."

"You see you were mistaken," replied the woman, drawing herself to her full height, while a dark scowl of contempt flitted across her handsome brow. A weak, frail woman, eh?"

There was a mocking tone, a derisive intonation about the woman's speech as she spoke.

To portray accurately, and without omitting one single incident, the strange career of the Marquis of Aguado, would take volumes.

Our readers know already some of the deeds which he had perpetrated, and from the perusal of such would doubtless believe that he could be astonished at nothing.

Yet they would be mistaken were they to form such an opinion.

There are certain epochs in the life of man when he witnesses scenes which so much astonish him that he fancies himself in the mystic land of impossible reality. Like the play-goer, he gazes upon some transformation scene, which, for awhile at least, bewilders him, and leads him, for a brief while only, to believe that he is himself one of the inhabitants of the fairy land which is being exhibited for his benefit. He wonders, and although he knows that that which he sees belongs to the domain of fiction, yet he cannot help taking pleasure in persuading himself that it does not.

And thus it was with the Marquis of Aguado.

He knew that he was but a common mortal—he knew that the woman before him was also one—yet he could not dismiss the idea that there was something superhuman about her.

He thought, and very wisely too, that if the Brethren of the Crystal Dagger, whose chief he was, had been baffled in the attempts which they certainly had made to save him from the scaffold, he or she who could do it must be a most wonderful being indeed.

Meanwhile the woman remained at a standstill, and, conscious of the admiration to which she was subject, she tried not to destroy it by any useless word.

Languidly she strode on, bidding 557 to follow her.

"When they find that you have escaped,"—the woman said, flinging herself upon a luxuriant mount of moss, and allowing the silken tresses of her wavy hair to fall in disorder upon her neck while the faultless symmetry of her perfectly modelled limbs became visible to the Marquis d'Aguado's eyes— "they will do their best to capture you."

Mechanically the convict had allowed himself to sink by the side of his saviour.

The words of the speaker were the means to cause him to rise suddenly to his feet, as if he had been suddenly pricked by some concealed serpent.

"Will they?" he hoarsely exclaimed, "Will they?"

A low musical laugh was the woman's reply.

"Of course they will," she went on, and as if she was perfectly unconcerned with the fate of the man whose life she had saved, she began to gather the wild flowers which grew in luxuriant abundance by her side.

This was a behaviour which was unaccountable and terrible in the extreme.

The Marquis of Aguado was fairly astonished.

"Tell me, unknown friend," he said, clasping the woman's hands in his own, "your name, and your objects for having acted as you have done."

"I am called Lady Shepherd by some," she replied, "for others I have different appellations; my calling in life is not one which a mother would like her daughter to follow, and my object for—

"Yes," gasped Aguado, "for saving my life?"

"Was to bind you to me?"

"And can I be useful to you?"

"In more ways than one."

"What will I have to do?"

"To help me in all my schemes."

"And are they numerous?"

"Sometimes."

"Why, then, strange being, did you think that I was just the person to suit you?"

Here the woman's glance swept once more around her.

"Because," she said "I read an account of your early life in the newspapers; a lower villain, in my opinion, could not have existed. Satan on earth could not have played a more loathsome *rôle.* Then I pondered over the account. 'Bella,' I said to myself, 'you have two hard things on hand to accomplish—One is prompted by revenge, the other by cupidity, and both must yield gold—a help is needed.' Hitherto I have been unable to find it. A chance offered itself, and I seized it."

"And what will be my reward? what will you give, me Bella, if I act implicitly according to your orders?"

"My love—my love, such as it is!"

The Marquis of Aguado breathed with a sigh of intense satisfaction.

"Are you satisfied to accept my terms?" asked Bella.

"Oh, angel! oh, beautiful seraph! why question me thus?" the Marquis suddenly exclaimed, in an ecstasy of sudden bliss. "You are only playing with my feelings; you know an answer to be futile; say what you wish me to do, and I'll obey."

And he endeavoured to clasp the beautiful woman towards his palpitating breast.

"Not yet; not yet!" proudly ejaculated the woman. "You are my servant now. Not yet; not yet, my lover."

And with these words she retreated a few steps backwards, gazing with a bright and piercing expression upon the convict, whose eyes soon cowed before the spell of his preserver's.

At that instant a shrill whistle was heard.

"What's that?" asked Aguado.

"My chaise is ready," replied Bella. "Come."

The Marquis followed. Quickly he bore upon the woman's footsteps.

After three minutes' walk she halted.

There was now the open country before Afluado, and, awaiting the arrival of some one stood a handsome postchaise.

Bella was soon in the vehicle.

She bade the convict to sit by her side.

And then another whistle was heard—and the whip rattled—and away went the horses with a swiftness which the Marquis of Aguado had never seen equalled.

CHAPTER XLI.

ALONE IN LONDON.

It was about nine o'clock in the evening and a week after the period when we parted company with Velvet and Nancy.

Dressed in what had once been a snuff-brown coat—but which had faded to the hue of bricks imperfectly baked—could have been seen a youth.

His was not strictly speaking a ragged coat, though it had lost its cuffs—a bereavement which obliged the wearer's arms to project through the sleeves two long inelegant inches.

The coat altogether was too small, and was only made to meet over the chest by means of a bit of twine.

This wretched garment was surmounted by a bird's-eye handkerchief of cotton, wound about the throat hangman fashion—above was a battered billy-cock hat with a dissolute drooping brim.

The youth's hands were plunged into his pockets, and he shuffled hastily along in boots which were the boots of a tramp indifferent to miry ways.

Suddenly he stopped, and then he clasped his brow and reflected deeply.

"Ah! London," he murmered, "ah London!"

And he could say no more. His throat became choked—his eyes filled with tears, and despondingly he shook his head.

The youth to whom we are now devoting our attention was the farmer's son—Velvet, in fact.

The place where he was standing was in the Princes-road, Lambeth.

"I thought," he muttered to himself, "that I should have succeeded in making a living for Nancy and myself, and yet I have failed. As long as I could I kept her, I have sold all my clothes, my new clothes, and bought old ones, and cleared a few shillings by the bargain. That has prevented us to starve. We tried to get work—we besought employment, but nobody would have us, and now I have no money; and Nancy, poor Nancy, has disappeared—she has been stolen from me. I saw it and yet could not help—I saw the carriage approach, I saw the man emerging from the door—I heard her shrieks—I witnessed her supplications—I howled Police! Police! Police! but no one came—and Nancy, Nancy, she's gone, and I am alone."

"Alone! friendless, penniless, in the City of London."

Such was Velvet's soliloquy.

"Truly," he resumed, after a moment's respite, "I can return to the thieves—but I will not do so —sooner die of want—die in the path of honour than thrive in the smooth garden of infamy."

And he stood there musing.

Poor boy!

Presently an old woman, pushing before her a small stand, with coffee and slices of bread and butter upon it, passed before Velvet.

She gazed upon him.

Velvet threw a hungry, famished glance upon the victuals.

"Give me a cup of coffee and a slice of bread and butter," he asked beseechingly.

"Where's your three-halfpence?"

"Oh! trust me; I'll pay you by-and-bye."

"Trust you, young vagabond! Trust the likes of you! What else would you like? Perhaps the next thing you will do is to ask me to lend you half-a-crown?"

Velvet looked threateningly at that old woman who was mocking him in his misery—who was helping him to sink lower still in the Slough of Despond in which his imagination had fallen.

"If you are hungry," said the woman, "you had better go there."

"Where?" asked Velvet.

"To the big house," resumed the coffee merchant, and with her finger she pointed towards a gloomy, ominous building in the distance.

"What place is that?" asked Velvet.

The woman laughed loudly.

"You are a very clever young vagabond," she said, after a while, "but all the same for that, you do not get over me. Doubtless your next step will be to tell me that you are a young man from the country."

While scanning the annals of history from time to time, we are loth to proceed with our narrative, loving to commune with our own thoughts, and feeling a sweet satisfaction in pondering over the deeds of great warriors, who, knowing that their doom was certain, nevertheless feared not to attempt the forlorn expedition when they were told.

It was the case with Velvet.

He knew that he would receive no sympathy at the hands of the woman, and yet he persisted in remaining by her side.

"I am a young man from the country," said Velvet, remembering with bitterness that remark which had been made to him in the thieves' den, and once more sinking upon a stone beneath him.

"If you go to the workhouse," the woman said, they are bound to take you in, for such places are made for tramps and vagrants like yourself."

Thus speaking, the woman glanced around her, and seeing no customer near she wheeled the barrow away.

Velvet looked at her retreating form.

"I can stand it no longer," he said; "I am famished, faint, weary, and exhausted. I'll go to the workhouse."

CHAPTER XLII.

THE "BIG HOUSE."

Velvet was not long in carrying out his determination. With tottering steps he walked slowly towards the building which had been pointed to him.

Here we will take an opportunity of showing our readers how casual paupers are lodged and fed, and what the "casual" is like, and what the porter who admits him and the master who rules over him, and how the night passes with the outcasts whom we have all seen crowding about workhouse doors on cold and rainy evenings.

Much has been said on the subject—on behalf of the paupers, on behalf of the officials; but nothing by any one with no motive but to learn and make known the truth.

We will, then, describe the manner in which Velvet was treated.

The day had been windy and cold. The night was bleak and chill.

In less than a minute Velvet was standing outside the workhouse door.

He feared to advance close on seeing about a dozen ragged wretches, male and female, who were also seeking admission.

Some were standing with a bold face, others were hiding their heads in their hands, others were squatting about the steps.

They had all been refused admission, so Velvet gleaned from their conversation, the beadle having refused to take them in.

Velvet also learnt that they were habitual customers—slept in the house regularly—that is to say, when they were admitted, which was not always so, as with the case in point.

"What did he say to you?" asked a squalid-looking wretch from an old man with a strong smell of liquor about him.

"Why he told me that I came here too often, and that I was a drunken old vagabond, and should look after my wife and familo instead of behaving like a ruffian.

"Did he?" retorted the squallid wretch, a young individual of about seventeen years of age, reminding one very much of a low billiard marker; "Did he?"

"Yes."

Now this promising young gentleman seemed to have received an education superior to that of his companion, and proceeded in a most business-like manner to inform the drunkard that the beadle had no right to use his own discretion in matters connected with the parish; he spoke, also, of the heavy taxes paid by the tradesmen for parish purposes, and in one word gave all his learned opinions upon churchwardens, parish beadles, and so forth.

"And how is it, then, that if *you can* make the beadle suffer, my worthy, you have failed to obtain admission for yourself?"

"I'll explain that; he said; that I was too much of a gentleman, and he could not take me in.

With this remark the young gentleman drew himself to his full height, and called his companion's attention to his coat, which once was black, but now had lost that colour, the grease and dirt upon it placing you very much in mind of a waterproof gutta-percha.

Although highly interesting in its tone, Velvet did not stay to hear more of the above conversation, and, taking no heed of the catechising eyeing to which he was subjected, he lifted the big knocker and knocked.

The door was promptly opened, and he entered.

Just within a healthy, strong-looking clerk sat at a comfortable desk, comfortably holding a pen in hand, smiling comfortably at Velvet, and looking very comfortable altogether.

Before him was a desk.

The spacious hall accorded itself with the appearance of the clerk, for it was in every way as cheery as cleanliness, and great mats, and plenty of gaslight could make it.

"What do you want?" asked the man who opened the door.

"I want a night's shelter," replied Velvet.

"Go and stand before the desk," said the porter.

The boy obeyed.

"You are late."

"Am I, sir?" dolefully asked Velvet.

"Yes; if you come in you'll have a bath, and you'll have to sleep in the shed."

"Very well, sir."

"Who are you?"

"Who am I?"

"Yes: in fact what's your name, And drop questioning me. I am the party to question you; and remember that you are not the party to question me."

"My name is Harry Spaldings."

"Harry Spaldings," the clerk repeated.

"What are you?"

"Nothing."

"Nothing! we cannot have you here then. Have you no calling in life—no trade?"

"Oh! yes, I have," quickly and feverishly exclaimed Velvet, seeing the porter about to open the door; "I am a brickmaker."

This Velvet said to account for the look of his hands, which were rather rough, he having lately helped a mason to carry some building materials for him.

"Your answers are fishy, very fishy, sir—yes, sir, very fishy," slowly said the clerk. "Porter, have you seen him before?"

"Never, sir."

The clerk continued—"Where did you sleep last night?"

"In the streets."

"The porter does not know you; he sees so many faces that I can easily understand that. Answer me candidly—Have you ever been here before?"

"Never."

"What do you mean to do when you are turned out in the morning?"

"Look for work."

"I hope you may get it," concluded the clerk; and then he took down Velvet's name in the book.

"Porter."

"Sir."

"Take him through; you may as well take his bread with you."

"Thank you, Sir," said Velvet innocently.

Near the clerk stood a basket containing some pieces of bread of equal sizes.

Drawing one of these from many, and unhitching a bunch of keys from the wall, the porter led Velvet through some passages all so scrupulously clean, that the most serious misgivings were laid at rest.

At last he had bed for the night, and he would have food also.

Oh! you boys who would feel inclined to run away from home, listen to poor Velvet's trials, and if you have any thought of leaving good parents, good board and lodging, let the following make you alter your resolution.

The porter and Velvet passed in a dismal yard.

Crossing this, Velvet's guide led him to a door, calling out "Hillo! Daddy! I have brought you another!" whereupon Daddy opened to them and let a little of his gaslight stream into the dark where they both stood.

CHAPTER XLIII.

SEEING LONDON LOW LIFE.

"Come in," said Daddy very hospitably. "There's enough of you to-night, anyhow. What made you so late?"

"I did'nt like to come in earlier; I never slept in a workhouse before."

"More's the pity," muttered Daddy. "Ah! that's a pity, for you've missed your skilley (gruel)."

"Just like my luck," muttered Velvet dolefully.

The porter went his way, and Velvet followed Daddy into another apartment, in which were ranged three great baths, each one containing a liquid so disgustingly like weak mutton broth that a sickening feeling of disgust crept over the poor boy's frame.

"Come on; there's a dry place to stand on up at this end," said Daddy kindly. "Take off your clothes, tie 'em up in your hanksher, and I'll lock 'em up till morning."

Accordingly, and in compliance with the request made, Velvet took off his coat and waistcoat, and was about to tie them together, when Daddy cried—

"That a'int enough. I mean *everything*."

"Not my shirt, sir, I suppose," said Velvet.

"Yes, shirt and all; but there, I'll lend you a shirt," quickly followed Daddy. "Whatever you take in of your own will be nailed, you know. You might take in your boots, though—they'd be handy if you happened to want to leave the shed for anything; but don't blame me if you lose 'em."

With a fortitude for which Velvet hoped some day to be rewarded, he made up his bundle (boots and all) and the moment Daddy's face was turned away he shut his eyes, and plunged desperately into the mutton broth.

He wished from the bottom of his heart his courage had been less hasty; for hearing the splash Daddy looked round and said—

"Lor, now, there was no occasion for that; you look a clean and decent sort of chap. It's them filthy beggars that want washing. Don't use that towel—here's a clean one! That's the sort! and now here's your shirt."

Here Daddy handed Velvet a blue striped one from a heap.

"Here's your ticket," he continued. "Number 34 you are, and a ticket to match is tied to your bundle. Mind you don't lose it. They'll nail it from you if they get a chance. Put it under your head. This is your rug—take it with you."

"Where am I sleep, please, sir?" asked Velvet.

"I'll show you," replied Daddy.

And so he did.

With no other rag but the checked shirt to cover him, and with his rug over his shoulders, Velvet was accompanied by Daddy to the door at which he entered, who, opening it, kept him standing with naked feet on the stone threshold, full in the draught of the frosty air, while he pointed out the way he should go.

It was not a long way, but poor Velvet would have given much not to have trodden it.

It was open as the highway — with flagstones below and the stars overhead; and a frosty wind meanwhile blowing in smart cutting gusts.

"Straight across," said Daddy, "to where you see the light shining through. Go in there and turn to the left, and you'll find the beds in a heap. Take one of 'em and make yourself comfortable." Straight across Velvet went, his naked feet seeming to cling to the stones as though they were burning hot instead of icy cold (they had just stepped out of a bath, you should remember) till he reached the space through which the light was shining, and he entered in.

No language with which I am acquainted, reader, is capable of conveying an adequate conception of the spectacle he then encountered.

Imagine a space of about thirty feet by thirty, enclosed on three sides by a dingy whitewashed wall, and roofed with naked tiles, which were furred with the damp and filth that reeked within.

As for the fourth side of the shed, it was boarded in for (say) a third of its breadth; the remaining space being hung with flimsy canvas, in which was a gap two feet wide at top, widening to at least four feet at bottom.

This far too airy shed was paved with stone, the flags so thickly encrusted with filth, that he mistook it at first for a floor of natural earth.

Extending from one end of his bedroom to the other, in three rows, were certain iron "cranks" (of which he subsequently learned the use), with their many arms raised in various attitudes, as the stiffened arms of men are on a battle-field.

Velvet's bedfellows lay amongst the cranks, distributed over the flagstones in a double row, on narrow bags scantily stuffed with hay.

At one glance his appalled vision took in thirty of them—thirty men and boys stretched upon shallow pallets which put only six inches of comfortable hay between them and the stony floor.

These beds were placed close together, every occupant being provided with a rug like that which Velvet was fain to hug across his shoulders. In not a few cases two gentlemen had clubbed beds and rugs and slept together. In one case four gentlemen had so clubbed together.

Many of Velvet's fellow-casuals were awake—others asleep, or pretending to sleep; and shocking as were the waking ones to look upon they were quite pleasant when compared with the sleepers.

For this reason: the practised and well-seasoned casual seems to have a peculiar way of putting himself to bed.

He rolls himself in his rug, tucking himself in, head and feet, so that he is completely enveloped; and, lying quite still on his pallet, he looks precisely like a corpse covered because of its hideousness.

Some were stretched out at full length; some lay nose and knees together; some with an arm or a leg showing crooked through the coverlet.

It was like the result of a railway accident: these ghastly figures were awaiting the coroner.

From the moral point of view, however, the wakeful ones were more dreadful still.

Towzled, dirty, villanous, they squatted up in their beds, and smoked foul pipes, and sang snatches of horrible songs, and bandied jokes so obscene as to be absolutely appalling.

Eight or ten were so enjoying themselves—the majority with the check shirt on and the frowsy rug pulled about their legs; but two or three wore no shirt at all, squatting naked to the waist, their bodies fully exposed in the light of the single flaring jet of gas fixed high up on the wall.

Velvet's entrance excited very little attention.

There was a horse-pail three parts full of water standing by a post in the middle of the shed, with a little tin pot beside it.

Addressing Velvet as "old pal," one of the naked ruffians begged him to "hand him a swig," as he was "werry nigh garspin'."

Such an appeal of course no "old pal" could withstand, and, with his kindness of heart Velvet gave him a pot full of water.

He showed himself grateful for the attention.

"I should lay over there if I was you," he said, pointing to the left side of the shed; "it's more out of the wind than this 'ere side is."

Velvet took the good-natured advice, and (by this time shivering with cold) stepped over the stones to where the beds or straw bags were heaped, and dragged one of them to the spot suggested by his naked comrade.

But the poor boy had no more idea of how to arrange it than of making an apple-pudding; and a certain little discovery added much to his embarrassment.

In the middle of the bed he had selected was a *stain of blood* bigger than a man's hand!

To lie on such a horrid thing seemed impossible; yet to carry back the bed and exchange it for another might betray a degree of fastidiousness repugnant to the feelings of his fellow lodgers.

THE
DANCE OF DEATH;
OR,
THE HANGMAN'S PLOT.
A THRILLING ROMANCE OF TWO CITIES.

No. 13.]   SATURDAY, JANUARY 27, 1866.   [ONE PENNY.

THE MURDER IN THE WOOD.

CHAPTER XLIV.—CONTINUED.

He knew not how to act; but fortunately, and just in the nick of time, in came that good man Daddy.

"What! not pitched yet!" he exclaimed; "here, I'll show you. Hallo! somebody's been a-bleedin'!

Never mind: let's turn him over. There you are you see! Now lay down, and cover your rug over you."

There was no help for it.

It was too late to go back.

Down he lay, and spread the rug over him.

No. 13.]   [PRIZE TICKET.—No. 13.

Now it should be here mentioned that Velvet had brought in with him a cotton handkerchief, and this he tied round his head by way of a nightcap; but not daring to pull the rug as high as his face.

Before he could in any way settle his mind to reflection, in came Daddy once more to do him a further kindness, and point out a stupid blunder which he had committed.

"Why, you *are* a rummy chap!" said Daddy. "You forgot your bread! Lay hold. And look here, I've brought you another rug; it's perishing cold to-night."

So saying, Daddy spread the rug over Velvet's legs and departed.

CHAPTER XLV.

THE POOR BOYS OF LONDON—A YOUNG THIEF TELLS A GOOD STORY—THE CONVERSATION OF THE "CASUALS."

Velvet was very thankful for the extra covering, but he was in a dilemma about the bread.

He couldn't possibly eat it; what, then, was to be done with it?

He broke it, however, and in view of such of the company as might happen to be looking made a ferocious bite at a bit as large as a bean, and munched violently.

By good luck, however, he presently got half way over his difficulty very neatly.

Just behind him, so close indeed that their feet came within half a yard of his head, three lads were sleeping together.

"Did you 'ear that, Punch?" one of these boys asked.

"'Ear what?" answered Punch, sleepy and snappish.

"Why, a cove forgot his toke! Gordstruth! you wouldn't ketch me a-forgettin' mine."

"You may have half of it, old pal, if you're hungry," Velvet observed, leaning up on his elbows.

"Chuck it here, good luck to yer!" replied his young friend, starting up with an eager clap of his dirty hands.

Velvet "chucked it here," and, slipping the other half under the side of his bed, lay his head on his folded arms.

It was about half-past nine when, having made himself as comfortable as circumstances permitted, Velvet closed his eyes in the desperate hope that he might fall asleep, and so escape from the horrors with which he was surrounded.

"At seven to-morrow morning the bell will ring," Daddy had informed Velvet, and then he had told him he should give up his ticket and get back his bundle.

Between that hour and the present full nine long hours had to wear away.

But he was speedily convinced that, at least for the present, sleep was impossible.

The young fellow (one of three who lay in one bed, with their feet to Velvet's head) whom his bread had refreshed, presently swore with frightful imprecations that he was now going to have a smoke, and immediately put his threat into execution.

Thereupon his bedfellows sat up and lit their pipes too.

But oh! if they had only smoked—if they had not taken such an unfortunate fancy to spit at the leg of a crank distant a few inches from Velvet's head, how much misery and apprehension would have been spared him!

To make matters worse, they united with this American practice an Eastern one: as they smoked they related little autobiographical anecdotes—so

abominable that three or four decent men who lay at the farther end of the shed were so provoked that they threatened, unless the talk abated in filthiness, to get up and stop it by main force.

Instantly the voice of every blackguard in the room was raised against the decent ones.

They were accused of loathsome afflictions, stigmatized as "fighting men out of work," and invited to "a round" by boys young enough to be their grandsons.

For several minutes there was such a storm of oaths, threats, and taunts—such a deluge of foul words raged in the room—that Velvet could not help thinking of the fate of Sodom; as, indeed, he did several times during the night.

Little by little the riot died out, without any the slightest interference on the part of the officers.

Soon afterwards the ruffian majority was strengthened by the arrival of a lanky boy of about fifteen, who evidently recognised many acquaintants, and was recognized by them as "Kay," or perhaps I should write it "K."

He was a very remarkable-looking lad.

Short as his hair was cropped, it still looked soft and silky; he had large blue eyes set wide apart, and a mouth that would have been faultless but for its great width; and his voice was as soft and sweet as any woman's.

Lightly as a woman, too, he picked his way over the stones towards the place where the beds lay, carefully hugging his cap beneath his arm.

"What cheer, Kay?" "Out again, then, old son!" "What yer got in yer cap, Kay?" cried his friends.

To which the sweet voice replied, "Who'll give me part of his *doss* (bed)? —— my —— eyes and limbs if I ain't perishin'! Who'll let me turn in with him for half my *toke* (bread)?"

Velvet feared how it would be! The hungry young fellow who had so readily availed himself of half his "toke" snapped at Kay's offer, and after a little rearrangement and bed-making four young fellows instead of three reposed upon the hay-bags at his head.

Velvet was gazing upon these scenes which we are describing, and truly indeed did he regret having taken the old coffee woman's advice.

He would have preferred a sleep in the open air —bitter, bitter cold as it was.

"You are too late for skilley, Kay. There's skilley now, nights as well as mornins."

"Don't you tell no bleeding lies," Kay answered, incredulously.

"Blind me, it's true! Ain't it, Punch?"

"Right you are!" said Punch, "and spoons to eat it with, that's more! There used to be spoons at all the houses, one time. Poplar used to have 'em; but one at a time they was all nicked, don't you know."

("Nicked" means "stolen," obviously.)

"Well, I don't want no skilley, leastways not to-night," said Kay. "I've had some rum. Two glasses of it; and a blow out of puddin'—regler Christmas plum puddin'. You don't know the cove as give it me, but thinks I this mornin' when I come out, Blessed if I don't go and see my old chum. Lordstruth! he *was* struck!

"'Come along,' he ses, 'I saved you some puddin' from Christmas.'

"'Whereabouts is it?' I ses.

"'In that box under my bed,' he ses, and he forks it out.

"That's the sort of pal to have.

"And he stood a quarten, and half a ounce of *hard-up* (tobacco)."

"That wasn't all, neither; when I come away, ses he, 'How about your breakfus?'"

"'Oh, I shall do,' ses I."

"'You take some of my bread and butter,' he ses. "And he cuts me off four chunks buttered thick. I eat two on 'em comin' along.'"

"What's in your cap, Kay?" repeated the devourer of "toke."

"Them other two slices," said Kay; generously adding, "There, share 'em amongst yer, and somebody give us a whiff of 'bacca.'"

Kay showed himself a pleasant companion; what in a higher grade of society is called "quite an acquisition."

He told stories of thieving, and of a certain "silver cup" he had been "put up to," and avowed that he meant to nick it afore the end of the week, if he got *seven stretch* (? seven years) for it. The cup was worth ten *quid* (? pounds), and he knew where to melt it within ten minutes of *nicking* it.

Nor was there any affectation of secrecy in another gentleman, who announced amid great applause that he had stolen a towel from the bath-room: "And s'help me! it's as good as new; never been washed more'n once!"

"Tell us a 'rummy' story, Kay," said somebody.

And Kay did.

He told stories of so "rummy" a character that the decent men at the farther end of the room (some of whom had their own little boys sleeping with them) must have lain in a sweat of horror as they listened. Indeed, when Kay broke into a "rummy" song with a roaring chorus, one of the decent men rose in his bed and swore that he would smash Kay's head if he didn't desist. But Kay sang on till he and his admirers were tired of the entertainment.

"Now," said he, "let's have a swearing club! you'll all be in it?"

The principle of this game seemed to rest on the impossibility of either of the young gentlemen making half a dozen observations without introducing a blasphemous or obscene word; and either the basis is a very sound one, or for the sake of keeping the "club" alive the members purposely made slips.

The penalty for "swearing" was a punch on any part of the body, except a few which the club rules protected.

The game was highly successful.

Warming with the sport, and indifferent to punches, the members vied with each other in audacity, and in a few minutes Bedlam in its prime could scarcely have produced such a spectacle as was to be seen on the beds behind Velvet.

One rule of the club was that any word to be found in the Bible might be used with impunity, and if one member *punched* another for using such a word the error was to be visited upon him with a double punching all round.

This naturally led to much argument; for in vindicating the Bible as his authority, a member became sometimes so much heated as to launch into a flood of "real swearing," which brought the fists of the club upon his naked carcase quick as hail.

These and other pastimes beguiled the time until, to Velvet's delight, the church chimes audibly tolled twelve.

After this the noise gradually subsided, and it seemed as though everybody was going to sleep at last.

We forgot to mention that during the story-telling and song-singing a few "casuals" had dropped in, but they were not *habitués*, and cuddled down with their rugs over their heads, without a word to any one.

CHAPTER XLVI.

DADDY THE NURSE'S SERVICES ARE ONCE MORE CALLED INTO REQUISITION—FRESH ARRIVALS.

In a little while all was quiet—save for the flapping of the canvas curtain in the night breeze, the snoring, and the horrible, indescribable sound of impatient hands scratching skins that itched.

There was another sound of very frequent occurrence, and that was the clanking of the tin pannikin against the water pail.

Whether it is in the nature of workhouse bread or skilley to provoke thirst is more than Velvet's limited experience entitled him to say, but it may be truthfully asserted that once at least in the course of five minutes might be heard a rustling of straw, a pattering of feet, and then the noise of water-dipping; and then was to be seen at the pail the figure of a man *(sometimes stark naked)*, gulping down the icy water as he stood upon the icy stones.

And here we may remark that we can furnish no solution to this mystery of the shirt.

We only know that some of Velvet's comrades were provided with a shirt, and that to some the luxury was denied.

We may, however, further say this, that *none* of the little boys were allowed one.

Nearly one o'clock.

Still quiet, and no fresh arrival for an hour or more.

Then suddenly a loud noise of hobnailed boots kicking at a wooden gate, and soon after a tramping of feet and a rapping at Daddy's door which, it will be remembered, was only separated from our bedroom by an open paved court.

"Hallo!" cried Daddy.

"Here's some more of 'em for you—ten of 'em!" answered the porter, whose voice Velvet recognised at once.

"They'll have to find beds, then," Daddy grumbled, as he opened his door. "I don't believe there are four beds empty. They must sleep double, or something."

This was terrible news for Velvet.

Bad enough, in all conscience, was it to lie as he was lying; but the prospect of sharing his straw with some dirty scoundrel of the Kay breed was altogether unendurable.

Perhaps, however, they were *not* dirty scoundrels, but peaceable and decent men, like those in the farther corner.

Alas! for Velvet's hopes.

In the space of five minutes in they came at the rent in the canvas—great hulking ruffians, some with rugs and nothing else, and some with shirts and nothing else, and all madly swearing because, coming in after eleven o'clock, there was no "toke" for them.

As soon as these wrathful men had advanced to the middle of the shed they made the discovery that there was an insufficient number of beds—only three, indeed, for ten competitors.

"Where's the beds? D'ye hear, Daddy? You blessed truth-telling old person, where's the beds?"

"You'll find 'em. Some of 'em is lying on two, or got 'em as pillows. You'll find 'em."

With a sudden rush the new comers plunged amongst the sleepers, trampling over them, cursing their eyes and limbs, dragging away their rugs; and if by chance they found some poor wretch who had been tempted to take two beds (or bags) instead of one, they coolly hauled him out and took possession.

There was no denying them, and no use in remonstrating.

They evidently knew that they were at liberty to do just as they liked, and they took full advantage of the privilege.

One of them came up to Velvet, and shouting, "I want that, you ——," snatched at his "bird's-eye" nightcap and carried it off.

There was a bed close to Velvet which contained only one occupant, and into this one of the new comers slipped without a word of warning, driving its lawful owner against the wall to make room.

Then he sat up in the bed for a moment, savagely venting his disappointment as to toke, and declaring that never before in his life had he felt the need of it so much.

By the time the churches were chiming two, matters had once more adjusted themselves, and silence reigned. to be disturbed only by drinkers at the pail, or such as, otherwise prompted, stalked into the open yard.

Kay, for one, visited it.

We mention this unhappy young wretch particularly because he went out without a single rag to his back.

Velvet looked out at the rent in the canvas, and saw the frosty moon shining on him.

When he returned, and crept down between Punch and another, he muttered to himself, "Warm again! O my G—d! warm again!"

CHAPTER XLVII.

THE SINGER : HIS OPINION OF THE COLUMBINE—THE WEARY HOURS OF NIGHT—THE WORKHOUSE CLOCK.

Whether there is a rule which closes the casual wards after a certain hour Velvet did not know : but before one o'clock the number was made up, the last comer signalising his appearance with a grotesque *pas seul*. His rug over his shoulders, he waltzed into the shed, waving his hands and singing in an affected voice, as he sidled along—

"I like to be a swell, a-roaming down Pall Mall,
    Or anywhere,—I don't much care, so I can be a swell"—

a couplet which had an intensely comical effect.

This gentleman had just come from a pantomime, where he had just learned his song, probably.

Too poor to pay for a lodging, he could only muster means for a seat in the gallery of "the Vic. ;" where he was well entertained, judging from the flattering manner in which he spoke of the clown. The columbine was less fortunate in his opinion—

"She's werry dickey!—ain't got what I call 'move' about her."

However the wretched young woman was respited now from the scourge of his criticism ; for the critic and his listeners were fast asleep : and yet Velvet doubted whether any of the company slept very soundly.

Every moment some one shifted uneasily ; and as the night wore on the silence was more and more irritated by the sound of coughing.

The conversation was horrible, the tales that were told more horrible still, and worse than either (though not by any means the most infamous things to be heard—I dare not even hint at them) was that song, with its bestial chorus shouted from a dozen throats ; but at any rate they kept the blood warm with constant hot flushes of anger ; while as for the coughing, to lie on the flagstones in what was nothing better than open shed, and listened to that, hour after hour, chilled one's very heart with pity. Every variety of cough that Velvet ever heard was to be heard there : the hollow cough ; the short

cough ; the hysterical cough ; the bark that comes at regular intervals, like the quarter-chime of a clock, as if to mark off the progress of decay ; coughing from vast hollow chests, coughing from little narrow ones—now one, now another, now two or three together, and then a minute's interval of silence in which to think of it all, and wonder who would begin next. One of the young reprobates above Velvet coughed so grotesquely like the chopping of wood that he named him the Woodcutter. Now and then Velvet found himself coughing too, which may have added just a little to the poignant distress these awfully constant and various sounds occasioned him. They were good in one way : they made one forget what wretches they were who, to all appearances, were so rapidly "chopping" their way to a pauper's graveyard.

Velvet did not care about the more mature ruffians so much ; but, though the youngest, the boys like Kay were unquestionably amongst the most infamous of his comrades, and in every respect worthy of a place in the thieves' den from which Wild Will had taken him away, yet to hear what cold and hunger and vice had done for them at fifteen was almost enough to make a man cry ; and there were boys there even younger than these.

At half-past two, every one being asleep, or at least lying still, Daddy came in and counted Velvet one, two, three, four, and so on, in a whisper.

Then, finding the pail empty (it was nearly full at half-past nine, when Velvet entered), he considerately went and refilled it, and even took much trouble in searching for the tin pot which served as a drinking cup, and which the last comer had playfully thrown to the farther end of the shed.

We ought to have mentioned that the pail stood close to Velvet's head, so that he had peculiar opportunities of study as one after another of his comrades came to the fountain to drink, just as the brutes do in those books of African travel.

The pail refilled, Daddy returned, and was seen no more till morning.

It still wanted four hours and a half to seven o'clock—the hour of rising—and never before in his life did time appear to creep so slowly.

He could hear the chimes of the parish church, and of the Parliament Houses, as well as those of a wretched tinkling Dutch clock somewhere on the premises.

The parish church was the first to announce the hour.

Westminster came next, the lazy Dutchman declining his consent to the time o'day till fully sixty seconds afterwards.

It may seem a trifle, but a minute is something when a man is lying on a cold flagstone, and the wind of a winter night is blowing in his hair.

Three o'clock, four o'clock struck, and still there was nothing to beguile the time but observation, under the one flaring gaslight, of the little heaps of outcast humanity strewn about the floor ; and after a while Velvet found that one may even become accustomed to the sight of one's fellow-creatures lying around you like covered corpses in a railway shed.

For most of the company were now bundled under the rugs in the ghastly way we have already described— though here and there a cropped head appeared, surmounted by a billy-cock like Velvet's own, or by a greasy cloth cap.

Five o'clock, six o'clock chimed, and then Velvet had news—most welcome—of the world without, and of the real beginning of day.

Half a dozen factory bells announced that it was time for working men to go to labour ; but Velvet's companions were not working men, and so snored on.

Out through the gap in the canvas the stars were still to be seen shining on the black sky, but that did not alter the fact that it was six o'clock in the morning.

A little while, and doors were heard to open and shut; yet a little while, and the voice of Daddy was audible in conversation with another early bird; and then Velvet distinctly caught the word "bundles."

Blessed sound!

He longed for his bundle—for his brown coat—for his warm if unsightly "jersey"—for his corduroys and liberty.

*   *   *   *

"Clang!" went the workhouse clock.

"Now, then! wake 'em up!" cried Daddy.

Velvet was already up—sitting up, that is—being anxious to witness the resurrection of the ghastly figures rolled in their rugs.

But nobody but Velvet rose at the summons.

Doubtless they knew what it meant well enough, and in sleepy voices cursed the bell and wished it in several dreadful places; but they did not move until there came in at the whole in the canvas two of the pauper inhabitants of the house, bearing bundles.

"Thirty-two," "twenty-eight!" they bawled, but not Velvet's number, which was thirty-four.

Neither thirty-two nor twenty-eight, however, seemed eager to accept his good fortune in being first called.

They were called upon three several times before they would answer; and then they replied with a savage "Chuck it here, can't you!"

"Not before you chucks over your shirt and ticket," the bundle-holder answered, whereon "thirty-eight" sat up, and, divesting himself of his borrowed shirt, flung it with his wooden ticket; and his bundle was flung back in return.

It was some time before bundle No. 34 turned up, so that Velvet had fair opportunity to observe his neighbours.

The decent men slipped into their rags as soon as they got them, but the blackguards were in no hurry.

Some indulged in a morning pipe to prepare themselves for the fatigue of dressing, while others, loosening their bundles as they squatted naked, commenced an investigation for certain little animals which shall be nameless.

CHAPTER XLVIII.

MORNING AT LAST—"NOW FOUR BOYS"—THE TOILET —THE BREAKFAST—THE CASUAL WITH ONE LEG— THE TASKMASTER—THE "CRANK"—THE TAILOR.

At last Velvet's turn came; an1 "chucking over" his shirt and ticket, he quickly attired himself in clothes which, ragged as they were, were cleaner than they looked.

In less than two minutes he was out of the shed, and in the yard; where a few of the more decent poor fellows were crowding round a pail of water, and scrambling after something that might pass for a "wash"—finding their own soap, as far as Velvet could observe, and drying their faces on any bit of rag they might happen to have about them, or upon the canvas curtain of the shed.

By this time it was about half-past seven, and the majority of the casuals were up and dressed.

Velvet observed, however, that none of the younger boys were as yet up, and it presently appeared that there existed some rule against their dressing in the shed; for Daddy came out of the bath-room, where the bundles were deposited, and called out, "Now four boys!"

And instantly four poor little wretches, some with their rugs trailing about their shoulders and some quite bare, came shivering over the stones and across the bleak yard, and were admitted to the bath-room to dress.

"Now four more boys!" cried Daddy; and so on.

When all were up and dressed, the boys carried the bed rugs into Daddy's room, and the pauper inmates made a heap of the "beds," stacking them against the walls.

As before mentioned, the shed served the treble purpose of bed-chamber, work-room, and breakfast-room; it was impossible to get fairly at the cranks and set them going until the bedding was stowed away.

Breakfast before work, however; but it was a weary while to some of the paupers before it made its appearance. For Velvet's own part, he had little appetite, but round him were a dozen poor wretches who obviously had a very great one: they had come in overnight too late for bread, and perhaps may not have broken fast since the morning of the previous day.

The decent ones suffered most.

The blackguard majority were quite cheerful—smoking, swearing, and playing their pretty horse play, the prime end of which was pain or discomfiture for somebody else.

One casual there was with only one leg.

When he came in overnight he wore a black hat, which added a certain look of respectability to a worn suit of black.

All together his clothes had been delivered up to him by Daddy; but now he was seen hopping disconsolately about the place on his crutch, for the hat was missing.

He was a timid man, with a mild voice; and whenever he asked some ruffian "whether he had seen such a thing as a black hat," and got his answer, he invariably said "thank you," which was regarded as very amusing.

At last one sidled up to him with a grin, and showing about three square inches of some fluffy substance, said, "Is *this* anything like wot you've lost, guv'ner?"

The cripple inspected it.

"That's the rim of it!" he said.

"What a shame!" and hobbled off with tears in his eyes.

Full three-quarters of an hour of loitering and shivering, and then came the taskmaster: a soldierly-looking man over six feet high, with quick grey eyes in which "No trifling" appeared as distinctly as a notice against trespassing on a wayside board.

He came in amongst the poor forlorn creatures, and the grey eyes made out the number in a moment.

"Out into the yard, all of you!" he cried; and all went out in a mob.

There they all shivered for some twenty minutes longer, and then a baker's man appeared with a great wooden tray piled up with just such slices of bread as Velvet had received overnight.

The tray was consigned to an able-bodied casual, who took his place with the taskmaster at the shed door; and then in single file all re-entered the shed, each man and boy receiving a slice as he passed in.

Pitying Velvet's unaccustomed look, Mr. Taskmaster gave him a slice and a large piece over.

The bread devoured, a clamour for "skilley" began.

The rumour had got abroad that the morning to which we allude and on all future mornings, there would be skilley at breakfast, and "Skilley! skilley!" resounded through the shed.

No one had hinted that it was not forthcoming, but skilley seemed to be thought an extraordinary concession, and after waiting only a few minutes for it, they attacked the taskmaster in the fiercest manner.

They called him thief, sneak, and "crawler."

Little boys blackguarded him in gutter language, and, looking him in the face, consigned him to hell without flinching.

He never uttered a word in reply, or showed a sign of impatience; and whenever he was obliged to speak it was quite without temper.

There was a loud "hooray!" when the longed-for skilley appeared in two pails, in one of which floated a small tin saucepan, with a stick thrust into its handle by way of a ladle.

Yellow pint basins were provided for the paupers and large iron spoons.

"Range round the walls!" the taskmaster shouted.

All obeyed with the utmost alacrity; and then what was about three-fourths of a pint of gruel was handed to Velvet.

He was glad to get his, because the basin that contained it was warm and his hands were numb with cold.

He tasted a spoonful, as in duty bound, and wondered more than ever at the esteem in which it was held by his *confrères*.

It was a weak decoction of oatmeal and water, bitter, and without even a pinch of salt to flavour it.

But it was hot; and on that account, perhaps, was so highly relished.

It was now past eight o'clock, and as Velvet knew that a certain quantity of labour had to be performed by each man before he was allowed to go his way, he was anxious to begin.

The labour was to be "crank" labour.

The "cranks" are a series of iron bars extending across the width of the shed, penetrating through the wall, and working a flour mill on the other side.

Turning the "crank" is like turning a windlass.

The task is not a severe one.

Four measures of corn (bushels they were called —but that is doubtful) have to be ground every morning by the night's batch of casuals.

Close up by the ceiling hangs a bell connected with the machinery; and as each measure is ground the bell rings, so that the grinders may know how they are going on.

But the grinders are as lazy as obscene.

The paupers were no sooner set to work than the taskmaster left us to our own sweet will, with nothing to restrain its exercise but an occasional visit from the miller, a weakly expostulating man.

Once or twice he came in and said mildly—

"Now then, my men, why *don't* you stick to it?"— and so went out again.

At least one half the gang kept their hands from the crank whenever the miller was absent, and betook themselves to their private amusements and pursuits.

Some sprawled upon the beds and smoked; some engaged themselves and their friends in tailoring, and one turned hair-cutter for the benefit of a gentleman who, unlike Kay, had *not* just come out of p ison.

There were three tailors; two of them on the beds mending their own coats, and the other operating on a recumbent friend in the rearward part of his clothing.

Where the needles came from is a query; but for thread they used a strand of the oakum (evidently easy to deal with) which the boys were picking in the corners.

Other loungers strolled about with their hands in their pockets, discussing the topics of the day, and playing practical jokes on the industrious few; a favourite joke being to take a bit of rag, anoint it with grease from the crank axles, and clap it unexpectedly over somebody's eye.

CHAPTER XLIX.

THE "SLAP BANG" CLUB.

The consequence of all this was that the cranks went round at a very slow rate and now and then stopped altogether. Then the miller came in; the loungers rose from their couches, the tailors ceased stitching, the smokers dropped their pipes, and every fellow was at his post.

The cranks spun round furiously again, the miller's expostulations being drowned amidst a shout of "Slap bang, here we are again!" or this extemporised chorus—

> "We'll hang up the miller on a sour apple tree,
> We'll hang up the miller on a sour apple tree,
> We'll hang up the miller on a sour apple tree,
> And then go grinding on,
>   Glory, glory, Hallelujah, &c., &c."

By such ditties the ruffians enlivened their short spell of work.

Short indeed!

The miller departed, and within a minute afterwards beds were reoccupied, pipes lit, and tailoring resumed.

So the game continued—the honest fellows sweating at the cranks, and anxious to get the work done and go out to look for more profitable labour, and the paupers by profession taking matters quite easy.

Now Velvet felt convinced that had the work been properly superintended the four measures of corn might have been ground in the space of an hour and a half.

As it was, when the little bell tinkled for the fourth time, and the yard gate was opened and all were free to depart, the clock had struck eleven.

Velvet had seen the show, spent a night in a workhouse, and never, never again, did he swear to himself, would he undergo the same ordeal.

He had had a bed, that's true—he had supper and breakfast, such as they were—yet he thought that he could for the future master hunger and the cold night air with a brighter heart than that which he had passed through.

When Velvet left the workhouse the sun shone brightly on his ragged figure, and showed its squalor with startling distinctness.

Without all was rejoicing. Then Velvet breathed satisfactorily the morning air.

"What awaits me?" he muttered sadly, gazing upon the blue sky above his head. What can be my fate?

And he remembered his home in Bournemouth—and he remembered the happy hours he had spent as a boy, and he appealed to Heaven in his distress.

He had seen London life.

If anybody had he had, and he regretted bitterly the rash step which he had taken.

Now, reader, there are many incidents which

occurred in the workhouse, and which escaped us while writing this narrative.

We ought to have told you of two quiet elderly gentlemen, who, amidst all the blackguardism that went on around, held a discussion upon the merits of the English language—one of the disputants showing an especial admiration for the word "kindle," fine old Saxon word as ever was coined.

Then there were some childish games of "first and last letters," to vary such entertainments as that of the swearing club.

We should also have mentioned that on the dissolution of the swearing club a game at "dumb motion" was started, which presently lead to some talk concerning deaf and dumb people, and their method of concerning with each other by means of finger signs, as well as to a little story that sounded strangely enough coming from the mouth of the most efficient member of the club.

A good memory for details enables me to repeat this story almost, if not quite, exactly.

"They are a rummy lot, them deaf and dumb," said the story-teller. "I was at the workhouse at Stepney when I was a young un, don't you know; and when I got a holiday I used to go and see my old woman as lived in the Borough.

"Well, one day a woman as was in the house ses to me, ses she, 'Don't you go past the Deaf and Dumb School as you goes home?'

"So I ses, 'Yes.'

"So ses she, 'Would you mind callin' there and takin' a message to my little girl as is in there deaf and dumb?'

"So I ses, 'No.'

"Well, I goes, and they lets me in, and I tells the message, and they shows me the kid what it was for. Pooty little gal! So they tells her the message, and then she begins making orts and crosses like on her hands.

"'What's she a doing that for?' I ses.

"'She's a-talkin' to you,' ses they.

"'Oh!' I ses, 'what's she talkin' about?'

"'She ses you're a good boy for comin' and tellin' her about her mother, and she loves you.'

"Blest if I could help laughin'!

"So I ses, 'There ain't no call for her to say that.'

"Pooty little kid she was!

"I stayed there a goodish bit, and walked about the garden with her, and what d'ye think?

"Presently she takes a fancy for some of my jacket buttons—brass uns they was, with the name of the 'house' on 'em—and I cuts four off and gives her.

"Well, when I give her them blow me if she didn't want one of the brass buckles off my shoes.

"Well, you mighn't think it, but I gave her that too."

"Didn't yer get into a row when you got back?" some listener asked.

"Rather! Got kept without dinner and walloped as well, as I wouldn't tell what I'd done with 'em. Then they was goin' to wallop me again, so I thought I'd cheek it out; so I up and told the master all about it.'

"And got it wuss?"

"No, I didn't. The master gave me new buttons and a buckle without saying another word, and my dinner along with my supper as well."

All the incidents which we have related came before Velvet's mind in rapid succession, and a sickening feeling of depression came over him, and caused his heart to sink within his breast.

"Hitherto," he soliloquized, "I have been unsuccessful. Wherever I have tried I have failed. People say that the world is wide; and yet I cannot make my way in it. But never mind, I will not be beaten."

With these words he cast one last look upon the Lambeth Workhouse.

Before him a crowded thoroughfare.

Before him men, women, boys, girls—all with some occupation, doubtless some remuneration for their labour,

And he, he alone, friendless, penniless, in the large town.

Will he sleep again in a workhouse?

And what will he do?

But more of that anon.

CHAPTER L.

THE BEAUTIFUL WOMAN—THE VILLA—LADY SHEPHERD AT HOME.

Lying luxuriously upon a Turkish divan of a most expensive make, and playing listlessly with a beautiful spaniel by her side, could have been seen a woman on the evening which followed the day when Velvet left the Lambeth Workhouse.

Dazzlingly handsome was she, and the numerous attractions which she possessed were considerably enlivened by the fanciful costume which she wore.

There was a certain steadfastness about her eye, however, and a peculiar voluptuousness about her movements which we believe we have seen before.

Who was that woman?

It would have been no easy matter for a stranger to have answered that question.

For had an envious individual felt inclined to knock at the door of the pretty villa in St. John's Wood where she lived—and where, in fact, we pay a visit—and had he made inquiries, he would not have learnt much.

He would have been told by the servant that the name of the inhabitant of the house was Lady Shepherd, and that she had lived in the house for three years.

More he would have been unable to glean from the servant who would have answered the call.

But as it is not our business to keep our readers in suspense, we will inform them that Lady Shepherd was no other than Bella, the strange wayward creature who had saved the Marquis of Aguado from an impending doom.

Bella—the beautiful Bella—who had entered into a secret compact with 557—with the fratricide—the Captain of the Knights of Satan!

What her object was for having acted as she did up to the present period is but partly explained. The sequel remains to be dwelt upon in the course of this story.

Captivating, indeed, was Bella, as, like some sultana, she reclined voluptuously upon the spring cushions of her sofa, and glanced uneasily around the room, as if she were trying to discover in some by-nook some object which she had apparently lost.

Presently she rose from her stooping position, and walked towards the bell pull.

Then with a feverish movement she rang.

Mute, a servant, appeared. Silent he stood upon the threshold of the room awaiting his Lady's command.

"Thomas," said Lady Shepherd, in a quick hurried voice, "Have you received any messages for me?"

"No, my Lady," replied the servant in a respectful submissive manner, "I have not. Had any communication been sent I would not have delayed in bringing them to you!"

"That will do, Thomas, that will do. To night I am expecting Lord —— ; be sure to have some of my champagne ready?"

The Flunkey bowed his head, and without saying another word disappeared.

"Valuable fellow, that," muttered Lady Shepherd when she was alone. "He is a great rogue, but unless people previously knew it I would defy them to find it out."

With this flattering opinion of *her help*, as the Americans would say, Lady Shepherd sank upon her couch with the indolence of a pert courtesan, and tried to sleep.

Now it is perfectly impossible to say whether or no she would have succumbed to Morpheus, the God of Sleep, had she been allowed to remain undisturbed, but as it was she did not slumber, for very shortly after she had closed her eyelids, a heavy knock at the door roused her attention.

"It is him," she muttered, and passing her warm hands athwart her brow, she waited.

The bang of a door being closed—the sounds of footsteps creaking against the carpeted staircase—soon told her that she was not mistaken.

Louder and louder became the steps, and shortly afterwards an old acquaintance of ours entered the room.

An old acquaintance?

Who can it be?

And how does it come to pass that Lady Shepherd, a woman whom we have seen but a short while ago, should happen to know one of the characters of this tale?

Was it the Marquis of Aguado?

Or was it the Earl of Mountcarsden?

Reader, the latter. Yes; it was his lordship. He whom we have met in his gorgeous residence in Belgrave-square.

"How do you do to-night, Bella?" asked his Lordship in a drawling tone of voice. "How do you do? Did you expect me, Bella?"

"I did!" replied the dazzling woman of mystery. "I did. The time is rapidly approaching when you must take a decision!"

The Earl of Mountcarsden became very attentive.

"You can help me, Bella," he said, "can't you?"

And there was a strange intonation in the nobleman's voice as he spoke.

Bella smiled.

"Perhaps," she went on languidly.

"Perhaps!" re-echoed Lord Mountcarsden. "Perhaps! You must not use that word; you must say *certainly.*"

And he dwelt upon the last phrase.

Now, although to any other woman Lord Mountcarsden's manner would have been offensive in the extreme, yet upon Lady Shepherd it produced no impression whatever.

And so she heeded not the nobleman's behaviour.

"And what do you require of me, my lord?" she asked, after a moment's silence.

"*Get* rid of her by all means. Heavens! heavens!" he shrieked, his mouth meanwhile foaming with rage; "if she lives, why I will be a ruined man. Three days ago I lost ten thousand pounds upon my favourite horse, and that money must be paid, or my most sanguine dreams of glory and of honour will be dashed to the ground."

"Get rid of her!" said Lady Shepherd, in a slow measured tone; "I can do so, but it is a dangerous game to play."

"How so?"

"She is in a mad-house, that is true enough. The physician there can be bribed, that's true also; but she has friends."

"Not many."

"But she has one."

"Curse that Lawyer Workirk!" now uttered Lord Mountcarsden. "Curse him! I wish that I could get rid of him also."

Lady Shepherd laughed loudly.

"How many more do you wish to dispose of?" she asked, in a jeering voice. "You are plotting nothing more or less than *wholesale murder.*"

His lordship became deadly pale and his teeth chattered.

"And to carry out your fiendish work you come to me!"

A half suppressed ejaculation, whose real nature no one could have well described, now issued from the livid lips of the nobleman.

"Bella," he said, drawing the beautiful woman to his breast; "Bella, I love you."

With the *nonchalance* of some of those Roman courtesans, who were said to be so feelingless and yet so dazzlingly attracting, Bella made no resistance to his lordship's loving caresses.

"I must indulge him," she soliloquised to herself, "I must indulge him, and I may yet be Lady Mountcarsden."

Perhaps a few of our readers may be at a loss to understand the relation which existed between a nobleman and Lady Shepherd, whose title, we need not tell our perusers, was an assumed one.

Owing, therefore, to the knowledge which we possess, we will enlighten them on the subject.

Doubtless many remember the scene which took place in the early part of this story,* and they can bring back to their minds her ladyship's sorrow at the loss of a son who had been stolen from his cradle a few days after his birth.

Now since then many things had occurred. Lord Mountcarsden had succeeded in getting his wife incarcerated in a lunatic asylum, and his great object was to get her out of the world, so as to enable him to inherit the large property which would revert to him in the event of her death.

On the other hand, Lawyer Workirk had not been idle, and if Lord Mountcarsden had succeeded in his foul plot, the former had lost no opportunity in watching all that had taken place.

Lady Mountcarsden had, therefore, a staunch friend in the attorney—a bitter foe in her own husband.

News had also reached Lord Mountcarsden to the effect that the lost son's whereabouts had been traced, and that it was not at all unlikely that he should turn up when least expected.

The great purpose, then, of his lordship was to have some one to side with him, and to help him in his schemes.

For that help he looked to Lady Shepherd—to Bella, his own paramour.

But Bella knew that a plot such as his lordship contemplated could not be wrought with success without confederates, and she had chosen the Marquis of Aguado.

She had saved him from the gallows—from an ignominious death—and she knew that she could require everything from him.

Even cold-blooded murder!

She was thus thinking when she heard a rush of footsteps.

Shortly afterwards a servant entered the room, and walking straight towards Bella he muttered a few words in her ears.

* See No. I. of "DANCE OF DEATH," with which is presented No. II. gratis, and a splendid presentation plate.

THE
DANCE OF DEATH;
OR,
THE HANGMAN'S PLOT.
A THRILLING ROMANCE OF TWO CITIES.

No. 14.]   SATURDAY, FEBRUARY 3, 1866.   [ONE PENNY.

"IS SHE DEAD?"

CHAPTER L.—CONTINUED.

"What!" she exclaimed, "is it him?"

The servant bowed.

Then turning towards the nobleman, Bella summoned one of her pleasantest smiles.

"Mountcarsden," she said; "I am called away."

"Called away!" the patrician repeated, in a drawling tone of voice. "Called away from me, Bella; what a confounded bore!"

And his lordship made a frightful grimace.

Bella, however, swept across the room; but she suddenly stopped upon the threshold.

"Mountcarsden," she said, "try to amuse yourself while I am away."

"Will you be long ? "

"No."

"And what am I to do in the meantime ? "

"Drink champagne."

"Oh ! Bella, you are a good girl." And the nobleman thought he had said quite enough, for he reclined upon the sofa without uttering another word.

Bella and the servant were now outside the room.

"Fellow," she said, in a haughty tone of voice, to the flunkey, "know you where the champagne is ? "

"*The drugged champagne !* " knowingly retorted the servant.

"Yes."

"And am I to give one to his lordship ? "

A nod of Bella's head was her only answer, and with the rapidity of a phantom she glided downstairs.

CHAPTER LI.

THE MEETING—THE TALE—THE STARTLING ADVENTURE
—THE MURDER IN THE WOOD—THE DEEP-LAID
SCHEME.

"What brings you hither ? " asked Bella, as soon as she found herself face to face with one of the characters of this tale.

The Marquis of Aguado !

The escaped convict was pale as death.

Although dressed in the height of fashion, yet his clothes were soiled and wet.

"Is it raining outside ? " asked Bella.

The Marquis nodded in the negative.

"No ; it is not," he replied.

"And yet," pursued Bella, laying her soft, velvetty white hand upon the convict's coat, "you seem to have gone through some shower."

The Marquis smiled.

"Ah ! " shrieked Bella suddenly. "Ah ! "

And she looked at her hands.

They were covered with *blood !*

"Have you committed a murder ? " she asked feverishly, "and if so, why come you beneath my roof ? "

"I had my reasons for doing so."

"And what were they ? "

"I am hunted by the myrmidons of the law, and I knew that you would save me if you could."

"You felt sure of that ; did you ? "

"I did."

"Why so, I ask once more."

"Because you want me to do for you that which very few people could accomplish."

"Speak not so loud," now whispered Bella, "your words might be overheard."

"Overheard ! " repeated the Marquis of Aguado, with a startled shudder.

Lady Shepherd remained mute and silent for awhile.

"Come on with me," she resumed.

"Where ? "

"Never mind ; follow."

With these words Bella led the way.

The Marquis of Aguado was too much in dread of being discovered for him to raise the slightest objection to his beautiful saviour's request.

So he abided at once by her wishes.

Bella pushed a door before her and walked into a small closet.

"What a delightful scent there is here ? " ejacu-

lated the Marquis. "Why, the carpets must be soaked with perfume."

Bella pointed to a hothouse which could be plainly seen. and where the most exquisite flowers were confined in splendid vases ; and this explained the mystery.

"And what have you done ? " she asked from the convict, as soon as she had closed the door and felt certain that she was alone with her companion in crime.

"Listen," said the Marquis. "I have a passion which years of degradation have not cured. I am desperately fond of gambling. I love it. For me it has a mystic fascination. Well, when we reached London you gave me money."

"I know."

"Five hundred pounds."

"Exactly."

"I went into the first hell I came to."

"Yes."

"And there I lost all. What was I to do ? "

"You should have asked me for more."

"I knew not that you could afford to be generous."

Again Bella smiled.

"You are not acquainted with my affairs," she said ; "money to me is no object."

The Marquis breathed satisfactorily.

"Go on, go on," quickly went on Bella, while her breast heaved with excitement, "Go on ; the very fact of you losing your money does not account for the blood which I see upon your garments."

"I'll explain."

Bella was getting more and more interested.

"In the gambling house where I wended my way," the convict resumed, "I saw an old man. He was lucky in the extreme. Fortune, that would remain dumb to my entreaties, seemed to favour him. Every piece of gold which he placed upon the green baize became in a few instants converted into piles of sovereigns. This galled me. I had but one pound left, the last of your £500, and I resolved to risk it ; but I took an oath at the time, should it be snatched away by the old man, I swore to myself I would have his life."

"How very kind and considerate of you," muttered Bella, and a Satanical smile played upon her pouting lips.

"Yes," hissed the Marquis between his clenched teeth, "I resolved that if Fortune smiled on the old gambler, soon I would change the tide of events against him."

"I can foresee the conclusion," Lady Shepherd now followed, with the slow, steady demeanour of an experienced politician, "you lost your last sovereign."

"Bella, you have guessed the truth."

"The next thing you did was to make the old fellow's acquaintance."

Again the convict nodded his head in the affirmative.

"How did you manage that ? Did you know him ? "

"Personally I did not. I had seen him, though, in Florence, and I believed that if my recollection did not deceive me, he was a foreign nobleman. I saw him picking up his gold, and as he placed the banknotes and the glittering coin in his pocket, I reckoned that he must have won at least one thousand pounds, and I longed to obtain possession of it. I remembered having seen him once on the piazza in company with a lady friend of mine."

"Yes."

" 'Baron,' I said, approaching him, 'perhaps you have forgotten me.'

"The old sinner looked at me minutely and

searchingly, and then he wound up by saying that he had, and that, although my features were familiar to him, yet he could not bring back to his mind the place where he had first seen them.

"'In Florence, Baron, we first had the pleasure of meeting each other,' I said, after a moment's silence, during which I pondered over the answer which I should give him.

"He at once held out his hand.

"'Delighted to make your acquaintance,' he said to me; 'Dame Fortune treated you very badly to-night; but she will occasionally withdraw her favours. Now I won to-night, but three days ago I lost a very considerable sum.'

"We both went out.

"'Whither are you thinking of going, Baron,' I asked, as soon as we stepped out of the gambling saloon.'

"'To see a few lady friends,' he replied, in an off-hand manner.

"'Ladies, I suppose, Baron.'

"'Yes, ladies,' he repeated.

Lady Shepherd had sunk down upon an easy chair, and was looking attentively at the narrator.

"And where do you think the old sinner with his hoary locks took me? That vile specimen of humanity who had lived over eighty years in the world."

"I know not."

"To Rupert-street, to a dazzling den of infamy. We remained indoors for a couple of hours, and when we left it was about one o'clock in the morning.

"A splendid, costly carriage was standing at the end of the street.

"'I wish,' said I to the Baron, 'I could call myself the owner of such a turn-out, and what fine horses to be sure.'

"Then the Baron remarked that there was not much in having carriages and horses, and thereupon hailed the coachman, who turned out to be his own servant.

"We rattled away at racing pace, and we presently came to a gate.

"The noise of the horses' hoofs beating the ground soon awoke the keeper.

"In an instant the horses were dashing along a gravelly avenue, lined on both sides by a row of stately elm trees.

"'My house is about five hundred yards from this place. The coachman is rather tired, and we will alight and he can attend to the horses; a little walk will do us both good, and may be give us appetite for our supper.'

"After having uttered the above words, the Baron pulled the string which communicated with the coachman.

"We were now at a standstill.

"The door of the carriage was shortly afterwards opened, and we both jumped out.

"The vehicle rapidly drove away.

"Around us stretched a small park, thickly studded with a profusion of vegetation.

"I thought now that my opportunity had come.

"And so I listened, and hearing nought but the sighing of the breeze, I grasped the old man by the throat.

"His struggles were terrible, frightful to witness.

"He would not die.

"He supplicated me to let him live. He would do anything—part with the whole of his fortune—for a few hours' existence.

"But I would not hear him. My passion was once more kindled by the sound of the golden pieces.

"With my left hand I kept the old sinner beneath me, with my right I plunged my poniard to the hilt in his breast.

"The blood spurted upon my garments.

"And then his agony was of short duration.

"There was a gurgle and a rattle in the old man's throat, and he lay motionless at my feet—a cold, stiff, rigid corpse.

"When I had perpetrated the deed I rifled his body.

"I robbed all his gold, and I ran away from the spot where he lay.

"And now I have come here to seek your protection."

CHAPTER LII.

TWO FIENDS TOGETHER.

"Since you take me for your confidant," Lady Shepherd resumed, in answer to the convict's words, "I may as well tell you who and what I am."

"I wish you would, for there is a mystery about you which I have hitherto failed to fathom."

Here the interest became reversed.

It was now the turn of the convict to wonder.

"Lady Shepherd is a strange creature," the woman went on, "and yet she has hitherto baffled the vigilant eye of the law. I go about town—frequent swell night-houses — and make young fellows' acquaintance. The world gives me credit for being handsome."

"And do you doubt the world, Bella?"

Lady Shepherd made no immediate reply, but the look which she gave to the querist implied a good deal.

"I have no reasons to do so," she said, "for at present I am handsomely supported by the wealthiest scions of England's boasted aristocracy. Above us is the Earl of Mountcarsden."

"The Earl of Mountcarsden," mused the Marquis of Aguado; "I think I have heard that name before."

"Where?" quickly asked Bella.

"Among the Knights of Satan—the Black Brethren of the Crystal Dagger, whose chief I am."

"And what relation can the dread order of which you speak have with a nobleman?" queried Lady Shepherd.

"More, perhaps, than you think."

"And where, once more I ask you, did you hear the name of Lord Mountcarsden mentioned?"

The convict clasped his brow and reflected deeply.

"Marian of the Glen—Marian, the old Gipsy Queen, is, I think, the only person who, if I remember aright, told me that she knew certain incidents connected with that nobleman's antecedents which would be worth thousands and thousands. What those things were she would never divulge. One thing she remarked also was that I was very much like that lord. Do you see any likeness, Bella?"

As he spoke the murderer drew himself to his full height.

"How strange; yes, how strange," now ejaculated Bella, "that I should not have seen that before; now it strikes me that you do."

"Is he rich, Bella?"

"He was."

"Now?"

"Poor; but why such questions?"

"I will answer you, Bella; I am one who never flinches, one who fears not the catechising looks of society. If the likeness between his lordship and myself is so great, any idea of mine might be carried out."

"And that idea is ————."

The convict seemed to take a great delight in prolonging his companion's suspense.

"I have often thought that I would like extremely to be an English nobleman. I am fond of adulation; I would like to hear lots of people 'my lording' me, and all that sort of thing."

The convict smiled as he concluded his sentence.

"What, would you dare to assume another man's name?"

"Not only his name, but his property, be it however trifling; and an English nobleman has, I should say, a great deal more to boast of than a felon, an outcast, a murderer hunted down, and who, if discovered, is extremely likely to *swing* for his past misdeeds."

"And how would you purpose to carry out your plans?" quickly asked Bella, who was anxious to hear the manner with which the Marquis of Aguado intended to proceed.

"Easily, enough; you say the Earl of Mountcarsden is within this roof."

"Yes."

"Well, he must not leave this house."

"Why not?"

"Because if you like to pull with me we can astonish the world."

"Preposterous!"

"Yet it can be done."

"And how about the wife and the children?"

"I'll manage that."

"Nonsense!"

"How about the servants? They would be sure to notice in you the peculiarities which, doubtless, characterised their late master."

"I fear them not."

"And what remedy have you against an inevitable occurrence?"

"I will discharge them for some trifling motive."

"But Lord Mountcarsden has a daughter, and she would be sure to find out that she has to deal with an impostor."

"Never mind, Bella, will you try?"

"And my reward?"

"If I succeed I will place a coronet upon your luxuriant wavy hair."

Lady Shepherd reflected.

"We could not get rid of Lord Mountcarsden except by murder.

To Bella's observation the Marquis at first made no reply.

"Is it worth a trial, Bella?" he asked, after a few moments' silence.

There was a pause.

"But I do not see how you can succeed," her ladyship went on. "The difficulties in your way are too great."

"I differ from you."

"How so?"

"Because I think that the difficulties disappear before a bold *coup d'état*."

"Explain yourself."

"Well, we murder his lordship."

"By what means?"

"Poison."

"He dies. What afterwards?"

"I take off his clothes."

"Yes."

"And wear them."

"So far so good."

"Then I send for the police."

"Is that advisable?"

"I think that when you will hear me out you will agree with me."

Lady Shepherd's nostrils were dilated, her lips quivered, and she gazed with a searching, penetrating look upon the speaker.

"The police come here?"

"If they are sent for they will come quickly enough."

"Then I say that I, Lord Mountcarsden, of Belgrave-square, was sitting comfortably here, when a great noise was heard outside the hall-door. I relate to them the story of the murder, and conclude by informing them that after having spoken the stranger fell dead at my feet."

"Not at all a badly concocted plot. The next thing is to carry it out successfully."

"It will be, Bella, if you leave it to me."

It was then finally decided between Bella and the Marquis of Aguado that the Earl of Mountcarsden should be disposed of.

Meanwhile his lordship was drinking the drugged champagne, and strange sensations were overpowering his brain, and he wondered from whence came the sickening feeling which crept over his frame.

CHAPTER LIII.

THE DARK DEED OF HORROR.

Bella had been relating to the Marquis of Aguado all that which she knew concerning the life of the nobleman whose death she was plotting with her companion in crime.

Previous to playing the bold game which he had on hand the convict wished to get thoroughly acquainted with the minutest incidents in the career of the distinguished libertine.

For he did not wish to assume the name of one who was hitherto a perfect stranger to him, without a certainty of his being able to play the difficult role which he had undertaken.

Thus it took Bella over an hour to answer the severe cross-examination of her lover the Marquis of Aguado.

Such he was!

It was a strange feeling—a feeling which can be scarcely explained, but which nevertheless existed.

For such anomalies in Nature it is difficult to account.

But it is not our purpose to inquire here into their causes.

Lady Shepherd had already given her reasons for having acted as she did.

She had told in a previous chapter of this story the objects which had induced her to save a convict from the gallows.

Now she was ready to help him in his nefarious schemes.

"Come upstairs, Aguado," said Lady Shepherd, laying her taper fingers upon the convict's shoulders.

"Will I see him there?"

He referred to the nobleman.

"Yes. I'll go in first and then you can follow me. But are you prepared with the poison?"

The Marquis of Aguado drew a ring from his finger.

"There it is." he said.

This was sufficient for Lady Shepherd.

She rose, and carefully opening the door, she glided up-stairs.

Cursing and swearing, and using most blasphemous language was his lordship at the time when Bella entered the gorgeous apartment, where the nobleman was sitting in an elaborately-carved arm-chair, stuffed with cushions of a most expensive material.

The Marquis of Aguado remained outside.

"Halloa! my Lady Shepherd. Is that you?" asked his lordship, on seeing the beautiful woman approaching the spot where he sat. "What have you been doing all this while? I was in hope you would not have kept me so long by myself. But since you are back again it is futile on my part to complain."

"My lord!" said Bella, "I was engaged with a man who is going to take your life."

Lord Mountcarsden laughed hysterically.

"Bella," he quickly ejaculated, "Bella, you are joking, I fancy."

"Joking!" repeated Lady Shepherd, "not in the slightest degree. What I state is true."

But a few minutes ago the nobleman was at a loss to account for the strange sensations which he experienced after drinking a part of the bottle of champagne which Lady Shepherd had sent him, but now he was really in a critical trance.

"And do you think it odd." Bella said, "at a man wishing to take your life. Were you not asking me but a few hours ago to get *your own wife* out of the way?"

His lordship trembled violently.

Like all cowards he felt uneasy at the approach of danger.

He did not like the glare of Bella's eyes. He did not like the uneasiness of her whole demeanour, and he was beginning to think that his hour was nigh.

He was thus thinking, when Bella made a bold dash upon him.

In an instant her fingers grappled his windpipe.

They were like iron screws.

He tried to scream for help, and just as he was about to open his lips he saw the Marquis of Aguado rushing in the room.

"Mercy! mercy!" he mumbled

But he was doomed to die.

The Marquis of Aguado was not one to retreat once he had advanced.

He placed his ring upon the nobleman's mouth, drew his lips apart, and poured in them a few drops of a liquid contained in the jewel.

The effect was instantaneous.

Lord Mountcarsden's head fell heavily downwards, his hands became cold, and his limbs stiffened.

Thus died the Earl of Mountcarsden.

Thus died the noble ruffian who had made a proposal to Lady Shepherd to destroy his legitimate wife.

But what is more terrible to relate remains to be told.

The toilet of the Marquis lasted for above five minutes.

And he was dressed in the nobleman's clothes, and he was just attiring the patrician with his own garments, when a heavy tramping of footsteps was heard in the street.

Exclamations, cries of horror, shrieks, and the loud hum of a thick crowd, reached Lady Shepherd's ears.

What can this mean? she wondered, darting across the room, and opening the window of her room.

One sweep of her glance was enough.

"Aguado," she said, "Look! look!"

"Mountcarsden for the future, my lady. Do not forget that I am Lord ——," cooly ejaculated the convict.

Thus speaking, he stood by the window-sill.

Sure it was plain enough there were over a hundred people outside Lady Shepherd's residence, and amidst men, women, boys, and girls, could be seen the green uniform of several members of the force.

"And they say he's gone in there.

"The murderer, is he?

"I would like to see him."

Such were some of the remarks which emanated from the mob.

"How very fortunate that I thought of all things in time, Bella. Had I delayed where would I be to night? Flung into some dark cell, and left there to rot until I would be led to the scaffold!"

"It may be so now, Mountcarsden."

"No, never Bella; hear you the row which the d—— scoundrels are making outside?"

The last words, of course, were specially intended for the enlightened members of the force, against whom ruffians and all classes have a great hatred.

Presently there followed a loud rat-tat-tat, and the hall door-bell was rung violently, and a stentorian voice, in no measured terms, sought immediate admission in Lady Shepherd's house.

"What is all this about?" asked the Marquis of Aguado, walking down stairs with Lady Shepherd, and reaching the landing at the very moment when the servant was flinging the door open.

"A murder has been committed two miles from here," said a man in private clothes, who, to the sham lord, appeared to be a detective.

"A murder!" Lord Mountcarsden exclaimed, and he raised his hands as if he were very much surprised. "Indeed! Perhaps this gentleman will be able to explain to us the strange adventure which occurred to us to night?"

The first part of his sentence had been addressed to the speaker, the second to Lady Shepherd, who was trembling from head to foot, and trying to appear as much concerned, as she deemed it wise, under the circumstances.

"Perhaps, sir," resumed the convict, addressing the detective (for he was one) "you will step inside with such of your friends as you think necessary to further the ends of justice."

"Oh, my lord, I hope that they will create no disturbance in the house," now muttered Bella, who wished to place the detective off his guard, having noticed his rather close survey of the murderer.

"Madam, you need not alarm yourself; we will proceed as quietly as we possibly can."

Lord Mountcarsden thought it right to speak a little more.

"Bella," he said, "you had better retire to your apartment. In the meantime I will acquaint the gentlemen with the strange events which occurred to us this night."

When the detective heard Bella calling the Marquis of Aguado "my lord," he gradually grew more and more civil, not to say cringing, which would be a more appropriate word to use here.

But we must not blame the detective.

With him it was the case of thousands and thousands. A man with a handle to his name in this country always commands respect.

Bella had retired to the drawing-room.

Lord Mountcarsden meanwhile was standing speaking to the detective and to the policemen who were with him.

"My lord," said the detective, "up to the present you cannot know the object of our visit, and so I will acquaint you with it at once."

The sham nobleman nodded his head in a very patronising manner.

"Proceed, sir," he said, "proceed."

The detective looked at the Marquis of Aguado.

He did not like the appearance of his lordship.

Yet, what could he say? Had he not heard her ladyship calling him "my lord."

Our experience of the police force is not limited.

I am a detective, and am writing this tale.

Whatever I state is correct.

"Would you be kind enough to favour me with your name," asked his lordship, "before proceeding any further?"

The detective bowed.

"I go by the name of Detective Brownlow," he said, "and I belong to her Majesty's force of Scotland-yard."

The Marquis of Aguado remained silent.

"Well, Mr. Brownlow," he said, "I am listening to you."

There was another detective in plain clothes besides Brownlow.

He was taking stock of the noble speaker.

The bobbies were, on the other hand, listening.

Policemen, as a rule, are very cute when taking in charge drunken youths, or handling a woman about, but when it comes to a matter of cleverness, they are generally found wanting.

And so, when they heard they were in a nobleman's house, they were civil in the extreme.

Lord Mountcarsden meanwhile was doing what we call riding the high horse.

He felt sure of his position, and indeed no one ould have played the character of a nobleman better than he did.

"My lord," began Detective Brownlow, "but a few hours ago a foreign nobleman was coldly and dastardly murdered in his own park; indeed, in the very sight of his own house."

The detective then related to his lordship all the incidents with which our readers are already acquainted.

Speech is silver, but silence is gold.

Remember those words. The Marquis of Aguado ever bore them in mind.

And right enough was he in doing so.

For it is too much talking that ruins the best speculation.

Oh! if a man could only keep his tongue to himself, and not talk too much—as a facetious, hard-working publisher of the best periodical of the day, a penny journal, says—what an immense amount of harm would be prevented.

Lord Mountcarsden was playing with the watchguard of his chain, and from time to time a satisfactory smile escaped his lips, as he glanced upon the valuable rings which he now wore, and which but an hour ago had ornamented the finger of the real Lord of the Mountcarsden family, whom he had murdered in cold blood.

"I am very glad," he said, "that you should have seen me on so very important a subject; I will do my best to help you in any way I can. As a humble man I dare say that I can serve you."

When the "blue bottles" heard the nobleman call himself a humble man, they smiled.

"What can I do to serve you?" asked his lordship; "but first hear me."

"What is it, my lord?" asked the detective.

The convict reflected.

"I am very glad," he said, "that you came here, gentlemen, for I had already given instructions to my servants to go to the nearest station."

"What for?" quickly queried Detective Brownlow, who thought he began to smell a rat.

Noblemen and policemen should never be connected, except under very peculiar circumstances.

"What were they?"

He listened.

"I was sitting with Lady Shepherd in the drawing-room," began Lord Mountcarsden, "when a man came in—his clothes were soiled, and his appearance was ghastly and terrible—and he told me and Lady Shepherd that he had soiled his hands with blood."

"Such a communication to us seemed impossible; we listened to him, and we found that there was truth in it."

"Where is that man?" now asked Detective Brownlow.

"Upstairs!" replied Lord Mountcarsden.

Then he acquainted the detective with a few particulars of his own concocting, and wound up by saying that after having spoken the man dropped dead.

Fancy, reader, the feelings of the convict. Fancy, reader, you being in the same position.

Having besides to play your part well.

Lord Mountcarsden mused deeply.

Then he led the way.

The detective entered the room.

Fully stretched upon his back he saw the real lord.

"That man looks like a ruffian," he muttered—loud enough, however, for his words to be heard by the nobleman.

Aguado smiled.

"The world! the world!" he muttered.

"Ah! ah! What a pity that beings of a same creed should not understand each other. Ah! ah! The world is cruel and bad."

"See! see!"

Hear us.

There was the nobleman dead; there was the real owner of the title, and yet people insulted his *corpse.*

Why?

Because his corpse was that of a supposed murderer.

The convict enjoyed the insults heaped upon his victim with feelings of delight.

He was the Angel of Evil, and yet people sided with him.

"Your business, I should fancy," the nobleman began, "would be to remove this man from my house."

As he spoke Aguado pointed to his victim.

"We must take him to the dead-house, my lord."

His lordship remained silent.

"Remove him," he said, after a moment's silence.

Then the corpse of Lord Mountcarsden was taken away.

Then it was carried to a neighbouring station.

With feelings of bitter fear Aguado waited.

When a man has committed a crime he fears detection.

The voice of conscience is loud in his ear.

What should he do?

Gradually and slowly the force departed.

He gave his name as the Earl of Mountcarsden in Belgrave-square.

Before that no one could speak.

And they took away the corpse of the real lord, and the sham swindler remained on the battle-field to face the world.

CHAPTER LIV.

VELVET FALLS IN WITH AN OLD ACQUAINTANCE.

Wearily and slowly tramping along the Black-friars-road was Velvet, a week after the night which he had spent in the Lambeth Workhouse.

He had met some strange characters there.

In the casual ward he had seen things which he hoped he would never see again.

Velvet yet was in London.

Alone, friendless!

Boys, can you not feel for him?

Fancy yourselves deprived of the means of living —of shelter.

What would you do?

Perhaps you do think that London is an hospitable place.

Make no mistake.

London—ah! London.

Come not to it if your imaginations are young and pure.

The days of Sodom and Gomorrah are not gone yet.

If the voice of some charmer lures you away from home, seek not London for such.

It is a place of corrupt pride and of grasping greediness.

In London a man without money is nobody.

Dress a mannikin in a millionaire's clothes and you will see that society—that contemptible courtezan—bowing before the recipient of filthy lucre.

But why dwell?

Why expatiate upon the truth?

Why bring forth opinions which the cleverest politician of the day could not contradict.

Take, for instance, poor Velvet.

He had been sorely tried by misfortune, and yet, withal, he had withstood the enormous temptations which a houseless tramp is sure to encounter.

Over and over again had he tried to obtain honest employment, but up to the time we see him he had been unsuccessful.

Perhaps it may seem strange to many of my young readers that a lad in a large city would be unable to earn himself a crust of bread.

Alas! it is too true.

It is no use for us to abuse the laws of the land or to cavil at the mysterious decree of Fate.

Velvet is there to show us that providence sometimes is wrong.

For what right has a boy who has never done wrong, what right has he to starve?

And we see that poor Velvet was not far from starvation.

It was late.

Dark!

He was thinking, when a well-known voice smote upon his ear—

"Velvet?"

"What?"

"What about Wild Will?"

The boy turned round.

Before him stood Big Ned.

"I don't know where he is gone too," he said.

"He came to the crib yesterday."

Velvet became puzzled.

"Is Will in town still?" he asked.

Big Ned replied in the affirmative.

Here poor Velvet's heart sank within his breast.

For a week he had battled against misfortune.

For a week he had sustained all sufferings which a poor lonely boy has to experience.

And then he must succumb at last.

"Ned," he asked of his companion, "I am going in the public-house. Will you wait for me?"

The bully took stock of the boy.

"Have you taken to drinking, then?"

"No."

Surely his words were unnecessary; for were those bright eyes those of a drunkard? Was that thin, emaciated face the one of a besotted worshipper of Bacchus?

"And what are you going to do in a public-house?" asked Big Ned.

"I am hungry and thirsty, and I will ask the publican to give me something to eat."

"And do you know what his answer will be?"

Velvet shook his head.

"Try if you like, and I will wait for you outside. If you do not succeed you can come with me."

Velvet did not like to make any rash promises.

"Very good," he said, and he walked towards the public-house.

Big Ned meanwhile waited outside.

When Velvet stood before the bar his resolution gave way, and his heart sank within his breast.

The landlord was a pompous, fat, bloated, self-opinionated sort of a card, and he was too much engaged in serving quarterns and half-quarterns of gin over the counter to notice at first the new comer's entrance.

"That man seems very happy," soliloquised Velvet; "I wonder whether he will be charitable to me."

There is no class of men in the world, we believe, more inclined to grasp money than those who trade by retailing adulterated stuff, which, although it goes under several names, might nevertheless be more appropriately termed poison.

When the landlord had drawn all the liquor which had been ordered, and had taken the money for it, and given change for the same, his glance rested upon Velvet.

He then discovered that he was standing before the bar without anything to drink.

"What will it be for you, sir?" he asked from Velvet

Bland was his smile, and courteous in the extreme was the bow which he made to Velvet, as he wished to know his pleasure.

Velvet heard the words of the publican.

"I am thirsty," he faltered, "and would feel very much obliged to you if you were to trust me with half-a-pint of porter."

Now let it be noticed here that this worthy gentleman, who, while Velvet had been in the house— and it was not above four or five minutes—had received at least five shillings, took a long period to consider.

Of course Velvet fully expected that his answer would be in the affirmative.

Inwardly the poor boy swore to himself that, should he obtain a glass of beer and a bite of supper, he would reject Big Ned's offer to go back with him to the thieves' den.

Otherwise what was he to do?

"There is no credit given here, sir," roughly ejaculated the publican, after he had made up his mind as to what he would do, "unless to well-known customers."

"If you give me a crust of bread and cheese and glass of beer, upon my honour, sir, I will pay it to you as soon as I can."

"And what means have you got to pay me?"

This was too much for Velvet.

He cast one long look of contempt upon the publican, and swiftly emerged from the public-house.

As he left the place he heard several remarks which were made by the frequenters of the house concerning his appearance, which, had he been in a different position, he would not have allowed to pass unnoticed.

"If a man is down in this world, it would seem as if every one wished to crush him," now soliloquised Velvet.

As he concluded this sentence—which is, alas! too true—Velvet felt a heavy hand laid upon his shoulder.

It was Big Ned's.

"Any luck, old pal?"

"No."

"He refused to give you that which you asked for; did he not?"

"Yes."

"And did you expect that he would be such a flat as to have acted otherwise?"

Velvet nodded in the affirmative.

"Come down with me, old cock, and, by George, you will have enough to eat and to drink."

Velvet had no choice.

There was but one path for him; one alternative.

Either he must remain honest and starve, or he must mingle once more with the thieves and live.

"We had a grand lark the other night at the crib, Velvet," the thief began, "and Wild Will, by the Lord Harry, proved himself to be quite the gentleman."

"In what manner?'

"Why, he lushed us all up, and, further, he lent ten pounds to the firm. Oh! you should have seen Bob O'Link singing out as loud as he could the tune to a song which h composed—

> 'For there are no joys
> On earth, my boys,
> Like the life of a London thief.'"

"And where is Will?" asked Velvet.

"Living at the West-end."

"What part?"

"Brompton."

"Is he in lodgings?"

"In lodgings? Not he. He has taken a furnished house, for which he paid six months' in advance"

"And where did he get the money?"

"Perhaps you forgot the little game that he played at Long's Hotel. It turned out to be a very profitable one, for it appears that he got a good deal of money for the jewellery which he stole from some foreign nobleman. He took it to old Markam in the Mint. The watch was broken up, all the gold was melted, and I believe that the diamonds were also paid for at the time."

"And how does Will look?"

"First class. He drives a trap in gay style."

"Does he?"

Velvet did not know whether Big Ned was telling him the truth or no, yet he had seen enough of Wild Will to credit the most extraordinary stories attributed to him.

As the two boys spoke together the time quickly passed away.

At length Velvet saw in the distance the alley which led to the place from where he had taken his departure with Wild Will some time ago.

Big Ned led the way, and Velvet followed.

When the latter entered the room where all the boys were sitting together, loud exclamations of surprise rented the air.

Hip! hip! hurrah!

"Here he is back again."

"Ned, where did you meet him?"

"Well, old fellow, shake hands now," said Bob O'Link, grasping Velvet's taper fingers in his huge palm. "How have you been since? You do not look well. Tell us all about it? Why did you not come here?"

These were the only kind words which Velvet had heard since the night when we last saw him.

To him it was like the drop of water which refreshes the parched lips of the shipwrecked mariner; like the soothing balm which is laid upon the bleeding wound and alleviates the pain.

Velvet could not speak.

Whereupon came the only kindness which he had received since his arrival in London.

From *thieves*.

"There was some one inquiring after you the other day?"

"Who was that?"

"Your friend Will!"

"And what did he say?"

"That he would give a great deal to see you again!"

"Faith, that's no lie, either," now began Pat Nowlan.

"And what does he want to see me for?" asked Velvet.

"He has got a deep game on hand, and he wants you to help him, I think."

"Do you know his address?"

"I'll give it to you."

"Well, then," boldly ejaculated Velvet, "I'll go and see him. It is too late to-night."

"Too late! I rather think it is, too. Besides you require some fresh toggery, and I dare say that I'll be able to give you enough to rig yourself out."

Thus Velvet had supper, and a bed for the night.

In the morning he would have some clothes.

What more could he want?

And he got by sinning that which he had been unable so obtain otherwise, after having been a week in the metropolis.

That night Velvet dreamt about early days, and fancied himself once more in Bournemouth.

Little, indeed, did the poor boy know the changes which had taken place, and which some day he should learn with sorrow.

That night also Velvet dreamt about Old Marks, and somehow or another he fancied that some girl whom he loved was connected with a paper which he had lost.

A paper which he believed to be in Wild Will's possession; and so when he rose from his bed he determined that he should go and see Wild Will.

In the meantime we may as well ask what had become of Nancy?

 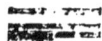

THE
DANCE OF DEATH;
OR,
THE HANGMAN'S PLOT.
A THRILLING ROMANCE OF TWO CITIES.

No. 15.]   SATURDAY, FEBRUARY 10, 1866.   [ONE PENNY.

"I'LL DISFIGURE YOU!"

CHAPTER LV.

THE YOUNG THIEVES TOGETHER—INTELLECTUAL PAS-
TIME—THE FIGHT PREVENTED—VELVET IS PLACED
UPON HIS METTLE.

The life of a London thief is at all times one which, if it possesses its attractions, is not without its drawbacks; and although we look upon human nature as being most decidedly inclined to wicked-ness and sin, yet we believe that there are many who would reform if they could—martyrs to cir-cumstances not those of their own choice, which, step by step, have brought them to a state of degradation, to a fall in the social scale, which have left them prostrate and weak, and thus prevented them rising once more to assume the rights of their own citizenship.

Writers may fill reams and reams of paper, publishers may buy their works and sell them, a free-thinker may assert that there are abuses and anomalies in society which he would like to see corrected, and yet the world will remain as it is, and no one will ever be able to deny this striking truth—namely, that if you are down, one and all will do their best to prevent you rising above water —will, knowingly or unknowingly, help to drown you.

When Velvet arose in the morning—and it was early, for his mind was filled with painful thoughts —the above remarks flitted across his mind, and, glancing upon the young thieves around him who were soundly asleep, he asked himself whether he was doomed to become one of them.

"What time is it?" he muttered, and he listened as if he were anxious to hear the chiming of some neighbouring clock.

He had not to wait long.

Presently the monotonous click in an adjoining building told him that it was five o'clock in the morning.

"It is too early for me to go and see Wild Will," he soliloquised, "I'll try to sleep a little longer."

The mind often subdues the body, and thus Velvet closed his eyelids and soon began to snore soundly.

But how quickly the time passes when you are sleeping.

It was twelve o'clock before he awoke, and doubtless he would not have done so had he not been disturbed by the loud hum of several voices.

He rubbed his eyes and looked about him.

The thieves were practising upon the dummies, and every time the bells sounded there were loud laughs to mortify the unsuccessful apprentice.

"I say, Velvet," Big Ned ejaculated, addressing the boy, "have you ever tried your hand at this caper?"

The boy glanced upon the mannikin which hung from the ceiling.

"I have not, Ned," he replied; "you know that very well."

"Well, then, you must make yourself as useful as ornamental for the future. We are not going to keep you here unless you do some work."

Velvet saw the force of the remark.

Then his pride got the best of him.

"Do you think," he asked, "that I could not rifle his pockets as well as yourself?"

"You!" Big Ned retorted contemptuously. "You! Why, it took me at least five weeks to learn my business."

"Some people are rather slow and thick-headed," Velvet replied sharply; "but I would not require five weeks to be as clever as you at it."

The bully's temper rose.

"To whom are you talking?" he asked.

"To you," replied Velvet.

And there was no fear in his intonation of voice.

"I will give you a d—— good hiding if you do not be more civil."

Velvet made no reply; but his lip curled defiantly.

At the same time the bully advanced towards the boy.

But Bob o' Link was on the look out.

"I say, Ned," he said, "I would advise you to be very particular, or——"

"What?" asked Ned.

"I will carry out the threatening which you just made to Velvet."

Bob o' Link had spoken like one who meant what he said, and the subject dropped before any one had come to blows.

But if Big Ned had been compelled to postpone his revenge against the boy, he was not an individual to forget in a hurry what he called a d—— piece of impertinence—and so he resolved to have it out with the boy at the first opportunity.

The dummies meanwhile were hanging in the room, and the young thieves were practising in great style.

"I say, comrades," Big Ned began, "Velvet just told me that he could rifle this 'ere covey's pocket without making any noise. What think you?"

"That it is a piece of boast on his part," followed one of the gang.

Velvet, who had sat upon a chair immediately after the time when Bob o' Link had come to his rescue, now quickly rose to his feet.

Cannibal Jack was grinning at him.

Johnny Crapaud, *alias* Monsieur Armand, seemed to enjoy the fun extremely, and the other "young gentlemen" were anxiously awaiting the finale of the scene which we are relating.

———

CHAPTER LVI.

THE ORDEAL—THE VICTORY—THE PRIZE—THE SWELL THIEF AND VELVET.

"*L'amour propre offense, ne pardonne jamais*"— "Offended self-pride never forgives"—so has said La Rochefoucault, one of the greatest French thinkers of the last century—a being who thoroughly understood human nature, and who, if he made allowances for the good qualities of mankind, was nevertheless also a severe judge of its defects.

The truth of the above sentence could not have been doubted in the instance which now comes before our own notice—namely, in the case of Velvet, who had been dared to pick a man's pocket, without any previous practice, as well as one who was an old hand at it.

Although we were all created from one image, and all more or less resemble each other in general outward appearance, yet the respective turn of our minds differs widely indeed in its tendency.

Some are inclined to be bad, others good.

But when one's pride is offended, and when his ability to accomplish a certain thing is doubted, it will be found that great exertions will be made by him to win the day.

Thus it unfortunately came to pass that Velvet was dared to do that which was wrong.

It was not a question, though, of propriety or impropriety—it was a challenge which he had accepted, and from which he hoped to emerge victorious.

The boys were all sitting together in the room, and upon a word of Big Ned the mannikin had been trimmed. Two handkerchiefs had been stuck deep in his pocket, the watch-guard had been fastened to the waistcoat, and he hung there in that room for the purpose of being rifled.

Bob o' Link was sitting close to Velvet, and he whispered a few words in his ear.

Bob had given him a wrinkle or two, and had enlightened him upon the pressure which he should use not to get the bells to ring.

Big Ned was impatiently waiting.

At length Velvet swept across the room and stood before the dummy.

"What is the first thing which I am to take?" asked Velvet.

"Begin with that which you like best," replied Big Ned.

Here Bob o' Link spoke.

"Ned," he said, "it is not right to make Velvet the laughing-stock of this place. If he fails he will be turned into ridicule. Let us weigh the other alternative. Should he succeed in pleasing us, what is he to get?"

"Why, the property on the dummy ought to be his own by rights. That's to say if we intend acting as fairly towards him as towards the others."

Velvet remained silent.

"Will it be agreed, boys, that if Velvet does his work well he is to be rewarded?"

"By all means," replied the boys.

There was but one dissentient voice, and it was that of the bully.

But he had to bow before the superiority of numbers.

And in conclusion, after a great deal of talking and discussing, it was settled that Velvet was to begin in earnest.

The interest of the boys was at its culminating point—for we need not tell our readers that, deprived as they were of indoor excitement, any novelty was hailed by them with no small amount of delight.

With a precision and a gentle touch, and the rapidity of an experienced conjuror, Velvet extracted the pocket-handkerchief from the dummy.

It moved slightly, but not one metallic sound was heard.

"Hurrah! hurrah! hurrah! hurrah!"

These exclamations, which came from Bob o' Link, were the means of bringing old Mother Conkless on the threshold of the room.

"What's all this about, my little duckies," she asked, in a honeyed tone of voice, which contrasted strangely with the hideous aspect of her repulsive countenance.

Then she recognised Velvet, and she saw what he was at.

Like the old procuress, who, after having trained some simple country girl to the brazen effrontery of a courtezan, rejoices at the fiendish handiwork of her polluted and depraved mind, so old Mother Conkless smiled with inward delight as she saw that handsome boy taking a deep interest in the work upon which he was engaged.

Had Velvet been by himself, and had the old woman appeared to him as suddenly as she did, doubtless he would have felt ashamed, and relinquished his task.

But her appearance, instead of discouraging him, gave him renewed pluck; and feeling already proud of his first success, he resolved to conclude his part as cleverly as he had begun it.

And then the rings on the dummy's hand were extracted, and his watch-guard was cleverly nipped, and his watch was lifted out of the waistcoat pocket, and Velvet came triumphant out of the ordeal.

It would be impossible to give here an accurate description of the scene which ensued—the congratulations which were poured upon Velvet's head—and the tight squeeze which old Mother Conkless gave to the boy for his cleverness.

Big Ned slunk away like a beaten cur, and was not heard of for the remainder of the day.

Velvet was in high glee.

He had won a very handsome watch. He was looking at it when an incident occurred.

It was the arrival of Wild Will.

The swell thief shook hands with the boy, and asked him what had become of him ever since he had parted company with him.

Velvet related the adventures which he had met with, and, after having got a new suit of clothes, and wished good day to the thieves, he went away with the swell thief.

CHAPTER LVII.

THE ARGYLL ROOMS—WILD WILL AT HOME—LIFTING GENTLEMEN'S WATCHES—THE ROW—THE CHARGE—TAKEN IN CUSTODY.

Reader, I must ask you to step with me up the Haymarket, to go to the top of the same, and to branch off in a street called Windmill.

It is late for some people.

Late for the thrifty artisan who, after his day's toil, seeks his couch and rest; late for the poor semptress who, with aching and cramped fingers, returns to her scantily furnished bedroom, and seeks in slumber a forgetfulness of her troubles; late for the needy clerk, who, upon his seventeen shillings a week, is bound to sleep when his mind would travel; late for the father of a family, who, with children clustering round him, sees the propriety of his offspring keeping good hours.

If it is late for some, it is early for others.

Eleven o'clock!

And it is in the evening.

It is early for the drivelling drunken sot in search of sensation; early for the libertine, to whom the hours of night are the hours of day; early for the swell woman who wishes to pick up "*good*" men; early for the low lodging-house keeper, who turns his house into a "hell;"* early for kangaroo of bygone notoriety; early for the barmaid who serves poison over the counter; early for the man of means at his club.

In the distance—less than a hundred yards on our right—stands a building called the Argyll Rooms.

We will walk up Windmill-street, and enter there.

There are sounds of revelry and merriment issuing from the building. The orchestra is at work. The talented Julien is moving himself in great style. He leads the musicians under him with that energy and *eclât* which brings back to our minds the days of the great Julien, his father.

We pay our shilling, and are admitted.

But when we get in we find that there is something to "fork out" if we wish to have the run of the whole place.

Mind you this is at the West End.

Willingly we do what's right.

Perhaps it may be suggested here that we have no business to bring our friends out of the way.

Is there anything very wonderful about to occur in the Argyll Rooms?

If we had waited a few minutes longer outside we would have seen a brougham driving up, and then coming to a standstill.

The coachman sits upon his seat with the dignity of a flunkey belonging to a big house.

He halts; and then he sees his master and friend alighting, and, without making any uncalled for observation, he drives off, goes to the neighbouring public-house, where he makes himself comfortable by imbibing sundry quarters of a stuff called gin.

In the meantime let us follow the two individuals

---

* Gambling-house.

who but a minute ago were the occupants of the vehicle.

One of them we know already, the other is also familiar to us.

Wild Will and Velvet are the two beings to whom we must revert our attention.

Wild Will, the swell thief, disgusted with life—in search of enjoyment—loth to remain alone in his house at Brompton—fidgetty about the future, for his resources are gradually diminishing—has taken it into his head to pay a visit to the Argyll Rooms.

The gaol-bird, the outcast, the ruined youth, feels sick at heart, and for a few instants muses despondingly as he gazes upon the spot which he knows so well—upon that room where years ago he entered with an unsullied name, with life before him, with the wayward sanguine dreams of a youth's imagination buoying his heart with the most extravagant projects.

One solitary thought of repentance for a second mars his ephemeral pleasures; but he soon dismisses it, as if he could not bear the weight of its truth.

Wild Will has taken Velvet with him; and all the women, as they enter the gallery upstairs, gaze upon that small boy, with bright eyes and wavy locks, in company with the swell thief, whom they at once put down to be a "swell."

"What could have induced Will to bring me here?" asks Velvet to himself. "Surely he must have an object in view."

What that object was will be shortly explained.

We do not think that many of our readers have visited the dancing rooms where we beg of them to accompany us.

Being a place of public resort which is acknowledged to be the most fashionable in London in winter, to dwell upon the same may not, perhaps, be out of place.

Velvet innocently gazed upon the fallen daughters of Eve—the nymphs of the pave, as they are called at the East End—and somehow or another his glance cowed before theirs.

It was all a wonder to him where they got all the jewellery which they wore, and wherefrom they obtained the money to buy the expensive dresses which veiled from mortal eyes the charms which, at a moment's notice, they were ready to sell to the highest bidder.

Another thing which did not strike Velvet, but which would have unquestionably caused us to reflect, was the fact that the oldest girls seemed to be the best dressed.

There are many fools in this world we doubt not, or how should this woman of forty, with her false teeth, with her *rouged* features, manage to live in the style which she does.

But Wild Will saw many fine women there nevertheless; and very shortly after Velvet had taken a launch arm in arm with him, he entered into conversation with rather a small woman, but beautifully made withal.

"Who have you got there with you, Captain?" this woman asked, eyeing Velvet, and addressing the thief by the name which he had assumed.

"A young Eton boy, my darling. He ran up to my hotel to see me, and I thought that I would bring him here for fun."

"A pretty boy! a very pretty boy!" mused the woman, and she kept on looking at Velvet so steadily that he blushed to the very temples.

"Baby," said the Captain, "I am d—— if you are going to make love to my friend; and so be steady now, will ye?"

Baby looked at the swell thief straight in the eyes, and then she broke out with the following—

"Well, old cock, it is all very well talking here; are you going to lush me up?"

The Captain nodded, and he offered his arm to the girl Baby, who was not long in reaching the bar.

"What will it be, Baby?"

"The same as usual," replied the lovely courtezan, addressing the waitress behind the bar.

Velvet was very anxious to know what this pretty woman was going to have. He fancied a bottle of lemonade, or even a glass of wine; what was his astonishment when he saw her polishing off, with the soundness of an old sailor, a tumbler half full of brandy.

"Captain," she said, "I am low-spirited to-night. I wanted something to make me smart. I have not taken any 'good money' lately, and I am frightfully hard up."

The Captain when at the West End became generous.

And now let us here state that it is not only the case with swell thieves, but also with people who earn their living in a less dangerous way.

For instance, we know of sundry instances where fathers of families, who would grudge a sovereign to their daughters in the morning, would think but little of giving the same to a "fast lady;" of merchants in the City grinding down their clerks to a very low salary, and spending a year's stipend of half-a-dozen of the same in nighthouses; of needy individuals forgetting their landlady's bill to lavish it in reckless extravagance; of young hopefuls in humble callings of life aping the "gentlemen," and wishing to be considered "fast men," for one evening.

Go it, old boys! Go it young and old! If you like it, have your own choice. It's all in the way of trade. And if you spend your coin in one way, you must do without it in another—that's all!

So you see, friend and reader, that we are not taking exceptional cases.

But we have said that Wild Will was generous. How so?

"I am sorry to hear, Baby," he began, after having called for a bottle of "cham," "that you are out of your usual luck; take this, and may it do you good."

As he spoke the swell thief gave Baby a sovereign.

Velvet had also been partaking of the champagne, and not being accustomed to it, he was getting somewhat excited—nay, getting a great deal closer to Baby than the Captain liked.

"I say, Captain, hark at him!" laughed Baby. "The young fellow is making love to me; give him a couple of quids, and I'll take him home.

The Captain laughed loudly.

Rather vulgar, you know, that sort of thing.

"Why the medals ought to be reversed, and it is you that ought to ——"

The conversation between Baby and the swell thief here came to rather an abrupt finale, for Baby had just been accosted by some fellow that she called "my lord."

Velvet was devilishly annoyed at Baby's abrupt departure.

"What's that woman's name?" he asked, as soon as the girl was far enough not to be heard by him.

"They call her Baby Jordan; she was one of the prettiest women when I first went on town. She has the whitest skin I ever saw, and bar none she is worth a dozen put together."

Here the swell thief related to Velvet a rigmarole concerning the woman, namely, that she had been married to a penniless spendthrift with "gentle blood." That she had kept him, and that in the end she had found out to her own cost that she had made a great mistake in linking her fate to his own.

Velvet listened attentively to Wild Will, who was telling him the above story in a most casual sort of manner, and he could not help feeling for Baby, who had produced quite an impression upon him.

"I say, Velvet, keep a sharp look out; we must begin to work very shortly; in half-an-hour it will be closing time. The swells will be coming in presently, and you must repeat this morning's performance upon 'a live mannikin.'"

Velvet understood it all.

The swell thief had brought him to the Argyll to help him to pick pockets.

But it was too late to retreat.

"I say, dear. I see no viscounts here to-night; what a parcel of paupers!"

On hearing these words the swell thief very naturally turned round.

The woman who had spoken was a girl who used to go under the name of Rose, with some appellation which we forget, but it was not Rose Young at all events.

Her friend, who was reclining voluptuously upon a chair, and who was displaying for public inspection a very pretty pair of feet, made at first no reply.

"Perhaps there are no viscounts here yet, dear," she replied languidly, "but I feel convinced that this extravagant fellow who comes here every night will not be long ere he turns up."

"Who do you mean?"

"A fellow whom they call the Earl of Mountcarsden?"

"And do you know the woman who is constantly with him?"

"Yes!"

"Who was she?"

"Don't you remember?"

"No!"

"Why, that Rosa Waters, who a few years ago was the means of ruining a young clerk in a bank; don't you remember that famous forgery case?"

Wild Will turned deadly pale.

Uneasily he glanced around him to see whether he had been recognised.

Then he drew a long breath.

"Mountcarsden," he muttered, "why that's the very house where ——"

But here the swell thief stopped suddenly.

"Velvet," he said, "come and let us have another drink?"

Velvet said "he did not want any more!"

But Wild Will insisted.

Yet Velvet refused.

"Well, then, if it is the case," he said to his companion, "go and sit down in one of those benches, and I'll soon return to you."

Velvet did as he was bid, and walked towards a single row of benches which runs on the two sides of the balcony, from which one could see the dancers below.

Meanwhile the swell thief returned towards the two women who had spoken about the forgery.

He longed to hear more.

"I heard you just now, my ladies," he said, bowing courteously to the two women, "complaining about there being no viscounts here."

"Yes, that I did," quickly retorted one of the beauties addressed; "the place is confoundedly slow, there is not one swell here."

The swell thief drew himself to his full height, and rattled a few sovereigns in his waistcoat pocket.

The last remains of the clever swindle which he perpetrated at Long's Hotel, and of which we have already spoken at full length.

"Do you know that you are a very nice looking girl?" he said.

"That'll do, that'll do, walk on!"

And the two women rose as if they wished to get rid of the captain's importunities.

This was provoking in the extreme, and the swell thief knew that if he wished to glean further information from the two lorettes there was but one way to do it.

Thus he persisted in speaking to them.

"Who the devil are you?" asked one of the women, taking stock of Will.

"Perhaps a viscount."

"And perhaps not," followed the friend.

"Never mind, you look a right sort; less palaver old boy, and now to the point, what are you going to stand?"

"Anything you like!"

"Really!"

"Anything; I am on for anything, from pitch and toss to manslaughter, and now what's it going to be?"

"Sherry and lemonade for one," said Will.

"The same for me and my pall," pursued the oldest of the two women standing boldly before the bar.

The order was given, and Wild Will paid for the refreshment.

Now, according to Cocker, the Captain had spent a pound in less than an hour.

The champagne, brandy, and three of sherry and lemonade, would make close upon that amount at the Argyll Rooms, to say nothing of the waiter.

While drinking, Wild Will questioned his two lady friends.

"Who is that Lord Mountcarsden about whom you spoke just now?" the sham Captain asked.

"I do not know him, but Polly does."

Wild Will turned towards Polly.

"He must have lots of money," she said. "As sure as God made little apples he treated nearly all the women here the night before last. He generally brings his woman with him, but when he is alone he goes ahead, and no mistake. But look here, when you speak of the devil you are sure to see him."

As she concluded her sentence, Polly pointed to a handsome woman who was leaning upon the arm of a cavalier dressed in the height of fashion.

"That's the Earl of Mountcarsden," whispered Polly.

Wild Will's brain was now in a whirl.

The woman who was leaning upon the nobleman's arm was no other than the girl who had been the means of his ruin.

Rosa Waters!

She with whom he had gone to Paris. She for whose sake he had forged his principal's signature. She for whose sake he had sacrificed the brightest dream of his youth. She who had helped him to glide on the slippery road to ruin!

For Rosa Waters was no other than Lady Shepherd.

Wild Will glanced upon the nobleman and his companion.

"I have seen that man before," he said, "but where I cannot tell. Of one thing I feel confident, when I last met him he was not then Lord Mountcarsden. There is a mystery somewhere. I must solve it if I can."

Wild Will had parted company with the two women about whom we have spoken.

Alone he resolved to watch Bella and her male friend.

But he did not wish his behaviour to be noticed. So he proceeded cautiously.

The Earl of Mountcarsden had gone in to one of the inner rooms, and Lady Shepherd had taken a seat by her side.

Wild Will, however, decided that he would do his best to overhear their conversation; but then his features might be recognised—for if, after a few years, he could know again the girl whom he had loved, was it not most likely that she would know him also?

He of course meant before the evening was over to speak to Bella; and since she was kept by a nobleman, as he believed her companion was until his doubts were set at rest, he fully intended to make her stump some of the "needful," as he was getting every day more and more hard up.

And there was another reason which would have prompted the swell thief to renew the girl's acquaintance.

Forlorn, friendless, houseless, we may well say here, he would have related to her all his troubles and his tribulations since he had left her, and sought consolation from her depraved wicked nature, were it capable of affording such, which to some may be a matter of considerable doubt.

Then, again, one seldom forgets his first—his only love.

Owing to the crowd of fashionable people who were every instant flocking in the Argyll Rooms, Wild Will succeeded in dogging the steps of the supposed nobleman and Bella.

Suddenly there rose a cry.

Somebody had lost his watch.

There was a commotion.

What could it mean?

Where was the thief?

The proprietor of the establishment—a very gentlemanly, worthy good fellow—was soon on the spot.

But although two or three detectives were sent for, the watch, of course, was not found in Wild Will's pocket, where he had placed it.

Habit is a second part of human nature; and so accustomed to thieving was this young gentleman, that even while his mind was bent upon one search, his fingers were bent upon another.

Although we may be accused of blending the sublime with the ridiculous, will it be denied for the future that is possible for a man to do two things at once?

Presently another incident occurred.

The exhilarating sounds of the orchestra had ceased.

There was a lull.

The corks of the bottles of lemonade were heard popping off, quickly followed by the loud laugh of the gay women "slightly on."

The swell thief was still alone.

He had lost Velvet in the crowd.

What had become of the boy he could not make out.

Doubtless he was in the building, and he would find him at the closing, waiting outside for him in the street.

So Wild Will thought.

Lord Mountcarsden was at the bar, and Bella, who had left "her man" for a few instants, was talking to two swell women of her acquaintance — swell women who had no idea of the dangerous game which she played at her villa in St. John's Wood.

Presently her glance met that of Wild Will.

"Rosa!"

"William!"

Such were the exclamations exchanged.

For let us here tell our readers that Wild Will had not changed his baptismal name, although he had dropped the family one of his forefathers.

The swell thief in an instant was by the side of Lady Shepherd.

"Is that you?" he asked of the woman, his heart beating fast, his eyes shining like two diamonds from their almond-shaped orbs.

"What do you want with me?" Bella asked proudly.

Hers was truly the tone of one who would wish to imply that further conversation was useless—of one who had forgotten all that a man had spent for her.

"I want to speak to you—alone!"

Bella summoned one of her most haughty smiles.

"Look sharp about it," she said; "I have no time to lose."

Wild Will paused.

"Is it you, Rose," he said, "that holds to me such language?"

That woman of marble had no heart.

She smiled derisively.

Bella cast a look around her, and she saw that Lord Mountcarsden was busy talking to some woman.

"Come on," she said, "and I'll listen to you. What is it?"

And they both sat down.

"Do you know what I am now?" he asked of the prostitute as soon as she had sat down before him.

"I don't know, neither do I care."

The swell thief could have wept.

Not out of sorrow, but out of baffled revenge.

There before him was a woman who could defy him.

She was a courtezan, true.

But she was kept by a nobleman.

As long as money lasted—as long as her beauty did not fade—she was not in fear of starvation.

Wild Will was.

For taken at the best, the life of a swell thief—or of a man about town—is indeed an unenviable one.

Attired to-day in the garb of a nobleman, to-morrow he must pawn the same for bread; lavishing money to-day in hollow display, to-morrow he regrets the follies of the previous evening.

"I am a thief, Rose," he said, and you are the cause of my fall."

Had Bella spoken to Wild Will he would have forgotten that himself.

When contempt was heaped upon him he remembered it bitterly.

"A thief?" said the swell woman, rising, "and you talk to me; why it is enough to compromise me."

Wild Will had been drinking.

We have seen him already indulging freely in various beverages.

The words of Bella exasperated him.

"Sit down," he said, "you ———," and he used a foul expression which we cannot write.

Bella rose, but with one quick movement Wild Will crammed her down to her seat.

"Be civil. I'll give you one last chance," he said.

But Bella took no heed.

Then the passions of the thief became aroused.

"I'll disfigure you, and deprive you of that beauty which is your bread," he said to himself.

And no sooner had the thought entered his head than he seized hold of the empty bottle of champagne which stood on the table before him.

Reader, note the engraving representing the incident to which we allude.

It is drawn by one who is, in our opinion, to astonish the world.

There is cleverness about that cut. Well engraved.
Idiots who run down penny numbers, beware!

The first men of the day began by illustrating cheap publications.

We could mention names, but we think it best to abstain.

Grasping the bottle with the tightness of an enraged youth, Wild Will was about to hurl it with all his might against Lady Shepherd, when it was suddenly snatched from behind by a new comer.

The shriek of Bella had brought a crowd.

Lord Mountcarsden had heard the voice of his accomplice.

Then there followed a great struggle between Lord Mountcarsden and the swell thief.

Willingly would we describe the same, but unfortunately it did not last long enough to make it worth our while to do so.

The Argyll Rooms you know, my friends, is not a low place for amusement.

It is conducted on first-class principles.

The proprietor there sees that there is no humbug going on.

Thus, no sooner had the row taken place than a very gentlemanly fellow stepped forward.

This was the identical individual who had been baffled by Wild Will at Long's Hotel.

"What's the present charge against this individual?" he asked, turning towards Lady Shepherd.

"Well, sir," said Bella, "this gentleman whom I have never seen before accosted me just now. He spoke to me, and without any provocation whatever threatened to assault me."

"You do not know me!" shrieked the swell thief. "Ladies and gentlemen, that woman *lies*—lies through her teeth."

This little event created quite a commotion.

Hundreds of people were standing looking on.

There could have been seen in the motley group who were watching that which we are describing men of every class and description.

Gentlemen just taking a stroll in the Argyll Rooms previous to going to the House of Commons; officers on leave spending their money previous to returning to Aldershott, and individuals connected with the law "blowing up" their client's costs.

All these gentlemen and their fair, but frail, companions enjoyed the row immensely.

And can you blame them?

No. For do we not one and all take a great interest in a fight?

If we are walking in the street, and if we see a mill, do we not stop to see the end of it?

And we like it.

The detective was very glad to have an opportunity to revenge himself against the swell thief.

Thus, with praiseworthy, equitable, and just discernment, he began to squeeze the swell thief's arm.

Wild Will was getting more and more excited.

"That woman says she does not know me—the low prostitute—the contemptible hound! Why, she was my evil genius, ladies and gentlemen; she drove me to ruin. For her I——"

The Captain was not allowed to speak any more.

He was fiercely dragged downstairs, closely followed by the Earl of Mountcarsden, who had been requested to press the charge.

Wildly and incoherently Wild Will spoke.

But it was useless.

The charge of assault was clearly proved.

But even had it not been, would he have got the best of it?

He had been charged by a swell prostitute under the protection of a nobleman.

Who could withstand that?

Surely very few.

For do we not remember reading in last Tuesday's *Daily Telegraph* a report of a police case, in which a respectable woman was charged by a drunken fellow with having stolen from him a bunch of flowers, worth twopence.

The inspector took the charge.

The woman was locked up. But in the morning the magistrate himself said that it was one of the most disgraceful cases which had ever been brought under his notice.

When Wild Will, strongly guarded by the detective, came out of that place again a large crowd swelled around him.

Lord Mountcarsden begged to be excused, and after having given the particulars and his residence, he wished good evening to the detective, and returned to the Rooms to meet Bella.

What had become of Velvet?

We think that, if we are not mistaken, he was taken care of by some very nice young lady who had not forgotten his bright eyes in a hurry.

But more of that in a future number of this story.

CHAPTER LVII.

RATCLIFFE HIGHWAY—THE ADULTEROUS WOMAN—THE CONVERSATION—COMING EVENTS CAST THEIR SHADOWS BEFORE THEM.

There is, in the East End of London, a spot which is known by the name of Ratcliffe-highway. It is in the vicinity of the Commercial-road, and densely populated by a large tribe of individuals, male and female, who, wishing to exist without work, are compelled to have recourse to thieving, and occasionally to doing worse than that, to keep themselves from starvation.

Poor Jack, when he steps from shipboard with his pockets full of his hard earnings, strangely enough is to be traced in that hell on earth; and as he likes to brag and get drunk, he generally finds many listeners who all the while are anxiously waiting for an opportunity to rifle his pockets—a thing which they never miss to do.

For a stranger who would like to see all that is to be seen, that peculiar spot in the great metropolis is not without interest—for it would show him that if England is supposed to be the first city in the world for wealth and industry, it is also the only city where you can witness so much vice, misery, and brazen infamy.

Ratcliffe-highway and Lambeth are proverbially known to be two of the most favourite spots for thieves to resort. Why they go there we know not, unless they like to be all together, and, believing in the old proverb, "Union makes strength," feel less fearful of detection when surrounded by their "pals."

In the vicinity of Ratcliffe-highway there is a street called Leman-street, if we remember aright, where outcasts are very fond of congregating, and where it will be our purpose to bring our readers; and not only will we walk along the street, but enter one of the houses situate in it.

To a casual passer by the outward appearance of the house would have presented nothing very remarkable. True, the windows were rather dirty, the area rather slovenly cleaned, the knocker rather greasy, but altogether it was not worse than the dwellings on each side of it.

Let us knock at the door and enter that house.

A girl of about thirteen years of age, pale and

emaciated, ragged and dirty, opens the door, and in reply to our inquiries tells us that the mistress is at home.

We are novelists—we walk upstairs unseen.

In a room upon the second floor, sitting upon a common chair, is a woman whom we have met before.

She is busily engaged in finishing a black mask—a mask which some individual with whom she is living is to wear in one of his midnight excursions.

One would have thought that if a woman sins deeply she is made to suffer for it.

Vice, we understand, is sure always to carry its punishment with it. In Jenny Spaldings' case it did not, however, seem to be so, for she looked as handsome as the day when we saw her in Bournemouth. Perhaps she was a little thinner, but her well-shaped eyes had lost nothing of their brilliancy; her skin was as soft and as white as of yore; her bust, still plump and firm, would have appealed to more than one lover of beauty, and not unsuccessfully either; and her pretty feet, which wandered restlessly to and fro, and were encased in a sort of slip-shod worn-out boot, were still as well-modelled as when she was Dick Spalding's faithful wife.

In a previous chapter of this story we have been told that Dick Spaldings had become a drunkard—whether he was playing a part or not we know not—and that Jenny had left him and eloped with young Will Spanton, the village schoolmaster. ;

Truly the life which she had led had not made much alteration in her personal appearance; and although Dick Spaldings had taken a vow of vengeance against her paramour and herself, he was, as our readers may suggest, a very long time in carrying it out.

William Spanton, since his departure from Bournemouth, had lived by means which at any moment rendered him liable to be arrested and confined in gaol.

"Where's Willy gone?" the woman asked herself, after a moment's reflection. "What a long time he has been away! What would become of me were I suddenly deprived of his protection?"

As she spoke the woman raised her eyes and looked towards the door. Then a sigh of satisfaction escaped her lips.

Willy Spanton had at last arrived.

"Jenny," said the youth, taking the woman's hand into his own, and clasping her to his breast, "I have a great game on hand. If I succeed I shall make at least a thousand pounds."

"What is it?" asked Jenny.

"I had better keep it dark for the present from you, Jenny, until I hear more."

"Will there be any danger, Willy?"

The woman spoke tenderly and lovingly, and in the tone of her voice could have been traced the passion which she entertained for her seducer.

We may be accused of immorality—God forbid that such should be laid at our door! for we always speak the truth. But we will ask, how is it that guilty love is always stronger and more powerful than the legitimate lover?

One consolation, it does not last so long as the former.

If Jenny was not much altered, the same could not have been said of the dissipated youth who had whispered sweet words of love in her ear.

He looked much older.

Still there was about him that same gentlemanly demeanour which we have noticed in the early part this story. Dressed with becoming elegance, there was nothing in his attire to which the most fastidious critic could have objected. He wore a plain signet ring and a gold watch and guard, and any one unacquainted with his way of living would have taken him to be one who derived his income through honest means.

"Yes," lovingly whispered Spanton in Jenny's ears, "if my speculation turns out trumps I'll make a good deal of money. Then do you know what I purpose to do?"

"No, Willy; how could I fathom your plans?"

"I then intend to place some money in the lawyer's hands to clear some mystery with which my birth is connected. With the remainder I purpose to live until the matter is settled."

"And if an unsatisfactory answer is given, Willy?" the woman asked.

The late schoolmaster bit his lips.

"I am rather sanguine of success," he said; "but should I be deceived, a man must live, you know."

"And would you remain in London, Willy?"

"No; I would start for Italy, out of the way."

After Willy had spoken a sudden pallor overspread the cheeks of the adulterous woman, and she placed her hands across her eyes as if she wished to hide some terrible sight from her gaze.

"Willy," she asked, squeezing the youth's hands in her own with nervous fear, "could you give up what you have on hand? I feel certain it is some burglary—perhaps some murder. Something tells me that you have sinned long enough. Sad forebodings cast their shadow before my mind. Willy, give up the career of recklessness which you are leading. Trust not to miracles for a change.'

After Jenny had spoken Will Spanton mused sadly.

"Do you know, Jenny," he asked, after a few moments' silence, "that your words sometimes cause me to reflect?"

A passing smile, like the sunshine which brightens a stormy day, flitted across the expansive forehead of the adulterous woman.

"Reflect!" she repeated; "of what use is that unless you reform?"

"Reform!"

Bitter, sad, gloomy, was the tone of the youth's voice.

"I have gone too far," he said; "I cannot retreat. But if what I have been told is true, I may one day come into a large fortune."

"What have you heard, Willy?"

Supplicating, affectionate, and kind was the woman's voice.

'Tis sweet to meet consolation from a human being when you are alone and friendless. 'Tis sweet to have balm poured upon a bleeding wound when you suffer—'tis sweet to gaze upon the features of one whom you love, and who holds her hand to you and cheers you on when you are about to fall.

In the course of this story we have brought our readers in contact with strange and various characters.

Some were low, vile, and heartless: the swell thief and the Marquis of Aguado to wit.

But the schoolmaster was not one of that stamp.

Love had been his ruin. Love! oh, how pretty that word—how sweet it sounds to young hearts!

The schoolmaster was not thoroughly bad. Within him he believed that he had the blood of a gentleman—something told him that he was not meant to be an usher in a parish school. His mind, like many other victims to hope, soared above his station.

LOOK OUT FOR THE PLATE
GIVEN AWAY WITH NO. 17,
"A FIGHT IN THE THIEVES' DEN."

THE
DANCE OF DEATH;
OR,
THE HANGMAN'S PLOT.
A THRILLING ROMANCE OF TWO CITIES.

No. 16.]   SATURDAY, FEBRUARY 17, 1866.   [ONE PENNY.

"A LONG ROPE SUCH AS THE HANGMAN USES."

CHAPTER LVIII.—CONTINUED.

After Jenny had asked her paramour to give her some information she had remained silent and thoughtful.

"Well, listen, darling," the youth began; "one evening that I was walking in Lincoln's-inn-fields I met a gentleman who, from his appearance, I believed to be connected with the law. He placed to me several questions relating to my whereabouts."

Here Jenny's nostrils dilated.

"I hope," she exclaimed vacantly, with a startled shudder, "that you did not tell him?"

"I did not, Jenny. I might have been mistaken, and he might have been some one wanting to take me in custody."

"Yes; but on the other hand he might have wished you good."

The youth smiled with a sad, weary, melancholy smile.

"What did you do then?" the farmer's wife resumed."

"I waited to hear more."

"Afterwards?"

"He began to question about my ways of living—asked me whether I was in want of money"

"Strange occurrence that!"

"Yes, Jenny, it was. After consideration I thought that I should have remained and listened to him. But, as the proverb says, 'A guilty conscience needs no accuser;' and so I foolishly ran away."

"Have you heard anything more since?"

"Not a word."

"And why has this induced you to think that you were the heir to a large fortune?"

"This adventure, and one or two others, Jenny, have confirmed my opinion upon the subject."

"If such is the case, why not wait patiently?"

"And in the meantime, Jenny?"

The woman cast a meaning look upon the empty cupboard.

"True," she muttered.

Although the schoolmaster lived by roguery and thieving, yet he was not so accomplished a vagabond as to manage things for himself as cleverly as others can do.

Occasionally he and Jenny wanted bread.

"Never mind that, Willy," she said. "I'll try with my needle to earn enough. In the meantime make inquiries."

"Jenny, your remark is senseless. Do you think that I would consent to live upon a woman's labour? No; never! I have met some parties to-day who were asking me to join them, and they guarantee me success."

"And what do they want you to do, Willy?"

"Not a great deal; but of course there are risks attached to our undertaking."

Jenny was getting more and more interested. But her interest was of a sad character indeed, for to her it foreboded no good.

"And who are the men who were asking you to join them?"

"Of that, Jenny, I know but little. But they are vagabonds, of that I feel confident."

"Stay with me, Willy," once more supplicated the woman, "and give up keeping bad company."

But the youth shook his head.

Then he looked at the clock.

"I have no time to lose, Jenny," he said; "I must be off."

As he spoke he walked towards the door.

"Willy," she said, seizing hold of the youth's arm and hindering his departure, "do you believe in dreams?"

"Dreams!" replied the youth; "No; I do not. But why such questions?"

Jenny's glance swept around the room, and having satisfied herself that there was no one nigh, she placed her hand athwart her brow, and mused for an instant or two ere she spoke.

She was evidently trying to bring back to her mind some recollection of the past.

"Do you remember, Willy," she asked, "that night when you took me to the fancy ball?"

"Perfectly," quickly retorted the youth; "and dressed in your costume you looked more bewitching than I ever saw you before. But what can this have to do with a dream?"

"Then if your memory does not fail you, doubtless you will remember that you left me alone for a few minutes."

"Yes; I went to the corner house to get a bottle of wine."

"Well, then Willy——"

"What?"

"A strange, wonderful thing occurred."

"Ah!"

"Yes."

"And you never said a word to me about it."

"I did not like to appear foolish in your eyes."

"And what was that wonderful occurrence to which you allude?"

"Well, as soon as I was by myself, strangely enough I began to revolve in my mind all those things which I had done. I thought of Spaldings, when——"

The words which the woman was about to speak died in her throat.

She became deadly white, and an ashy, sickening pallor overspread her countenance, and her whole being trembled with a startled shudder.

The youth took the girl's hand into his own and pressed it.

It was cold and clammy.

Then Jenny fainted.

The youth laid her on her bed, where she remained senseless for a few minutes.

But the schoolmaster loved Jenny too much not to do his best to bring her back to consciousness.

With a swift step he glided towards the washing-stand, and brought back with him a tumbler full of cold water.

He dipped his fingers in the water and bathed his paramour's forehead.

At first her breath was, as it were, choked, and she seemed to gasp for air.

But the coolness of the water soon wrought a change, and she recovered.

"Where am I?" she asked, as if she were awaking from some terrible nightmare.

Then she placed her hand across her eyes.

"There!" she said; "there it is again!"

The schoolmaster was lost in bewilderment.

Fixedly and steadfastly he looked in the direction towards which Jenny's finger pointed; but he saw nought.

"There! there! Look!" once more shrieked Jenny.

This time her voice sounded louder, and she shrank back as if she feared to meet some one.

"Jenny," said the youth, leaning over the woman's shoulders, "for Heaven's sake speak! What is it?"

"Well, then," resumed Jenny, "on that night of which I speak I was thinking over bygone times, when suddenly I heard a strange creaking sound!"

"Yes," faltered the schoolmaster, who was also beginning to think that there was something in what the woman said. "Well!"

"I looked up."

"Yes."

"And there in that corner I saw my husband."

"Richard Spaldings!"

"Yes."

"Jenny, I do not think that the very fact of seeing your husband ought to have produced such an impression upon you."

"Willy!"

"What?"

"Do you know what he held in his hand?"

"No."

"A *long rope* such as the hangman uses."

"But even then, Jenny."

"Ah! you know not what I suffered. Without a word he showed me the rope, and immediately above him was a gibbet.

"'What is the meaning of that?' I asked him.

"Again he pointed to another part of the room, and I dimly saw a boy in a felon's cell."

"What about that?"

"What about that, friend? You speak easily and take matters carelessly indeed. Do you know who that boy was?"

Willy nodded his head in the negative.

"No; I do not," he said.

"Why, Harry, my poor boy, whom I have not seen for months."

And here the woman's words were choked by her sobs.

"Willy," she muttered, "I beseech thee on my knees. Go not where you intend. You will meet your doom."

And wishing to give more strength to her words, Jenny fell upon her knees.

The youth raised her gently.

"Do not be so fearful of consequences. Your mind must have been labouring under some excitement when you witnessed the apparition to which you refer."

Jenny said that it was not.

"Did you see your husband again?" he asked.

"My mind," she said, "is constantly haunted by his presence. Awake or asleep, I hear him hissing the word 'Revenge!' in my ear. Yes, I feel certain that he will have a striking revenge out of you and me."

The schoolmaster made no observation.

"I fear him not," he muttered; "so farewell, Jenny for the present; farewell!"

And before the poor creature had time to say another word, the youth swept out of the room.

He had taken the *black mask* with him!

CHAPTER LIX.

THE TURK'S HEAD—THE OUTCASTS—THE FENCE—THE BOY KAY—THE BULLDOG—THE INSPECTION—STOLEN GOODS—THE "SWAG"—THE LANDLORD PUTS IN AN APPEARANCE.

With quick steps the youth descended the staircase which led to the street door, and when he found himself in the highway he stopped suddenly, and mused for an instant or two ere he proceeded onwards.

Although before Jenny he had not allowed his feelings to give way, yet when alone he pondered on that which he had heard, and he began to waver as to keeping the appointment which he had made.

Sometimes in this life forebodings may prove correct, and the schoolmaster dreaded to embark into an expedition the end of which he could not foresee.

But he was on his last legs, and to retreat would not only have looked suspicious in the eyes of those who had proposed to him to join them in a game which they had on hand, but also deprive him of whatever chance he might have had of doing something for himself.

The appointment which Spanton had made with the individuals that he was about to join was to be held in a low beer-house called the Turk's Head, where burglars, pickpockets, and thieves were wont to resort.

Will Spanton had just sufficient in his pocket to pay for a pot of beer, and he was not reluctant in spending the same, as he knew that for the services which he was ready to give he would receive some consideration in the shape of a few pounds to bind him in his bargain.

When the schoolmaster entered the pot-house, he saw on his right a small door with green curtains hiding the window, and at the top of the same was written "Tap-room."

The instructions which he had received in the course of the day had been too explanatory for him to make a mistake about their purport, so calling for a pot of beer, he paid for the same, and carrying the pewter in his left hand, he boldly entered the room.

The floor, which was covered with sand, was literally strewn with spittoons, but apparently the customers of the house took but very little notice of the purpose for which they were placed there, for they spat anyhow and anywhere. The room was reeking with an offensive aroma of bad tobacco, and so great was the number of smokers that the clouds which issued from their pipes literally hid their features from view.

Gradually and slowly, however, the smokers relinquished their intellectual occupation, and a few minutes after he had been among them the schoolmaster saw the class of individuals he had to deal with.

Some were grown up men, others were very old, others very young.

Strange to say, the Hallelujah Club mustered there in full strength, and Bob O'Link, first and foremost, was doing his gin in great style.

On the occasion when we pay them a visit they were accompanied by an old man whom we have not seen before.

That was "The Fence."

Their chief and master.

The man with whom Will had made an appointment.

"I am glad," said this gentleman, rising to shake hands with Spanton, "to see that you keep to time."

The schoolmaster said that whenever he made a promise he kept it.

Then he took a survey of those around him.

The appearance which Monsieur Armand presented struck him as being comical in the extreme, and he could not refrain a smile as he gazed upon him.

The Frenchman of late had greatly improved.

Now he wore a very fine moustache, which he was constantly twisting. The brims of his hat were somewhat more turned up, and his peg-top inexpressibles were so large at the top and so tight at the bottom that he could indeed have used the upper part of his trowsers as an overcoat.

The Cannibal, on the other hand, looked anything but prepossessing.

His face was just a whit dirtier than when we last saw him, and his knock-kneed legs were still more uncouth—to say nothing of his left eye, which had received rather a heavy blow upon it, given to him by a boy of the name of Kay, whom we have met in the Lambeth Workhouse, a few chapters previously.

Kay of late had been "done for a rump"—convicted for thieving, to use the proper English meaning of the slang expression.

Since he had left the gaol, and that was now a few weeks ago, he had not been doing well.

Lately he had fallen in with the Club, and being rather of a fighting disposition, having on one occasion paid a visit to Nat Langham's public-house in St. Martin's-lane, he had had a row with the Cannibal, in which he had come off the conqueror.

Black Kettle was also present.

Big Ned was still bullying everybody as usual, and when he saw the new comer he eyed him like a cur would have done some one trying to snatch from his paws a bone which he was picking.

For by this time our readers cannot have been slow in perceiving that Ned was always jealous of any fresh addition to the gang over which he reigned supreme when the Fence, that is to say, their master, was away.

"Who is that?" asked Ned, speaking to the Fence.

"A friend."

"That's all right then."

"Of course it is. Do you think I bring spies here?"

"No, Mat," submissively replied Ned, and he renewed his smoking, which he had interrupted to speak.

Mat, who was the Fence, was rather a strange-looking character.

He wore a white hat with a black crape around

it, a long drab overcoat, a pair of tight-fitting breeches of dark cloth, and he never went anywhere without his stick—a heavy bludgeon—and a bulldog, which he called by the name of Beauty.

Beauty was, at the time when we first see him, crouching at his master's feet.

When Spanton had entered he had given vent to an ominous growl, which was anything but pleasant to hear.

And had it not been for a severe kick which Mat had given him, he would doubtless have sprung at the throat of the schoolmaster.

"How is it outside, my worthy?" asked Bob O'Link from Spanton.

"Do you mean the weather?"

"Yes."

"Rather dark."

"That's the ticket, my lads!" now put in Mat; "a starry night wouldn't suit us."

Spanton was asked to sit down.

Reluctantly he did so.

If he could then have given some excuse for not joining them in that which they had on hand, he would willingly have done so.

But he had pledged his word.

Besides he knew that they would not have accepted his resignation.

"Now, are you going to sit here all night?" said Mat, drinking a "go" of gin which stood on the table before him. "What about the spoil?"

This remark brought all the lads together.

"Who has got the things?" asked Mat.

Black Kettle went towards one of the corners of the room.

Then, from beneath Kay's overcoat—and it was an overcoat! for you could see through it without much difficulty—he drew a carpet-bag, which appeared to be full of luggage.

What luggage was it?

Stolen goods of course.

But as they had been nailed in the course of the day, and information had been given to the police, it was rather a difficult thing to get rid of them.

Mat knew that.

And Mat was a prudent fellow.

Fences as a rule are; and it is but little risk they themselves run.

They pocket the lion's share, and get those under them to do the dirty work.

It may be asked, How is it that in London, when you take a body of thieves together, there is always one out of many who succeeds in becoming master?

We should think that if we were thieves we would work for ourselves, and not for others.

But evidently thieves do not think so.

They want a leader, and a man of experience.

Mat was one of these.

For five-and-thirty years he had been a professional thief, and he took a deal of pleasure in boasting of all the dark deeds he had perpetrated in his lengthened career of vice.

Again, it may be inquired how it was that our readers did not see Mat before?

Mat had been in Birmingham, whence he had only lately returned.

The carpet bag was brought by Black Kettle to the Fence.

He opened it.

"Who prigged this?" Mat asked, taking from the bag an old pair of trousers, in which was rolled very carefully a very handsome gold watch.

"I did," said Big Ned.

"You did not!"

"I did, Mat," the Cannibal quickly interrupted.

"Place this upon the table," said Mat.

The watch was accordingly laid upon the table.

All the thieves flocked round it to inspect the jewel.

"Ned, for the future I would ask you to tell the truth," Mat went on gruffly.

The inspection was resumed.

The next thing which Mat brought out was a pair of scissors and an old knife.

"Who bagged that?" the Fence went on.

Black Kettle answered the call.

"Of what use is that to us, you nigger, you? I have a great mind to stick you with the knife."

Black Kettle mumbled an apology.

Mat now smiled.

"Never mind, Black Kettle, this time," he said; "for the future be more careful in your selection."

Black Kettle accordingly held his tongue.

The Fence, however, did not seem to be much annoyed, and he continued extracting the articles from the bag.

"We got 'the swag' at last," Mat went on, alighting upon six diamond rings, which he triumphantly showed to the crew.

Spanton meanwhile was looking on.

"It is wonderful," said he to himself, "how these fellows manage to do it—but they do it, nevertheless."

His next query was to find out how they would get rid of the stolen articles.

Space forbids us to enumerate, one after the other, the various goods, which were minutely catechised by the Fence.

At a minute's notice, less even than that, he could tell whether a thing was worth anything or not.

Now there was a hair brush—now a tortoiseshell comb—even in one instance he found a hare, which had been stolen from a poulterer's stall.

"I am a novice in all these things," Spanton said, addressing Mat. "How will you manage to sell what you have got?"

"Young man, do not be too curious. You will soon see."

At that instant a rap was heard outside.

"Who goes there?" asked the Fence.

"A friend."

One of the young gentlemen opened the door.

The landlord's voice had been recognised.

"What is it?" asked Mat.

"A young woman wishes to speak to you."

"Think you it is square, master?"

"I think so. I have seen her here before."

"With me?"

"Once with you, and often with So-and-so."

"Let her in then."

The landlord said he should.

"Any orders, gentlemen?" he asked; but there being no reply he betook his consequential self away.

––––––

CHAPTER LX.

WHO GOES THERE?—COCKEYED SALLY—THE LETTER —NEWS FROM THE SWELL THIEF—A NEW DODGE— THE BUTTER—A SAFE PLACE TO STOW JEWELLERY —A FEW WORDS ABOUT THIEVES.

The stolen property was on the table, and no steps had been taken by the thieves to remove it out of sight.

Mat knew that the landlord would not have betrayed them.

For years he had patronised the house, and he always brought a good supply of drinkers with him.

That was a sufficient guarantee for Master Dutcher of the " Turk's Head."

He had a wife and seven children, and had to work hard for his family, so he said.

So it mattered very little to him whether people were respectable or not, so long as they paid their way.

Many people like Master Dutcher in the world.

Shortly after the landlord had gone, the tramping of footsteps nearing the room approached.

Another knock at the door.

Another " Who goes there ?" for precaution's sake, and the new comer was admitted.

" Holloa! what brings you hither?" asked the Fence.

" Business."

The Fence closed the door.

The new comer was a girl.

She could not have been above fifteen. We have seen her before.

It was she whom Velvet had noticed in the thieves' den.

Cockeyed Sally in fact.

She whispered a few words in the Fence's ears.

" Indeed," he said.

" Yes."

" Got any message."

" A letter."

" Where is it ?"

" Here, Master."

Cockeyed Sally then fumbled in her pocket and brought out an envelope which had once been white, but which was now of a brown colour—the stay which it had made in the girl's dirty and greasy pocket not tending much to improve its general appearance.

Mat broke the seal.

Then he read on aloud :—

" Mat I am in a pickle. I am down upon my luck. I was at a place of amusement called the Argyll Rooms. I had a frightful row with a woman there, and I have been locked up in Bow-street. I have bribed one of the messengers. Please devise some means by which I may be liberated, for if I appear before the Magistrate previous convictions will come out against me, and I may be condemned to a few years of 'the everlasting staircase.' Do your best ? "WILL."

" I say, Will is at Bow-street," the Fence said as soon as he had concluded the perusal of the letter. " Can we get him out ?"

" Awkward that," mused Bob.

" Damned provoking !" said another.

" What's to be done ?"

Cockeyed Sally meanwhile was glancing around her.

" By-the-bye, there are a few lines at the bottom of the letter !"

" What is it ?" asked all the thieves.

" Will wants to know whether you have seen a fellow he calls Velvet ?"

" What about him ?"

Bob O'Link related to the Fence all particulars connected with the boy.

" Sally," said Mat, " I am glad you came. You can be very useful to me. Has any one seen you coming here ?"

" I believe so."

" Who ?"

" A peeler of the K division. He looked devilish hard at me !"

" Did he ?"

" Yes, and no flies !"

The Fence resolved in his mind the step he should ake.

Suddenly he rung the bell.

The landlord soon answered the call.

When the thieves patronised his house, and it was very often that they did so, he always waited upon them personally.

He never allowed the pot-boy to do so. His reasons were very good ones.

He thought that he might hear too much.

" Got any butter in the house, landlord ?"

" Yes."

" How much do you want—a pennyworth ?"

" More than that."

" A firkin, perhaps ?"

" Not exactly !"

" Well, for the order, then ?"

" Bring me in a pound or two. I may not use them both, but I'll pay for what I use."

" Right, sir."

Spanton was at a loss to know for what purpose the Fence wanted a pound or two of butter. He soon returned with the provisions ordered.

It was placed on the table by the side of the stolen jewellery.

" And did the bobby watch you closely, Sally ?"

Sally replied in the affirmative.

" Never mind, we will do him."

Then the Fence cut the butter in the middle, and in the centre placed the gold watch and the rings.

The next thing was to settle the butter again without disturbing the print.

Mat was accustomed to do those sort of things.

It is by no means difficult to accomplish.

But a good deal of practice renders you perfect.

The butter was then placed upon a tray, and the girl was told to carry the same to the thieves' den, when in the course of the evening Mat would rejoin her.

The bobby was smelling about outside the public-house.

These worthy, illustrious, and enlightened members of the force generally do.

The landlord had been spoken with.

And he gave a pint of beer to the peeler, and while he drank it Sally passed under his very nose with part of the stolen property.

The remainder of the goods which the Fence had on hand was parted in a matter no less ingenious, and an hour after Spanton had entered the room he had become thoroughly acquainted with their ways and means.

Now it would scarcely be believed by our readers how very cute thieves are.

Considerable ingenuity is displayed by them in conveying their unlawful possessions from one place to another.

Hampers, clothes baskets, hat boxes, carpet bags, and brown paper parcels, containing stolen articles are carried by women dressed like servants, and by honest and unsuspecting errand boys and parties, who frequently have no knowledge of the contents of the luggage.

Stolen articles are booked regularly at the goods stations, and travel along our streets and railways in company with honest merchandise.

We have seen how the Fence had disposed of the butter and to what use he had placed it.

But there were many things besides the diamond rings and the gold watch to do away with.

The hare to which we have previously referred was subsequently cleaned, and some goods stitched within its carcase, and sent in that guise to one of Mat's pals in Birmingham.

With thieves it is not a case of quick return for their money. Often they are compelled to keep by them valuable property, as they are too closely watched by the police sometimes to have their own way.

Cockeyed Sally was on her way to the thieves' den. Cannibal Jack had been sent to the station with the hare, and the thieves were all together.

One after the other he called out the names of all those in the room, and he wound up with the boy Kay.

"Here you are, sir," said the youth.

"I know that very well," the Fence replied, wishing to be witty, "but I want you *here*."

Kay growled, and approached the Fence.

Everybody was listening.

———

CHAPTER LXI.

BEAUTY GETS PUNISHED—THE BOND OF CRIME—GEN-
TLEMAN SPANTON—FRANK PULLEN THE THIEF.

We do not know how it is, but when a man is about to speak he generally rises to his feet.

This Mat did before he began to address the fellow before him.

But when he did so Beauty rose also.

Evidently he wished to have a part in the conference.

He began by growling in a most ominous manner; he cocked his ears and shook his tail.

This was a sign that Beauty understood what was about to take place.

But Mat was not inclined to let anyone have his own way.

Under the present circumstances, therefore, he gave a strong kick to Beauty.

The dog howled.

Then it looked fiercely at his master.

Mat had his stick in his hand.

He raised it menacingly over the bull-dog's head.

Beauty seemed to understand that also.

For with praiseworthy prudence and a striking illustration of its instinct, it slowly wended its way beneath the table, and crouched silently in a submissive attitude.

There was nothing more now to hinder the Fence.

"Big Ned," he said, addressing the bully, "have you got your mask?"

"Yes."

"And have you seen that all the others were provided with it?"

"I have; but with one exception, and that's this new party who has joined us."

Big Ned referred to Spanton.

Mat turned round towards the schoolmaster.

"Have you done that?" the Fence asked Spanton.

The schoolmaster knew the meaning of the Fence's words.

"I have," he replied, and then he drew from his pocket the black mask at which we have seen Jenny working.

Spanton placed it upon his face.

It hid the upper part of his features, and only allowed the lower part to be seen.

"Comrades," said Mat, "now for the disguise."

No sooner had he spoken than the whole of the lads and their pals put on their masks.

"That'll do," said the Fence, smiling good-humouredly. "I like the precision and the rapidity with which you go through your evolutions. Talk about the British Harmy or the Volunteers, why, they couldn't hold a candle to the Hallelujah Club!"

This compliment, which was not undeserved, produced loud laughter among the boys.

"What's your name, friend?" asked the Fence, addressing Spanton, who was gazing with astonishment upon those who surrounded him.

Poor boys of London, who had been driven to crime against their will, and who were bound to keep in their lawless career, however anxious to reform they might have been.

"I would rather not give you my name," said Spanton. "Is it usual to do so when one joins your band?"

"I do not understand what you mean by asking whether it is usual," repeated the Fence; "only it shows a want of confidence in us."

The late schoolmaster mused.

"After all," he said to himself, "Spanton is a common name. I'll tell him so."

Then Spanton gave his name to the Fence.

"Gentleman Spanton will be your appellation for the future."

"Indeed!"

"Yes."

"Why so?"

"Because you've got the style about you."

Spanton smiled.

"What is the next thing I am to do?"

"To take this and to pocket it."

As he spoke the Fence handed two pounds to the youth.

His heart beat with joy as he clutched the gold which was to seal his villany.

He placed the money in his pocket.

Never looked at it.

The two sovereigns seemed to burn his fingers.

And then he remembered Jenny's words.

The purport of her dream.

And he asked himself whether it was not a warning of Providence sent just in time to bid him to reform.

But if he had been alone Gentleman Spanton might have had time to think.

Surrounded by the others the thing was impossible.

"Instead of feeling delighted at the gift which I have just made you," the Fence said, "you seem to be down in the mouth."

Spanton made no reply.

Of what use would it be for him to acquaint them with the inward thoughts which lacerated his brain?

While he was thus thinking another individual came into the room.

That was Frank Pullen, a well-known thief.

"Made any money to-day?" asked the Fence.

"Rather."

"Where did you go to?"

"Sir Charles Westmacott's and Lady St. Clair's."

"And what did you get?"

"Only two silver tablespoons and two silver forks."

"How much will they fetch?"

"Only £1 10s."

The Fence shrugged his shoulders.

"Any risk in getting them?"

"Not much."

"I see."

"Do you know my new game, Mat?"

The boys were listening.

"No. What is it?"

"I hire a horse and cart, and accompanied by my 'doxy,'* I visit all the good houses."

"What do you mean?"

"You know the Court Directory?"

"Yes, where they've got all the gentilmen's names down. Is that what you wish to say?"

"Exactly."

———
* Female thief.

"In the morning I settle in my mind the neighbourhood which I shall visit in the day."

"Well."

"I stop before the house of a nobleman."

"Yes."

"I say I wish to purchase bottles."

"Yes."

"The flunkey looks suspiciously at me."

"Afterwards."

"He sees my cart outside, and a respectable woman sitting on it."

"Yes."

"The flunkey takes me in the housekeeper's room, and it is devilish hard lines if I can't pick up something worth while."

"Did you do much lately?"

"Only seven pounds on Friday last!"

The thieves all laughed. They enjoyed the fun immensely.

Besides, Frank Pullen was a great favourite amongst them.

He had once been a great admirer of the art of self-defence.

Had fought twice in the prize ring.

Knew Jessie Hatton, Jem Dillon, Bob Travers, and all the good men on town.

Thus they looked up to him.

Besides, Pullen stood no humbug.

If any one quizzed him a little too much he gave him a knob upon his conk, and drew claret almost instantaneously.

"I suppose," he said to the Fence, "you wonder at my reasons for coming here?"

"Not a bit, Frank; you know you are always welcome amongst us."

"I say that I have made inquiries."

"About what?"

"You know."

Then he whispered a few words in his ears.

"You are a day after the fair."

"What mean you?"

"Why the expedition is already planned."

"Is it?"

"Yes."

"And when are you going to do the job?"

"To morrow or next day, please God."

"I say, Mat."

"What?"

"I understand that he has received a very heavy consignment from Birmingham."

"I heard something about it."

"How much?"

"Over seven thousand pounds worth!"

The truth flashed across Spanton's mind.

Mat had asked him to join the crew in a burglary.

And that it was upon the house of a jeweller he had no doubt.

The words which Mat subsequently spoke enlightened him still more on the subject.

"Gentleman Spanton," said Mat, addressing the schoolmaster, "to morrow morning I wish you to go to the city."

"At what o'clock?"

"Eleven sharp."

"Yes."

"Here are two pounds more."

"Thanks."

"You must go into Richard, the jeweller's. Get him to overhaul the whole of his stock. Take a good survey of the place, and buy a ring from him."

"Right."

"That will place him off his guard."

"Afterwards."

"You join us here at six in the evening. Report progress, and if there is a good opportunity we will go there together. Between this and that I'll do my best to glean further particulars."

"To-morrow at six I'll be here."

"I expect you to act according to my instructions."

"I will not fail."

"And now good bye."

"Good bye," repeated Spanton.

And with these words he wished farewell to the thieves and returned to Jenny, whom he found bathed in her tears.

The poor thing had wept since his departure.

The strange manner of her lover, the black mask which she had made for him foreboded no good.

"I am back again, Jenny, you see," said the youth, "and I have got money."

The woman looked at her paramour.

"Is it all over," she asked.

"Yes," replied Spanton, "and I am going to reform."

The adulterous woman fell upon her knees and thanked heaven.

It was the first prayer which she had made since she had left Bournemouth.

But little did she know what was to follow.

Almighty God is good, but he will punish vice and crime, and Jenny had sinned too much to be so readily forgiven.

CHAPTER LXII.

THE SCUFFLE—THE INSPECTOR—BOW-STREET STATION —THE DARK CELL—THE MESSENGER.

As soon as Gentleman Spanton had taken his departure the thieves began to consider as to the line of conduct which they should adopt.

The swell thief evidently was in a pickle, and he appealed to his pals to extricate him from the same.

Mat, the Fence, had one redeeming point. He stood by the others when they required his help.

"What's to be done about Will?" he said, helping himself to a huge draught of the stout before him. "Is it worth risking ourselves for him?"

Now it was a great query to know what would be the reply to the Fence.

"Who's Will?" asked the boy Kay, who, having lately joined, was not yet thoroughly acquainted with all the ins and outs of the Hallelujah Club.

"A first-rate chap, and no mistake about him—ain't he, Mat?"

The Fence nodded his head in the affirmative.

"And where is he?" the boy Kay went on.

"In the lock-up."

"Oh! crikey! and I guess he is likely to remain there."

"I am not so certain about that," said Bob o'Link. "More than once he has done us a good turn; why should we not return it?"

"And how are we to proceed?" asked one of the crew.

Big Ned had not yet spoken.

Silently he sat, without uttering a word.

At last he opened his lips.

"It is no easy matter," he went on, "to take him out of Bow-street. They are a sharp set of fellows there."

"Yes, they may be; but it would not be right to forget an old pal in his distress."

"And what do you propose?" asked Mat from Bob.

"Why, rescue him from the hands of the bobbies."

"This would be rather a dangerous game, my

boys; moreover when on the eve of a grand thing like we have got on hand."

"Never mind. Will is a good sort, and he is a very useful fellow withal."

"Will we rescue him?" asked Mat from the boys. "Will we rescue him from the bobbies?"

"Yes, yes!" replied the boys.

And they constituted themselves into a committee, and there was a chairman, and they came to a determination which will be illustrated in the course of this story, at no distant period either.

* * * * *

Having left the Fence, Pullen, and the young thieves together, it is necessary for the comprehension of this tale that we should revert our attention to the object of their conversation.

When the Earl of Mountcarsden had given the charge to the worthy and enlightened members of the force who had taken Will in custody, they lost no time in dragging this promising young gentleman to the station-house.

We have often heard of there being but little sympathy in this world for those who are in difficulties; but we will back a policeman against any other mortal individual alive for being the most heartless fellow when in the discharge of his duty.

"Do you know who I am?" asked Wild Will, as he was pushed to the station. "Do you know who I am?"

"Now just draw it mild, will ye?" replied the inspector, in anything but a conciliatory manner. "We know the likes of you too well. What you are is no mystery to me."

"Yes; do you know who I am?" once more interrogated the swell thief, who wished by his impudence to set all suspicion at rest.

"A well-known character, no doubt; but I take you to be, young gentleman, a member of the swell mob. Am I wrong?"

When certain promising youths find that their doings are discovered, many think that it is best to hold their tongue and to await the issue of the charge, but Master Will was not one of these.

"I am a householder in Brompton, and I can prove it."

"A householder!" sneeringly pursued the policeman in plain clothes; "more likely a housebreaker, or something of that sort. Why, what did the detective say? that he had seen you before, and he spoke about some clever, very clever dodge of yours at Long's Hotel."

"He was mistaken. I never was at Long's Hotel in my life, although some of my friends did lodge there, an I know that there is such a place."

Had the intellectual keepers of the public peace been young country recruits just enlisted in the force, doubtless Will's confounded lying might have had the effect of putting them on the wrong scent— also, had they been open to a little bribery, a sovereign would have been wisely laid out.

But as it happened, to the swell thief's misfortune, they were old hands, and they would manfully have refused any offer likely to compromise their promotion in the service.

The swell thief was not long ere he reached Bow-street in company with his stalwart keepers, who were not likely to allow their prey to slip from their grasp.

For the enlightenment of those of our readers who have never been inside a police-station, we will relate exactly what occurred.

When the thief saw the entrance of the station, he very naturally shrunk back, and he might indeed have been compared to the poor sheep, which, being about to meet his doom in the slaughter-house, instinctively refuses to be driven into the place.

But, willingly or unwillingly, he had to find his way within the station-house.

Wild Will knew the place well.

Surrounded by the three constables the thief was brought before the inspector.

He was a man of about forty, dressed in the inspector's costume, and he happened to be sitting at a desk when Wild Will was brought before him.

"What's the charge?" he asked, in a slow, steady manner, while his eye was rivetted upon Will.

"Drunk and disorderly, sir; besides he created a great disturbance at the Argyll Rooms. He was very violent, and offered so great a resistance that three men were required to bring him here.",

The inspector entered "Drunk and disorderly" in the book, and then he proceeded to question the prisoner.

"What is your name?" he asked.

Wild Will, since he had entered the station, had not said a word.

"Captain de Vere."

"What regiment do you belong to?"

"I have left the service."

"Where do you live?"

"In Brompton."

"What part of Brompton?"

"Brompton-square."

Here the policeman, who had taken Wild Will in charge, spoke to the inspector.

That was enough for the official.

He had been told two or three things which the Captain heard unflinchingly.

The policeman had spoken about Long's Hotel, and such words "as an old offender" did not escape Will's hearing.

"Take him away," said the inspector, "and the magistrate will deal with him to-morrow."

"I want to get bail," said the swell thief.

The inspector laughed, closed his book, and disappeared in a closet close at hand.

Meanwhile Will was dragged along by the policeman.

He would not be locked up.

He would send for bail.

But the constable would not listen to him.

"I tell you that I am a gentleman. Will you let me go?"

Instead of taking any heed of the thief's words, the constable became still more and more silent.

Knowing him to be without anything to defend himself with, one of them was even kind enough to give him a box on the ear.

At length, after having crossed a small paved alley, where there were several cells all full, the thief was huddled downstairs in a dark vault.

He felt that resistance on his part would be useless, so he made no further attempt to free himself.

Shortly afterwards the door was closed with a loud bang. The key rattled ominously in the lock, and he sat down despondingly upon one of the wooden benches provided for the accommodation of those in a similar position as himself.

When alone Wild Will began to feel his face.

His left cheek was bleeding profusely from a scratch which he had received in the scuffle with the bobbies.

LOOK OUT FOR THE PLATE

GIVEN AWAY WITH NO. 17,

"A FIGHT IN THE THIEVES' DEN."

THE
DANCE OF DEATH;
OR,
THE HANGMAN'S PLOT.
A THRILLING ROMANCE OF TWO CITIES.

No. 17.]　　　　　SATURDAY, FEBRUARY 24, 1866.　　　　　[One Penny.

THE BOY KAY AND HIS ONLY FRIEND.

CHAPTER LXII.—Continued.

Besides, he ascertained that his clothes were torn to rags, to say nothing of his left eye, where he felt a very severe pain.

Yes, there he was.

Locked up.

With a scratch and a black eye.

And his garments torn up.

But Will had been in more than one predicament in his life, and he yet did not give up.

"I will look a picture to-morrow," he said, "when I go before the magistrate. Why he is sure to commit me. My appearance would be quite enough for him. With my features disfigured, with a black eye, and my torn clothes, who would believe in the best contrived tale on record?"

And in so thinking Wild Will was not far amiss.

It was bitter cold in his cell.

He walked up and down the limited space allotted, but uselessly ; he could not get warm.

Oh, that night ! would he ever forget it ?

How he longed for the morning.

Suddenly a shriek—it was a shriek—any other word would be inappropriate here—escaped him.

By a most extraordinary oversight he had not been searched.

There in his trousers pocket was the watch which he had " lifted " at the Argyll.

How should he get rid of it?

It would never do for him to keep it until the morning.

And, yet, should he leave it in his cell?

This he considered to be unadvisable in the extreme.

Now, there was one chance left to him.

In the morning he had a right to call for something to drink.

If he gave the money for a cup of coffee, or tea, whether a thief or not, he was entitled to it.

How long the hours seem to you in a police cell !

We do not wish any of our readers ever to undergo the same ordeal as Wild Will.

The swell thief laid himself upon the bench and tried to go to sleep.

But he could not.

The picture of Rosa Waters as she appeared to him on the evening when we saw him in the West-end resort galled his heart to the core.

She had insulted him.

Not only had she insulted him, but she had been the cause of his incarceration.

How he gnashed his teeth !

How he clenched his fist in his impotency !

Talk about the tiger in his cage—talk about the wild beast frustrated in his attempt to carry a prey to its lair—they are nothing to Wild Will.

He rose.

He paced up and down the cell.

Then he drew a long breath.

Tried to hear whether any sound would reach him.

But no.

All around him was silent as death.

" God !" muttered Will to himself ; " I have been here over seven hours. It was twelve o'clock when I was placed here. How long the time hangs upon my mind."

He was thus deliberating, when he heard the sound of footsteps, with which was mingled the rattle of a bunch of keys.

Then the door of his cell was opened.

It was the inspector taking his morning round.

" I would feel very much obliged to you, sir," said Wild Will, addressing the inspector, " if you were to have me removed upstairs. I am dying of cold here."

The swell thief's face was literally pale as a ghost, his lips were of a violet hue, his teeth chattered, and he looked supplicating indeed.

The inspector took active survey of his appearance.

He noticed the clotted blood on his cheek, where he had been scratched. He noticed his black eye, his tattered garments, and moved by an unusual feeling of pity, he granted his request.

We have heard of men having been condemned for

years to the gloomy retreat of solitary confinement.

What must be their feelings when again they see the light of day ?

For although Will had only been in darkness for a few hours, yet, when he saw the light his heart bounded within his breast, and he could not help thanking the inspector for his kindness in a few grateful words.

Wild Will was, therefore, removed upstairs and locked up in one of the ordinary cells for those who are confined for a few hours previous to obtaining bail.

He felt more at home now.

Once in his cell he waited.

Presently he again heard a constable coming round.

" I say, gov'nor," he said, " can I have bail ?"

" Bail? I don't know. I'll send you the messenger."

With these words the bobby, who was not a bad sort, departed.

The messengers at Bow-street police-station, or at any other station, are a curious type.

Sometimes, when the cells happen to be pretty full, they reap a golden harvest ; at others it is anything but a remunerative game.

For we must inform our friends that police-cells are not always occupied by tramps, vagrants, and vagabonds.

Many a gentleman has been locked up for a few hours.

Parties will get drunk and become noisy, and parties will accordingly be locked up, and be fined 2s. 6d. up to 40s. by the magistrate, according to the nature of the offence.

Thus, when there are many gentlemen locked up, the messenger makes rather a good thing of it.

The messenger on the present occasion was a man of about forty years of age, and his face, which was covered with a variety of pimples which are occasionally called " grog blossoms," testified to a strong taste for alcoholic beverages.

Whether he knew the real character of the swell thief we are not in a position to say, but what we can state here without fearing to be contradicted is that he did not let his manner betray his knowledge, if that knowledge he possessed.

Indeed, he was extremely civil.

" Well, captain," he said, " what can I do for you ? I have been up all night without a drop of anything, and I feel rather thirsty."

It was a very lucky thing for the captain that he happened to have had a few shillings left, otherwise it is highly probable that the messenger's politeness would have melted down before his want to stump up the needful, like the snow before the warmth of the meridian sun.

" I want you to go and get me something to drink first."

" What will you have, sir ? "

" Nice fellow you are to be sure, for you know very well that they will not allow you to bring in any spirits."

Here the messenger looked quickly around him.

" Let us have some money, captain," he said, " and I'll square it *with them* ; of course, ostensibly I'll go out for a cup of coffee for you."

" I am all right," said the swell thief to himself ; that chap is open to business."

And as a preliminary he gave a crown piece to the messenger, bidding him not to forget to have something for himself—a very unnecessary advice we feel perfectly confident.

The messenger took the money and mizzled.

Shortly afterwards he returned.

His breath this time testified to the opinion which any observer of his physiognomy would have formed concerning him, for a strong perfume of rum rose as he spoke to the thief.

He had brought a cup of tea and a slice of bread and butter, besides a small bottle of brandy cleverly concealed beneath his garments.

Captain de Vere thanked the messenger, and told him he could keep the change as he wanted him to go somewhere else for him.

CHAPTER LXIII.

THE MESSAGE—HOPE—THE ROUGH BOBBY.

Captain de Vere drank his coffee and his brandy with a great deal of gusto.

Having then refreshed himself he renewed the conversation with the messenger. who had just told him he must not keep him too long talking, otherwise *they* might smell a rat.

By *they* the messenger respectfully alluded to the constable.

"Do you know where Pimlico is?" asked the thief to the messenger.

"Pimlico is a large place, Captain. Which part of Pimlico do you mean?"

"Stanley-street."

"Right, sir!"

"I want you to go there at once."

"Very good, sir."

Wild Will always carried pencil and paper in his pocket.

He wrapped the watch in the paper, and upon a card bearing the name of Captain de Vere he scrambled a few hurried lines.

"Can I reckon upon you," he said, "to take this small parcel and this note to the address I'll give you?"

The messenger swore that he would go through fire and water to oblige the Captain.

The letter which Wild Will had written was the identical one which he subsequently sent to Mat, the Fence.

"If you deliver this message right for me," he said to the man, "when you return I will make you another present."

The messenger bowed, and sallied on his errand.

Now, we may be asked to whom had Will forwarded his epistle?

To the wife of the old miser who lived in the lone house, where he had paid a visit with Velvet.

The lady was one who made her living in a less dangerous way than her husband, but not a whit more creditable.

She kept a house where noblemen and men of means for a few trifling pounds could be accommodated with fresh country girls, who, once ruined, swelled the ranks of prostitution in this large city.

The messenger had been too well paid by Wild Will not to baffle the inquiries of the police.

Besides he never intended to deliver the parcel, as he believed there was something wrong about it.

When Wild Will had sent the messenger away he felt somewhat more comfortable.

He believed that his letter would be given to the party to whom it was addressed.

That it would be forwarded afterwards to Mat, the Fence, he had no doubt.

Whether the thieves would do their best to rescue him from the hands of the police he knew not, still he hoped they would.

Hope! This is, indeed, a word which cheers us on in life's vicissitudes. Hope! a word which revives the drooping spirits of the shipwrecked sailor drifting in unknown latitudes upon a frail piece of timber! Hope! which bids the ensign to look forward to the day when he may command a regiment. Hope! which whispers words of consolation in our ear, and helps us to battle against the tide of misfortune, and makes us see cheering prospects looming in the distance—prospects which tell us that there is a good time coming.

Hope was the only thing which kept up the courage and the self-possession of Wild Will.

Without it he would have found himself already undergoing penal servitude for a period of years, the number of which he dreaded to think upon.

The hour had passed. The messenger had not yet returned.

And shortly he would have to appear before the magistrate.

Before the beak, as that illustrious dispenser of the law is sometimes called.

Wild Will listened.

It struck ten o'clock.

The Court-house would shortly be opened, and he would be taken across the street, and have to stand upon his trial.

Should the detective whom he had baffled at Long's Hotel be there—and he had no doubt he would—he would be remanded.

Remanded!

These three syllables, which Wild Will kept on muttering to himself, made him shudder.

Remanded! This meant giving the police sufficient time to look into previous convictions.

How could he help it?

This was surely an impossibility?

He placed a bold face upon the matter, and as he was rather tired after his spree at the West-end, he flung himself upon his bench for the second time, and closed his eyelids.

Now, if he had twenty hours before him to while away, the probabilities are that he would have remained thinking, but as he had only twenty minutes. as a matter of course he was not long ere he fell in a comfortable doze.

He was just beginning to feel some relief from his rest, when he was suddenly awoke by a rough voice.

This was one of the policemen.

"Get up! Get up! Get up!" he said.

The thief fancied himself at his villa in Brompton.

"I don't want to be called just yet," he said. "Give us another look up in a couple of hours time."

The peeler thought that the fellow was chaffing him.

"I don't want you to be poking fun at me, you young fit for nothing scamp; just shake yourself up a bit. and come along with me."

But Will heard nothing.

Infuriated by what he believed to be contempt for the cloth which he wore, the enlightened member of the force dragged Wild Will towards him, never believing that he was soundly asleep.

This caused the thief to lose his balance, and to fall heavily upon the cold stone slabs.

Quickly he rose to his feet.

The fall had awoke him.

"What the devil are you after, man?" he asked.

"I am arter asking you to come with me, and as you took no heed of what I said I was going to make you."

"And where am I about to be taken?"

"Over the way!"

" Where's that ?"

" To•the police station, where the magistrate will be shortly sitting !"

The swell thief pulled himself together, and then under a strong escort he was led to a low entrance door, which happens to be the Court-house.

Among the spectators in the crowd he had recognised Mat, Bob O'Link, Big Ned, Monsieur Armand, and all the other members of the club.

" At all events," said he to himself, " the messenger has delivered my letter, for how could they all be here unless he had ?"

Wild Will was not wrong in his cogitations—the message had been given.

Thus we can account for the presence of the club.

CHAPTER LXIV.

THE POLICE COURT—BEFORE THE MAGISTRATE—THE BOYS ON THE QUI VIVE—THE FIGHT—THE RESCUE.

The doors of the police-court had but lately been opened when the swell thief was brought under strong escort to receive his sentence.

The magistrate was not yet sitting.

Meanwhile the court was rapidly filling with those extraordinary beings who are always to be found in the precincts where the law punishes those who have outraged it.

It was with a sigh of satisfaction also that Will saw that the Fence was present among the lookers-on, and had he been inclined to be down in the mouth, a further survey round, which exhibited to his view Bob O'Link and Big Ned, would have buoyed his heart with sanguine anticipations as to his prompt freedom.

It was a bold game on the part of the Hallelujah Club to come to the rescue of their pal, but they were venturing a chance which might or might not turn in their favour.

The public, with expectant ear and anxious looks, were gazing upon the various prisoners in the dock.

Besides Will there were several others who had infringed the law.

There was a woman of about twenty-five, who had been given in custody for obtaining goods under false pretences ; a cabman, who had been prevented by the authorities—and very wisely, too—to knock his wife's eyes out ; and an old lady of a very respectable appearance, indeed, who had been found lying in the gutter in a state of beastly drunkenness.

Soon there was a hum of voices, a commotion, and an *employé* bid silence in court.

This was the rising of the curtain.

Presently a little man, with a little nose, with little ferret eyes, with a little hair on his head and less still on his face, entered the court.

This was the magistrate.

He looked up and down, and on his left, then on his right, before him and behind him, fumbled about some papers on the desk facing him, was a long time ere he sat himself down to his heart's content ; but there is an end to everything, and when that end came he asked whether there was a heavy day on.

The clerk respectfully bowed, and appealed to the policeman ; the policeman appealed to the inspector, the inspector to another inspector ; and the magistrate, after a little delay, was told that there were several lengthy cases on hand.

Wild Will's case was not the first.

The lady who had obtained goods under false pretences was remanded ; the cabman was fined 40s.,

or forty hours' imprisonment, besides being required to find bail for his future good conduct ; and the old dame who was addicted to strong beverage and slept in the gutter, came off with a fine of 5s., besides being sternly reprimanded by the magistrate for the looseness of her habits.

Then came Wild Will's turn.

When he was placed at the bar loud laughter rose in court.

He looked indeed a curious specimen.

With the marks of violence which he bore on his features, and his torn coat, through which could be seen his shirt, his appearance was anything but prepossessing.

The clerk read the charge.

The magistrate steadfastly looked at the prisoner. Then he listened to what the constable had to say.

John Mulligan, of the X division, said—

" Your worship, last evening I was on duty in Windmill-street, when Detective Smith informed me that I was required. In company with Constable Manfield we went into the Argyll Rooms, where there was a great disturbance. The prisoner was holding a bottle in his hand and was about to hurl it at the head of a lady who was present there."

" Was the prisoner violent ?" asked his worship.

" Very violent, your worship, and he threatened to stab a nobleman, the Earl of Mountcarsden, who gave him in charge."

" Is the prosecutor present ?" asked his worship.

" No, your worship."

The magistrate reflected.

" Prisoner," he asked, " what have you got to say ?"

" Well, your worship," began Wild Will.

Here there was another loud laugh in the court, followed by shrieks and yells.

" Silence in court," said the clerk.

Again the shrieks and the yells increased.

" If this occurs again," pursued the magistrate, " I'll order the court to be cleared."

" Well, your worship," resumed Wild Will, " I grant that I was guilty of a little too much excess I had been dining with some friends at the club, and overshot the mark. We began with sherry, continued with brandy, and wound up with whisky. I regret very much what has taken place, and I'll do my best not to fall into a similar plight in the future."

The magistrate rubbed his chin and was about to pass sentence when he noticed Mulligan's anxiety to speak.

" What is it ?" he asked.

" This is a well-known thief, your worship ; he has been convicted before, and I would ask for a remand to make inquiries concerning him."

Instead of fining the prisoner five shillings for being drunk and disorderly, as it had been his first intention, the magistrate granted the remand.

Wild Will tried to say a word or two, but the magistrate having spoken he was taken out of the dock, and another person walked in his place.

And now the most important portion of this scene requires to be told.

No sooner had the magistrate granted the remand than from the space allotted for the public emerged at least a dozen individuals.

Bob O'Link and Frank Pullen leading the way.

So quick had been their movements that they were only perceived when it was too late to prevent what they wished to do.

The thieves all crowded round Wild Will.

When the swell thief saw this unexpected assistance you may rest assured that he did not remain idle.

He tried to extricate himself from the hands of the police.

Happily he succeeded in doing so.

The staff which Mulligan wore was taken from him by Bob O'Link, and with it he inflicted a severe blow at the back of the head of the constable.

This felled him to the ground, where he remained senseless.

The magistrate knew not how to act.

The public offered no help to the force.

They evidently were accomplices of the thieves.

But if they were not it looked extremely like it.

We don't know whether any of our readers have ever seen a fight between bulldogs.

If they have, will they not grant that it is indeed a merciless struggle between them.

They growl, howl, and bite each other in furious style, and instead of confessing themselves beaten they keep at it with a courage truly astonishing.

To a fight between bulldogs we might have compared the struggle between the constables and the Hallelujah Club.

But it could not last very long.

Policy and prudence are the best parts of valour.

Two of the constables were now *hors de combat.*

Wild Will, meanwhile, owing to the disturbance which had taken place, very wisely had taken to his heels.

A reinforcement of constables soon came from over the way.

But by the time they reached the battle field they found that the thieves had flown.

Profiting by the confusion which had ensued, one after the other had quietly gone out; and when the bobbies came they took into custody the first men, women, and boys who came within their grasp.

The business of the court was interrupted for a while.

Then the magistrate's clerk was asked to identify any of the persons arrested.

But neither he nor the magistrate could swear as to their being the individuals who had taken part in the scuffle, so they were liberated.

The force foamed with rage. One and all swore that if they once more caught the swell thief they would murder him.

But little did he care for what they said.

The object of these execrations was far away.

And by the time the court was cleared Wild Will was in the Thieves' Kitchen, surrounded by the whole of his mates, and laughing boisterously over the day's adventures.

One person was expected by the Fence.

This was Spanton, and he had not yet reported progress, as he had promised to do.

CHAPTER LXV.

THE GAY WOMAN TAKES A FANCY TO VELVET—MRS. ST. GILES—THE SUPPER—POPPING ONE'S WATCH—FOUR POUNDS TO THE GOOD — THE COLLOQUY — VELVET IN STANLEY-STREET.

By a strange coincidence it just came to pass that on the night when Wild Will was arrested on the charge of the Earl of Mountcarsden, Velvet, who had no home in London, was very fortunately for himself taken good care of by Baby Jordan.

This young lady had not fallen in love with the boy, but she had taken a great fancy to him.

Very fast women in London are very often fond of that sort of thing.

To satisfy the cravings of their corrupt passions they do not want men who are so courted by society as to look upon them as a toy—men who, favoured by the wheel of fortune, can grant any desire which flits across their mind. They would rather have some youth upon whom their dazzling toilets would make some impression—some boy like Velvet, with whom they could amuse themselves, taking pleasure in perverting his morals and drawing the bloom from his rosy cheek—like the bee which sucks the honey from the flower, or more accurately speaking the rattlesnake, which instils his venomed poison in the heart of the unconscious traveller, sheltering beneath the shady foliage of the clustering branches of the mighty trees.

Baby Jordan had seen Velvet parting company with the individual whom she knew as Captain de Vere, and she had noticed him at the Argyll Rooms retiring to take a seat upon a lonely bench.

A woman like the fast lady to whom we are now alluding does not care about what she does—money to her is at times no object. Easy it comes, easy it goes. Thus. although there was a gentleman speaking to her, and wanting to have supper with her, yet she had made up her mind to take the boy home with her.

And leave a woman of the town alone for doing what she wishes to do.

The reasons for our alluding once more to Baby Jordan will shortly be paramount to our readers.

Shortly before the Argyll Rooms closed, and by the time that Wild Will was brought before the inspector at Bow-street, Baby, in a casual manner, wound her way towards the spot where Velvet was sitting.

"Where's your friend Captain de Vere?" she asked of the boy.

The woman knew that he had got into trouble, but it did not suit her purpose to acquaint him with that which had taken place.

Velvet had been so engrossed with the music, had been so busy in looking at the strange capers of the dancers below, that the row which had been enacted not a hundred yards from him had escaped his notice.

"I don't know," replied Velvet. "I expect him back every minute."

"You do?"

"Yes."

"Are you going back to your hotel?" she asked.

Velvet blushed crimson.

When we are in fault—when we have done something wrong—so even when we are in a position which we wish to keep a secret from strangers, we think that everybody surrounding us knows our business.

Velvet believed that Baby was aware of the character of the swell thief, and that she was speaking to him as she did with the purpose of quizzing him.

"To my hotel?" he asked evasively.

His indeed was an hotel! The street for a shelter, some dark alley for a bedroom.

For he knew not yet that a boy with anything valuable about him can at any time of day or night obtain money for it in London, or any other town for that matter.

If he had been cute he would not have been very slow in finding out the value of the gold watch which he had in his pocket, and he would have got money for it.

But suppose he was. He was not ignorant of his property being a stolen watch.

He would therefore have dreaded entering a place of amusement.

For should suspicion be aroused?

What then?

Inquiries would be instituted, and he feared the result.

Baby Jordan sat beside the boy.

"Will you come home with me?" she asked.

Velvet knew not what to say.

It is all very well for fellows who have been knocking about town all their life to tell us that a boy would not be shy before a girl.

We remember ourselves about ten years ago.

Alas! our minds then were not so depraved!

We had not gone through great wealth—sickening poverty. We believed in the world. Our sanguine aspirations had not been damped by a thorough knowledge of life. We had not witnessed the scenes which we have since. We had not mingled so freely as we have done with the high and the low. We had not been admitted into the lady of title's boudoir and the courtezan's lodgings. We had not learnt that money rules the world—that a man with it is respected, courted, admired, sought—without it abused, condemned, despised.

Then we were boys!

Our minds soared high. In the distant regions of the future we thought we could see a reward for energy, talent, and labour.

We were mistaken.

"_Errare humanum est,_" say the Latin words.

He was one out of many. Why, then, complain?

Like we should have done when our imaginations were young and pure, so Velvet did.

He felt small before the courtezan.

"Will," he began, but then suddenly he corrected himself,—"my friend is sure to come back again."

"But if he does not?"

Velvet paused.

"But if he does not," repeated the woman, "will you come with me?"

Still the boy made no reply.

The wily Child of Sin took the boy's hand in her own.

But Velvet was uneasy.

He was thinking of the girl Nancy whom he loved with all the ardour of youth—Nancy whom he would have given all he possessed to see once more.

The orchestra ceased. The National Anthem was played. Slowly and gradually the votaries of pleasure left the hall.

And Velvet and Baby found themselves together.

The only two beings left in the Argyll Rooms.

The waiter who saw them sitting together approached.

"Now, ladies and gentlemen," he said, "will you be kind enough to leave? We are about to close."

"Come on," said Baby.

Velvet rose, and mechanically taking Baby's arm, he walked outside with her.

A well-appointed brougham waited in the street.

"Jump in," said Baby.

Velvet was lost in wonder.

What could all this mean?

Yes, he was now in a dream.

He had come in a brougham with a swell thief.

He went away in a brougham with a gay woman. To him it was a riddle.

London was an unaccountable place.

He could not make it out.

He had been among thieves, he had been tramping wearily in the streets, he had slept in a workhouse, he had been unable to obtain a crust of bread, he had been refused honest employment, and yet those who seemed to prey upon the vices of humanity, or to baffle her laws, like the gallant Captain managed to do, thrived gloriously.

The brougham rattled swiftly over the pavement.

The drive did not last above half an hour.

Then the vehicle stopped in Stanley-street, Pimlico.

At the very house, reader, where Wild Will had sent a message in the morning.

But the Baby did not know that.

The miser's wife opened the door.

"Who have you got there?" she asked, eyeing Baby's companion.

"A young swell whom I saw with a fellow who calls himself Captain de Vere."

"And where is Captain de Vere?" asked the landlady.

Baby then related to the tax-payer all that had taken place.

Mrs. St. Giles laughed with a hearty, strong, good laugh.

St. Giles was the name under which the miser's wife was known.

In reading some old romance which she was in the habit of hiring for a penny a volume from the Circulating Library, she had noticed that name.

St. Giles sounded aristocratic to her, and she had assumed it.

"The fellow is in trouble again," she said, "just like him. But he is sure to get out of it, for he is a broth of a boy, and he would beat an Irishman any day to get in a mess and out of it with the same alacrity."

To relate here what passed between Velvet and Baby Jordan would, we believe, be perfectly useless.

We might then be accused of immorality, and justly, too, the critics would blame us for describing that which it is an author's duty to hint at, and a reader's intelligence to fathom.

Suffice it to say that Baby understood hospitality, and as Velvet was what they term "her spooney man," she took very good care that he should have a very nice supper and any amount of port wine, conducive, we believe, to the health and strength of those who have arduous duties to perform.

At about twelve o'clock next morning Velvet rose.

He told Baby that he was in want of money, and asked her what he was to do.

Now, a few hours before, it is highly probable that this lady would have placed a few shillings at his disposal did he want them, but after what had transpired she thought otherwise when the question was placed to her.

"You have got a watch," she said. "I'll get it 'popped' for you. Let me have a look at it?"

"What do you mean by 'popped'?" asked Velvet innocently.

"Send it to your uncle, of course."

"I have no uncle in town."

Baby could not help laughing.

"Oh, yes, you have," she said. "Any one who carries a watch about him need never be in want of that accommodating relative."

After a few words more of explanation Velvet then gleaned the purport of the courtezan's remark.

"Oh, send it to be 'popped' by all means," he said. "The watch is useless to me. I would rather have the money."

Baby looked at the ticker.

"Damn my eyes,
    If ever I tries,
    To rob a poor boy of his lever,"

she said playfully. "No kid about it either. Why it is a first-rate watch that. You will get at least five or six pounds upon it at the pawn-shop."

"Will I?"

"Yes."

"Send it there, then, by all means."

Baby rang the bell, and an old girl of about forty years appeared.

She was the servant.

" What's it, Missus ?" she asked.

" Take this round to the corner."

" How much am I to ask, ma'am ?"

" As much as you can get ; but here, before you go, there is a penny for the ticket."

The servant collared the copper.

And without another word she took her departure. Evidently she was accustomed to that sort of thing.

Five minutes passed.

Then the menial returned.

Baby had not been far out in her calculation.

She had five pounds ten shillings.

She gave the money and the ticket to Baby.

The woman handed it to the owner.

Velvet reckoned his coin.

" Give the girl something for cleaning your boots," said Baby.

Velvet parted with half a dollar like a man.

Then his feeling told him that since Baby had been the means of getting some money which he otherwise would not have had, he had better make her a present of something too.

So when he had settled all claims he found himself in the possession of four pounds nett.

To him that was a fortune.

With it he intended to go in search of Nancy.

His adventure with Baby was only one of those things which no one could help, and it had not diminished the sincere affection which he entertained for the girl whom he had met, and whose forlornness had greatly moved him.

He was just on the eve of departing when Mrs. St. Giles rushed into the room.

" I hope he will get off," she said hurriedly. " I hope he will get off."

" Who ?" asked Baby.

" Captain de Vere."

The heart of Velvet sank within his breast.

Once more was he to fall in his hands ?

For the benefit of Baby Jordan Mrs. St. Giles related in a half whisper the incarceration of the thief, the letter she had received, and the bold attempt which his mates would make to rescue him from the hands of the police.

Although Velvet appeared to be perfectly unconcerned, yet he listened to everything, and he now accounted for the mysterious disappearance of the swell thief.

But he was too clever to let any words escape his lips by which the old lady might have guessed the relation which existed between himself and Captain de Vere.

If he had done so he feared that his departure would have been delayed, and that again he should be thrown in the company of Wild Will.

The conference between Baby and Mrs. St. Giles lasted for some time.

Gay women have no intellectual occupation by which they can while away the hours of day. It is idleness and love and display which bring two-thirds of the prostitutes to grief.

So when Velvet saw that with her drop of gin by her side, which she had poured from a bottle which never left her, Mrs. St. Giles was in for a long gossip, he thought that this was a favourable opportunity for him to leave.

" I have some business to attend, Baby," he said. " I must be away for the present. I'll see you again before long."

The final kiss which is given by the woman with whom you have stayed for hours was then, in the usual course, imprinted by the rakish woman upon the boy's lips, and, having bowed and wished good day to Mrs. St. Giles, Velvet took his departure.

" Dear, I hope you will come again," were the last words which smote Velvet's ears as he left the gay woman's sanctum, and, quickening his steps, soon found himself in the street.

Before he sallied on what might well be termed " a goose errand," namely, in search of the girl Nancy, Velvet halted a few yards from the house.

His hand made his way to his waistcoat pocket and he drew his money.

His coin was right.

" I have four sovereigns on hand," he said. " Will it do me good, although it has been acquired through foul means ?"

And he shook mournfully his head and walked onwards.

CHAPTER LXVI.

VELVET IN SEARCH OF NANCY—THE WATERSIDE—THE DARK ARCHES—THE GIRL IN A SWOON—THE TWO POLICEMEN—ONCE MORE TOGETHER.

Unless Providence watched over the steps of man and guided him in the direction where it decides that he shall go, it would be an impossible task for many to accomplish the wondrous deeds which are every day performed.

On the same principle had Velvet told a stranger that he was going to try to discover the whereabouts of the girl Nancy he would have laughed at him and advised him to give up a task which, in the face of the difficulties which he had to encounter, would have seemed to him to be madness to attempt.

Nevertheless, Velvet would have persevered.

Something told him that ere long he would meet the partner of his sorrows.

But for this paramount idea, which was deeply rooted in his mind, he would not have sallied onward as hopefully as he did, and with so steady and so brisk a step.

But there have been, since the world has been created, instances where superior minds have unravelled before others the cloudy cipher lost in the mist of the future — minds who, although they were ridiculed by their fellow creatures, have prophesied for themselves things which no one would credit.

For take two Emperors of modern times—Napoleon the First and Napoleon the Third, the reigning sovereign of France. If we must believe history, the first Emperor, when at the Military School of Brienne, a mere student, dreamt of the Imperial purple, of battles fought and won as if they were already accomplished facts ; and his nephew, when walking through the streets of London with his acceptances which no money lender would cash, often said that one day he would be Emperor of the French.

We have mentioned these two incidents to show to our readers that if Velvet had one idea, and that if he felt confident of carrying it out, he was no exception to the rule.

But it does not follow that all sanguine imaginations—and, alas ! there are many—are certain to see at some time or another the realisation of the castles in the air which they may have built.

We take individual cases—with those we deal, and with those only.

There is no place in the world, we believe, more lonely than London, or any large town, for a stranger, or, even worse, for one who has no friends, no money, and is penniless.

The latter was not Velvet's case : but, with the

exception of the thieves, and the old lady in Bond-street with whom he had lodged, and to whose house he was ashamed to return, Velvet could not be said to have any one in London who wished him well.

Little, indeed, did the poor boy know the changes which had taken place in Bournemouth since he had left the village.

Could he have seen his mother in that house in Ratcliffe Highway where we paid a visit, how he would have wept.

This knowledge might have hindered the course of the stirring events which we are about to relate.

Velvet walked on, and walked on, until night came.

Not being thoroughly acquainted with the ins and outs of London town he was apt to lose himself.

And that he did.

The shades of night were beginning to fall, the sky obscured by passing clouds looked inky and ominous, and a damp fog was mingling with the evening's dark shrouds when Velvet stopped in h s wanderings and looked about and around him.

Not very far from the spot where he stood he thought that he could hear the splash of water.

Mechanically he advanced in the direction from which the sound advanced.

Why he did so he knew not.

As he paced slowly forward he saw a heavy mist rising from the water, and after looking around him he discovered that he was treading beneath the arches of a bridge.

How he had come there all the way from Pimlico he could not account, but being a stranger in London he had allowed his feet to guide him wherever they would.

Before Velvet rolled the Thames slowly and silently, and occasionally a gust of wind would drive a splash of water at his feet

He was beneath Waterloo Bridge.

"Who brought you hither, and what are you doing, young man?" were the words which suddenly attracted Velvet's attention.

He raised his head and was about to reply, when the yellow rays of a policeman's bull's-eye shone right in his face.

"I lost myself," said Velvet, "and I would like very much to find my way out of this place."

The constable was about to give Velvet the required information when another constable laid his arm upon the boy's shoulder.

"Holloa!" he said. "What's that? Have you done it ?"

As he spoke the policeman pointed to something at his feet.

That something, reader, was a handsome girl of about eighteen years of age fully stretched upon her back and evidently in a swoon.

The wavy tresses of her luxuriant hair fell in abundant clusters over her features, and to all outward appearance it would seem that life had forsaken the frail tenement where it once dwelt in all the prime of youthful energy.

Her face was pale as death, her lips were colourless, and her hand, which one of the constables took in his own, was of a ashy whiteness.

She seemed to be exhausted, for her weary eyelids were closed, and not a movement did she make at the time when she happened to be discovered.

"Is she dead?" asked Velvet, his heart beating fast as he recognised, by the light of the bull's-eye, the features of the girl whom he sought.

Poor Nancy !

One of the constables meanwhile had been raising the girl within his arms from the cold steps where she lay.

"I think not, my boy," kindly replied the constable. "The heart still beats."

It was a prayer of thanks which issued from the poor boy's lips as the welcome tidings dispelled from his mind the sad forebodings which had usurped it.

"Do you know her?" the fellow policeman asked of Velvet, seeing the attention with which he was gazing upon the girl.

"I do," said Velvet boldly, "and she's a good, honest-hearted lass, and, if you will allow me, I'll take care of her."

"Got any money to spare?" asked the policeman, while he was trying to restore consciousness to the forlorn maiden.

"A little—not much : but quite enough for us two."

The constable looked suspiciously at the boy.

"Where did you first meet her?" he queried.

The catechising look of the constable was one which no thief would have forgotten in a hurry, and as Velvet happened. against his will it is true, to belong to the confraternity, he thought that he should tell a white lie to prevent, if possible, the girl and himself being taken to the station-house, when, doubtless, his whereabouts and his doings would have been looked into.

"I was in service at a nobleman's house in Belgrave-square, and she was my fellow-servant. She was housemaid there.

This answer from Velvet had been so quickly given that it would have deceived many.

"You know her friends, of course, if such is the case ?"

"I do," said Velvet.

"And how would you account for her being here ?"

Velvet was not backward in telling one or two good ones, you know, when he had something in view.

"Don't speak too loud," he said. "She might hear you."

"What about that ?"

"Occasionally she is taken with fits of madness, and when that's the case, don't you see, she runs away from home."

"I see," said one constable.

"What a pity! Such a nice girl, too!" echoed his companion.

One of the policemen had placed his cloak on Nancy's shoulders.

Gradually she recovered.

Presently she opened her eyes, and a smile played upon her lips.

Then she held out her hand to the boy.

Velvet clasped it to his breast.

"Nancy," he said, "I am glad I have found you at last. How came you——"

Nancy placed her finger upon her mouth, as if to enjoin silence.

The constables saw her movement.

"How do you feel now, miss?" one said. "If we had not seen you, the tide would have gone over you and washed you in the Thames."

A shudder crept over the boy's frame as he looked upon the dark waters gliding past him, and a harrowing pain shot to his heart while he thought what Nancy's fate might have been but for his being the means of finding her in the romantic manner we have described.

N.B.—*Owing to delay on the Artist's part, we are reluctantly compelled to postpone our Presentation Plate for a week or two.*

THE DANCE OF DEATH;

OR,
THE HANGMAN'S PLOT.
A THRILLING ROMANCE OF TWO CITIES.

No. 18.]   SATURDAY, MARCH 3, 1866.   [ONE PENNY.

THE THIEVES' DEN.

CHAPTER LXVI.—CONTINUED.

"What shall we do with her?" said one of the constables to the other. "Is it necessary to take her to the station-house?"

"Oh! for Heaven's sake, do not do that," said Velvet; "she is a respectable girl; I'll see her home.

In the meantime we will go and have a cup of something to drink somewhere."

Nancy had risen, and she stood glancing at the boy who once more had come to her rescue.

"Thanks, young man, I've just had my tea," now replied the bobby to Velvet; "but if you have the price of a pint of beer, I and my mate will go and have it together."

Fearing that the two constables might alter their minds, Velvet readily took some loose silver out of his pocket, and gave a shilling to be divided between them.

Then, without any noticeable hurry, he wished them good-bye, and, accompanied by Nancy, he ascended the staircase which led to the bridge, and after having walked for a few minutes, they entered the first coffee-shop they came to.

Velvet was now satisfied.

The policemen were far away—he had money in his pocket—and Nancy was with him; and what was more, he believed that all his troubles were over.

Let us hope for the boy's sake that he was not in the wrong.

CHAPTER LXVII.

NANCY AND VELVET MEET WITH AN ADVENTURE—THE BAND OF MASKED MEN.

As we have not sufficient space here to give to our readers all the details we should like to, we will content ourselves by saying that in answer to Velvet's numerous queries as to the manner in which Nancy had lived since she had been taken from him and flung into a carriage, to be driven Heaven only knew where, the girl replied that it was the very foreigner from whose grasp Velvet had once before rescued her who had made another attempt to compel her to yield to a loathsome proposal, which she had rejected with disdainful haughtiness.

She subsequently related to him that, owing to the proud manner with which she had spurned his advances, he had given strict injunctions to have her confined to a bedroom, and fed upon bread and water only.

By depriving Nancy of society, and refusing to her all the necessaries of life, he had hoped to win from her, after many days' expectation, that which he required.

"And how did you manage to get away from him?" asked Velvet.

"My bedroom," replied Nancy, "was situated upon the first floor. More than once I tried to escape, but unsuccessfully. At last, one dark, cloudy evening, I saw a good opportunity. I tore the sheets off my bed, and tying them together, I let myself down in the street. I was just in time, for no sooner was I safe than I heard cries and exclamations. I had been discovered; so I ran and ran onward until I could run no longer."

"And what did you do for a living, Nancy?"

In reply to the boy's query, Nancy acquainted Velvet with the fact that, after a great deal of trouble, she had obtained a situation in a coffee-shop.

She further told him that, for all the work she had done, she had only been provided with her food, and that, after having exerted herself to her utmost to please everybody, she had been compelled to leave the place, owing to the bad character of the house.

Velvet listened with interest to the details which Nancy was giving him, and after he had made arrangements with the landlady for two separate bedrooms for the night, and paid for the same in advance, he proposed a stroll in the Strand, in the neighbourhood of which stood the place where the two beings had taken their temporary quarters.

The evening, which at first had been bright and clear, was now dark and chill—the heavens were deprived of the slightest appearance of a star—and the moon had long ago climbed up in the lowering inky clouds, which foreboded the approach of a

storm; but so enraptured with each other's society were the young couple, that they did not notice the change in the atmosphere, and found themselves in the heart of the city ere they thought themselves above a mile from their abode.

They had been over two hours in the street, and perhaps they would have forgotten even that had not the belfry of St. Paul's Cathedral reminded them with its loud hum that it was past the hour of midnight.

"How late it is, to be sure!" said Nancy, clinging close to Velvet; "it is time to return home."

Velvet and Nancy were now in a very deserted part of the city. Around them everything was as still as death. It was one of those spots where there is nothing but warehouses, which, in the day full of industrious artisans, are at night deserted and gloomy.

The gaslight—and it was the only one to be seen for a considerable distance—cast a lurid yellow glare upon Nancy's countenance, and owing to the light which it reflected upon the girl's features, Velvet noticed that her eyes shone piercingly and that her lips were blanched with fear.

"What's the matter with you, Nancy?" the boy asked. "Surely you are not afraid?"

The girl replied in the negative, but the tremor of her voice belied her words.

And how can we account for Nancy's forebodings?

Easily enough, friend and reader. Nancy of late had been so ill-treated by Fate or Providence, or whatever people like to call it, that she imagined she saw danger everywhere.

"Let us get out of this place quickly," said Nancy. "Methinks—"

And here a startled shudder crept over the girl's frame and she feared to speak.

"What?" asked the youth.

"Listen."

Velvet and Nancy relaxed their speed and stood still.

Close to them could be heard the tramp of footsteps, and the subdued whispers of several men.

Had it been a moonlight night the boy would not have minded those ominous signs, but where everything around you is of an inky darkness it, indeed, leads you to believe matters to be worse than they really are; and although Velvet tried to conceal from his companion the fact that he coincided with her in the truth of her remarks, yet he now regretted very much having sallied out totally unprovided with any weapon wherewith he could defend himself in case of attack.

Property in the days of which we write—and it is not so many years ago either—was not as safe as it is now. Burglaries, highway robberies, and even body-snatching were of common occurrence, and bold, indeed, was he who ventured out at night without having first loaded a pair of pistols to preserve his purse and person from the lawless attacks which were often made against both.

And Velvet thought that most likely, indeed, there was something wrong on hand—perhaps some burglary, or even an attempt at murder—for now that he glanced around him he remembered that he was standing in the rear of the warehouse of one of the wealthiest jewellers of the period.

While thus musing his arm was squeezed by Nancy, and drawing herself close to him she muttered in his ear to look right ahead.

"Well, Nancy, what is it?" asked the boy, trying to appear bold.

"Don't you see them there beneath that doorway yonder?"

Faintly, and in a scarcely audible tone of voice had the girl spoken, yet her words were heard by Velvet, and his glance uneasily wandered in the direction to which she had alluded.

Then a heavy sigh escaped his lips and for an instant he stood transfixed with fear, his feet rooted to the ground.

"There," said Nancy, again pointing to a group in the distance.

What was Velvet to do?

He could no longer be mistaken.

For not ten yards distant before him he could see a band of *masked men* holding in their hands glittering poniards, and all the various implements necessary for a burglary.

CHAPTER LXVIII.

VELVET IS ABOUT TO SHOW FIGHT—A SETTLER—THE VIOLIN CASE—WHATS TO BE DONE—THE COMMITTEE—THE PRESIDENT—A CONVERSATION INTERRUPTED.

Evidently Nancy's words had been heard by some one keeping watch on behalf of the band, for no sooner had she spoken than a pocket handkerchief was placed across her mouth, and she was dragged away from Velvet.

The lad remonstrated, and was about to show fight, when he felt the cold steel of the barrel of a pistol upon his forehead, while his hands were simultaneously fastened together by some unknown foe, who had unaware pounced upon him behind his back.

This was a settler.

A settler of which the force was further increased by the following words, "Say not a word, or you are a gone coon," pronounced by a voice which Velvet thought was familiar to him.

And he had scarcely recovered from his surprise ere he was surrounded by at least a dozen individuals, young and old, tall and short,—at least so Velvet thought—having no means of judging with certainty, their features happening to be concealed by black masks, all of one size, and of one shape.

"Settle him, settle him!" now whispered one of the masked individuals. "'Tis a spy, and he is here to betray us."

"I am not a spy; you lie in your teeth whoever you are," defiantly retorted Velvet, drawing himself to his full height, while in his impotent rage his lip quivered at the undeserved slur he was compelled to put up with.

"Bravely spoken! By the lord Harry, he tells no lie either," pursued a third mask. "Death to him who says that Velvet is a spy; by God I tell you he is one of our mates. What the devil brings you hither at this hour of night?"

Had a thunder bolt fallen at Velvet's feet he could not have been more astonished.

The last speaker was no other than Bob O'Link.

Velvet opened his eyes wide, and inquired after Nancy.

"Be not afraid, my lad," said the Fence, advancing towards the boy, "I'll see that no harm will be done to her, but she must play her part, and become useful to us?"

"In what way?" asked Velvet.

"That's my business, not yours, and do not bandy any more words uselessly, for silence is the motto for a few hours at least."

As he spoke Mat glanced meaningly upon a violin case which he carried beneath his arm.

To a casual observer it would only have led him to believe that within the same was a musical instrument, but as we happen to know what were the contents of the "violin case" we will tell our readers the truth.

The violin was nothing else than a crowbar, made in pieces so as to be carried in a manner which would not be awkward to the bearer.

The burglars, for we cannot be mistaken in telling those who have the patience of perusing us that they were such, now formed themselves in a committee.

The Fence, as a matter of course, had the rank of a president.

"This is the house, my boys," he said, turning round to the lads who were gathering round him, "but we have got to enter without making too much noise."

"Who's to keep watch, Mat?" Big Ned sharply asked. "The 'wandering blue' is on to night here, and I am sure that he will keep a sharp look out. I know what I heard but a few days ago; he means that he will have us all locked up."

"He will if he can, I have no doubt," chimed Bob, "for I do not think that he will ever forget that memorable day when I introduced my bootmaker to his tailor, and gave him one on the knob which he is not likely to forget."

The Hallelujah Club laughed.

They did not forget that incident which we have described in a previous part of this story, when Velvet was rescued from the bobbies by the gallant behaviour of the boys.

"Yes, said the Fence, he was rather slack at one time, but now by —— he does his duty, and nobody can deny that to him, but we must *do* him nevertheless."

Then Mat mused for a few instants.

"Who shall I appoint to keep watch? We are all known by the 'slops.'"

"No, we are not!"

"Who is there, then?"

"Velvet. He is rather a sharp one, too, and he has eyes like a ferret."

"Why, that chap?"

"Bob, you are a valuable fellow. That's the ticket. We must make him as useful as he is ornamental."

"Hark!" now said the boy Kay, rushing up to the Fence, "I think I hear him."

"Nonsense; he just came round."

"Perhaps he suspects."

Then they all listened.

Sure enough the measured, steady, unmistakable tramp of the constable was plainly heard in the distance.

But should the boys have been deaf they could not also have been blind.

And if the warning was not enough, what was the meaning of that yellow glare lighting the pavement?

But one thing could produce it, and could it have been anything else than the bull's-eye?

Slowly, yet steadily, the constable was advancing.

But the Hallelujah Club was not composed of individuals who would wait to wish good evening to a chap who was in for "business."

"Godstruth!" whispered Big Ned, "that's him."

All the things which we are describing took place in much less time than we can take to commit them to paper.

No sooner had the word been given than all these gentlemen parted.

Where did they go?

We are unable to tell.

Under doorways, crouching beneath the shadows of the shutters, seeking refuge in a bye lane, anywhere but in the immediate vicinity of the policeman did these distinguished gentlemen slimly betake themselves away.

And little, indeed, did the wandering blue suspect that but a few yards from him the Hallelujah Club mustered in strength.

Little, indeed, did he suspect that a daring robbery was about to take place.

Velvet, meanwhile, was anything but pleased at the turn of his midnight stroll.

Mournfully he was shaking his head.

Go wherever he would it looked very much as if he was doomed to fall in with bad companions.

Big Ned knew that if he gained an opportunity "to cut" he was not the boy to lose it; so, foreseeing all, in due course the bully stuck to the boy like a leech.

Thus, when Velvet had learnt from the other that the bobby was close at hand, he took to his heels in gallant style.

When one's freedom is threatened he is not very particular as to what he does, and he had to put up with Big Ned's companionship.

He would have preferred any one else besides him, but the option had been denied to him.

Big Ned was not one to spoil matters by too much impatience.

For everything he did he took his time, and firmly believed in the fact that too much hurry is anything but productive of success.

Velvet and Big Ned remained together for about six minutes.

They were at the end of some court, whose name they did not happen to know themselves.

"Let me see—think," said Big Ned, "it is time for us to return to the crib."

Velvet, in reply to Ned, made no objection.

Big Ned had been longer in the world than he had; his experience, therefore, was more to be relied upon than his own, and he, in conclusion, fully conceded whatever his companion suggested.

While the thieves had been away the bobby had made his app arance.

He had carefully and slowly looked before, behind, and around him.

Brought his lamp downwards and upwards against the door of the jeweller's warehouse, and finally stopped to listen, to hear whether any sounds would reach him.

But hearing nought he was soon away from the spot where a few minutes after his departure the band were once more together.

CHAPTER LXIX.

THE FENCE BEGINS WORK—THE BOY KAY FALLS IN
LOVE—THE HOUSE ENTERED.

The time was pressing, and unless the Fence gave immediate instructions for entering the dwelling — before which the Club were standing—the morning would leave the thieves still deliberating, and without having obtained the booty for which they longed.

The cracking of the jeweller's crib was a work which, if it was likely to prove remunerative, was also strewn with difficulties.

In many instances where houses—either those of tradesmen or of private individuals—are broken into, bribery is set to work beforehand, and the burglar has but little to do, since he has agents inside to make everything smooth for him.

But in the present emergency the Fence had no one to rely upon except himself and the help of the young thieves, who were not likely to be found wanting in the hour of need.

To force your way into a city warehouse, which is generally so well watched, is by no means an easy task; besides, you should bear in mind the fact that occasionally there are heavy iron shutters which protect the windows from any attempt which would be likely to be made against them.

After the Fence had satisfied himself that there was no one in the immediate vicinity, and he had posted several members of the tribe at various spots to keep a sharp look-out, he very coolly opened the violin case, and from it withdrew a bunch of skeleton keys, and several iron bars, which, being joined together, one would have fancied would rend the mouth of a cannon asunder, so powerful was the bar on its outward appearance, and so likely did it seem to level all impediments.

"Lay hold of this, Jack," the Fence said, turning round to the Cannibal, and handing him the box to which we have alluded, "in the meantime, I'll speak to the lass."

By the lass, the Fence meant Nancy, who was safely guarded by the boy Kay, who was an admirer of beauty whenever he saw it.

But, unfortunately, Nancy did not think much of Master Kay.

He looked such a thorough rogue that she could not buckle to him; whether he was *de facto* or not will be told in the course of this tale, when the true story of the boy Kay, as related to us by his own lips, will be graphically described for the benefit of our readers.

At the time, when Mat crossed the street and went over to the spot where Nancy was standing, he discovered that Kay was not very mindful of his business, since he was trying very hard to get a kiss from Nancy, an attempt in which he not only met with a signal failure, but also with a very good smack, which the girl gave him on the left ear.

Kay did not seem to relish the punishment, and being rather hot-tempered, it is very likely that he would have tried to revenge himself against Nancy, had not the sudden arrival of Mat stayed his intention, should it have been such.

"Is this the way you are looking after my interest, you young varmint!" said Mat, and but for the sudden abject appeal he made for mercy, the hero of the Lambeth Workhouse would very probably have got another thump.

Kay swore that he was only "having a lark," and said that the girl had provoked him.

Upon which statement, Mat, in a very gentlemanly manner, called him a "sanctified liar," and told him to mind what he was about, as he did not wish for any more of his tarnation humbug.

All the little details which as faithful chroniclers we are jotting down upon paper did not take long to be enacted; still we relate them not to skip any incidents, which, however trifling they may appear at first, can nevertheless be looked upon as criterions of the characters of the strange beings who figure in our narrative.

The end of this was that the boy Kay was left to himself, and Nancy was led away by the Fence before the entrance of the jeweller's warehouse.

At first she felt somewhat inclined to resist, but after having heard a remark issuing from the Cannibal to the effect *that if girls would talk their tongues must be cut out of their mouth,* she soon cooled down, and resolved to submit herself to any order given to her, however irksome and loathsome to her feelings it might have been.

Happily, Velvet was not near when the cowardly

threat was made by the Cannibal, otherwise it is very probable that he would have shown the speaker that he did not give him leave to lacerate a girl's feelings, who was too inoffensive to be thus gratuitously insulted.

But Velvet was too busy in his watch to hear anything.

And after half an hour's hard work, many interruptions on the part of the police, several unsuccessful trials with the skeleton keys—after having used the crowbar and the jemmy, and sundry other articles, the burglars found that the door yielded before the pressure which was placed upon it, and that the key ralled in the lock and worked in a very satisfactory manner indeed.

Spanton in the course of the day had closely examined the premises, and his had been an information which was heartily welcomed—although to be candid we may well say that, strictly speaking, it might have been dispensed with, since Mat had been looking after the job since his discharge from Milbank Prison.

Two more endeavours, and one more interruption, which proved a false alarm, and the Fence and the band were safely in the premises.

The Fence had to walk along a small corridor, and then he came to another door.

There again great precaution was to be used, since there might have been a warehouseman within, to salute their entrance with a goodly discharge of some effective tell-tale revolver.

Bob o' Link had been told that the keeper employed by the jeweller was a drunken sort of a fellow, and that he never stopped on the premises.

The truth of that remained to be proved, for his informant's report might not be correct, and where the band expected safety they might have to encounter danger; and treacherous, indeed, it would prove to them since it was unexpected.

Bob o' Link, Big Ned, and the Fence, who were the leaders in the expedition, held their breath while they stood outside the second door.

With regard to their footsteps being heard, that was an impossibility, for housebreakers generally provide themselves with a slipper which they wear over the boot, and while they walk only produces a faint sound which few, indeed, would succeed in catching, were they not previously forewarned of the fact.

Nancy, also, who was standing by the side of the Fence, was shivering with fear.

What was to be the result of the burglary in the perpetration of which she had been made an unwilling actor?

CHAPTER LXX.

THE BURGLARY.

The room in which the burglars now obtained admittance was rather a wide one, and in the corner stood a desk, with several letters addressed to Mr. Samuel, jeweller.

This was the name of the tradesman whose wealth had attracted the envy of the housebreakers.

These letters, which had come by the evening post, had not been opened, and remained to be answered.

"I say," began the Fence, taking one of the envelopes, "let us get initiated with the private business of Mr. Samuels. Maybe we shall fall in with a check or a post-office order. 'Qui ne risque rien n'a rien,' as the French wisely observe."

Thus speaking, Mat opened a letter, which ran thus—

"Dear charmer,—You never sent me that five pounds you promised me. I am very hard up, and I never paid our dear boy's last month's nursing. Dear duck, forward the remittance at once, or Dorothy will die of a broken heart.

"Your heifer, "DOROTHY SNOOKS."

Even Nancy, who was listening to the burglar's perusal of the note, which was a curious specimen of caligraphy, every single word in it being mis-spelt, could not refrain a smile.

Mat sat down, and, with a pencil in his hand, wrote at the top of the letter—

"Will be attended to out of proceeds of the sale realised by the jewellery."

Bob smiled good humouredly.

It might, perhaps, be thought that in a case of burglary people would be very cautious. The reader naturally would fancy that it would be subdued whisperings, and spectral-like gliding movements, and that the burglars would fear to open their mouths, so awe-stricken would they be.

Where danger would exist, not unlikely the above would take place; but if there is no apparent danger, all fear ceases, and man assumes his real character.

Mat was something of a wag, and he liked a joke whenever he could crack one.

On the left-hand side of the desk, and with the help of the bull's-eye which Big Ned carried, the latter saw a washing-stand.

"It's dirty work," he said, "fiddling with locks. I'll wash my hands."

And without any further parley he carried his words into execution.

The room where the party stood was not the one where the valuables were to be found.

Spanton, who now arrived, acquainted them with the information he possessed, and told them that all the jewellery was locked up during the night in safes on the first floor.

Accordingly the party went upstairs.

Mat led the way.

Reluctantly did Nancy follow.

But she had no choice.

When they came upon the ground-floor the burglars breathed satisfactorily.

By some mistake the door was opened.

They walked inside.

There were two large safes in the room, and a case of wine which Bob o' Link was not long in opening.

Things were going on smoothly enough.

Bob was thanking his stars, and Spanton was sincerely hoping that he would in a few hours' time return to Jenny with his pockets loaded with jewellery.

Nancy was wondering whether house-breaking could be always so successfully carried out as it was in the present instance.

Everybody was apparently satisfied and happy, when a peculiar knock sounded against the shutters.

Immediately afterwards the sounds of a party running away were perceptible.

"This is a signal," said the Fence, "and there's no time to lose."

"What shall we do?" asked Spanton, and he trembled violently.

"Stand still and do not say a word."

Spanton became as silent as the grave.

The tramp of several footsteps were heard outside.

It was a patrol of policemen taking their rounds.

With fast beating hearts and their minds filled with dread and anticipation, the performers of the scene which we are relating stood in mortal agony by the side of the safes where thousands of pounds were locked up.

The Fence was an old hand.

Thus he did not feel very frightened.

Not so with Spanton.

He was exceedingly uneasy.

And with regard to Nancy?

Not one writer, however experienced and facile his pen, could adequately describe the poor girl's feelings as she remained in that room.

Knowing not whether the next moment would herald the entrance of a batch of police.

Also she wondered whither Velvet was.

She had met him and lost him twice, and was she again to be left alone to the world?

She hoped not.

Her nature could ill have withstood another series of such severe trials as she had already undergone.

The patrol halted before the house.

Then followed the hum of several voices.

"Did you fasten the door after you?" asked the Fence of Big Ned, "for if you have not it is all up with us, and we must prepare for action."

Nancy heard the words.

She heard the question.

Also the reply, which was satisfactory.

Big Ned had closed the door.

A few minutes passed.

Nancy's heart was beating fast.

At length the policemen resumed their walk.

The sounds of their measured tread dying away in the distance soon followed.

But people should make sure of things.

The Fence swept across the room on tiptoe.

Then he halted by the window sill.

A sigh of relief escaped him.

Through the interstices of the shutter he saw the boy Kay standing beneath a door-way.

The promising youth had just lit his pipe, and was doing a smoke.

"Now to work, boys, and let us look sharp," said the Fence.

"First, we must test the safe," said Big Ned.

"Yes, with the wedge."

"Here you are, my bold boy."

As he made the reply, Bob O'Link drew from beneath his under garments an instrument about two inches long and one inch and a half broad, and could it have been seen by the blaze of gaslight instead of that of a single eye, it would have been found to have been as sharp as a knife.

Big Ned gave his assistance.

"Where is the wood, Bob?" asked the boy thief.

Perhaps our readers may wish to know why wood was wanted.

A few words of explanation are necessary.

When the wedges are used there is a piece of wood put at one end to deaden the sound when striking them.

"Does it hold?" asked the Fence, after the wedge had been driven between the door and the frame of the safe.

"I think so," replied Bob.

"Where is the light?"

The bull's-eye was then placed close to the safe.

The wedge did hold good.

Success renders man bold.

Had the wedge fallen out of the frame it would have been unsatisfactory.

The door, then, could not have been opened.

As it was, to open the safe was only a question of time.

And time to the burglars was precious.

"Where is the 'alderman,' Bob?"

By the "alderman" the Fence meant an iron bar, which, once introduced in a safe, will open it, however good it may be.

The "alderman" was taken out of the "violin case."

But it was found to be too large.

"We can't use the 'alderman,' Mat."

"It is too big."

"Slightly so."

"Try again."

There was another attempt.

But it failed.

A smaller tool was then brought forth.

That was the "citizen," a tool very similar to the other one, only smaller.

It took at least half an hour ere the "citizen" could be introduced in the frame of the safe.

Another signal!

Another tramping of footsteps!

Again the burglars were interrupted in their work!

Heavy beads of perspiration now trickled down Spanton's forehead.

What was to be the issue of the second search?

Perhaps the policemen would take into their heads to walk upstairs.

If so, detection was certain.

For, if they were to see the burglars in a room where they had no lawful business, would they not walk them off to the station?

Besides, what about the tools?

The time the stay which two policemen made before the house was of a longer duration than before.

They stopped there talking together for over half an hour.

"Could they have suspicion of that which was going on?" the Fence asked himself; "but no, if they had, they certainly would walk upstairs."

It is very provoking for any one to have to wait to satisfy the cravings of some entrancing, absorbing desire, and thus it was with feelings of disgust and of mortification that the burglars in general, and Mat, the Fence, in particular, awaited the issue of the confab which was being heard between the policemen, who would not have been half so cosy and so unconcerned as they apparently were, relating to each other their adventures with the servant girls in the neighbourhood, did they but know what was taking place so close to them.

But policemen, like every one else, must at some time or another exhaust their conversational powers, and in due course it came to pass that they had no more to say to each other; they parted, each following a contrary direction; they took their way, one westward, and the other towards the north.

When everything was once more quiet, the Fence, who had been squatting down like a tailor, rose to his feet.

"Bob," he said, addressing our acquaintance, "let us have one of these bottles uncorked."

As he spoke the burglar pointed to the case to which we have alluded.

It was full with Martell's best Cognac.

Bob O'Link smacked his lips.

Then he withdrew a strong pocket-knife, which he carried with him, from his coat, and with the back of the blade knocked off the top of the bottle.

This was Bob O'Link's way of uncorking.

Here we must not forget to mention that Bob had, before uncorking the bottle, gone downstairs, not only to ascertain how the land lay, but to provide himself with a tumbler, which formed part of the toilet apparatus of Mr. Samuels.

Bob had a drink, so had Ned and the Fence, and while we are stating things in full force we must not omit to tell our readers that Nancy partook of the stolen goods, and that Spanton had no objection either to a glass of Martell's best.

Under the circumstances we think that they are entitled to some excuse.

"I feel much better now," said the Fence. "This has given me new energy; at one time I thought that I should be compelled to 'give up the job.' but, dead or alive, I swear that before morning I'll pocket Mr. Samuels' jewellery."

And the Fence renewed his weary task.

And then he found out that his clothes were in his way.

To sit hindered him in his progress.

So he stripped, and stood upright before the safe.

At last he was about to succeed.

After an hour's work, and after having successively used the wedge, the "citizen," and the "alderman," there was a chance of the safe coming asunder.

The "alderman" was now placed in the safe.

"Now for the aggregate strength of all of us," said the Fence.

These words brought Bob; Spanton and Big Ned were by the side of Mat.

They gave one steady, tremendous pull.

Then there was a creaking sound, followed by a smash, and at last the safe yielded, and it was fairly opened.

The lock was broken, but that mattered but little to the burglar.

The bull's-eye was once more placed into requisition.

They looked inside the safe.

There in small boxes, and wrapped in silk paper, were hundreds and hundreds of watches, besides gold bracelets, rings, brooches, &c., of all descriptions.

"There is at least three thousand pounds' worth here," said the Fence with a broad grin of satisfaction; "after all, the foreman did not tell me a lie."

"And now for the spoil," said Bob O'Link. "I'd better tell the 'interlopers *' that in a few minutes we will be with them."

The Fence was about to speak, but several rat, tat, tat's were heard outside the shutters.

"They are coming! they are coming!" exclaimed Velvet.

"I see a batch in the distance," said the boy Kay.

And one and all the thieves rushed to the door which was now ajar, and which Bob O'Link had opened to admit his mates within the premises.

But the last one gliding in the warehouse had been too late.

He had been seen!

Surely there has been a spy somewhere.

For now came at least twelve policemen, followed by a large crowd.

The policemen had their staffs threateningly in their hands.

Behind them the mob yelled furiously.

There was a burglary somewhere.

"Where was it?" were the words in everybody's mouth.

CHAPTER LXXI.

THE ARRIVAL OF THE POLICE.

Friend and reader, have you ever been in a crowd —and have you ever, while gazing upon some sight

* INTERLOPERS.—Thieves who are called upon to help others in a case of emergency.

of interest, been disturbed and startled in your contemplation by the words, "Fire! Fire! Fire?"

Like one man thousands and thousands of people all rush towards the same spot—towards the direction where the fire is supposed to take place—and then the engines come rattling along, the pumps begin to work, the water spouts from many unknown sources, the flames creak and burn brightly, and the mob, pushing each other, gossipping, remarking, swearing, enjoys the treat.

But if the signal of a fire possesses in itself the elements of a disturbance—if it is calculated to bring many people together—how very powerful and how very certain to effect the same object in a much quicker time are the mystic syllables, "There is a robbery going on!"

It spreads like wildfire, and curious individuals would go any distance to see it, since they know that the chances are that perhaps the burglars will be gone, a contingency which in their own minds enhances the interest of their errand.

"They are coming! they are coming!" had said Velvet.

"I see a batch in the distance," had warned the boy Kay.

Full of meaning!

Beyond a doubt were those words hurriedly spoken by the two youthful thieves.

No time, therefore, had been lost.

The door had been opened.

The Hallelujah had been admitted.

And there, headed by the Fence, they stood still.

We would be the last ones in this wide, wide world to fight the cause of our criminals. We would be unfit to wield a pen; rightly and justly we ought to be held up to public scorn. Like the soldier who disgraces his uniform by conduct unbecoming the cloth which he wears, we would deserve to be drummed out of the regiment of letters, were we to place vice upon a pedestal of fame and bid public opinion to bow before it. We would then be accused of immorality, of instilling erroneous ideas into minds unable to discern the right from the wrong; but we do not do so; we only relate. And if we ask our readers whether there was not something sublime and manly in the attitude of these outcasts awaiting the arrival of the force instead of trying to flee, will anybody give us a denial?

"'Tis a pity if we lose all our booty" said the Fence, as he gazed upon the open safe, and the different tools which they had used to open it; "the devil a bit of luck have I had lately."

Spanton, meanwhile, was sadly reflecting.

Poor Jenny's forebodings had again come to pass.

After all, there might be some truth in her warning.

Her dream, then, was not only the ephemeral conjurings of a diseased brain.

So thinking, a tremendous noise downstairs startled the youth.

Grasping their poniards in their hands the Hallelujah Club waited in dread suspense.

Could an artist have been hidden in one corner of that room, what a fine subject for the display of his facile pencil.

Never before on canvas would so effective a sketch have been made.

The different expressions which animated the features of these men and boys were truly of a terrifying aspect.

The door of the warehouse entrance had been carefully locked.

Nancy had been told to remain by the side of it, and to let the burglars know as soon as it would have the appearance of yielding.

The poor girl was at her post.

At first she had felt weak, sick, and desponding.

Not so, indeed, now.

A revulsion of feeling had come over her.

To her the arrival of the police was a godsend.

She would tell them the truth.

Hence she feared not.

And yet she did not like to betray the burglars.

Had she done so, she would not have been able to save Velvet, and she knew that he had been among the thieves before.

Suddenly Nancy rushed upstairs.

The force had arrived before the door.

They also were provided with instruments to break the lock.

And now it sounded very much as if the iron shutters had been rent from the grooves, and as if there were people stepping in the room.

These ominous sounds were not the only ones.

Shortly afterwards they were followed by a loud bang of a door.

By loud voices.

It was all over.

They were coming upstairs.

And now listen.

Hark!

What's that?

They are on the roof.

On the roof of the house.

"What's to be done?" asked Bob.

"Let us seek shelter on the top of the house."

"Yes."

"And then we can perhaps escape."

"Never! never!" said a stentorian voice. And a man, tall, wiry, slim-built, but extremely pale, with eyes darting fire, and a quivering lip, entered the room first and foremost.

Spanton gave the new comer one glance, a glance rapid, swift, and passing.

But it was enough.

The new comer was Richard Spaldings!

Behind him were a long batch of policemen.

"They are too many for us," said the Fence. "Away! away!"

And simultaneously the burglars darted upstairs.

But there their progress was also interrupted.

Somebody must have watched the burglars.

Must have known the day, the very hour upon which they purposed to visit the jeweller's warehouse.

Who was that?

And could it have been the farmer?

Faithful to his oath.

Bent upon his revenge.

Mindful of the words he had promised in the neighbourhood of the haunted mill.

But perhaps we anticipate.

The robbers were baffled.

The Fence gnashed his teeth.

Bob O'Link swore he would draw blood.

The boy Kay hoped there would be no fighting.

The fact was, that several detectives, armed to the teeth, had entered the warehouse situated close to the jeweller's place, and had found their way upon the tiles, awaiting a signal from the street to rush to the spot where the burglars were, so as to make sure to capture them all.

There is no accounting for certain individuals' behaviour.

Thus, when the robbers found a superior force opposed to them, they became wild, desperate, and bloodthirsty.

They would sell their lives dearly, or escape with their spoil.

"Let me pass," said Bob O'Link, to a policeman who placed his hands upon his shoulders and forbade him to advance.

The constable refused.

"Take this, then, you hound," said Bob.

And quickly drawing the small poniard from its sheath, which was slung to a belt encircling his waist, the youth plunged it to the hilt in the courageous constable's breast.

The steel had entered the heart.

The man fell down dead!

"There is one at all events," said the Fence.

And then Big Ned, amidst immense difficulties, raised the corpse from the ground and flung it down stairs, after having, however, smashed out the brains of the unfortunate murdered man, who presented truly a terrible ghastly sight.

"If this does not cool their ardour a bit," the bully soliloquised to himself, "'tis a query."

But Big Ned was sadly at fault in having acted as he did.

Show to a famished tiger a piece of raw meat, and it will be the means of driving him to frenzy.

The corpse of their disfigured mate, which fell at the police's feet like a mere log of wood, stun their feelings to the quick, and thirsting for revenge they rushed to the help of the force upstairs, who were engaged in a severe struggle with the burglars on the house tops.

There a scene which we must accurately describe met their sight in all its ghastly and terrible distinctness.

It was indeed a deadly affray on the house tops!

But a good deal of blood was to be spilt on that morning.

Up to the present the burglars had had the best of it.

They had slain six policemen.

And Spanton, to preserve his life, had been compelled to commit a murder.

And he had been seen in the act by the farmer.

By his bitterest foe!

So when Spanton got a chance he attacked Richard Spaldings.

But the end of their struggle was not doubtful from the first.

The farmer was by far the strongest man of the two.

Accordingly, after a few instants' fighting, Spanton yielded.

And his hands were screwed in irons, and he was dragged downstairs.

There to await the arrival of a reinforcement of police.

Afterwards to be taken to the police station.

To be tried.

Judged.

Sentenced.

Condemned to death!

Was it to be so?

And would the farmer succeed in his revenge?

So far as we have gone he had proceeded but slowly.

Was he coming to a crisis now?

It looked very much like it.

Spanton was now a prisoner.

But to revert to the house-tops' affray—a plate illustrating which was presented gratis with No. 1 of this stirring tale.

The burglars tried to escape.

N.B.—Owing to delay on the Artist's part, we are reluctantly compelled to postpone our Presentation Plate for a week or two.

THE
DANCE OF DEATH;
OR,
THE HANGMAN'S PLOT.
A THRILLING ROMANCE OF TWO CITIES.

No. 19.]   SATURDAY, MARCH 10, 1866.   [ONE PENNY.

LORD MOUNTCARSDEN'S SURPRISE.

CHAPTER LXXI.—CONTINUED.

But once victorious, new difficulties arose.

Richard Spaldings, the farmer, followed by the force, now appeared on the tiles.

What did he see?

Bob O'Link apparently drunk, holding a bottle in his hand, and singing a song, sitting as comfortably as you please upon a chimney.

He was doing no harm, so people did not mind him.

But Big Ned's fate had come.

This worthy gentleman was just in the act of

kicking a cat in the street, and he was raising a heavy bludgeon above his shoulders, when he was asked by a stern voice to surrender.

Big Ned turned round, and saw it was a policeman.

Not believing that he was armed, he was about to fell him to the ground, when the constable was before him this time.

He raised his arm.

Took a goodly aim.

And fired.

There was a sharp detonation.

Then a gurgle and rattle in Big Ned's throat.

And he reeled and fell heavily upon the ground.

The bullet had entered his forehead.

And so died Big Ned.

No one pitied him, and slanting downwards the rigid and stiffened limbs of the bully rolled off the tiles, and fell from a height of several hundred yards upon the stone pavements in the street.

Afterwards to be carried off in a stretcher to the hospital a mutilated body, the charred remains of as great a scoundrel as ever lived.

*　　*　　*　　*

Thus big Ned met his doom.

Spanton was arrested in less time than we can take time to describe it.

Velvet in the meantime was looking after Nancy.

At length he alighted upon her.

She was about to be carried away in a fainting fit by Frank Pullen, the thief.

But Velvet arrived just in time.

In time to rescue her.

And bring her downstairs.

The farmer was nowhere to be found.

Otherwise it is not unlikely that father and son would have met.

For it was now morning.

Richard Spaldings had seen that Spanton was led under a strong escort to a place of safety.

It had been a bloody contest.

"Where are you going?" asked Pullen from Velvet.

"Downstairs."

"What for?"

"To go out."

"And do you think the police will let you?"

"I hope so."

"Try then?"

"I shall."

Thus speaking, Velvet carried Nancy to the first floor, where the body of the policeman was to be seen.

"Where are you off to now, young man?" asked one of the bobbies who kept watch.

"Home."

"Please stop here, will ye?"

This was the "wandering blue" who spoke.

Frank Pullen meanwhile was doing the obsequious.

He would have liked to cut.

But all the ways of exit were too closely guarded.

"I am not a bad one," said Velvet.

"Neither is she?" asked a detective in plain clothes, pointing at Nancy, while he looked at the boy with a sneer.

"No, that she is not!" replied Velvet.

"That chap lies; she is one of our mates," Pullen said. "Nancy, just *flash* the watch you got upstairs."

The reasons which induced the thief to talk as he did are obvious.

He was jealous, and he knew that Nancy was partial to Velvet.

Frank Pullen was of an envious disposition.

Nancy looked beautiful now.

And this was the reason why Pullen turned so revengeful.

The white softness of her skin enhanced her attractions.

Interesting in the extreme did she appear.

When she had heard her name pronounced she had looked up.

Limpid then was the mellow and honeyed expression of her almond-shaped eyes.

Surely, thought the policeman, she cannot be a thief.

But appearances are deceitful.

The constable was admiring the girl.

"Is she really one of your mates?" he asked of Pullen.

"Of course she is," said Pullen sullenly. "Why should I say so if she wasn't?"

"Do you hear?" asked the policeman.

Velvet was too thunderstruck by Pullen's impertinence to say a word; at length he spoke.

"Mr. Policeman," he said respectfully, "I assure you that she is harmless, and that she is not what that chap wishes you to believe of her."

Between such conflicting statements what could anyone have done?

The policeman would have been inclined to be lenient.

But could he take the responsibility upon himself?

Besides his companion would have objected to it.

The girl swore, in reply to other queries, that she was innocent.

"Very well performed. Miss Nancy," said Pullen; "you would do well on the stage. What a face she has, godstruth; forgive me for swearing."

And now the policeman laid hands upon Nancy.

The girl retreated proudly.

"Do not touch her," said Velvet.

But the policeman laughed.

And so, notwithstanding all their entreaties, Frank Pullen, Nancy, and Velvet were walked away in custody.

The other members of the Club had flown.

Certainly Velvet and Nancy were doomed to be baffled in their expectations.

Was it to last for ever?

CHAPTER LXXII.

THE SHAM NOBLEMAN PLAYS A NEW PART.

Having related the thrilling incidents of this story as they occurred, and having spared ourselves no trouble to establish in their true light the real characters of those who successively appeared before us, we must ask our readers to follow Lord Mountcarsden on his departure from the Argyll Rooms, where we last saw him.

It was, it must be granted, a bold feat on the part of the murderer to assume a rank to which he had no right; for although, with Bella's assistance, he had become thoroughly acquainted with the minutest peculiarities of the real lord's nature, yet he was aware of the difficulties in his way.

What the convict had done was not, however, a new feature in the annals of crime, since we remember in real life a case very similar, where a carpenter from the island of Java personified for fifteen years the *rôle* of a foreign prince, and for that period imposed upon the credulity of Continental Europe.

Had the Marquis of Aguado left the country after he had become an Earl, he might indeed among strangers have relied upon success; but when we tell our perusers that the real lord when alive had friends, or such people as the world so calls, acquaintances, relations, servants, and even a wife and a daughter, it may be asked, could so bold a scheme as his own last long?

There was, however, one point which weighed in the favour of the impostor—a point upon which Bella had dwelt when the murder had been resolved upon.

Bella had, we know, been acquainted with his lordship for several years.

Women are generally speaking talkative and inquisitive, and she had not therefore failed to fathom the deepest of his thoughts.

It is, therefore, as well to tell those who may have the patience of perusing us, that the knowledge which she possessed was not amiss, since without it but little could have been done.

Owing to the influence which the real lord possessed, the convict had learnt that, after several attempts which had failed, the late nobleman had obtained from the Court of Chancery an order to incarcerate his wife in a lunatic asylum.

His object for doing so needs no explanation.

In the event of her death, and he had planned it more than once, the real lord would have come into possession of a large fortune.

Her ladyship out of the way, the claim of a child who was supposed to exist could easily have been set aside.

But did that stolen child still live?

If so, he must have been a grown youth.

And Lawyer Workirk, with his manly and generous nature, had often tried to ascertain his whereabouts.

Perhaps one day, and with that perseverance which never forsook him, he would obtain a clue to the birth.

All these things were to be considered.

Lord Mountcarsden, at least the sham lord, had often pondered over them.

To delay would have been unwise.

The Marquis of Aguado resolved not to keep things in suspense.

It would not be to our purpose here to dwell at too much length upon matters which can easily be disposed of.

So we will at once tell our friends that on the night when Wild Will was given in charge to the policeman, the nobleman parted company with Bella.

From the villa in St. John's Wood he had not yet paid a visit to Belgrave-square.

He had, through the courtesan's servant, sent word that he would not be at home for a few days.

The person to whom the message had been delivered had not been astonished.

Often his master absented himself.

Occasionally he went to race meetings.

And stopped away for days, sometimes weeks.

Blanche, the daughter, never wondered.

Her father was such a strange man.

He might have told her of it, so she thought, and on the instant she accepted an invitation which had been sent to her by a lady friend of hers.

The Belgrave mansion was thus left entirely to the care of the servants.

Often the sham lord wondered what reception he would get.

Once or twice he had passed before his gorgeous mansion and had smiled with pleasure.

Yet he had not summoned sufficient strength of mind to enter.

But at some time or another he would take the bold step.

The morning that he had paid a visit to the club of which the late lord was a member, he returned to the villa in St. John's Wood.

"Bella," he said, exultingly, "I have a good deal to tell you"

With an intense feeling of curiosity Bella listened. She wished to know how her paramour had succeeded.

A goodly stake depended upon it.

Let her lover become the owner of the property settled upon the son, who had never appeared for many years, and whom many people believed to be dead, and she would be wealthy.

She would be Lady Mountcarsden.

But the wife and daughter, what about them?

Bella was one who thought that in this world nothing was impossible.

She sat down.

"Well, my lord," she said, derisively, accentuating her phrase, "what reception did you get at the club?"

His lordship smiled.

"I must confess," he replied in answer to the woman's query, "that I was rather bashful when sitting in the cab which was driving me to the club."

"Bashful," retorted Bella.

"Bashful, yes Bella, you must understand me."

"You use a wrong word, my Lord."

"Well, say diffident."

"That's more correct."

"*Continuez*," said the Marquis, assuming one of his pleasantest smiles, and bidding his friend to proceed finding fault with him.

The convict knew French.

He had learnt that language in France, as our readers, doubtless, do not forget that he came from that country.

There was a pause.

After awhile the nobleman resumed.

"On alighting from the cab in Pall Mall, Bella, I ascended the steps of the club."

"Yes."

"You know the Carlton?"

"I do."

"Splendid entrance."

"Very. But you are keeping me in suspense."

"I'll proceed. As soon as I entered the hall where several gentlemen were standing, I walked towards the porter."

"What for?"

"For my letters, of course."

"Did you ask him whether there were any?"

"I would have done so, but—"

"But what?"

"The fellow guessed my intention."

"You were lucky."

"Yes, my star is in the ascendant; I can perceive that. I heard the fellow 'my lord-ing' me, and I took three letters which he handed to me in a most obsequious manner."

"And what was your next step?"

"I went into the reading-room."

"And then?"

"Proceeded to become acquainted with the contents of my correspondence."

"Anything important?"

"No. They were three letters from the country —all applications. One of them wanted a pound for a church about to be built; the other solicited my name to a subscription for a sporting novel about to be published; and the third, having understood through some source or another that I was in need of a jockey, forwarded me his testimonials with a sincere hope that I would give him a vacancy in my stable."

"What did you do, then, my lord?"

"Replied at once."

"In what may."

"Told the clergyman to put my name down for five pounds."

"And the author of the book?"

"Never answered his letter."

"And the third?"

"Told him to come up to town, and that I would look at him."

"Well done, Mountcarsden."

Here the courtesan burst into a violent fit of laughter.

"This, Bella, is how we do it."

"And were those the only letters you had?"

"To-day, yes."

"Anything else occurred to you?"

"Yes."

"What was it?"

"I shook hands with several individuals, who asked me my opinion about the Derby."

"Do you know anything about horses?"

"Not a bit."

"And what was your answer?"

"That at present I thought that Lord P——'s stable contained the winner."

"Ah!"

"And they asked you to name it?"

"Of course."

"Well."

"I said that I should reserve my opinion—speech is silvern, but silence is golden—and as I went to glance over the paper I heard a party say, 'Lord Mountcarsden is a shrewd fellow, and I daresay he has a good thing on hand.'"

The conversation between Lord Mountcarsden and Bella did not last much longer.

To the woman who had been his partner in crime he had no more to say.

She gave him a few instructions.

And wishing him luck returned to her dressing-room.

His lordship hailed a cab.

Drove to Belgrave-square.

If his feelings on entering the club were such as would require a cleverer pen than ours to describe, what must have been those which usurped his mind as he stopped before his mansion?

The coachman gave the usual rat-tat-tat.

But for the worthy gentleman the knock was not sufficient.

So he violently rang the bell.

A powdered footman answered the call.

The likeness between the late nobleman and the present one was so great that they would have been taken for twin brothers.

Nature sometimes takes freaks.

We see an instance of it.

His lordship paid the cabman.

Then stood in the hall.

The only thing by which his lordship's scheme might have been discovered was his tone of voice.

But he had done the best to disguise it.

For hours and hours he had practised in Bella's boudoir.

And she had told him that he was perfect.

"Has my daughter returned?" he asked from one of the menials, as if he was *au fait*.

"No, my lord."

This was a load off the nobleman's breast.

But there was something in store for him.

"My lord."

"What?"

"A gentleman has called here several times in your absence."

"Do I know him?"

"Yes, my lord."

"What name did he leave?"

"Here is his card, my lord."

The nobleman took it.

A white, lurid pallor overspread his countenance. It ran thus:—

    Mr. James Workirk,

        Lincoln's-inn-fields.

The late lord's bitterest enemy.

"Ah!" he said.

The servant remained silent.

"Did he leave any message?"

"Yes, my lord."

"What was it?"

"He will call again."

"When was he last here?"

"Yesterday, my lord."

"Very good."

"Will you be 'at home' when the gentleman calls again?"

"Yes, I'll see him."

With these words the sham nobleman walked upstairs to the drawing-room.

"How very much altered is my master?" said the servant, as he swept down the pantry to communicate his ideas to his fellow menials.

When the nobleman of his own making entered his drawing-room, he gazed with satisfaction upon the beautiful pattern of the paper which ornamented the walls, the sumptuous, polished French looking-glasses, the golden candelabras, the magnificent mantelpiece of Carrara marble, and he took pleasure in treading the soft Brussels carpet beneath his feet.

"Many men," he soliloquised to himself, "have risked the scaffold for much less than this; my game, at least, is a bold one."

And so it was.

"It is provoking," he continued to himself, "that I am not allowed to have all my own way; confound that fellow Workirk."

But there were, perhaps, other men besides Lawyer Workirk with whom the Marquis would have to contend.

He rose.

Paced up and down the room with quick, hurried steps.

Then rang violently the bell.

He called for some refreshment.

Shortly afterwards the servant brought him a sandwich and a glass of sherry upon a metal salver.

The next thing which the nobleman wished to ascertain was where the apartments were situated.

Of that he had no idea.

He drank his sherry.

Then looked full into the servant's face.

"I wish you," he said, "to come with me into my study."

The servant stood aside to let the nobleman pass.

But this was exactly the thing which he wished to prevent.

But he could ill do so.

He prepared to walk downstairs.

But the servant stopped him.

Now it just happened that the study was on the first floor.

"Decidedly my master is gone mad," thought the servant.

"Show me the way," his lordship said.

The menial obeyed.

Then his lordship reached the placed he wished.

He sank down in a seat.

An idea had flashed across his mind.

Surely the servant's suspicion must have been aroused.

What should he do to dispel it?

Some mysterious power came to his help.

"John," he said, taking for granted that John was the name, and it luckily happened to be, "I am very unfortunate."

The servant now thought that his master had some family trouble.

His lordship was about to make him his confidant.

Then he could no longer be mad.

So reasoned the flunkey.

"John," repeated the nobleman, "I have had heavy losses on the turf, very heavy losses."

John here sympathised very much with his lordship, and related to him a long story how Jim, Tom's brother, who was closely connected with Mr. Jones, the bookmaker, was addicted to gambling, and lost all his earnings, and finally backed the winner for the Derby, and with one sovereign got back every farthing that he had ever spent on horseflesh.

The noblemen smiled good humouredly.

"It is not yet the case with me, John," he said.

"Let us hope, my lord, that you will have the same turn of luck as that ere party which I spoke to you about,' the flunkey retorted, and off he went.

Let any of our readers fancy themselves in the same position as the Marquis of Aguado.

Since we have introduced him he has found himself in strange and critical positions.

What would he do?

Left once more alone the nobleman mused.

So far as he had gone he had no reason to complain. He had faced the club, and from the manner with which he had proceeded with his servant he believed that he had placed matters upon a more substantial basis than they hitherto were.

And he remained thinking, building castles in the air, levelling difficulties, and feeling confident of success. And now that we know that the Earl is at last in Belgrave-square we will leave him for awhile to attend to other matters which also require our immediate consideration.

CHAPTER LXIII.

A BEAUTIFUL SPOT IN THE METROPOLIS—THE WANDERER—THE DANCING-ROOM.

Not far from the spot where William Spanton lived with Jenny the faithless wife there was, and there is still, a place called "Tiger Bay."

It is indeed one of the worst dens at the East End of London!

The horrors that are perpetrated there would baffle description.

Only think of unwary mariners betrayed to that craggy and hideous shore by means of false beacons, and mercilessly wrecked, stripped, and plundered —of continual bloody fights between white men, plug-lipped Malay, and ear-ringed Africans—of savage assaults in the shape of an ear snapped off a human head by human teeth, and decently wrapped in a cool cabbage leaf for the magistrate's inspection when the case is tried at the court—of besmattered brains—tousled female hair—of highway robberies and vile prostitution stalking forth in its ragged filthiness! Imagine to yourself the worst horrors that are perpetrated in God's defiance beneath heaven's canopy—dark deeds—and then, then only can you have some idea of the place.

People indeed say that at times it is even unsafe for policemen to perambulate the neighbourhood, except in gangs of three.

There was one man, however, who had not been afraid to venture in that locality on the evening when our chapter opens, and which was precisely the one when Will Spanton had met the Fence in the public-house where we saw all the thieves together.

In the appearance of the individual to whom we now revert our attention there was nothing very remarkable but for the care which he evidently took to conceal his features, for he kept his hat hard down upon his brow and looked at the ground as he walked along.

He was doubtless a stranger, for from time to time he stopped to inquire his way from the policemen on their respective beats.

But this did not satisfy him.

To make matters still worse a heavy fog now fell, and it became so thick that the names affixed to the street corners could not be made out.

We would never have noticed this individual but for the reason that we believe that he has something to do with this tale.

After having walked for several minutes the unknown individual stopped.

"It must be close here," he said to himself.

And he plodded onwards.

He was walking up the Highway.

Again he stood still.

Perplexed as to the direction he should take.

Then he saw a labourer walking past him.

"My friend," he said, "can you tell me where is Leman-street?"

"Don't know," surlily replied the man, and he walked off.

Presently another individual crossed his path.

"Holloa!" he ejaculated.

"What! Mate?" asked a stout, burly-looking man, whose costume bespoke him to be a seafaring man.

"Do you know this neighbourhood?"

"Rather, I lost my clothes here yesterday."

"How so?"

"Easily enough."

"Explain."

"Only got three sheets in the wind, half-seas-over if you like it better, as we say on board, and my reefing jacket was took off my back. Know it, rather? But I have had enough of it, so good night, mate."

And this second person went away without answering the question put.

The stranger thought that he would never reach his destination.

"Never mind, I'll not give it up," he soliloquised, and pursued his way.

"Presently, while pottering along in the thickening fog, the enlivening strains of music greeted the wayfarer's ears, and looking towards the spot whence they proceeded, he beheld the following sign, "The Globe and Pigeon," inscribed on a lamp, the gas within which was struggling bravely in its consumer's interest against the foggy odds heavily pressing it on every side.

The stranger then halted.

He had been unable to glean the information which he required. It would be very extraordinary if he could not do so in a place where many were assembled.

Accordingly, without further reflection on the matter he crossed over, and pushing the swinging door before him, found himself in view of a frouzy bar, (still adorned with the garlands and misletoe of the last Christmas), and before which an old woman was sitting.

The stranger knew that the spot and its vicinity went under the name of "Tiger Bay."

Had he not, he would have felt inclined to give the house in which he entered the appellation of the "Tiger's lair."

By the side of the woman stood two girls, drinking gin.

One quite a cub—you could see that her baby teeth were yet serrated and ungrown, when she opened her mouth to swear, which she did very often.

The stranger noticed that a mariner had stood the gin.

He was a specimen of a sailor, indeed!

There he leant against the counter, with his face on his folded arms, his cap on the back of his head, and his favourite forelock dabbling in the glass of liquor that had generously been allotted to him out of the half pint he had paid for.

He looked as though he was crying.

Spoke as if he was.

And with gin in his heart, gin in his head, gin in his hair, he was murmuring complaints against the eldest cub of the two.

Blamed her for her infidelity.

After what he had done for her, too!

It was a d—— tarnation shame.

The sailor's language was every instant getting stronger.

And the stranger dreaded every instant a row, for the oldest of the two girls was for growling and showing her claws.

But the landlady had an eye to business.

She suggested peace.

And Jack thanked her, and gave another dollar which went towards more gin, which was poured in the purchaser's glass to console him, and in that of his peaceable paramour, who wanted doubtless a little drop to help her to bear against the sailor's unjust aspersions.

The stranger had gone in to ask a question.

Being interested in the sight he thought he would see more.

Passing, therefore, the party, he spied a passage, across the end of which hung curtains of dirty chintz, through the chinks of which shone the glare of gas beyond.

This in itself was not very attractive.

But there was something else.

A concert was going on.

For the scraping of feet against the floor, and the twanging of a harp, and the shrill playing of a cornopean could be heard.

Curiosity impelled the stranger.

He looked at his watch.

He was, doubtless, too early for some appointment on hand.

So, there being no one hindering him or requiring to know whither he was going, he approached the calico barrier to the realm of bliss, raised it, and entered.

If the spectacle revealed was not enchanting it was at least highly curious.

It was like being behind the scenes at a theatre during the pantomime season.

A barn-like long narrow building, with white-washed walls, on which in flaming colours were a series of hideous pictures illustrative of the domestic habits and customs of the Chinese.

There was a big fire-grate in the place, with a broad mantel-piece, on which reposed short pipes and splints, and a quart pot with beer in it, and with one of her naked arms resting lovingly against the pot, and a foot on the fender, stood the most beautiful female that ever disgraced womanhood.

Her hair was economised in its ornamentation of her fair head by a coronet of green leaves and pearls, and her maiden blushes were modestly screened from public gaze by a substantial coating of some ruddy pigment; her bodice was low, as were not her skirts, and she wore scarlet shoes with brass heels.

Yet, for all these fairy-like attributes, she was not proud. For with his foot on the fender, and his elbow on the shelf, and a particularly short and dirty pipe in his mouth, stood a loutish, clumsy, dirty-faced, unpleasant-looking person, who was talking to the beauty.

This personage was the potman of the establishment.

The dance was just finished as the stranger entered.

But no one took any notice of him.

Besides he was sober, and he appeared like one who was not on for joke.

In addition to this his muscular strength would have secured him respect.

The mob, composed, as far as the stranger could see, of the lowest class of prostitutes, with swollen lips which betrayed frightful diseases scarcely cured, and of sailors of the merchant service, mingled freely together and partook of each other's beer.

A perfect freedom as regarding the morals of either sex, male or female, seemed also to reign in an atmosphere where the smell of beer and tobacco pervaded all other aroma, not to say stench, for the nymphs of that modern Eden had their bare arms entwined round their mates' necks; others sat upon the gallant tars' knees; while a few, still bolder, with their bodices unfastened, permitted their worshippers to go a great deal further than common decency would, in many people's opinion, have permitted.

The stranger, meanwhile, had taken a seat in one corner, and he had scarcely settled himself satisfactorily, when a fairy came up to him and asked him the following question, "Did you say bacca?"

These words now recalled to the stranger the fact that he had a pipe in his pocket, and so he withdrew it at once.

"I did not say bacca," he replied, "why did you think I did?"

The fairy wished to be attractive.

"'Cause I got it," she replied, with a slight pout of the under lip, while she scratched her hair in anything but a reassuring manner to any one fond of cleanliness; "screws and 'arf ounces; you take what ye likes, you pays your money, and Loo asks no more."

"Is your name Loo?" asked the stranger, at the same time drawing a dirty piece of brown paper from a greasy tumbler, which was Loo's "bacca" store.

"That's my name. Are you going to let us have a peep at the ceiling?"*

"Yes, on one condition."

Loo reflected.

"I hope it ain't a hard one," she said, after awhile.

"No."

"What is it? Out with it then?"

"Can you come along with me?"

Loo stood up proudly.

"You make a mistake, sir," she went on, evidently highly offended.

---

* Have a glass of gin.

The stranger seemed puzzled.

At first he did not understand the girl's meaning.

But it soon dawned upon his mind.

"You are labouring under a misapprehension," the stranger went on.

"Under what?" the girl pursued. "Speak English."

The stranger gave full particulars.

"Oh, I axe your pardon."

"Granted, but hear me."

"What?"

"I promised some gin."

"You did."

"I want a service for that."

"Name it?"

"Do you know Leman-street?"

"Rather."

"Is it far from here?"

"Not very."

"Will you take me there?"

"If you stand the gin."

"How much?"

"Whatever quantity you feel disposed to drink."

"Half-a-pint."

"Done."

The order was given, and a black bottle containing the "Blue Ruin" was soon on the table.

The stranger drank a wine-glassful, and then rose.

Loo was a girl who kept her word.

She was not long in taking the stranger where he wished to go, and shortly afterwards she came tripping back as pert as a daisy, and as light as a feather.

But follow the stranger we must.

And as a good deal is to be said let us here wind up our chapter, and begin a fresh one to that effect.

CHAPTER LXXIV.

WHEREIN WE MEET OLD ACQUAINTANCES.

Loo had been born and bred at the East End.

She knew Ratcliffe Highway (Tiger Bay), and there was not one bye-lane, nook, corner, court, or street, with which she was not acquainted.

As soon, therefore, as she had put on her bonnet she bid the stranger to follow.

Nowise undaunted by the bad character which the neighbourhood bore, or fearful of danger amidst the foggy darkness which reigned, he quickly followed her who, with hurried, quick steps, led him through a labyrinth of noisome, loathsome, slimy, stinking lanes until she reached Leman-street.

She cleared the distance in a very short time.

"Very few," she said to the stranger, "could have shown you this short cut. If you have money to spare, don't forget Loo."

"Tell me how the numbers run first," he asked.

She swept across the street, and straining her eyes made out the number of the house before her.

"This way," she said, pointing to her left. "No. 1 is here. What house do you want?"

The stranger placed his hand in his pocket.

"Never mind," he replied, "I'll find out what I want. This for you; good-bye."

Loo at once placed the coin which the stranger had given her to her mouth.

"'Tis a good one," she laughingly observed; "thanks for the half-crown."

And she swept away out of the stranger's presence.

The man then walked on until he came to the end of the street.

At length he halted.

In front of the house where Jenny lived with the schoolmaster.

He listened intently.

And presently, hearing no sound, gave a peculiar knock against the pane of the parlour windows with a stick which he carried.

The door was soon opened.

And upon the threshold appeared a pale, emaciated little girl of about thirteen years of age.

"You have come at last," said the child, who was the maid of all work in the house; "I believed you had forgotten me."

"No, dear, you were wrong to think so," quickly retorted the man; and aside he whispered, "Shall I lose so good a chance?"

There was a great change for the better in the girl's attire since the day when we last saw her.

Since that day when we paid a visit to Jenny, whom we visited in a poverty-stricken room on the second floor.

Money had been given to her by the stranger.

And in exchange he wanted but little—correct information.

"I expected you to-night."

"You received my note, then?"

"I did."

"And why tell me so?"

"Because I can go out with you."

"It is cold, girl."

"But I know a very nice place."

"Where is it?"

"Not far from here."

"What do you call it?"

"The Gun Boat."

"Do sailors go there?"

"Sometimes."

"And why do you wish me to pay a visit to the Gun Boat?"

"Because it is such a rum place."

"A rum place!"

"Yes."

"And do you want me to go to a rum place, then?"

"Yes, because I know that it would amuse you. You have been kind to me, you know, and I am grateful to you. Besides—"

"What?"

"I expect to see a friend of mine there."

"Yes."

"And he can—"

"Yes."

"Give a good deal more information that I could within doors."

The last words had a mystic influence upon the stranger.

"Come on," he said.

The girl returned in an instant.

The poor thing was not bad-looking. She was one of the many white slaves in England who are ground down by misfortune.

Give them good food, plenty of fresh air, any amount of exercise, and then they are different creatures, indeed."

Kate was quite proud of the stranger's company.

She led him to the Gun Boat.

Accompanied by little Kate, the stranger then walked along a passage exactly similar to the one pertaining to the Globe and Pigeon (screened by exactly similar curtains), except that it was somewhat larger and had a sort of raised platform at the end, and stepped into an exactly similar barn, just as dirty as to its walls, and bespattered with saliva as to its floor ; just as uncomfortable in every possible respect, and as suggestive of the wonder how it could prove attractive to any class of men possessed of the least degree of sense or decency.

But he saw one thing which he little expected to see—hundreds and hundreds of dancers in various costumes.

The fact was that on that particular night there was a masquerade.

" Did you know, you little vixen," the stranger asked, turning towards the girl Kate, " that there was a bal masque going on here ? "

" Of course I did, or why should I have brought you hither ? " she replied playfully, and glanced rapidly around her, evidently much amused with the sight.

The most imaginable costumes were to be found in that hall.

The men who were dancing, and they were many, were mostly sailors.

A sword dance was taking place when the stranger and Kate entered the room.

But this was a failure.

And it was quickly followed by a hornpipe.

This was most creditably performed.

" Do you like this place ? " now asked the stranger, whispering in the girl's ear.

" Like it ? Not overmuch. But have I not told you I have an object in coming here ? "

The stranger remained silent.

Kate was but a girl, it is true ; still she was very cute.

" Kate ! " the stranger said, gazing with a melancholy smile upon his companion, " do you know that you are the prettiest girl here ? "

Kate blushed.

" So a chap that comes here often tells me," she went on slowly.

" Does he ? "

And the stranger became thoughtful.

" Take care of yourself," he said, after a moment's respite, " men are great flatterers, and he does not mean any good."

" Oh, yes ; I believe he does."

" And what is he ? A respectable trade, I hope."

Kate made no answer.

The stranger would not be beaten.

" No, he is not," she said, " and that's why I think he is genuine."

" Kate, you are a riddle."

" No, sir."

" I say you are."

" And don't you see, sir, he has told me his story from beginning to end ; and when I said to him that I wanted such and such information—"

The stranger bit his lip.

" Speak lower," he said harshly.

The girl looked uneasily around her.

" Well," she resumed, " when I asked him to find out all that you told me of, for my sake he promised he would, although he is running great risk in so acting."

" He is a detective, then, I presume."

" Often tracked by them."

" What ? "

" Yes, sir, do not betray me if I tell you the truth. He is—he is a *thief !* "

At that instant a hand was laid upon Kate's shoulder.

She trembled violently.

By her side stood the poor girl's sweetheart.

Monsieur Armand, the French thief.

The youthful member of the Hallelujah Club.

He that for a mere girl was to betray the secrets of the gang to which he belonged.

" I have found out everything about that William Span—"

The girl placed her finger upon her lips.

" 'Tis the party," she said, pointing to the stranger, who was now glancing upon a group of females before him, which are, indeed, worthy of a few lines.

They were women.

But did they deserve that name ?

For in glancing upon decrepit humanity—upon the decayed remains of fallen womanhood now in view—could any lover of the beautiful and fair have soiled his lips by bestowing the name of woman upon such as they ?

It would then be a blasphemy of the word, or an implied doubt of the existence of Providence ; for could it ever have been meant by the Omnipotent when He created the world—when from man He drew a rib and made a sweet sylph-like semi-goddess to ornament terrestrial Eden—that those short bull-like throats, those high-cheeked bones, deeply-set eyes, retreating foreheads, and straight wide mouths, should ever be allowed to disfigure beings who, on the plea of Christianity, claim descent from weak mother Eve ?

Monsieur Armand was in want of funds.

He asked Kate whether she had any money.

The girl replied in the affirmative.

Then the boy took her aside.

And for at least five minutes, while the discordant sounds of the music were vibrating high, and while gallant tars with their Mollys were dancing *vis-a-vis*, the former stamping as hard as they could upon the floor—while the masqueraded women, whose breath was pestilence and their foul-mouthed language poison, were " mopping up " the adulterated gin which was burning their inside and clearing Jack's pocket of his hard-earned wages—Johnny Crapaud kept on talking a good deal to Kate, she drinking in every word, since it was all good, genuine information, for which she would be paid on delivery with sterling money.

Why relate all the horrors of that den ?

Why call our reader's attention to that ticket-of-leave man, who fifteen years ago, with a hand of his own murdered a man in a low lodging close at hand ?

Why ask him to gaze upon him—upon that blot on humanity—who laid a man upon a wooden plank and stabbed him to the heart for the sake of a few shillings ?

We could not tell more than we have already done, and we should fear to exhaust our readers' patience by dwelling at too much length upon details.

" Who is he ? " asked the thief, glancing upon the stranger, after having puzzled his mind to ascertain the object which could have brought him to the Gun Boat.

" I can't tell," replied Kate.

" But you ought to let me know."

Kate mused.

" Why should I ? " she queried quickly.

" He might be looking after *me.*"

" Not he."

" Perhaps he is a detective."

" I can answer for that in the negative."

Mr. Armand felt more comfortable.

Like all Frenchmen, he was fond of the Terpsichorian exercises, and encircling Kate's waist, he was soon lost with her amongst the giddy whirl of dancers.

N.B.—Owing to delay on the Artist's part, we are reluctantly compelled to postpone our Presentation Plate for a week or two.

THE
DANCE OF DEATH;
OR,
THE HANGMAN'S PLOT.
A THRILLING ROMANCE OF TWO CITIES.

No. 20.]   SATURDAY, MARCH 17, 1866.   [One Penny.

A SAD SCENE.

CHAPTER LXXIV.—Continued.

"And now, mate, what are you going to stand?" asked a sailor, coming up to the couple after they had sat down. "I haven't a 'rap' left in the locker."

Mr. Armand proved generous.

Meanwhile Kate ran up to the stranger and acquainted him with all the details given to her by the French thief.

He listened to her with the greatest attention.

And how did it come to pass that Armand proved a traitor?

No. 20.]   [Prize Ticket.—No. 20.

There were two reasons.

Love.

Revenge.

Powerful reasons, indeed!

In the first instance the Frenchman had become deeply enamoured with Kate on the day that, pensive and melancholy, he had seen her with tears in her eyes, standing outside the house in Leman-street.

The young vagabond, with a boldness which never forsook him, had then spoken to the girl.

Had heard from her that she had been beaten by the landlady for not scrubbing the bottom part of the staircase.

Monsieur Armand had sympathised with her.

And poor Kate, having no one to love or to speak to, gave her affections to Monsieur Armand for better or for worse.

Love, therefore, had a good deal to do with the betrayal of the Hallelujah Club secrets.

And if it had been that alone but little correct knowledge, perhaps, would the stranger have gleaned from Kate.

But there were also motives of vengeance!

And Monsieur Armand had sworn to take a striking revenge at the first opportunity against Big Ned and Cannibal Jack.

How could he have done so?

They were both heavier built than him.

How often he had received a kick or a blow and been compelled to gnash his teeth—powerless to resent the injury.

If he betrayed the club Big Ned and the Cannibal would be sure to die, and he would obtain pardon by having turned Queen's evidence, and with his earnings take Kate to Paris, where he longed to return.

Suddenly Mr. Armand turned round.

"Where's my gal?" he asked.

"Here she is."

And it was true, for Kate was coming back towards the thief.

"I hope you are not going to leave me again," the thief said reproachfully; "it is not so often that I see you."

Kate tapped the thief on the shoulder.

"Don't be ridiculous, you great booby," she said, "wasn't I earning money?"

"Where is it?"

"Here—look."

And Kate drew from her pocket a piece of gold.

The thief smiled.

"That ain't bad work, lass," he said.

The girl nodded her head in the affirmative.

"But where's the stranger?"

"He is gone."

And so he was; for, notwithstanding the search which the French thief made, nowhere could he see him.

But he soon thought of something else.

For now tripping along came Jack and Molly, and then in the midst of the barn they began an Irish gig.

The cornopean, the guitar, and one creaking violin formed the instruments which enlivened the evening's concert.

And then the hours passed, and male and female became drunk, and an old gentleman with a wooden leg, and a black patch on his left eye—the chairman of the extempore-got-up "free and easy"—began a song of the sea, winding up with—

"Britons never, never shall be slaves."

It would really have greatly served any of *Mr. Punch's* artists had they been present when the chorus was repeated, for the mariners, who hitherto had been stupid, foolish, and recklessly extravagant, now were still worse.

Hiccupping, and still drinking, taking their purses from their pockets and allowing the nymphs by their sides, in their idiotic insensibility, to pick them, they looked truly degenerate specimens, and one would indeed have felt inclined to know whether—like the one above alluded to—these besotted seafaring individuals belonged to Nelson's gallant tribe, who fought for years under England's proud banner, and spilt the best of their blood in the defence of her outraged nationality.

But closing time came.

And so, after witnessing several little scenes of interest, representing one man knocking another's eye out, a reefing jacket pulled off a man's back and bartered for an ounce of "bacca," a fight between two "tigresses," and sundry other little sights of no less interest, the curtain dropped, and Monsieur Armand saw Kate safely to her home.

And now that the door of the house is closed, and that Kate is asleep—now that the thief has returned among his palls—now that Jenny prays for her lover's safe escape—we may ask, in conclusion, who was the stranger, and did we ever see him before?

CHAPTER LXXV.

A FEW WORDS SAYING A GOOD DEAL—THE TRIAL.—THE VERDICT—OUTSIDE AND INSIDE NEWGATE—THE MORNING OF AN EXECUTION—TRUE DETAILS.

A few weeks have elapsed since the incidents which we have related in the previous chapter of this narrative.

A great trial had taken place at the Old Bailey, and the court had been sitting for several days, and eloquent speeches had been made for the prosecution and the defence, and a verdict had at last been given.

It had been one of those trials which at once engross public attention, and which as long as it lasted was capital food for the newspapers.

The City burglary had been the trial.

A daring case of burglary had been committed by a gang of lawless ruffians—murder had been perpetrated, and a youth of the name of Spanton having been found guilty of wilful murder, the judge had put on the black cap and sentenced him to death.

Our readers remember the burglary in the City.

The result of the same was sad, gloomy, terrible.

The least guilty of all had to suffer.

Everything was against him. Richard Spaldings, once a farmer in Bournemouth, Hampshire, had been the party to give the information which had led to the capture of some of the burglars, and he also had been the one who on his oath swore that Spanton had wilfully murdered a policeman.

In France the youth of the burglar and the murderer might have weighed more heavily than it did in this country, and a verdict with extenuating circumstances might have been returned, and our friend Will Spanton might have been spared the ignominy of a death on the scaffold, but an English body of impartial men had thought otherwise, and he had been confined in Newgate since his trial.

And on the morning when we bring our readers outside Newgate the late schoolmaster and Jenny's seducer was to be hung by the neck until life was totally extinct.

A great crowd was expected round the gallows, and a great crowd came.

The barriers to check the crowd had been begun two days previously, but yet there had been hovering round them a dismal crowd of dirty vagrants.

Newgate! what a terrible word.

One would think that it is with feelings of awe that the mob glanced upon that ominous looking building, that small door which leads to the scaffold.

No!

What were the people assembled on the morning of the execution?

Were young beginners in the career of crime, whose immature tastes were satisfied with catcalls in the dark, fondling the barriers, or at most a hurried scrambling throw of dirt at the police when they dispersed them.

Among these could be seen many well-known young thieves, and once we thought we saw Frank Pullen, the thief who, with Bob O'Link, the Fence, and Cannibal Jack, had succeeded in escaping from the hands of the police.

Suddenly the rain fell.

Let it not be thought that it dispersed the anxious sight-seers.

Perhaps there was a thinning of the fringe about the beam, but on the whole they stood it out very steadily, and formed a thick dark ridge round the enclosure kept before the debtors' door, where Spanton was to die.

We have forgotten to state that it was a winter morn, dark, dreary, and cold, and leading you to believe that it was night instead of day.

Newgate looked black enough in its blind massiveness, except at one point, high over the walls, where one window in the new wing showed a little gleam of light, to which it seemed the crowd was never tired of pointing?

Why so?

Because truly enough the mob had learned that that was the spot where Spanton lay in his condemned cell.

The youth whose bright dreams of future happiness were to end upon the scaffold.

All eyes were turned towards the direction of the light.

But little did the youth who stood behind this miserable flicker in the black outline of the great gaol, know that he was already the observed of all observers.

Certainly he heard strange noises outside, which faintly reached his ears, and he believed he dreamed as one long revelry of song, and laughter, shouting, and often quarrelling, was wafted to him by the chilly wind.

Sick would he have been to live had he seen the scene outside. Crowds of loungers, as well as drunken men, who stood the miserable drizzle with tolerable patience—the public-houses flaring brightly through the mist—a rough mass of indescribable beings, moving to and fro with a painful indecision—a dirty chaos of curiosity, crime, and villany, settling itself down at last, silence on one side, boisterousness on the other, caused by noisy groups whooping and wrangling away—a thick, dark, noisy fringe of men and women settled like bees around the nearest barriers, eager for the forthcoming morbid sensational exhibition.

The hour drew nigh.

Only one quarter of an hour more and the bell would toll.

The death knell sound!

Worse in ruffianism then became the conduct of the rapidly-increasing throng.

Ranting preachers vainly attempted to yell reform and repentance in the ears of the hardened sinners by their side.

The Word of God was smothered beneath the mud, and the name of Christ drowned amidst obscene jokes and coarse laughter.

Why send missionaries abroad?

Would, could such scenes be performed in barbarous countries?

And yet you have it in the heart of civilisation?

But still, to go on with our description.

Perhaps the preacher might have been genuine, for finding himself compelled to cease speaking he began to sing.

It was the old familiar hymn of the "Promised Land."

For a little time this man was allowed to sing alone, but at last he was joined by others, who howled out some English or Irish song, ending with

"Oh my!
Think I've got to die,
But Paddy don't care."

After the singing followed a lull, diversified by shouts and obscene remarks, or cheers, or hisses, as the humour took the crowd.

And still the light burned grimly in the cell where Spanton was, and where we will pay him a visit.

In a cell of gloomy appearance was the prisoner.

He sat upon a wooden stool and was reading.

Occasionally he would glance upwards and listen to the row outside.

The schoolmaster knew that he was about to die.

He paid dearly for his sinful career in this world.

He was pale, but quite calm and collected.

He repented.

By his side was a letter which he had written to Jenny, beseeching her to alter her ways, for his dying sake.

And now Spanton's attention was devoted towards another channel.

The officials were doubtless coming round.

And so they were.

The Sheriffs of London and the Under-Sheriffs had arrived from the London Coffee-house, Ludgate-hill, to the court-house of the Old Bailey, where they remained until a quarter to eight.

Then, when the time came, they were met by the Governor, who led them from the sessions-house to the gaol.

The way lay through a series of gloomy passages, some of them subterranean and dimly lighted, and over the graves of the malefactors who had been buried there during the last thirty years.

Emerging at length into an open courtyard within the precincts of the gaol, the mournful procession paused.

They were expecting some one.

The culprit!

He soon came.

For a door at the further end of the court-yard was suddenly opened and Spanton presented himself attended by a single warder, on his way from his cell to the scaffold.

Spanton's heart beat rapidly.

But he resolved to behave manly.

So he walked with a somewhat measured tread, with his hands clasped in front of him, and looking upwards with a touching expression of countenance.

Not a word did he utter.

For a mist was over his eyes, and a choking sensation was at his throat.

CHAPTER LXXVI.

THE TOILET—ON THE GALLOWS—THE BEHAVIOUR OF THE CROWD—THE OCEAN OF WHITE FACES—THE DEATH-KNELL — THE HANGMAN — REVENGE—TOO LATE!—BENEATH THE SCAFFOLD.

A feeling of sympathy filled the breasts of the officials, as their gaze met that of the culprit, who without the slightest touch of bravado, bowed respectfully his head before them, and resumed once more his quiet and self-possessed demeanour.

Truly it was a sad sight indeed, many thought, to glance upon that handsome youth who was about to atone for his brief career of sinfulness upon the scaffold.

Since Spanton had been confined he had much improved in appearance—an appearance which was greatly enhanced by the tidy clothes which he wore.

From the court-yard the culprit passed with his attendant into the press-room.

The authorities, and among them the Governor of the prison, were visibly touched.

The condemned man noticed their sympathy, and a tear stole from his eyes.

At this trying moment the clergyman approached Spanton, and endeavoured to sustain him again and again.

Repeating in a docile and affectionate manner words which the rev. gentleman put into his mouth, the convict said, "Christ the Lamb of God have mercy upon me."

And as he spoke he believed he heard the voices of angels singing a gentle lullaby in his ears, bidding him smile, for although he was leaving the world he was slowly about to ascend to a blissful home where cares and troubles are unknown and where life is an eternal paradise.

And so absorbed was he with his thoughts that he took but little heed of the executioner.

Then the hangman removed his neckerchief and shirt-collar, and stuffed them within the breast of his coat.

The process of pinioning over the Governor asked the convict to take a seat.

The prisoner did so.

And sank down upon a chair, his head bent downwards, until the prison bell would summon him to his doom.

Here an incident occurred which should be mentioned.

Did anyone notice it?

And why should the executioner keep aloof from Spanton when once his work was done?

Why should he remain behind him as if he feared his gaze?

Information—the hangman had been newly appointed.

And now the signal was given to the Governor.

The prisoner rose.

The bell of Newgate began to toll, and loud did it sound upon the ear of the culprit.

Outside this was the signal for fresh disturbances.

The muffled and foggy boom heralded to them the approach of the prisoner.

Escorted by the Sheriffs and Under-Sheriffs, Spanton stepped forward.

At the little porch leading to the gallows the officials stopped.

Alone with the guilty man the clergyman ascended the gallows.

When the culprit appeared there were cries of "Hats off! Hats off!"

Then the whole mass of pale but dirty faces commenced, amidst yells and struggles, to wriggle to and fro, passing remarks.

The clergyman at once took his place on the little line of sawdust which had been laid to mark the outline of the drop which falls, and which, without such a signal to denote its situation, might easily have been overlooked in the duskiness of the whole well-worn apparatus.

Spanton gave one last look around him.

He saw sharpers, thieves, gamblers, betting men, the outsiders of the boxing ring, bricklayers, labourers, dock workmen, with a fair sprinkling of what may be called as low a grade as any of the worst that might be met—the rakings of cheap singing-halls and billiard-rooms, the fast young gents of London.

But to the fast-dying man it appeared that all, whether young or old, men or women—and there were also many of the last denomination—seemed to know nothing, feel nothing, to have no object but the gallows, and to laugh, curse, or shout, as in their heaving and struggling forward they gained or lost in approaching the spot where he stood.

Before him, far up even to Smithfield, the keen white faces rose rank above rank, till even where the houses were shrouded in the thick mist of the early dawn the course of the streets could be traced by the stream of the faces alone; and all, from first to last, from nearest to farthest, clamouring, shouting, and struggling with each other to get as near the gibbet as the streaming mass of human beings before them would allow.

With his arms pinioned close behind him and a sickening pallor overspreading his countenance—with roguery, thieving, blasphemy, bonnetting, swearing, and all sorts of lewd behaviour, and pocket-picking, going on beneath him— Spanton with a steady step took his place beneath the beam.

Then, looking up, he saw that he was not exactly beneath the proper spot where the short black link of chain depended; so he shifted a few inches, and stood quite still.

Since the sight of the crowd was being gratified not one sound was heard.

The hangman then did his duty.

Spanton turned round.

A shriek escaped him.

The crowd yelled.

The schoolmaster had recognised in the hangman's features those of

RICHARD SPALDINGS!

*   *   *   *   *

He had heard him whisper, "I am the cause of thy death! You have ruined my wife! Revenge is sweet!"

*   *   *   *   *

What Spanton would have said it is impossible to tell.

He had no time to speak.

For no sooner had the farmer uttered the above words than with quickness he pulled the white cap over the culprit's face, fastened his feet with a strap, and shambled off the scaffold amidst hisses.

Immediately afterwards the drop fell.

Those who stood close to the apparatus could just detect a movement twice—so slight, indeed, that it could scarcely be called a movement, but rather an almost imperceptible muscular flicker that passed through the frame.

That was all!

*   *   *   *   *

But another scene was being enacted inside the prison.

A message had come from the Home Office.

A respite obtained for the culprit.

So amidst laughing and oaths the hangman came round and cut the rope, and took Spanton's body away from view.

But alas! it was too late.

Life had fled from its frail tenement.

The youth was dead!

*   *   *   *   *

And now—when the crowd has dwindled off—when the publican who has let his window for the spectacle to some morbid "swell" reckons his money—when the unwary mariner who has been assisted to the sight is dragged off in his besotted drunkenness to "Tiger Bay" by grasping Molly—when the thief with his mates "chucks up" the watch he has lifted to the careful and prudent Fence—when Newgate place is about to resume the bustle and activity of everyday life, and the casual way-farer thoughtlessly crosses the thoroughfare where in the morning the ghastly scene has been enacted—when the large multitude has been scattered away and the carpenters come to remove all traces of the ominous scaffold—from whence arises this sudden commotion?

Why is the policeman sent for?

Stay; let us see.

A woman has been discovered beneath the scaffold!

She tears her hair, and scratches the fair skin of her breast, with violent execrations, with loud curses!

She raves!

She is evidently insane!

For why should she be so lavish in her anathemas against the hangman?

Does she know him?

Who is she?

How explain this mystery?

The scaffold is removed.

The woman is dragged away.

The rapidly-collected mob once more disperses.

Every one wonders.

Something strange about this occurrence!

Is the reader getting interested?

Perhaps he is; so let him summon a little patience, and follow gently the thread of our narrative, for the chapter of explanation is close at hand.

CHAPTER LXXVII.

THE SHAM LORD AT HOME—A FAMILY SCENE—MR. WORKIRK—THE THREE VISITS—MERCEDES REVENGES HIMSELF.

For the comprehension of this tale it is necessary that we should pay a visit to the Earl of Mount-carsden on the evening which preceded the execution of William Spanton, which we have described in the foregoing chapter.

The returned convict had a difficult rôle to play, for he knew that he had enemies, and he felt convinced that if he was not careful in the extreme a day would come when the mask which he wore would be dashed from his face and his imposition revealed to the world.

The Marquis of Aguado, musing over the bold feats which he had perpetrated in his lengthened career of crime, was sitting in his drawing-room, when a noise outside the door of the apartment attracted his attention.

Quickly he turned round.

On the threshold of the room stood a girl of about eighteen summers, of imposing appearance, and dressed in a travelling costume.

On seeing her the sham Earl rose.

Who could she be?

But no time was left for reflection, for the girl ran towards him, and encircling his neck in her beautifully-shaped arms, she imprinted a kiss upon his forehead, and quickly exclaimed,

"How are you, father?"

The Marquis of Aguado guessed all. It was she before whom he had to play a most difficult part indeed—the daughter of the man whom he had murdered.

Murdered in cold blood, with the help of Bella, the shameless prostitute, who shrunk before no deed, however ignominious, if gold could be made by it.

We may be told that it was an impossibility for the sham lord to act as he did.

An event, however, occurred which came to his help, and diverted the girl's attention at the most critical moment of his position.

Vivid flashes of lightning cleared the air; the thunder rattled ominously; heavy drops of rain began to beat against the broad windows of the mansion, and distant peals of the unchained elements seemed in their loud wrath to threaten the murderer with a retribution which was close at hand.

"Now to the startled eye the sudden glance
Appears far south irruptive through the clouds,
And following in explosion vast, the thunder raises
  its tremendous voice.
At first, heard solemn on the verge of heaven,
The tempest growls; but as it nearer comes,
And rolls its awful burthen on the wind,
More and more the noise astounds,
Till overhead a sheet of flame, disclosing the etherial
  world,
Follows the loosened aggravated roar."

Blanche ran to the window.

"Oh, father," she said, gazing upon the deserted square, and listening sadly to the rain pattering against the smooth glass before her, "what weather!"

The nobleman knew not what to say.

He had not spoken yet and feared to do so, for he thought that his daughter might detect in his intonation of voice accents which she had never heard before.

But he resolved to speak.

"It is indeed sad weather for the poor of the metropolis, Blanche," he replied, "and I am glad indeed that you returned before the storm broke out. You would have caught your death of cold had you been out in a cold carriage. Sit down, now darling, and tell me how you spent your time while away from me."

The girl did as she was bid, and related to her father the manner with which she had wiled away the hours in company with the person with whom she had been staying on a visit.

Occasionally her father would question her.

Then Blanche would wonder.

She thought that her father's voice sounded strange; that he had greatly altered; that he was a different man, indeed, from him whom she had seen but a few weeks ago.

But, had she been told the truth, could she have believed it?

Then it was not extraordinary that she did not guess it; for could any imagination, however fertile, have conceived to itself the terrible drama which had been enacted by the returned convict.

No, never. For there are things in the daily occurrence of the incidents of the world which would baffle the belief of the greatest advocate of the supernatural and of the impossible.

"Blanche," said the nobleman, gazing upon his daughter, "do you know that you look very pretty indeed this evening ? The country air has done you good."

A smile played upon the beauty's lips.

" Think you so, father," she replied coquettishly, and as she looked at her father, and her glance rested upon the fixed sunken eye, upon the compressed lips, the low retreating forehead, she could not but think that the expression of her parent's countenance had indeed undergone a great change in a very short time too.

" I have been very unhappy since I left you, father," Blanche resumed. " You know I was without you, and when away from you I feel forlorn and disconsolate, and I cannot but think that you did not act right towards my poor mother."

" Mention not the name of her," the sham nobleman went on.

As he spoke a dark frown furrowed the convict's forehead.

Blanche became silent.

Her father had spoken roughly to her.

And for the poor girl that was a terrible blow, for she loved him dearly, although she often thought that he had behaved badly indeed towards her mother—towards the Lady Mountcarsden, who for some time past had been, as we have already stated, incarcerated in a lunatic asylum.

We have often heard people run down womanhood—nay, not so very long ago we listened to a young gentleman well known in the literary world who compared women to cattle !

But we think that such words are unbecoming any one provided with the slightest particle of intelligence.

For is not woman a sweet companion given to man to enliven the weary hours of his solitude ? Within a woman's breast often beats a heart which can feel for pleading misery—for forlorn destitution. She is constant, faithful, and loving—she toils hard sometimes for the object of her choice—she is never to be beaten in a work before which many others would succumb. Although weak and frail, we find that she has often performed deeds which have been a credit to her sex—deeds which have rendered her illustrious in many instances—instances which are not wanting either, whether we refer to the annals of the present day, or the voluminous records of past ages, embracing the history of mankind.

Blanche, however, was resolved to revert once more to her mother.

She felt that she had not acted towards her as she should have done.

She knew that she had sided with her father in the carrying out of a dark scheme which had resulted in a woman, endowed with all her mental abilities, being flung among lunatics, and for no reason whatever, except those of being legally entitled to a large fortune coveted by somebody else.

" Father," said Blanche, approaching Lord Mountcarsden, " do you know that when I think of my poor mother —"

The nobleman rose and uneasily paced up and down the room.

" Well, then, what ?" he asked, feverishly, wishing to appear annoyed.

" Yes," replied Blanche, resolving not to be beaten by the sulky mood of her supposed father ; " tears come to my eyes and I cannot help weeping."

" A very natural feeling on your part, my child," replied his lordship, wishing to appear concerned by his daughter's words ; " but your mother of late had become so very violent towards me that it would have been dangerous for me to allow her to remain indoors."

Blanche wondered.

Could it be true ?

Was she hearing aright ?

Was it her father who spoke ?

No, she could not believe it.

Her mother !

Her own darling mother !

To hear her thus abused was repugnant to her feelings.

And by her speech she soon told her father that he was not acting right in speaking as he did.

" Father," she said, " would you do me a favour ?"

" What is it, darling ?"

" Will you promise me to abide by my request ?"

" Speak."

Blanche mused as she spoke.

She knew that she might utter words which might be the means of kindling her father's wrath.

Yet she determined that she would make a clean breast of the feelings of remorse which for weeks past had been lacerating her soul.

His lordship was getting impatient.

" Speak, Blanche," he went on, affectionately. " If your wish is one with which I can comply, I'll yield to it."

Blanche's features became radiant with hope, and her beautiful eyes sparkled brilliantly.

" Do you know, father," she pursued in a coaxing friendly tone, " that I have often thought that if my poor mother was to be back here we would be much happier."

Lord Mountcarsden reflected.

What should he do ? Should he make a rash promise to his daughter, or on the other hand should he adopt another ?

He determined upon the latter.

" Your mother, Blanche," he said, " is one who has acted in a very unjust manner towards me. She was ever blaming me for behaving in a feelingless way. I never did so. I was always kind and affectionate to her. She would confuse in her mind things that had never taken place. Of late a whirl came over her. It was a sad task for me to perform the rôle which I did. The world blamed me, but I had no other alternative. She became mad, and there was but one step left to me, to have her placed in an asylum where every care would be bestowed upon her. Sincerely do I hope that under the treatment of expert physicians she may recover her health."

Slowly had his lordship spoken.

" Father," said Blanche.

" What ?"

" Are you certain that mother is mad ?"

" Mad, of course she is, or——"

" My lord," said the menial, " a gentleman is down stairs, and wishes to see you."

Thus speaking he presented a metal salver to the nobleman.

Lord Mountcarsden quietly took up the card.

" Mr. Workirk," he muttered ; " show him upstairs at once."

The servant withdrew.

When the message announcing another visitor was conveyed to the earl his features grew livid, a sickening sensation nearly choked his throat, and he wished he could have hidden himself away from the gaze of the new comer.

He had heard from Bella that Lawyer Workirk was one who had sworn to take a bold revenge against the late Lord Mountcarsden, who had related to the courtesan the scene which he had had with the man at law, a scene upon which we have dwelt in one of the early chapters of our narrative,

But there are moments in life when to assume boldness is certain to ensure victory—a moment during which often the freedom of man hangs upon a thread.

The Marquis of Aguado was a good actor. That he had hitherto acted like very few others could have done has been shown to us, and now that matters were gradually becoming more entangled he firmly resolved that he would not by any untoward act of his forfeit the position he had gained.

During the time which we have taken to commit to paper the above details the lawyer was ascending the staircase, and he soon walked into the room and faced the nobleman.

" Good evening to you, Mr. Workirk," said the nobleman, holding out his hand in a friendly manner to the lawyer.

" Good evening, my lord," repeated the man at law.

" Pray take a seat, Mr. Workirk," resumed the false earl, pointing to a sumptuous easy chair by the fireside, " and be kind enough to let me know the object of your visit."

As he spoke the Marquis of Aguado's glance met that of the lawyer.

Unflinching was the look of the returned convict as he prepared himself to listen to the remarks of his visitor.

But the false earl did not like to have anyone in his confidence. He feared that during the conversation which was about to be held he might say things which would betray the imperfect knowledge which he possessed of the late lord's family matters, and so he bid his daughter to retire from the room.

Unwillingly did Blanche depart.

She wished she had been allowed to remain.

But she knew that it would have been unwise in the extreme to rebel against her father's orders, and so with a slow measured tread she sought the privacy of her bedchamber.

When alone with the lawyer the returned convict drew a long breath.

There was a load off his breast, a load which he could have ill borne much longer.

As soon, therefore, as his daughter Blanche had left the room the sham nobleman rose and opened the door to see whether anyone was lingering behind it; but having satisfied himself that there was not a human being nigh besides the lawyer, he retraced his steps towards the seat which he had vacated.

There was a moment of silence which followed the prudent steps which the sham nobleman had taken.

" And now, Mr. Workirk," he resumed, " what might be your pleasure?

With his feet upon the fender facing the hearth, and with his eyes rivetted upon the burning embers Lawyer Workirk was doubtless resolving in his mind the answer which he would give to the nobleman's query.

At length he spoke.

" You remember, my lord, he said. the interview which we had together in the presence of her ladyship. It is some time ago. Since then many strange things have occurred.

" Perfectly," replied the sham lord drily.

" You have gained your point, my lord."

" How so ? "

" You have succeeded in incarcerating in a lunatic asylum a lone woman."

" I have."

" You have succeeded in committing a base deed."

" Mr. Workirk ! "

" My lord ! "

" Really, sir, if you have come here to insult me I must ask you not to do so again, pursued the sham nobleman in a cool, collected tone, wiping his brow, from which trickled heavy drops of perspiration. My actions have been prompted by the best of motives, and I fear not any paltry accusations."

" You do not ? "

" No, certainly."

Here the Marquis of Aguado breathed easily.

It was evident to him from the lawyer's manner that he was upbraiding him for actions which he had never perpetrated, and he preferred such accusations from any remarks which might have led him to believe that he had discovered who he really was.

" Then you think yourself very strong, my lord," the lawyer retorted.

The returned convict bit his lips.

" Strong enough to fight my own part."

" Indeed, my lord."

" Yes."

" Well, then, listen to me, my lord."

" With the greatest of pleasure."

" If you have gained your point I have also *gained mine*."

" In what way, pray ?"

" Her ladyship will be liberated this night."

" Ah !"

" I do not believe it."

" You don't ?"

A satanical smile played upon the white lips of the sham lord.

" Deeds are stubborn things, for look here."

As he spoke the lawyer drew a parchment from his pocket and read it aloud.

It was an order from the Chancellor, giving the lawyer permission to remove Lady Mountcarsden from the place where she was confined, her sanity having been pronounced to exist beyond a doubt by a board of three of the most eminent physicians that London could produce.

The returned convict turned deadly pale.

Difficulties were every instant rising before his path.

Would he be able to level them all ?

Of that he had strong doubts indeed!

" But this is not all, my lord. The long lost son has been found. I will bring him hither, and he will baffle you in your schemes. He will inherit the large estates which you have been doing your utmost to deprive him of."

" His name ?" gasped the nobleman.

" William Spanton," replied the lawyer.

A loud, derisive, mocking, satanical yell escaped the returned convict's lips.

" I do not fear him," he said ; " he is a *felon*."

" What ? "

" Have you read the newspapers?"

" No."

" Have you seen the report of the famous burglary case ? "

" No."

" The trial—the verdict ? "

" No."

" Well, Mr. Workirk, I daresay that you are not in a hurry for a moment or two. I happen to have the papers."

Thus saying the sham nobleman rose and opened a desk which was lying in one of the corners of the room.

From it he withdrew a bunch of newspapers Picked one out of many and read on—read on with a flowing voice, with a triumphant smile—read the trial, and wound up by informing the lawyer that the heir to the princely fortune had been found guilty and was now in Newgate, and was to be executed the following morning.

This was enough for the lawyer.

He had the interests of her ladyship too much at heart to delay one instant.

"I am not beaten yet, my lord," he said. "You will hear from me again. I'll save her ladyship from your unmanly persecution; with the help of Heaven I'll save her son."

He spoke with hope.

But the good lawyer was doomed to be disappointed.

He went to the Home Secretary.

Explained to him the whole bearings of the case.

But as we have seen in a previous part of this work he had acted too late. A reprieve had been granted, but when it came William Spanton had ceased to exist.

* * * * * *

It was a long time ere the sham nobleman retired to his bedroom.

There he remained in the drawing-room, unable to calm the torrent of wayward thoughts which was usurping his brain.

At length midnight came.

There was a deathlike stillness in the mansion.

Blanche had retired to her apartment.

The sham nobleman thought that he should do the same.

So he walked slowly to his bedchamber.

But he could not sleep.

The bitter pangs of remorse were beginning to lacerate his heart—his brain was in a whirl. He trembled violently. What a sad farce his existence had been! That he could carry on his difficult game he believed impossible, and so he began to think. Then the dark deeds which he had committed appeared in rapid succession before him. He thought he could see his headless body claiming vengeance; and then again he revolved in his mind the murder in the wood, so quickly followed by his assumption of a title which he had purchased with the price of blood.

He was soliloquising aloud when his bedchamber door opened, and a man in a servant's clothes creeped in the room.

"Who are you," feverishly asked the Marquis of Aguado, bending before the stranger.

The unknown divested himself of his garments, pulled off a wig and a flesh mask which he had been wearing, and disclosed to the Earl of Mountcarsden the features of Mercedes.

Mercedes! the man who had been his accomplice in getting rid of his brother.

"Well, my lord," said this man, "you have kept your promise, eh?"

"What do you mean?"

"Mean what I say."

"Man, I know you not."

Mercedes laughed loudly.

"I suppose, my lord, you did not expect me here."

"Expect you!"

"Yes."

"Once more, I repeat, I do not understand you."

"Is that your game?"

The sham lord's teeth chattered.

"Man, I never saw you before."

"I did you, though."

"When and where?"

"In a lone field."

"You are making a mistake."

"In France."

"I am not the party."

"Do you deny it still."

"I do. Your words are so many riddles to me."

"I helped you to murder your brother."

"My brother!"

"Yes."

"I never had a brother."

The impertinent manner with which the Marquis of Aguado was receiving his old confederate galled him to the core.

He took a rapid survey of all the valuables in the room.

He saw that his lordship was unarmed.

"My lord," he said, "I know you. You are the fratricide—the convict who escaped from the bagne of Toulon. How you became a nobleman I know not. Am I not speaking truly, No. 557?"

Had the sham Earl of Mountcarsden acted wisely he would have made friends with his former companion, but so confident of success did he feel that he thought that submission would be beneath him.

"No, man, I do not know," he said. "You are making a mistake. And now, allow me to ask you, how came you here?"

"By the door, of course."

"Well, then, you must go."

"I shan't."

"Leave my presence."

"What else would you like?"

"Do you hear me?"

"557, beware."

"What would you do."

"Do you refuse to know me."

"I never saw you before."

"I'll sit here until you do."

"Will you."

"Yes."

"I'll see about that."

"What then?"

"I'll have you expelled by my servants."

"Are you joking."

"I'll keep my word."

"Nonsense."

"Unless you leave at once I'll summon assistance."

And the Earl of Mountcarsden meant what he said, for he prepared himself to ring the bell to summon assistance.

But some cool impertinence had exasperated Mercedes. He was wild beyond description.

He rushed towards the sham nobleman.

"Die, then, you liar!" he exclaimed. "Die the death of a traitor."

In vain did the sham nobleman try to make a dart towards one side of the room, where a pair of swords hung. In vain did he try to remove the screwy-like fingers of Mercedes, who held him tightly by the windpipe. In vain did he endeavour to yell for assistance. Mercedes was too much for him.

With a heavy knock he felled the Marquis of Aguado to the ground, and quickly withdrawing a dagger from his undergarments, he plunged it to the hilt in the sham nobleman's breast.

Then Mercedes glance swept quickly around him, and having seen that nothing of importance was to be carried away he rifled the nobleman's clothes of whatever jewellery they contained, and by some well contrived means managed to effect his escape.

NOTICE.

A List of the Successful Winners of our Prizes will be shortly published. Any communications relating to the same to be forwarded to the Editor of " The Dance of Death."

THE
DANCE OF DEATH;
OR,
THE HANGMAN'S PLOT.
A THRILLING ROMANCE OF TWO CITIES.

No. 21.]   SATURDAY, MARCH 24, 1866.   [ONE PENNY.

IN PRISON.

CHAPTER LXXVIII.

RELATING WHAT OCCURRED THE MORNING OF THE MURDER—THE GOOD LAWYER AND LADY MOUNT-CARSDEN — NANCY IN FASHIONABLE QUARTERS—EXPLANATIONS.

The convict Mercedes was one of those men who would not have shrunk before any ignominious deed; he delighted in cruelty. Thus it was with no pangs of remorse that he left the mansion of the sham lord. He had detected him playing the rôle of an impostor, and 557 had refused to know him. There is a code of morals and honour among thieves rogues, and vagabonds. What that is must be left for some other to describe. Our object is to attend to our characters; with them we find we have quite enough to do. So let us tell our readers that Mercedes' idea was that if one of his creed and of his own calling refused to acknowledge him, he was doomed to die. He had wrought justice; he cared for no more. He had got rid of a man who knew his secrets, and he felt happy. So he managed, after considerable manœuvring, to leave Belgrave-square without exciting any suspicion.

We must attend to matters of detail. It may be

162

asked, how had Mercedes found his way upstairs? The answer is simple. Mercedes had not been idle. He had watched his former companion; had frequented the public-house where his servants were in the habit of going, and had learnt from them all particulars.

But now he is gone—we may not have occasion to see him again; we must, therefore, again attend to our story.

Early in the morning, Blanche, whose mind had been filled during the night with strange apprehensions, rose from her bed, and after having entrusted to her ladyship's maid the care of her toilet, roamed about the house, anxiously expecting the sound of the clock striking ten, a sound which would inform her that the meal was ready and that breakfast-time had come.

But ten o'clock came, and yet her father did not appear.

At first she did not fret; but as the minutes passed and the half-hours followed, she began to think that it was strange that her father did not put in an appearance, for he had always been remarkable for great punctuality, a peculiarity which, if it failed him during business hours, never failed him at any other.

Blanche violently rang the bell.

A servant answered.

"John," said the girl, addressing the individual whom we have seen before, "my father has not been down yet; go and see whether he is unwell, and whether I can do anything for him."

"I hope that nothing has occurred to his lordship," replied the valet, obsequiously; "last night I saw master, and he seemed perfectly well."

"Never mind about what you saw; act as I bid you, and delay not."

The flunky felt by his young lady's manner that she did not wish to be kept waiting, and so, bowing ere he departed, he went straight to his lordship's bedroom.

John was one of those men who, having no feelings or no enthusiasm, cannot either be frightened or be moved by anyone or anything. They take one thing and everything as a matter of course. To suppose for one moment that his lordship was out of the same health which he had seen him enjoy the night before would be the last idea which would come into his head. He looked upon life as a pleasant sort of thing—never tried to ascertain that which he could not understand, and so altogether he was very happy; and knowing it so to be, jogged along peaceably and a great deal more smoothly than many people would have done.

John fully expected to find his master in bed, snoring soundly, and looking very annoyed to be disturbed.

We do not know whether we shall again have occasion to see Mr. John, but for the present we must remain in his company (we hope that nobody will blame us), as he is bent upon an errand of some importance.

Importance for Blanche and for us, but trivial enough, God knows, for anybody else.

John gave one gentle tap against the door.

"My lord," he began, after he had waited for above a quarter of an hour.

To this interrogation there was no answer.

"My lord," again renewed the flunkey.

Still his voice remained without an echo.

"Decidedly," said John, to himself, "my master is the most extraordinary being out. Not only does he alter his face, but also his manner. At one time he was a civil, decent sort of chap. What changes of late!"

John, therefore, blessing his master all the while, waited.

But a man cannot be so deaf as not to hear the strong pummelling which the servant was inflicting upon the door.

But evidently his lordship was.

The servant felt disgusted. Still it would not do for him to remain all day outside his master's bedchamber. So John resolved to enter the sacred premises, where during many years of service he had never ventured, except on peculiar occasions, when the earl was out.

John accordingly summoned courage, and resolved to obtain immediate admission on his own hook, since he could not do so otherwise.

The servant knew that he was taking a great liberty, for his lordship had before now given strict orders not to be disturbed in his privacy; but Blanche had expressed a desire, nay, a command, and in the event of the Earl of Mountcarsden blaming him for intruding, the worthy flunky fully determined to lay all the blame at his young mistress's door.

But how can we describe John's features when he entered the bedchamber? He gave way to a low groan, and ran hurriedly down stairs like a madman.

"My lord has been murdered!" he exclaimed wildly to the first person whom he met, and who happened to be the housekeeper.

"His lordship been murdered, John!" this good dame replied. "Why, man, you must be dreaming!"

In reply to the woman's remark John opened his eyes wide and muttered, "Go and see."

It will be clearly understood by our readers that such an event as that which had taken place, and to which we have assisted, was likely to create a great commotion.

In less than a minute the whole household knew of the news.

One and all, therefore, flocked to the master's apartment.

Yes, there could be no doubt about it! The false earl to all outward appearance seemed to be dead—his eyes were closed, and his lips were of a livid hue. There he lay, supine upon his back, with rigid limbs and motionless body.

"What is to be done?" asked the housekeeper from one of the under servants. "We can't break the news to Miss Blanche, for it would be enough to kill her."

"But she is sure to hear of it sooner or later," put in another.

"Never mind that, we must keep matters quiet," suggested a third.

"A sad ending to our master, now," soliloquised the housekeeper, shaking wisely her hoary locks; "but I often thought that he would be punished some day for the manner with which he acted towards our poor lady. And now that I begin to consider, why it strikes me that her ladyship is expected to return this day."

At that instant a loud noise was heard outside the bedroom door, and the attention of John was called to the cause which produced it.

This worthy had been afraid to remain in the room with a corpse by himself; but with company round him he rather liked the gossip which was taking place on the supposed dead body of the sham lord.

"What's the meaning of that?" asked the housekeeper.

John had rushed upon the landing.

Out of breath, excited, panting, he returned to the earl's room.

"Lock the door," he said, "and let us break the terrible tidings to Miss Blanche bye and bye, and through her own mother, for the carriage is outside the house, and I expect that her ladyship is returning among us."

"Her ladyship! God bless her!" were the words which were uttered in quick succession by the numerous persons who composed the Earl of Mountcarsden's household; and being anxious to welcome their mistress home, they followed the track of the menial whose duty it was to answer the door.

Meanwhile Blanche was sitting pensively in the breakfast-room, every instant expecting the return of John, who would inform her of the cause which had detained his lordship so much beyond his time.

But she was not likely to see him return as quickly as she anticipated, John having resolved not to join his young mistress again during the course of the day.

Blanche, however, was getting impatient, and was about to summon the servant once more, when the door of the breakfast-room opened, and Lady Mountcarsden appeared on the threshold, accompanied by Lawyer Workirk and a sweet pretty girl, whom we believed we had seen before, and whom we have introduced to our readers under the name of Nancy.

The meeting which took place between Blanche and Lady Mountcarsden was one of the most affecting scenes which it was ever the novelist's duty to chronicle. She questioned Lady Mountcarsden—hoped for forgiveness—blamed herself for having never tried to love her—and, in conclusion, wept and wept until her eyes were sore.

Lawyer Workirk meanwhile was standing by Lady Mountcarsden.

"I bring your mother back to you, Blanche," he said, after a while, "and I will entrust her to you and to this young girl, who will act as a lady's maid to Lady Mountcarsden. Have you any objection to that?"

"Oh, Mr. Workirk, how can you be so crossed and so matter of fact towards me?" Blanche replied enthusiastically. "You know not the debt of gratitude which I owe you in having restored my mother to me; for I often thought of her, and in the silence of my own room prayed for her safe return. I am proud to think that you believe me still worthy of my mother's affection; and with regard to the young person, I can only say a thing which you ought to have guessed long ago—namely, that the friends of Mr. Workirk are also mine."

As she spoke she looked towards Nancy, relating whom we must say a few words, explaining how it came to pass that the girl finds herself in the lawyer's company.

The last time we saw her it was on the morning which followed the burglary.

We left her in the hands of the police—with Velvet and Frank Pullen.

How had she managed to get out of them?

This we must tell.

With tottering steps and a faint heart Nancy had been dragged to the station.

When in the gloomy cold cell her heart sank.

The feeling to her was terrible—something akin to that of William Spanton, when in the gaol of Newgate he was visited by the Crown Lawyer, who was to take his case in hand and defend him upon his trial.

But, gradually, Nancy's feelings took a more cheerful tone—she relied upon the truth of her story—and hoped that by relating all things as they came to pass her innocence would be clearly proved.

In so thinking she was not mistaken.

The magistrate, before whom she was brought, discharged her, and remanded Velvet to cause inquiries to be made concerning him.

The sad story of the girl Nancy was published in all the newspapers, and a long account appeared in the *Daily Telegraph* about the difficulty existing for hard-working laborious girls to obtain an honest living in London.

Among the many hundreds of thousands of readers before which the account of Nancy's trial found its way was Lawyer Workirk. He ascertained her address, and, as he wanted a good trustworthy girl to watch her ladyship (who was, in a few days, leaving the lunatic asylum), he resolved to pay her a visit.

Nancy, who had been provided with a few shillings out of the poor-box, had secured a very modest bedroom, at 2s. 6d. a week, in a poor neighbourhood of London, and it was there that the wealthy lawyer sought her.

When the girl saw a perfect stranger to her appearing before her she at first was not a little alarmed, as it may easily be fancied; but when he told her his motives the forlorn creature would have been ready to kiss the ground on which he stood, impelled by the noble enthusiasm of elevating gratitude.

Then the lawyer told the girl that if she liked to become the companion of a lady of title, he would place her in a position to do so.

Need it be told that Nancy readily assented to the proposal?

There was nothing very extraordinary in the occurrence.

The Hand of Providence could be traced even in this trifling incident.

Lawyer Workirk had there and then insisted upon the girl coming with him.

It mattered little to Nancy whither she went.

So she had accepted. And the good lawyer, after having provided Nancy with a few pounds wherewith she had purchased herself a wardrobe, finally introduced her to Lady Mountcarsden.

Nancy's story was a sad one.

But how her heart clung to her patrician friend—to the lord's wife—when she heard from her own lips the narration of her trials—when she heard from Lady Mountcarsden how she had been incarcerated for years in a place where she was surrounded by mad people of all descriptions.

So Nancy had become Lady Mountcarsden's companion.

And this is how it was that she went with her to Belgrave-square.

But, think not that her career was thus to be ended.

There were other things in store for the poor girl.

She battled long enough against the storm. Was she not to have days of calm?

She had been sorely tried.

Before great temptations she had remained virtuous. Was she to have no reward?

Perhaps it may be found that the sun was to shine upon her path, and that after having walked for years in a barren moor she was to enter a garden teeming with Nature's most abundant gifts.

We have deemed the above explanations necessary.

Return to Blanche and to her mother, therefore, now we must.

"My poor child," said Lady Mountcarsden, gazing upon her daughter, who was weeping as if her heart would break, "do not thus give way to sorrow. I hold you perfectly free from all blame. You had nothing to do with that which I suffered. All now is forgotten—yet we may be happy. But say where's your father?"

"He has not been down to breakfast yet," replied Blanche, "and I have sent John to his room, but he has not returned yet."

Her ladyship walked across the room.

She was about to sing.

But she found it useless to do so.

For John at that instant appeared.

"Where is your master?" asked her ladyship.

"My master!" repeated the flunky, and he began to reflect.

"Will you give me an answer, John?"

"Why, my lady," John replied, "that is what I was trying to do."

"Trying to do!"

"Yes my lady."

"Are you dumb, then?"

"No, my lady."

Lady Mountcarsden looked round the room.

John was evidently mad—so Lawyer Workirk thought; but it was not so. The menial was revolving in his own mind the best means of acquainting his mistress with the news of which he was the bearer, and dreaded to speak for fear that he should break out the intelligence with too much abruptness, and thus inflict a severer blow upon her ladyship than she would perhaps be able to bear, after the serious illness which Lord Mountcarsden had purposely said, and falsely too, that she had undergone.

"John, how is it that your master is not downstairs? Have you told him that breakfast is ready?"

"Told him, my lady!"

"Yes."

"It would be useless to tell him; he would not have heard me."

"What do you mean?" her ladyship resumed, more and more puzzled.

"God help me!" now muttered John at his wits' ends, and then he said, "why I mean—I mean, my lady, that his lordship——"

"Yes."

"Is dead!"

Had any one been listening he would have heard a "Thank God!" issuing from one who was very much like Lawyer Workirk.

"Dead!" retorted her ladyship, with a low intonation of voice.

The servant shook his head mournfully in the negative.

"That he is, my lady," he went on gloomily, "and what is worse, it looks very much as if he had been murdered."

And with these words John swept out of the room, leaving his listeners to conjecture upon the strange revelations which had been made to them.

CHAPTER LXXIX.

THE MARQUIS OF AGUADO'S DEATH-BED—THE CONFESSION—NANCY HEARS SOMETHING ABOUT WHICH SHE HAS SOME KNOWLEDGE.

There are moments in life which it would be difficult for any one to describe, for the very reason that they must be experienced for their real nature to be well understood—moments which, however short of duration, nevertheless often leave a lasting impression upon the mind. These moments are not brought on by trivial incidents; they are the results of either unexpected happiness, or untoward, crushing calamity. The feeling which one then experiences could be compared to that which usurped the brain of Wellington on the field of Waterloo, when he wondered whether the victory would be on the English side or not; to that of the playwright, who anxiously awaits the rising of the curtain to see whether his drama will be cheered or hissed by the audience; a feeling somewhat akin also to the sensation of the sporting man, scanning the course and following, yards and yards from his gaze, the swift track of the horse upon which he has laid his all; and by those whose welfare depends upon a crisis of which the result is doubtful.

We have begun our chapter with the above short remarks to prepare our readers for the information which we are about to give them, and which consists in telling them that those brief moments, so short and yet so powerful, were exactly those which hung heavily upon two hearts—those of Lady Mountcarsden and her daughter Blanche.

Her ladyship was really puzzled—nay, more properly speaking, undecided, thoughtful, and pained. She could not believe that on the morning which heralded her return to the house from which she had been rejected by her worthless husband, she would hear of his being no more.

For a few minutes the actors in the drama which we are narrating remained at a standstill—Lawyer Workirk not speaking for fear of offending his lady friend; Nancy too bashful to utter a word without having been previously spoken to by those whom she believed to be her superiors in rank and birth.

Lawyer Workirk, however, was one of those who would have allowed things to remain in suspense, moreover when so great a stake as that of the death of a lord whom he had always despised depended upon it.

"My Lady Mountcarsden," he said, "turning blandly towards her ladyship, "I would deem it a great favour if you were to let me know when I can ascertain the truth of the servant's words."

The words of the lawyer were not thrown away upon Blanche.

"Oh, come with me, sir," she exclaimed, "and I'll take you upstairs."

Lady Mountcarsden was so thunderstruck for a while at least by the news which she had heard that she said nothing to prevent her daughter from taking Lawyer Workirk into the nobleman's bedroom, where they both expected to find him dead.

Lawyer Workirk, with a greater agility than one would have given him credit for, considering his time of life, cleared the flight of steps with the quickness of a youth of twenty.

Blanche and he soon reached the landing.

The lawyer entered the room.

But, like John, he was not easily frightened; but if he had been there was this time full reason for a bold man to retreat.

Standing upright upon a bed was the supposed Earl of Mountcarsden.

"Oh, come here," he ejaculated, in a weak tone of voice, as soon as he saw the lawyer. "Come here, I want to speak, to say a good many things of importance before I die."

Although the words were pronounced in a very faint intonation, yet they reached the lawyer's hearing; and knowing that betimes many an important secret is revealed on one's death-bed, he resolved not to lose the opportunity which offered.

It required, however, all Lawyer Workirk's strength of mind to approach the dying man's bedside, for the spectacle which met his gaze when he entered the room was ghastly and horrible in the extreme.

The sheets of the bed were literally saturated with clotted blood—with the blood which had issued from the wound which Mercedes had inflicted upon the Marquis of Aguado, and which was to prove mortal.

The returned convict's features also were repulsive to behold. His forehead was of a clammy whiteness, and he shook like an aspen leaf when he spoke, his teeth all the while chattering with the shiver which precedes the hour of death.

But Lawyer Workirk was not one to lose easily his self-possession; and so when he saw him whom he believed to be his greatest enemy he held out his hand.

"My lord," he began, " I see you in a sad plight, and allow me to see whether I can give you any help. You have a wound? What has occurred to you?"

The Marquis of Aguado shook mournfully his head, and a ghastly smile played upon his pale lips.

The lawyer retreated.

A thought had flitted across his mind.

" I hope, my lord," he said, " that you did not intend to commit suicide."

Again the Marquis nodded in the negative.

" Do not call me my lord," he went on; " I am an impostor—a murderer! "

And he hissed the last words between his teeth.

Now came the lawyer's turn.

" What were you, my lord? " he asked.

But the convict made no reply.

Then it was that the man at law began to catechise the features of the man before him; and then it was that Blanche rushed into the room, followed by her ladyship and the girl Nancy.

"Oh, father! " exclaimed Blanche.

But a shriek escaped her lips, and she sought protection in her mother's arms.

The glance of the returned convict had met hers, and she had been frightened by it.

" Workirk," said her ladyship, squeezing the lawyer's arm, and drawing him towards her, " this is not my husband."

" Who can it be, then?"

" I know who that is," now put in Nancy; "that's a foreign gentleman, and they call him the Marquis of Aguado."

Can any one fancy the consternation which was depicted upon the features of all those who were standing in the room?

" The Marquis of Aguado," muttered her ladyship.

" Not Lord Mountcarsden?" pursued the lawyer. " Am I asleep or am I dreaming?"

Under any other circumstances, doubtless, the police would have been sent for, but so strangely situated was her ladyship that she never thought of the only step which at any other time she would have taken.

"You are astonished," now began the convict; " and I am not surprised at it. To you my appearance must be a riddle. But there is no time to be lost. I am dying—yes, dying fast; and I have several important communications to make."

" Shall I leave the room?" asked Blanche, whose head was in a whirl.

No notice was taken of her request by her ladyship, and so she remained.

" Well, speak," said Lawyer Workirk, approaching the murderer, for whose momentary recovery it is not difficult to account.

The Marquis of Aguado had been mortally wounded by Mercedes.

No sooner had he received the blow than he fell like a log of wood on the carpeted floor of his apartment.

For several hours he remained in a swoon, and when the servants had seen him he was unconscious.

But when he had been handled by the servants a change had taken place, and he had opened his eyes to find himself alone, having, it is needless to state, not the remotest idea of the visit which had been made in his room by the whole of the household.

"Oh, heavens " ejaculated the convict in a faint tone of voice, " I wish I could live to repent; but God will not give me time. I have sinned too much to be so readily forgiven."

It was, indeed, a sad scene which was being enacted in that handsome mansion in Belgrave-square, and few of the passers-by could have believed that that which we are relating was occurring not many yards from them.

Lawyer Workirk was a Christian.

The sight of the dying convict moved him deeply, and although her father's murderer was before her, Blanche could not help gazing with pity upon him.

" I wish," continued the convict, " that I could speak more fluently, but my tongue becomes parched and my breath draws short, but I'll do my best to acquaint you with a most important communication."

Then the convict related to the listeners the murder which he had perpetrated, and the bold manner with which he had assumed the rank of the late lord.

Lawyer Workirk believed himself in a box at the theatre, listening to some far-fetched performance. He could not realise to his mind the fact that the things which he heard belonged to the annals of daily life.

Long and sad was the convict's conversation.

He spoke much clearer than he or his companion had anticipated.

Occasionally, however, he would stop short and draw breath; for it was perceptible that every word which he uttered caused him no small amount of pain.

Presently the convict placed his hand across his eyes and reflected for a few instants.

Then a strange expression flitted across his pallid countenance.

" Hark! " he said, tremulously; " I hear Satan's bell summoning me to everlasting punishment; but before I go to him—to my master—I must——"

Here he stopped.

" Yes," he resumed, after awhile, " I must tell you one thing which may be the means of righting one whom I have deeply injured."

" Proceed, proceed," quickly whispered the lawyer in the convict's ears.

The Marquis of Aguado went on—

" I was not always an outcast of society," he said bitterly. " Once I was an honest man, but a terrible passion followed me through life, and has been my ruin. To satisfy the cravings for gambling, which ever haunted my whole being, I would have shrunk from no amount of villany. In truth, I sold my soul to Satan through it. Yes, I hear him! I see him waiting for me, but I——"

Incoherent at times was the Count's speech.

But he, however, succeeded in relating the murder which he had committed in the wood in France— how he had lately taken his brother's life. And he went on slowly until he came to this part, " but my brother had a daughter alive."

" Yes," said the lawyer, anxiously.

"Upon her was settled an immense property—a quarter of a million of money. To obtain it I forged deeds."

"Yes."

"And should the will of her father be recovered she could inherit it, as all the documents which I used were worthless."

"Do you know, then, in whose hands it is?" asked the lawyer.

"Yes. I left it in the possession of a man of the name of Marks."

"Where does he live?"

"I know not."

"Oh! Mr. Workirk," now ejaculated Nancy, "I know something about the paper."

"You do?"

"I heard some one speaking about it."

Perhaps the reader may be at a loss to fathom the meaning of Nancy's words. To refresh his memory we will beg of him to recall to his mind the scene which took place in the thieves' den—a scene we did our best to describe in one of the early chapters of this work.

"And where is that man, Marks? Think—try to recollect—give us all particulars," continued the lawyer, anxious to get as much information as he could from the dying man.

But no powers of speech could have got another word from the convict's lips now.

His voice had left him, and it was visible that the stream of life was rapidly ebbing from its tenement.

Once more the convict tried to rise.

But he had not strength to do so.

Presently his eyelids closed. Then the chill of death rapidly followed, and he was quickly hurrying on to that bourne from whence no traveller returns.

"Pray leave the room, my ladies," said the lawyer, "and leave me here. You have heard enough. Your presence here is no longer necessary."

Her ladyship did as she was requested.

In company with her daughter she sought the privacy of her own apartments.

Nancy meanwhile stood upon the landing.

What strange things she had seen enacted in London!

How odd also that she should have been present when a dying man mentioned the existence of a will relating to which Velvet had more than once spoken to her.

Was she concerned in it?

Could she have any interest in a long-lost parchment which would ensure the owner a colossal fortune?

She was thus thinking when Lawyer Workirk tapped her gently upon the shoulder.

"The man is dead, darling," he said; "the heart has ceased to beat. Do you know, child, that God does everything for the best? The individual who has just expired was a great villian, but not a whit worse in character than the nobleman whose name he assumed. People must save appearances. It would never do to relate in the papers the story to d to us by a murderer. As he was Lord Mountearsden to all intents and purposes, he will remain so for the public; for I will announce his death in the *Times*, and the outcast and the murderer will have a patrician's tomb! And now come and see her ladyship."

Here it is necessary to quit the Mountearsden family to revert to other characters of this story, who also claim part of our attention.

CHAPTER LXXX.

HUSBAND AND WIFE — A PRAYER REJECTED—THE PARTING.

Whither was taken the woman who had been discovered beneath the scaffold? This is the question which we fancy we hear our readers asking us, and fully conscious of our duty we shall not delay in answering it.

Whenever and wherever they are not wanted the police are sure to appear. For what right had they to detain one who had committed no theft, and who was only guilty of being beneath the scaffold—a place certainly where she could not have done much harm.

When Jenny (for it was the farmer's wife) had been led away. A large crowd had followed until she was asked to step into a shop until the people had dwindled off.

A mob is always curious, but also very impatient, and so it mostly happens that when its wish is not satisfied at once, it seldom waits for the gratification of the sight which has caused it to deviate from the path which it should otherwise have taken.

Jenny was very handsome, and when alone in the shop with one of the policemen she began to weep as if her heart would break.

There is something very touching, very appealing to a manly heart in a woman's tears; moreover, when the mourner is endowed with no small amount of personal attraction.

The constable felt moved by the sight, and he asked Jenny whether the man who had suffered the last penalty of the law was one of her relatives.

The woman made no answer, but she hid her features in her hands.

"Now, come," said the policeman, who was a good sort. "do not cry like that; what's the use of it, eh? It won't mend matters."

Jenny's lips quivered, and again she gave vent to a flood of tears.

Then she rose, and her heart being too full she thought she would relieve it by acquainting the policeman with the whole of her story, since she had left Bournemouth.

The constable reflected.

"Ah!" he said, in a friendly tone, "it might have been worse. Where does your husband live? If I were you I would go to him and ask him to forgive me."

"Would you?" said Jenny; "but I fear he would not hear me."

"Never mind, you can but try."

There was a pause, during which the shopkeeper appeared with a glass of brandy, which he had got out of his own cupboard.

Seeing the foriornness of the creature who had entered his abode, like a kind-hearted man he had prepared a tumblerful of spirit and water for her acceptance.

Jenny thanked the shopkeeper but refused the proffered draught. In vain he tried to persuade her to accept, but she would not, and so at last, annoyed at her obstinacy, he left to attend to his business.

The constable meanwhile was thinking in his mind how he could carry out a scheme which had just entered his head.

"What's your husband's name?" he asked of Jenny after a while.

Jenny, at first, refused to answer.

"Why, won't you tell a friend the truth?" the constable resumed, "you know that I wish you well, and look here, I am not rich, but if a few shillings are of any use to you you are welcome to them."

And as he concluded speaking he withdrew his purse and was about to open it to give to Jenny whatever money she might have been in need of.

But Jenny again refused this mark of kindness.

"She's a rum one," thought the constable, "but I'll not be beaten yet."

So he resumed.

"What's your husband's name?" he asked once more.

"Why do you want to know?"

"To tell him that he has a repentant wife, and to ask him to forgive her."

"But he would not listen to you, perhaps. However, since you have acted friendly towards me I must not show a want of confidence in you. Richard Spaldings——"

"Are you married to Spaldings, then?" quickly followed the City constable, fearing to have guessed right, and interrupting Jenny in her speech.

The farmer's wife said that she was.

"Why that's the newly-appointed hangman! and you are his wife?"

All feeling of sympathy seemed to have left the constable.

"Go to Newgate," he said, "it is not far from here, and you will be sure to find him, for he must identify the corpse of the youth that he hanged this morning, and that will take him sometime; so good by.

And the constable left.

A sickening sensation now found its way in Jenny's breast, and a mist fell on her eyes.

Her husband was the hangman !

And William Spanton, her lover, had been executed that morning.

She would see him then—she would go to the prison.

She made a determination, and wishing good day to the shopkeeper for his kindness towards her, she strode with quick, hurried footsteps towards Newgate.

What awaited her ?

The unfortunate woman was not long in making her way from the shop where she had sought shelter to the ominous-looking building which goes under the name of Newgate prison.

After a few minutes walk she reached the outside of the place where she expected her husband was to be found.

Slowly she ascended the steps which led to the door, and rang the bell.

She had to wait some time.

To her every instant was a moment of bitter suspense.

What reception would she get ?

Would her husband prove merciful ?

And would he tell her the whereabouts of her son, about whose welfare she naturally was very anxious.

At last a turnkey appeared.

Previous to opening the door he looked at Jenny through the iron bars.

"What do you want ? " he asked, in a very business sort of manner.

"I want admission."

"Admission ?"

"Yes."

"I cannot let you in."

"Why not ?"

"Because you must show me some document warranting your right to come here."

Jenny did not expect this difficulty.

But she resolved to smooth it.

" I have important business."

" Have you ?"

" Yes."

" Upon what motives ? "

" Private ones."

" I cannot open the door, then."

" Pray do."

" I dare not."

And the turnkey was preparing to depart.

Jenny, however, fearing that the last' chance of seeing her husband would escape her, called back the official.

" Good sir," she said, " listen to me."

The turnkey retraced his steps towards Jenny.

" You have already told me whatever I wanted to know, so why take up my time? I have my duties to attend, and I cannot stay here much longer."

Such was the speech which emanated from the turnkey's lips.

"If I tell you my business, will you allow me to come in ?"

"That depends entirely upon what it is."

Unless she made the turnkey her confidant Jenny plainly perceived that she would have to remain in the street, and that the object of her errand would be baffled.

She had made up her mind to carry out a certain thing, and she firmly resolved that she would do it.

" I know some one connected with the prison," she said slowly.

" Why did you not say so before ?"

" What's his name ?"

"Spaldings," replied the farmer's wife.

Sadly and pointedly had Jenny spoken the name which she herself bore.

"And do you want to see him ?" asked the turnkey, eyeing the woman who had made a request to communicate with the hangman.

" I do."

" That is a different thing, then. If you had told me that at first there would have been no occasion for my having kept you out waiting."

So saying the turnkey opened the door of the prison.

Jenny stepped inside.

It was with a strange feeling that she followed the gaoler, who led her through long, gloomy, dark corridors to the left wing of the building.

"You will not be able to see Mr. Spaldings for some time," the turnkey went on. "He is rather busy just at present."

"Never mind, I'll wait."

"You may please yourself about that. But you must not stand here."

The words, "he is rather busy at present," sounded terribly upon Jenny's hearing.

She understood their ghastly meaning.

He was looking after the duties of his vile office.

"Will you give me your name and I'll take it to Mr. Spaldings," said the turnkey, minutely catechising the features of Jenny, for whose appearance in Newgate he was at a loss to account.

He had been many years in the prison and never before, during his experience as a gaoler, had he witnessed a similar occurrence.

He had known well the former hangman, and he was not often troubled with visitors.

"Now, my friend," said Jenny, addressing the turnkey, "will you do me a service ?"

"With all my heart."

"Take this message to Mr. Spaldings."

"Which one ?"

"That a poor woman wishes to see him."

"Is that all ?"

"Yes."

"Well, I do not mind doing that, but I fear it is not of much use. However, you seem chagrined, and I'll do my best to meet your wishes. That is to say, so long as it does not interfere with my duty."

Jenny was then conducted to a dark, square room, when she was told to wait.

Then, having seen Jenny taking a seat, the turnkey sallied forth on his errand, bearing to the hangman the message which had been given to him.

Anxiously Jenny waited.

What would be the result of her interview?

Such was the query which she was ever placing in her mind during the instant that she sat in that cold, dreary waiting-room where we have left her.

She could not, however, realise to herself the following fact, namely, how it happened that her husband had become the hangman.

Ere long, however, she would learn the truth.

Become acquainted with details of a revolting character.

Jenny was thinking deeply, when sounds of footsteps were heard approaching her.

So engaged with her reveries was she that she did not heed the noise.

However, as it grew nearer and nearer she was compelled to look up.

She did so.

Then her glance met that of a man, who was standing before her.

Richard Spaldings had arrived.

"What brings you hither, madam?" he said, derisively. "I expected not the honour of your visit."

There was an intonation of bitter hatred and of avowed contempt in the man's words.

Jenny was not slow in detecting the above.

"Richard," she said, slowly drooping her eyebrows, and allowing her glance to sweep far beneath her, "I have come to ask you to forgive me."

"Richard!" returned the farmer; "please address me by some other name than that. I am known under a different appellation here. Jack Ketch they call me. Ah! ah!"

Had a dagger been thrust in Jenny's breast the pain which she felt in the immediate vicinity of the heart could not have been keener than the one inflicted by the speech of the man whose lawful wife she still was.

"What induced you to become the public executioner, Richard?" Jenny resumed, and the sound of her voice grew fainter as she finished speaking.

"I had a motive—a powerful motive!"

"Oh, pray, Richard, do not keep on speaking thus."

The hangman's lips were compressed.

Ire darted from his sunken eyes.

"I understand your meaning, Richard."

"If you did not, perhaps this would leave you no doubt as to its purport."

Jenny now raised her glance from the ground.

An ejaculation of horror escaped her lips.

Richard Spaldings was showing the rope.

"This little thing did it," he hissed between his teeth; "this little thing was round William Spanton's neck this morning."

Could any behaviour have been more brutal?

Could any act be more horrible?

"Oh, Richard," she said, "why torture me so?"

And she receded a few paces.

There he was, Richard Spaldings, the public executioner.

There he stood before her as she had seen him in her dream.

And, alas! it had come to pass.

"Spanton is dead?"

"Hung by the neck, madam."

"Ah!"

"And by my own hands."

The farmer seemed to gloat over his words.

"With his death, Spaldings, let my guilty behaviour be ushered into oblivion."

"Never."

"Oh, Richard do not forsake me?"

"My work is not done yet."

"What do you imply?"

"Look at this little rope."

There was something fascinating in the sight.

Jenny would have wished to hide it from her glance.

But she could not do so.

All power of movement had forsaken her.

Her arms hung stiffly by her side.

"Your work is not done yet! What do you wish me to infer from that observation?"

"That you will perish by the rope."

"Be hanged?"

"Yes."

"What for?"

"For crime."

"And by whom?"

"By me."

The farmer hissed the last word.

Such was the reception which Jenny got.

She would, however, make another effort.

"Richard," she began, taking no heed of the request which her husband had made to her not to address him by his name; "I have sinned greatly, and I repent."

"Repent!"

"Yes, Richard."

"What's that to me?"

"Are you so cruel as not to forgive me?"

"Do I look like one that appears to have forgotten the faithless wife?"

Ironical in the extreme was the farmer's manner.

"Richard, I am lonely and friendless, and I come to you."

"Too late!"

"Why?"

"Because as long as you have lived you remained with your lover."

"I knew not where to find you."

"Richard, I admit my guilt, and I ask you to forget and forgive."

"I daresay you do. But I will not."

What could Jenny do?

"For the sake of our child, Spaldings."

"Ah! ah!"

"For the sake of bygone times."

"Ah! ah!"

"For the sake of the happy years which we have spent together."

"Ah! ah!"

These were the only derisive sounds which Jenny received for her answer.

There was a moment of silence.

Richard Spaldings was thinking deeply.

"Your child, your boy," he said, "you speak about him!"

"Yes, Spaldings, where is he?"

"And do you come to me for the information?"

Jenny nodded her head in the affirmative.

"Away, then, for I do not know."

NOTICE.

All our Subscribers are requested to send in the yellow Prize Ticket which appeared attached to our First Number and the 19 following Numbers.

THE
DANCE OF DEATH;
OR,
THE HANGMAN'S PLOT.
A THRILLING ROMANCE OF TWO CITIES.

No. 22.]   SATURDAY, MARCH 31, 1866.   [One Penny.

"A YOUNG GIRL OF ABOUT FIFTEEN YEARS OF AGE."

CHAPTER LXXX.—Continued.

"Richard," resumed the wife, approaching her husband, "I have behaved badly towards you, and I wish you to tell me that you have forgiven me."

"No; never—never!" hissed the farmer between his clenched teeth. "I took a vow and I will carry it out. You will die, and by my hands! Remember my words. Think you I can be so easily reconciled? Little indeed do you know my character. Faithless woman, you have turned my heart to ashes, prostrated my mind, ruined my brightest hopes! Can I forget that you have been the cause of my fall?

Lightly indeed do you consider your sin. Once I had a peaceful, happy home ; you broke it. Once I was respected ; you brought contempt upon me. Once I was wealthy ; I am now a beggar. Once my life was a sunny morn ; now it is a dark, murky evening—and I have but one hope left, and that is one of revenge ! "

" Oh ! Richard, do not remain thus. By the great heaven above our head—by the name of our boy Harry, do not forget that I was once a faithful, good wife to you ! Oh ! do give me your hand ! "

And Jenny flung herself upon her knees, and appealingly tried to shake her husband's determination.

The farmer glanced upon the poor woman, gave vent to a loud mocking laugh, and left the room.

All her endeavours had been useless.

In her husband Jenny had a bitter foe.

He had cruelly insulted her !

Spurned her !

And that was too much !

And now there came within her breast a revulsion of feeling.

She rose from her stooping position.

" I have done all that I could to reform." she said loudly. " Richard Spaldings, I am no longer the weak, frail woman. You have left me—flung me away from your presence ! But hear—hear me ! It is war between us—bitter war for the future ! "

" I accept the challenge, madam," replied a voice which seemed to issue from under the cold slabs. " You will die by this, madam ! "

It was Richard Spaldings who had spoken, and he was holding the rope for Jenny's inspection.

Jenny looked at it.

This time proudly and defiantly.

Then with quick, hurried steps she wended her way towards the door by which she had obtained admittance.

Were husband and wife to meet again, and under what circumstances ?

CHAPTER LXXXI.

THE HALLELUJAH CLUB.

" Lor, do you say it is so ? "

" No kid about it either, mate."

" Discharged ? "

" Yes."

" And do you tell me that you saw Velvet driving in a carriage ? "

" That I did."

" Dressed in young swell's togs ? "

" And it was a swell's too."

" How did that come to take place ? "

" I don't know, but methinks I guess."

' Speak then, lass."

The above conversation occurred between a young girl of about fifteen years of age, who was a strolling player, and a roguish sort of a man in company with several of our old acquaintances.

The girl was one of those town gipsies who for a living do anything that offers itself. The other was the Fence.

The Fence, who had managed to keep clear from the law's grip, was not a little annoyed at hearing that Velvet—a boy whom he hoped some day to render one of the boldest thieves of the day—had, by some unknown means, left the gaol, and was now in affluent circumstances.

The place where the following particulars took place was a pothouse of a very low stamp, frequented only by costers and thieves.

For many days, or rather many weeks past, and since the Hallelujah Club had been compelled to leave their old quarters, and to remove them to the neighbourhood of Strutton Ground, Westminster, the house where we now see the thieves had been their rendezvous.

The girl, who has hitherto been a complete stranger to us, and who is likely to remain so, and that for two reasons—first, because she is not to occupy any part in this narrative beyond appearing and disappearing, and secondly, because our story is rapidly drawing to a close—was one who had once or twice been thrown in Velvet's company.

Johnny Crapaud was present on the night we pay a visit to the weakened strength of a once flourishing club ; and so were Cannibal Jack, the boy Kay, and the illustrious Bob O'Link, not drunk yet, but very much that way we are going to say.

" And do you know the particulars ? " asked the Fence from the girl who had been telling him that she had seen Velvet.

" I do not," replied the girl ; " but I was told that a good gentleman came to his help."

" A good gentleman ? "

" Yes."

The Fence was at a loss to understand.

" You know what a lawyer is, Mat ? "

" Yes."

" Well, then, a lawyer, and a lawyer of the name of Workirk, went bail for the young fellow."

" Did he ? "

" Yes."

" And he obtained his liberty ? "

Then it was explained that Lawyer Workirk had obtained all particulars from the girl Nancy, and that Velvet was no longer in prison.

To tell our readers what became of him is a matter upon which we must subsequently dwell.

" Velvet has gone," said one.

" Big Ned got settled."

" Cannibal Jack is still with us. We are getting less and less every day ; let us know each other. The Fence told us he would relate us his story ; why should he not ? "

" I will, boys."

" If Kay tells his."

" I shall."

" Listen then."

And the Fence began in the following terms :—

CHAPTER I.—THE STORY OF MAT THE FENCE.

It was in the height of the season—many, many years ago—that the first act of the drama of my life was performed.

Time—but never mind that ; hour, eleven o'clock p.m.

Then there was a youth, handsome, rich, hitherto honoured—a youth whose happy lot everybody envied.

Hitherto for him life had been a sunshine—no cloud in his sky ; his star shone brightly. Proud patricians would have been glad to see him leading their daughter to the altar.

A yearly allowance of a thousand a year—a commission in the guards—a member of the fashionable West-end clubs—horses to ride—what more could he want ?

Will the present company believe it ?

That youth was Mat the Fence.

Yonder stands a gorgeous, noble, stately-looking mansion.

Sweet strains of music are heard — splendid

equipages dash towards it. There is a ball—a grand ball being held at the Earl of ——

Towards that mansion the youth is wending his way.

At length he reaches his destination—enters the hall—walks upstairs—is ushered into the drawing-room by a powdered footman.

What a galaxy of beauty!

England's fairest daughters are to be seen within the small compass of four walls. The scions of aristocracy—dukes, princes, foreign ambassadors, lords, members of parliament—all elbow the fortunate youth.

Now Mat the Fence!

Why should the youth wander through these rooms in search of some one—some one to love—some one to fill a blank in his existence? And why should he at last halt before that girl dressed so exquisitely and with a countenance so dazzlingly attractive?

That is Laura Fitzwalter, the youngest daughter of a poor Scotch lord, the creature that the youth loves.

"Laura," says the youth, with a sad voice, "Laura, I told you I would come. My father is dying. To be present at a ball when such calamity hangs over my home is not the duty of a faithful son. But I longed to see you. I received your note. To-morrow you inform me you are returning to Scotland. What's your answer?"

The patrician maiden smiles, and her glance sweeps across the room. Is it in search of a reply, or in search of ——?"

But we must not anticipate.

"You say you love me, Frank!"

"Can you doubt it?"

A smile of unfathomable description plays upon the questioner's lips.

She has spoken slowly, coldly; and neither in her intonation of voice nor in her demeanour can be traced the slightest shade of that feeling which the youth entertains for her.

Is it her disdain, her seeming indifference, which so kindle the sparks of that fire which burn the youth's brains, which racks his heart.

"To-morrow my father may be dead, Laura."

"Is he very ill?"

"The doctor said that he would not go over the night."

The peer's daughter's eyes brighten—her bust heaves at times broadly as she sits upon her chair—at others languidly, carelessly, she plays with her fan.

The youth before her will inherit a colossal fortune if his father dies. She is proud to be courted by him. She gloats upon the large means which will become her own if she succeed in becoming his wife.

But how different are the feelings of the two beings.

And now the orchestra strikes up a waltz—the supper follows—a bargain is made—Laura elopes with Frank—and next day they are married at Gretna Green.

CHAPTER II.

It was in the dull season, many, many years ago, that the second act of the drama of my life was performed.

It was a bleak, wintry, November night.

The sky was dark and grey, and the snow was heavy upon the ground.

In the drawing-room of one of the most fashionable and celebrated houses of the west of London two beings were seated.

One was Laura Fitzwalter, the peer's daughter.

The other the youth—now a man.

Seven years had elapsed since the marriage chronicled in our last chapter.

"Wasn't it strange, Laura?"

"What, dear?"

"Wasn't it strange, Laura, when we compare the time, that my poor father died at exactly the same instant as that at which I placed the ring upon your finger and you became my wife?"

Laura resumes the perusal of a book which she holds in her hand.

The husband repeats his query.

"Yes it was rather odd—but those things will occur."

"Seven years ago, Laura, I was very rich."

"Oh, are you going to begin again? Another scene, of course."

"Laura?"

"Sir."

"If I am ruined —"

"Yes."

"It is through your own fault."

"Or your own extravagance, which?"

Laura quickly leaves the room, and closes the door with a bang.

And the husband remains.

And plots.

That was myself, your humble servant, Mat the Fence.

Still the love which the youth once entertained for Laura was ever the same.

She had been the cause of his squandering his fortune, of nearly reducing him to beggary; and yet he still clung to her.

"Laura, I'll go to Crockford's,* and see whether I can get luck to be once more in my favour," mutters the husband to his wife, quickly following her to her apartments, where she had gone on leaving the drawing-room.

"May you never return," is the fervid prayer of the peer's daughter.

The story is soon told.

The husband lost.

Poverty and distress succeed in the home—rows were of frequent occurrence—and one morning Laura absconded.

Whither had she gone?

People said with a certain Captain Franklin—a former rival of Frank—a confirmed rake—a man without any principles—and with a heart as black as Satan.

Was it true?

CHAPTER III.

The sun shone brightly, the birds sang merrily, the sky above head was of a limpid blue, Nature's bountiful harvest teemed with varied profusion. Green was the foliage, verdant and luxuriant the broad prairies—in one word, as beautiful a landscape as any lover of nature could have wished, as Laura's husband drove to Ascot races, a year after she had left his home, to go where he knew not; but, alas! he feared to take a road which leads to ephemeral pleasures for awhile, to dishonour and to ruin for ever.

How grand the sight on the course.

Gaily attired pedestrians, male and female—sumptuous carriages—fearless riders—the grand stand filled with anxious sightseers and morbid sportsmen—betting men howling, screaming, shrieking—the flower girl—the gipsy telling Flash Polly her good fortune—the young swells drinking champagne and kissing their frail companions—the blue, cushioned seats of the vehicles—the sounds of the

---

* A noted gambling-house.

bell—the rainbow colours of the riders in the distance—the cattle with their wiry legs and swan-like shoulders—all combined to show that everybody should make merry on such a fine day.

But among so many there is one whose heart sinks in his breast—there is one in search of his wife. And if he find her, alas! alas! what's to happen?

The bell has rung. "They are off! they are off!" is the cry which towers above the universal hum, and away with a swift canter the horses fight hard for the prize in store for them.

And so is he?

For swiftly towards a four-in-hand drag, on the top seats of which he thinks he has seen his wife, darts Laura's husband.

"Who is that fellow who has just alighted from the drag?" asks the husband of an old friend whom he happened to meet on the course.

"A Captain Franklin."

"Enough."

And the two friends part. The informer thinks rather abruptly.

Laura's husband walks towards the drag.

On his way he hustles against the captain.

"Sir!"

"I beg your pardon."

"What's your name?"

"Franklin."

"Would you like to know mine?"

"Perfectly indifferent to me."

"A word with you, sir."

"Not the pleasure of your acquaintance."

"Listen. You live with the daughter of Lord ——, the wife ——, a fellow, I am told, that used to drive the poor thing mad with illtreatment."

"Do you love her, then?"

"Why such question?"

"Do you love her, sir? Oh, answer me like a gentleman."

Captain Franklin looked steadfastly at the questioner.

"I'll tell you the truth. Will you tell me your name, sir? You are a stranger to me. You are not a *madman*."

"I will."

Captain Franklin had been drinkly freely.

"Who wins?" he exclaimed. Then turning round he said hurriedly:—

"Laura was my first love—I seduced her—had a child by her—then she got some fool to marry her—and she wants to have another by me."

"My name, sir?" hissed Frank. "The newspapers will fling it to the world."

Then he swept away.

He understood all. His love had been a dream—a deep-laid scheme on Laura's part. She had never loved him; he had been duped.

To win the cup that day the jockey might have been very anxious. To win the cup that day the winner may have run very fast. But not faster did the mind of man and beast travel than the step of Frank anxious to revenge a blighted life.

With his manner, with his clothes, with his speech, Frank had no difficulty in ascending the drag.

Once on the top of the vehicle he asked for the captain.

"He has just gone down on the course, he will be back directly," replied Lord B——, offering the new comer a glass of champagne from a bottle which had been handed out of the hamper.

Laura saw her husband.

Heavy beads of perspiration trickled from her forehead.

She would have shrieked, she would have flung herself from the top of the drag, had she had time to do so.

But she could not.

"My Lord Butler, I'll have an idea of that champagne with you. Please pour it out slowly, as I do not like froth."

And while diverting the attention of his lordship Frank drew a small pocket pistol from his undergarments, cocked it, and placed the steel muzzle straight upon Laura's forehead.

The intention was guessed too late.

There was a flash in the pan, then a detonation, then a small hole in Laura's forehead.

The blood oozed slowly from the handsome brow.

The crimson ruby saturated the white dress which the peer's daughter wore.

The straw bonnet looked comical and ghastly, towering above the livid, pallid, ghastly features, distorted by the anguish of death.

"My Lord Butler, this will be a very good subject for you at the club to-morrow. What horse have you backed?"

"Leonore."

"See, the numbers are up. She has lost."

"Mine has won."

Then the murderer pointed to the card.

"Avenger was the beast I selected."

*   *   *   *   *

Well, gentlemen, who do you think perpetrated the foul murder above related? Well, young and old, who do you think was condemned to thirty years' penal servitude for it? Well, who do you think returned to this country and tried to work, and could not, and had to turn to sin and crime to live?

Mat the Fence, your humble servant.

Here there was a cry for more.

"Tell us what followed."

"What you did afterwards."

"What for?"

"It will interest us."

"No, it is no use my doing so. Kay, I have told part of my story, now tell us yours."

Kay said he would.

At a future period we will return to him—in the meantime, let us revert to the other characters of the tale.

———

CHAPTER LXXXII.

WILD WILL IN IRELAND.

There is a very promising young gentleman, who has figured from time to time in the course of this story, to whom we must revert, as we will have occasion to connect him with a point of this narrative of no small import.

By one of the early trains from Kingston to Dublin this intellectual member of the swell mob arrived in the latter named city. London was getting too hot for him, and being fond of country scenery he had taken it into his head to pay a visit to the Emerald Isle.

The cognomen under which he went at the time was that of Major Dowling, but as we will have to remain in his company for a few hours we will follow him in his peregrinations.

With a majestic gait the swell thief issued from a particular carriage. "Porteer! Partarh! Here," he said, alighting from the train, "here!"

An obsequiously-looking railway official answered the call.

The major's disguise was complete, having a pair of false Dundreary whiskers and a very fine whig which he bought in London.

The major wished his luggage carried to a cab.

Therefore to insure civility he tipped the porter sixpence.

A cab was hailed and the swell jumped in, having, however, previously told the driver the address of the Prince of Wales Hotel, in Sackville-street.

Distances in Dublin are not so great as they are in London, so the worthy gentleman soon reached his destination.

He was shown into a very nice bedroom, and had some breakfast. Eggs and bacon, and any amount of buttered toast and coffee, formed the bill of fare of this gentleman's early meal.

While eating with a voracity which would have done credit to one who had been starved to death, Wild Will began to consider as to what he should do next.

He glanced over the papers.

A thought came into his head.

"By Jove," he said, rising and walking to and fro in the room, "that's the next tack; every man in this life ought to have some object on hand; egad, I'll be a Fenian!"

But, of course it did not suffice for him to say so; he should, as a preliminary, have received an insight into the secret orders of the craft.

With his quick discernment he doubted not that if he went carefully to work he would have no difficulty in finding some patriotic individual, with more money than brains, who would join him in the scheme, which he hoped to see carried out; and which was nothing less than he, Wild Will, becoming King of Ireland, the confederate in the matter holding the highest post under the Crown.

The idea of the swell thief may seem preposterous, but there is nothing very unusual about it, for at the present moment there are in Ireland many weak-brained individuals who believe that at some period or another they will succeed in becoming great guns in their own country.

While musing over the thoughts which we have just dotted down, and sipping a basin of coffee, Major Dowling's glance ran over the morning newspaper.

For some time he had been attentively perusing an advertisement which appeared in the first column of "Saunders's News Letter."

It ran thus :—

"Whereas, some party possesses the information which may lead to the discovery of a will made by a Count Duplessin in Calcutta, in the year '78, entitling his daughter sole heiress to the fortune which he had to dispose of. This said party is requested to communicate with W., Lincoln's-inn-fields, who will pay one thousand pounds for the production of the document."

This was the passage of the newspaper which had so kindled Wild Will's curiosity.

"I believe," he said, looking satisfactorily around him, "that I am going to be in luck's way. I wonder whether the advertisement is genuine? if so, I am as certain as I stand here of a thousand pounds."

So soliloquising, Wild Will walked towards an expensive yellow-leather trunk, which was in the corner of his room, and withdrawing a bunch of keys from his pocket he opened it.

From a large bundle of papers he took a piece of parchment, which, from the many folds which it possessed, and the red tape which surrounded it, looked very much like one of those things which are of some importance to the owner.

He unfolded it.

Then he read.

But why should we ask our readers to follow with us several folios of technical law terms? Suffice it to say that Wild Will saw the name of Count Duplessin in bold letters.

He saw, besides, a bold array of figures.

Saw how over half-a-million of money was being disposed of.

There were lands, money in the funds, and sundry other valuables described one after another; and all of them were bequeathed to Mademoiselle Rachel Duplessin, a child of four years of age at the time that the document was penned.

"This man who signs himself W., and who offers a thousand pounds for the recovery of the will," the swell thief went on, "must have paramount reason for doing so. Why should not I try to find out where Rachel Duplessin is? Doubtless it is the old story—a girl entitled to a large fortune, to be met with in a garret. If I could only see her I would say nothing to her about the will. I would introduce myself as some respectable young fellow, and marry her; and once her husband, the fortune becomes mine."

This was certainly a very sensible way to look into the matter. But there was a difficulty in the way, and that difficulty was to find out the heiress.

Wild Will, however, with that foresight which characterised him, and which had enabled him to get out of sundry unfortunate critical positions, from which very few would have emerged as securely as himself, carefully folded the paper which contained the advertisement and a signed it to his innermost pocket.

Do our readers remember the death of old Marks?

Do they remember the loss of the document—which had been given to him—by Velvet?

If so they will have no difficulty in placing the two incidents together, and in coming to something like the truth.

The fact was that the document which Wild Will had in his possession was nothing else but the piece of parchment which the convict Marks had given to the boy Velvet, but, unfortunately, had not time to read it.

If he had many of the things which we have related would not have been required to be told.

But everything in due course.

Wild Will rang the bell.

A servant appeared.

"Are there any letters for me?" he asked.

"No, sir."

"Have you got a billiard room in the house?"

"Yes, sir."

"Any gentlemen playing?"

"I am not certain, sir, but I think so."

Wild Will then inquired the exact situation of the billiard room. So he intended to pay a visit to it.

There he wished to make acquaintances.

He was a total stranger in Dublin.

A man cannot form another's acquaintance in the street, but in a billiard room it is quite different.

People do talk to each other—play together—and if one has at all good manners and enticing ways it is but seldom that he fails in his object.

From the success which has always attended Wild Will's schemes in his attempts, he doubted not that all would go on smoothly with him.

Besides, he was going to be a Fenian, and if he meant to be one he should not lose any time about it, as the democratic feeling was raging high at the period when he honoured Dublin with his presence.

When Wild Will, or Major Dowling, entered the billiard room he saw several gentlemen who were engaged in playing a game of pool.

Patiently he waited until the game was over, and as they apparently were about to begin another, he asked them whether they would have any objection to his joining them.

Such a request on his part being a very natural one, it was quickly granted.

But the game did not last much longer, and at the conclusion of it the conversation between the gentlemen became general.

Orders were given for various refreshments, and the wine and whisky getting into the heads of the imbibers, they very soon began to let each other know their respective business.

The company, which numbered about six gentlemen, including Wild Will, is not such as is to be passed over without a few words of description.

Two of the heaviest losers at the game of pool were farmers from the South, who had run up to Dublin on business and cared not, seemingly, how fast the money went, if such an opinion can be formed from the careless manner with which they dropped their golden effigies of her most gracious Majesty, Queen Victoria.

Two of the others were bagmen, or, more properly speaking, commercial travellers; and the last, but not least, was an American gentleman, of no small rank and smell—at least so one would have felt inclined to think, from his bombastic talk.

"Well, stranger, you come from London?"

"Yes."

"And what do they think of the Queen there?"

"The Queen?" repeated Wild Will, "Why, they think her the woman in the right place."

"Do they, stranger?"

"Yes."

"Now I guess, that in America they would not; people are too fond of their rights and their freedom to tolerate all the humbug which goes on in England.

"Indeed!"

"Have you ever been in Amerika?"

"No."

"A great country, that!"

"So I believe. But how is it that you Americans all come to England?"

"Ireland, Sirree."

"And you object to go to England then?"

"I have no business there?"

"Any business here?"

"Perhaps."

Wild Will knew that there were certain American gentlemen who came to Ireland with an object which, although it would go down with weak-brained enthusiastic Irishmen, was not likely to wash with sober, intellectual Christians.

Fenianism, adopted in a pecuniary point of view, appeared to Wild Will to be the game of his Transatlantic friend.

As his game was the same in purpose, although not in practice, he resolved to get this man in his confidence, so as to glean from him whatever information he possessed.

Wild Will was a clever fellow.

He felt that if he appeared to the American to be a good dupe, the latter would not lose an opportunity to cultivate his friendship.

But of course Wild Will reserved to himself the right of parting with his money—a point upon which he was very shy, except under very particular and peculiar circumstances.

Therefore he asked him to step upstairs with him to his rooms.

The Yankee did so.

When the two men found themselves together, between them it was a deep game to play.

They both wanted to fathom each other's thoughts, but neither had any suspicion of each other's genuine behaviour.

If they had the matter would soon have been settled, for they would not have gone on with it.

"Pray take a seat," said Wild Will, pointing to a chair close to the table, which stood in the middle of the room.

The Yankee did so.

When the two men were sitting together the Yankee thought he would begin the conversation in earnest.

"Do you know what brought me hither, friend?" he asked.

"No, I have not the slightest idea."

"Can you guess?"

"Perhaps."

"Well," said the Yankee, "I came here to enlist as many friends as I possibly can in a great cause."

"What's that?"

"Can I be candid with you?"

"Friend, I am a gentleman, and you will not find that I will betray you."

"And that cause?"

"Yes."

"By what name do you call it?"

"We call it Patriotism."

"Yes."

"And others?"

"Fenianism—though the latter term is one of derision."

Wild Will thought that he could not have been more successful in his endeavours had he been for years in search of the very object which he was now meeting with.

"And what would you like me do?" asked Wild Will.

"To join us."

"Willingly would I do so but I fear that there may be certain things with which I may not be able to comply."

"What things?"

"Oaths."

"There are no oaths."

"I would not like, don't you see, to pledge myself to any one, unless I knew exactly what I was going in for."

"Perfectly natural."

"And you will have no objection to a preliminary?"

"What preliminary?"

"Your subscription."

"How much is that?"

"Only two guineas."

Here Wild Will made rather a wry face.

"Are you the treasurer of the Patriotic Association, then?" he asked.

"I am."

"And yet you are an American?"

"And I love liberty besides."

The swell thief inwardly thought that the American was much more a lover of coin than of liberty; but, fearing to be detected, he forbore his speech.

"I have no objection," he said "to pay my subscription. Here it is."

The Yankee took the money.

In exchange he gave to Wild Will a receipt upon a piece of paper, at the top of which "Down with

Queen Victoria!" and "The Irish Republic for ever!" were conspicuously displayed.

On seeing the receipt, and on afterwards consigning it to his pocket, Wild Will could not refrain a smile.

"If you like," said the American gentleman, "I'll introduce you to the head centre to-night. We are going to have a meeting, and you can be present."

"Where is it to be held?" asked Wild Will.

"Will you come?"

"With all my heart."

"Ten o'clock to-night will be the hour."

"I'll be your man then. In the meantime I'll go about and see the city."

Then the two men separated.

The swell thief left his hotel and walked up and down Sackville-street, which is, beyond doubt, one of the finest streets in the world.

The sight of the town was strange indeed.

The large, long street looked so dull when compared to the bustle of a London thoroughfare.

The jaunting cars also, with their peculiar make, astonished him greatly.

At length the evening came.

Wild Will returned to his hotel, and he was sitting comfortably having a glass of Irish whisky, when the American stepped into his room.

"I have got a car outside," he said. "Will you come?"

"Yes."

And the vehicle rattled away in the direction of Rathmines.

There was no caution observed.

The house before which the two men stopped was one which had nothing very extraordinary in its appearance.

The American knocked at the door.

A man answered.

And the two individuals entered the precincts of the house.

We will here describe the appearance of the room and its occupants.

There was a large table, round which at least forty men were sitting.

One at the head of the table was the chairman.

"Mr. Andrew O'Flaherty," said the American, introducing Wild Will to the chairman, "allow me to inform you, on behalf of my friend the Captain, that he is anxious to join us."

"Has he paid his subscription?" whispered the chairman to the American. "If he has not, see that he does."

"Oh! that's all right," replied the American.

Wild Will was then told that he should sit down and watch the proceedings.

The chairman rose.

"Gentlemen and Brethren of the Irish Patriotic Association, formed for the purpose of filling our own pockets at the expense of individuals who may be stupid enough to join us, I rise here to place before you the results of our progress since our last general meeting.

"It is with feelings of the highest gratification, indeed, I consider this day one of the proudest of my life, since I can tell you that so rapidly are our brethren joining us, that for the last fortnight I have never gone to bed without getting as much as I can drink of the real mountain dew, to say nothing of the gorgeous feeds which I am required to take to help me to support the high responsibility of my important office, and to keep myself strong and healthy, to enable me to discharge conscientiously and to your general satisfaction the high post which I have the honour to fill."

Here there was a general "Hear, hear," calls to let in some whisky, followed by a thumping of sticks and fists upon the table.

The American having allowed the noise to subside, requested in very bland terms silence, so as to enable the hon. chairman to proceed.

"My name, gentlemen and brothers of the Irish Patriotic Association, is Andrew O'Flaherty, and I glory in it—I am proud of it—I—I—Yes, gentlemen, I am—I am proud to be one of the O'Flaherty's, and, I fear not to state, one of the descendants of the old kings of Ireland of that name!"

"Hear! Hear! Hear!"

And the same tokens of approbation as previously described were now renewed with still more vigour.

"But, gentlemen," the chairman resumed, "let not our enthusiasm carry us away—let us not wander from our subject, and like the bird that soars above the prairie and glances at the sky, *rino della parridetuda*. But excuse, gentlemen, the flow of my language—old associations gather fresh upon my mind—I remember the days of my boyhood, and my Latin returns freely."

Although it would have been difficult for any one to make either head or tail of the latter part of the chairman's speech—which was, indeed, deprived of the slightest particle of fear—yet it was loudly cheered, and such exclamations as, "By St. Patrick his honour is a great scholar!" were not found wanting from the company.

Andrew O'Flaherty at this stage of the proceedings then withdrew a pinch of snuff from a large silver box (bought out of the proceeds of the Irish Patriotic Association), and having inhaled it with that slowness and decorum which belonged to one of his rank and smell, sneezed once, wiped his nose twice, and resumed.

"Like ominous clouds gathering in the dark vaults of the sky, and ready to burst with a heavy pelting shower—a shower welcome to the duck, unwelcome to those who have no umbrella—so the English vampires await the moment when they can suck our blood, and the innocent ruby which flows in the veins of our darling little children, and of the spotless mothers of the Emerald Isle's rising generation."

It would be impossible here to convey an adequate idea of the shrieks, howlings, and applause which welcomed the hon. chairman's last remark.

Like one single man the whole company rose to their feet, and flourishing their bludgeons in a most expressive manner (whereas one of the American's eyes was very nearly knocked out), they all swore death to the English.

"Brothers of the Irish Patriotic Association, formed for the purpose of filling our own larder, and wetting our whistles at the expense of others, once more let me entreat you not to display in such a powerful manner the noble and sublime feelings which exist in your patriotic and free breasts. The day is not far distant, my friends, the hour is not so very remote, my brothers, when you will be called upon to show that you are not contemptible curs only, but that you are noble, jolly, jolly dogs, and that if you do bark you can also bite, and bite in a manner to extract blood—English blood."

It should be here remarked that the hon. chairman hissed the word blood in so powerful a voice that he was shortly afterwards compelled to expectorate, which he did by mistake upon the breast of a fellow patriot, who resented the insult by inflicting a blow upon the chairman's left ear, and subsequently accepting an apology for not giving him another.

This little incident for a few instants caused a stay in the proceedings, but the chairman, after a few minutes' discussion, again resumed.

"Gentlemen and brothers of the Irish Patriotic Association, it would be unfair on my part," resumed the chairman, "if I were to take up your valuable time. I will only say a few words more."

" Go on, Go on."

"Since you wish me to proceed, gentlemen,—and it is with no slight gratification that I witness such marks of your approval—I'll do so, and acquaint you as briefly as I possibly can with whatever information I have to give you. And at the conclusion of my speech the treasurer and secretary will let you know how the balance sheet stands."

Andrew O'Flaherty then resumed :—

"The instructions which have reached me from Stephens, the Head Centre, are of a most satisfactory nature. He says that he has received several heavy sums from his fellow countrymen and sympathisers in America, and that he intends to devote it to a fund called the Bath of St. Patrick's—"

"What of that ?" a voice inquired.

"That the moneys be placed in a bank, and be kept there to bear interest,—at the end of a year to buy a statue of St. Patrick. That statue to be hollow, and to be filled fifty times with whisky, until every loyal member becomes as drunk as an owl before it, so as to pay the great saint a yearly mark of their respect."

To this proposal there was several dissenting voices, and it was finally agreed that the proposal, which was of a very good nature, should not be postponed but carried out within the present twenty-four hours.

"Now, my friends, I must conclude my speech," resumed the chairman. "The time has not yet come for us to act. In the meantime let us plot and prepare ourselves for the action."

The hon. chairman concluded his speech in his usual manner and was followed by the treasurer and secretary, who informed the company that the funds of the Association being rather low they would have to call upon the members for a fresh subscription before the end of the week.

"What has been done with last month's moneys?" asked one of the members.

" Spent."

" How so ?"

"For the general welfare of the Association."

" Have you got the items ?"

" No."

" Then I will not give another stiver,"

" Order, order, gentlemen."

But the request was not likely to be attended to this time, for there was a general scramble between one and all, followed by a fight, and the bludgeon flew about, and many a severe blow was inflic'ed upon the heads of the Fenians, who, a few minutes ago, were so friendly towards each other.

Wild Will had seen enough. Profiting by the row which had taken place, he took to his heels and returned to his hotel, altogether giving up the idea of becoming a Fenian.

A few days elapsed, and again we find Wild Will at breakfast.

He had received a letter in reply to the advertisement relating to the will.

Within it the writer promised Wild Will a thousand pounds for the document.

He was happy in the extreme, and was about to go to his box when the servant entered his room.

"Captain," he said, "there is a gentleman who wants to see you."

" What's his name ?"

" I don't know his face."

" What does he look like ?"

"A very gentlemanly man."

" Indeed."

" Yes."

" Let him up, then."

But the permission was perfectly unnecessary, for the gentleman downstairs, accompanied by a friend of his, had already entered the room.

The Captain looked very restless and very uneasy.

"Well, Captain," said one of the men, sitting himself down, "how have you been since we last met ?"

"Oh! pretty well," replied Will.

The new comer was no other than the detective whom we have seen before.

"How do you like Ireland ?"

"Right enough."

"I say, you gave me the slip the other day in a very clever manner, old boy ; but now you mus come,"

Wild Will said not a word.

"Jack," said the detective, addressing his companion, "just drag that box to the centre of the room."

Jack, a powerfully-built sort of fellow, laid hold of the trunk, and withdrew it from the place where it was situated.

"Wild Will, have you got the keys?" asked the detective.

"No."

"Break it open then, Jack."

Wild Will now stepped forward.

"What's the use," he said, "your doing that ?"

"I want to see the contents of the box."

"I tell you there is nothing in it."

"Perhaps you will allow me to form my own opinion.

Jack was in the middle of the room.

He was ready to proceed.

At last Wild Will opened the box.

On the top of the swell thief's wardrobe he saw the document of the will.

The detective read it.

"I have heard something of this paper ; how came you by it ?"

Wild Will remained sullen, and refused to give an answer.

"I'll stick to that," said the detective ; " there is a large reward offered for the same."

The swell thief bit his lips in disgust.

Jack was overhauling all his clothes.

"I say, young man, what do you call that ?' asked Jack, showing a hat-box to Wild Will.

"My hat-box."

"Is there anything in it :"

"Yes, some of my jewellery."

"A very strange place to keep jewellery."

And then Jack opened the box.

Out of it he withdrew at least twenty gold watches, sundry pairs of earrings, and twelve gold chains, in addition to several diamond rings.

"Ah! ah! Master Will; have you been at your little game here ?"

"No."

"Where do these things come from ?"

"I bought them."

"From whom ?"

"From a friend of mine."

THE
DANCE OF DEATH;
OR,
THE HANGMAN'S PLOT.
A THRILLING ROMANCE OF TWO CITIES.

No. 23.]   SATURDAY, APRIL 7, 1866.   [One Penny.

HAPPINESS AT LAST.

CHAPTER LXXXII.—Continued.

"What's is the name of your friend?" said the detective.

"I beg to decline answering that question."

"Have you any objection to come with me, then, to give the proper information to the proper parties?"

Wild Will looked at the window; then he looked at the detective and his companion Jack.

The detective, however, had guessed the thief's intention.

"What! young man," he said, "would you think of destroying your valuable carcase? for from such a height you would be sure to do so."

Wild Will drew himself to his full height.

"No," he said, "I was not thinking of that."

"It looked very much like it then."

And as he spoke Jack approached Wild Will and laid his hand upon his shoulder.

"You are my prisoner this time," he said, "and I'll take care that you do not escape."

This had been a plan concocted between Jack and his confidant, for no sooner had Jack spoken than the detective came to the rescue, and seizing Wild Will's fingers, encircled them in a pair of iron wrists which he had brought with him for the purpose.

Here it need not be said that the jewellery which was stolen was returned to the Irish tradesman to whom it belonged, and that Wild Will suffered for the theft.

Previous convictions having been brought against him, he was condemned to five years' penal servitude. There we will leave him and wish him all success, since we shall not have occasion to see him again in the course of this story, which is shortly coming to a close.

CHAPTER LXXXIII.

THE BOY KAY'S STORY.

Owing to more pressing matters which claimed our attention, we were compelled to quit the Hallelujah Club, and therefore our readers were deprived of the perusal of the story of the boy Kay, which we will relate for their benefit, such as it is, being the one which we heard from his own lips one day that we met him in one of the purlieus of the Seven Dials, where this young individual is prone to saunter—it being the resort of several of his pals, and of several of the workhouse *habitués* whom we have had occasion to meet in the course of this narrative.

When Mat the Fence had concluded his story, which was, in our opinion, common-place enough, there was a cry for that of the boy Kay.

For a long time he refused to comply with their request, but at last he yielded, and began in the following terms:—

"I was born in the month of September, in the year 1848, in a dark narrow alley branching off the Gray's-inn-road, where my parents kept a greengrocer's shop.

"I was not an orphan, but had a father and mother, besides a sister, whose various characters I will endeavour to describe.

"Although I was very young at the time of which I speak, I still can remember that we never did a large trade, and that the paternal shop was anything but a remunerative one.

"But that can perhaps be accounted for by the fact that, with the exception of a few turnips and potatoes and a scanty supply of coals, there was seldom any great choice in store for our limited number of customers.

"The result was that gradually the neighbours who used to patronise my father and mother dwindled off, and that they found at the end of one week that not one customer had entered their shop on business, their stock-in-trade being still the same, with the exception of the vegetables which they had used for their private consumption.

"'Betsy,' said my father, turning round to my mother, 'this evening will be Saturday night, and I have got no money for you. What will you do for to-morrow's dinner?'

"Betsy was my mother's name. By the neighbours she had been called 'Blossom Betsy.' I did not know them why such an appellation had been bestowed upon her; but I subsequently learnt that it was owing to several red spots which she had upon her face, and which had been produced by the frequent visits which she was in the habit of paying daily to the Admiral Tom, a public-house in the immediate neighbourhood of our tenement.

"'What will I do about to-morrow's dinner, dear?' she asked, in reply to my father. 'I don't know; but it looks very much as if we are to go without one.'

"At the period when the scene which I am describing was taking place, I was seven years of age, and my sister, who is now dead, was one year younger.

"'Are we going to have no dinner, father?' my sister asked. 'Why, I have had nothing to eat since morning, neither has Charlie.'

"The remark of my sister, which, upon any kind-hearted man, might have been the means of kindling up his energy, was thrown away upon my father; nay, not only was it thrown away, but it had the effect of souring my mother's temper, which at all times was not of the best.

"'Carry, you little slut,' she said vexedly, 'what are you complaining of? Had you not some potatoes before going to bed last night?'

"'It was not last night, mother—it was on Thursday night; but then they were cold and diseased, and Charlie and I had to divide the only one between us.'

"There was something very appealing in Carry's words, and if her distress could not then be relieved, she at least deserved to be pitied, and it would not have hurt either my father or my mother to have spoken kindly to my poor sister, instead of the manner in which they acted towards her.

"'Only a potatoe between you two!' my mother said irascibly. 'Well, you little wretch, you ought to think yourself very lucky. Is not half a loaf better than none at all?'

"'Yes, mother.'

"And Carry burst into tears.

"Here a neighbour of my mother, who was known to be the mistress of a well-known ticket-of-leave man, came into the shop with a bottle of gin under her arm.

"'What is the matter with ye?' she asked. 'Are ye in trouble?'

"Now my mother had one redeeming point—if one redeeming point it can be called—she never allowed any one to become acquainted with her affairs. She was proud to a degree, and would have starved sooner than let any one know how she was situated—although her subsequent behaviour, and the orders which she bid me and my sister carry out, were not such as one would have expected to hear emanating from her lips.

"'No; thank God!' said my mother, hypocritically, 'we are doing very well; and see that little Carry, she has had so much at her dinner that she is suffering from indigestion, and is crying it off.'

"Here Carry raised her glance and looked at the new comer.

"Up to this day it is impossible for me to say whether Mrs. George (such was the ticket-of-leave's companion) guessed through the truth. Perhaps she did; she must have been very blind if she did not, for poor Carry's features were pale and emaciated, her cheek hollow and sunken, her arms thin and cold, and glassy and vague was the expression of her dark eye.

"However she sat down upon a stool in the room, and working her gin, asked my father and mother to join her.

"The white, thick, liquory stuff was poured into a huge tumbler (the only one in the room, my mother protesting that she had lost the key of the cupboard and that she every instant expected the smith), and my parents drank it with that gusto which never forsook them when gin was in the way.

"For I believe they would have done anything for gin. The greater part of their time was spent at Admiral Tom's; and then when they were not drinking gin there they were drinking gin at home.

"Since I have been a roving Arab, a houseless boy of the street," Kay went on, "I have, on more occasions than one, noticed that my parents' vice, namely, drunkenness, was excessively prevalent among the destitute classes—a fact which would account for the numerous diseases which infect every over-populated tenement, the inhabitants invariably buying gin with whatever chance money they get, however deprived they may have been of food for the previous days.

"Mrs. George remained with us as long as the liquor lasted; but when the bottle had become a 'dead 'un,' and two shillings and twopence, which would have set us agoing for two days with food, poured down three throats, she rose, and said that she should go and get a fresh bottle, as her old man wanted a drop before he went out.

"With these words Mrs. George left us.

"When my father and mother were by themselves they began to talk about Mrs. George. From their conversation I gleaned that Black George, her husband (so he was called in the alley) was in the habit of sallying out at night on expeditions which kept him out for hours and hours together—expeditions which must have proved remunerative, if Mrs. George's daily expenses at the Admiral Tom could have been looked upon as a criterion.

"Such was one of my mother's best friends. Can it be wondered at that, under such tutorship and with such associations around me, I followed the only line of conduct which was left open to me?

"'Now, Betsy, what do you think of that woman?' asked father, as soon as Mrs. George had gone out of the room. 'She spends all her money in drink; could she not have lent us a few shillings, which she would not have missed, instead of blowing them out as she does?'

"'My dear,' replied my mother, 'why talk thus of one who has always treated us well? I would not for the world let her know that we are hard pushed.'

"'And think you she don't see through it?'

"'Never mind about that. At all events she cannot say among the neighbours that I beg from her, a thing which she would be the first to circulate had she a chance to do so.'

"Now although the quantity of gin which had been drunk by father and mother would not have produced any effect upon them had they had some food in them, yet in course of time it told greatly against them.

"With his head drooping listlessly upon his breast my father was gazing at me, when my mother shook him rudely by the shoulder, and in not very smooth terms asked him to wake up.

"'I say, dear,' he said, 'let us think of to-morrow.'

"'There are the mattresses of the bed, shall we pledge them, and see what Monday will bring forth?'

"Before doing anything my mother invariably appealed to my father, who advised her by all means to see how much she could get at the corner.

"This being settled, I had to accompany my mother to the pawnshop, When I entered the place a feeling of shame crept over me—I did not know why—yet it existed; and after having waited for at least ten minutes in one of the boxes, we at last succeeded in getting as much as we could upon the bedding.

"The few shillings which the pawnbroker lent to my mother did not, I need not state, last very long. On the following day, however, which turned out to be Sunday, we had a good dinner—namely, a sort of Irish stew, composed of potatoes and turnips and a few odd pieces of meat, commonly called block ornaments, which had been bought the previous evening.

"Two more days passed on, and then gradually the whole of the furniture was disposed of, and father and mother, and Carry and myself, had to sleep upon the floor, huddled all together in a heap, the warmth of our respective bodies acting as a very good substitute in the absence of any fire, there being no fuel, and no money to purchase any.

"Poverty was now to be our lot, and unless something was done towards improving our position I saw nothing but the workhouse for my parents.

"A noble idea then entered my head. If I could only obtain a broom I would sweep a crossing, where I thought I could get a goodish bit of money daily.

"This, I thought, would be an honest way of obtaining a livelihood. I had no trade, no education—for I can neither read nor write—what could I do? And so I resolved that I would mention the proposal.

"In a sort of hole hacked in the grimy wall sat my father, tailor fashion, and warming his long, bony fingers at the fire, which had been provided out of one shilling which Mrs. George had lent my mother.

"My mother was bustling about the room with no settled purpose, and Carry was looking out into the alley at the passers by.

"Wretched was the sight which the poor girl presented as she stood shivering outside the broken down threshold, where one slab was missing, attired in a shockingly old and dirty cotton gown, the tatters of which, scattered by the wind, enabled you you to see her build high above the knee.

"'Father,' I said, after communicating to him my idea of the broom, 'what do you think of it?'

"'It is not practicable,' he said. 'We have no money, and the work'us is the only place which remains for us.'

"'The work'us!' exclaimed my mother irascibly, the high-pitched passionate tone of her ire flashing in her eye. 'No; I shan't go to the work'us—I'd rather swing than do that.'

"Then my mother remained at a standstill.

"A minute afterwards she flew towards Carry.

"'Is it raining outside?' she asked abruptly.

"'Yes, mother.'

"'Well, then, you and your brother go out at once. Before to-night you must have some money. I shan't go to the work'us—no; not if I can prevent it.'

"'What am I to do to get money?' I asked dolefully.

"Go into the street and look out for some. Take Carry with you. Beg—steal—do whatever you like; *but I must have money!*'

"'Carry,' said I, turning round towards my sister, 'do you hear your mother? Will you come?'

"A faint 'Yes' was Carry's reply; and after having tried to settle her dress, which at the best was but a parcel of rags (a task in which she did not succeed), we both left the house.

"As we passed through the long and narrow passages which led to the Gray's-inn-road, poor Carry blushed to her very temples; and the poor thing said that she was ashamed of walking about, since she feared that everybody who looked at us knew the object upon which we were sallying.

"With the rain pattering in our faces we walked up the Gray's-inn-road until we reached that part of Holborn which faces Chancery-lane.

"I have been in several unpleasant situations in my life, but I do not recollect having experienced anything more painful than the feeling which invaded my whole being when Carry and I halted together to decide whither we should go.

"'I say, Carry,' I began, 'what shall we do? Shall we beg together, or separately?'

"This suggestion was made by me because I thought that by so doing we might succeed in making more money, and not be compelled to do the same thing the next day; but I was obliged to alter my mind, and that very quickly too.

"'Oh, Charles!' Carry said to me, the warm tears flowing fast from her eyes, 'how unkind you are, to be sure. By myself I could never do it. Let us try together, and may be when I get accustomed to the work I'll feel stronger. At present I could not do it.'

"We had left the alley at one o'clock, and it was slowly indeed the time passed away. As yet we might have remained at home for the good which we had done by coming out. And now the old clock of St. Paul's struck two.

"'Carry,' I said, turning to the poor girl, 'I hope we will shortly be in luck's way. How long do you think you will be able to stand the work?'

"'As long as it be necessary,' replied Carry, dolefully. 'But I wish they would give something, don't you, Charlie?'

"But we were not to be in luck's way. Yet, for now huge flakes of snow began to obscure the air with a white mist, lodging in the strangest and strangest places the fancy could suggest. It continued so for hours. No flitting shower, coming in whirling gusts, but an even down descent of the icy particles, until for yards and yards before us nothing was presented to the eye but an uninterrupted sheep of white.

"Thick and fast fell the snow, until it enveloped in its white mantle the steeple of Sir Christopher Wren's great monument, and the tops of the houses which reared their proud heads behind us. On and on came the descending shower, noiseless and steady, until all objects were alike confounded and impossible to be distinguished each from each. The night too was coming, coming with a strange and sullen gloom, the cold becoming more intense, and now and then a hissing cry swept moaningly over our features, carrying with it in its progress clouds of frozen articles, small, and cutting, colder than rain.

"Deep in the snow were poor Carry's swollen naked feet, and pallid was her hollow cheek, while her white teeth chattered convulsively as the gusts of the wind swept in merciless blasts through the raven tresses of her silky hair, which protected the back of her small neck from the inclemency of the weather.

"'This will never do, Carry,' I said, 'we are getting nothing. Let us appeal to the footpads, and they may not be deaf to our prayers.'

"Then, impelled by hunger, and the dread which supervened at seeing poor Carry and myself beaten on our return home, I strode with Carry towards the first individual that came in our path.

"'Repeat what I will say, sissy,' I added quietly, 'and something tells me that we will be successful this time.'

"'For Heaven's sake help us, good lady,' I began, addressing a kindhearted looking dame, all wrapped up in furs, and with a huge umbrella towering high above our heads. 'We want bread. Do not say no. Oh, do, good lady. Do help us!'

"Carry's voice joining mine had the desired effect. The lady addressed halted and looked at us both. She asked us a few questions. We answered them quickly and openly, and it seemed to move her heart.

"'Poor things!' she said, opening the purse which she carried, 'take this, and may it do you good. I have a large family, or I would give you more.'

"With the greediness of a famished cur clutching a long-coveted bone, I immediately grasped the money, without even thinking of thanking the lady, so great was my joy.

"'O, Carry! Carry!' I exclaimed, my heart bounding within my breast, "we will not be beaten to-night, at all events.'

"'How much is it?' asked sissy, whose eyes began to sparkle with anxious expectation within her hitherto glassy but now glittering orbs. 'How much is it?'

"'Half-a-crown,' I said, but I had no time to finish the sentence which I had began for an iron hand was placed upon my shoulders, and a harsh voice called my attention.

"'Deliver that money at once,' it said, 'you young begging vagabond, don't you know that mendicity is forbidden within the precincts of the city?'

"I looked up—I was in the power of a feelingless, burly, constable, who had been watching me for some time past.

"'If you let me go this time,' I said, ' I will not beg again, and I'll give up the half-crown.'

"Look sharp, then, young one, where is it?'

"The constable relaxed his grasp, and I feigned to place the hand in my pocket in search of the piece—but this was only a scheme on my part—I was not going to lose so quickly the hard earnings of my days' labour—'oh, here it is! I went on, and whispering a few words in Carry's ears, I added in an undertone, 'let us run for it.'

"So impressively had I spoken, and so confident did Carry feel that to linger would have been endangering not only our freedom but our bread, had we remained at a stand-still, that with the swiftness of a cat she darted off from the constable's sight. How long we ran I know not. Tightly clutching my half-crown in my closed palm and ever and anon turning round to see whether we were followed and fancying that we were; we at length branched off in the Grays-inn-road.

"'Charles, do not walk so fast,' Carry said to me, as she laid her hand upon my shoulder, 'I am so faint that I cannot step any further.'

"It was late—beneath a dark doorway we halted. Then it was that I noticed Carry's face was as pale as death.

"'Cheer up, girl,' I said, 'we will have a nice fire and a nice supper when we get in. Lean upon my arm and let us make our way home, the atmospere is frozen. It would be dangerous to remain here much longer—you would get your death of cold, darling.'

"Carry smiled sadly, and with her thin emaciated hand she laid hold of the skirts of her tattered garment and wiped the thick drops of perspiration which were slowly coursing each other down her pale, careworn features.

" There was nobody within when we reached home. I feared to spend part of the money for fuel, and yet poor Carry was very cold, and shivering all the while.

" An hour passed, and father returned.

" 'Got any money,' he asked, archly—and I advanced towards him to communicate the result of our days' tramping.

" 'Yes, father, we have,' timidly returned Carry, ' a good lady gave us half-a-crown.'

" 'Where is it ?' roared my father.

" He had been drinking—1 could guess that from his manner, from his hot breath reeking with gin—from the vacant expression of his eye.

" ' Here, father.'

" The sight of the money seemed to sober him in an instant.

" 'This is not a flash one ?' he stammered stupidly, I'll go after your mother, I left her at The Admiral Tom.'

" Poor Carry and I gazed with melancholy upon his retreating form. The Admiral Tom, the public-house—I knew what that meant ! No fire, no supper for us that night.

" Carry looked at me—her glance was full of meaning. There and then she gave vent to a flood of tears, and, helpless to prevent it, wept as if her heart would break.

" Our anticipations were not without their foundation, for when night came—when the honest painstaking citizen is in his house at rest—the theatres, and the various places of amusements have disgorged their multitudes—when the night robber, like some hideous phantom of humanity, sallies out from the dismal haunt which conceals him during the day on his errand of crime—when exhaustion has compelled the night wanderer, be he whom or what he may, to lay down in some dark alley—when the gin palaces, bound by law to close at a certain time, have, for a few hours only, suspended the sale of their poisoned stuff—then father and mother, arm-in-arm, with besotted faces—hiccupping—and singing incoherent snatches of a drunken chorus, reeled in to our poverty-stricken cellar.

" The worst part remains to be told. The half-a-crown was spent, Carry and I were starving, and now could it be possible that I, who was suffering all the bodily pains that we poor mortals are heir to, should be doomed to witness that, which even now causes my blood to curdle within my veins, and which shot so cute a pain to my heart, that I became for a while paralysed in all my movements, and unable to prevent the accomplishment of one of the darkest deeds that ever disgraced humanity.

" Huddled together upon the boards of the abode where we four slept—with nothing beneath us beyond a few rags and several greasy newspapers, poor Carry and I tried to seek in slumber a forgetfulness of our troubles.

The loud snoring of my mother was a sufficient guarantee to me that no sooner had she laid down than she was asleep. Not so with my father, restlessly he moved to and fro, and bid me not to keep on talking to Carry and be sure to hold my tongue if I did not wish to get a —— good hiding.

" The fear of the threat being carried out, and the fatigue which I felt after my days' toil, were powerful stimulants indeed to compel me to close my eyes. Thus I did so. I previously, however, drew poor Carry's lips close to mine (she was sleeping by father's side), and sank into what I hoped would be an oblivion of my sad lot until the short rays of the morning sun shone full upon the broken panes of our windows and awoke me once more to life—its faults, follies, crimes, and virtues.

" Wafted by the fanciful turn that the mind sometimes takes even the body is lacerated by pain, it was a in sort of fairyland—when that nature's anomaly chose to lead the thinking powers of the outcast. Forgetful of what I had suffered I sank in a pleasant slumber. Methought the old lady that had so generously helped us had, on a mission of charity, discovered our poor abode—rescued my parents from the low degraded state in which they had fallen, and adopted poor Carry as her child.

" Why was not my dream to last for ever ? I was thinking of Carry, and it was her voice which awoke me.

" But it was not the voice of one appealing to you soothingly—it was not the sweet, soft, lullaby of the gentle girl, pleading in a low musical strain—it was the voice of Carry's, but it was harsh, strident. It was a shriek of agony—a shriek which told of incestuous infamy—a shriek which, as it vibrated despairingly above the midnight stillness, seemed to plead for help—fruitlessly and uselessly besought. The Unknown's just wrath against the drunken libertine who, not satisfied to nip in the bud the faded flower, fast sinking for want of food and care, had not feared in the pitchy darkness of a dreary noisome cellar, to renew in the nineteenth century the feast of Balthazer, had dared, like a new Satan on earth dispensing with all the pomp and gorgeousness of a criminal banquet, to gloat in his loneliness upon the means to be devoted to soil the spotless robe of a girl's purity by wrenching from an exhausted frame a submission to the unnatural passion of a base and fiendish parent.'

At this part of his narrative the boy Kay stopped abruptly, and withdrawing from his undergarment a soiled piece of rag—meant for a handkerchief—he wiped slowly the heavy beads of perspiration which were fast gathering upon his brow, and resumed in the following terms :—

" Romance writers, scholars, and learned gentlemen connected with the press have often tried to describe the manners and customs, sins and miseries of the London destitute poor. As yet, the tale is half untold. Why so ? Have the materials been wanting, or, loth to give the lie to civilisation and to its boasted progress, have they dreaded to approach the human sewers, from which spring the slimy reptiles called crime, incest, prostitution ? For the scene which had taken place was not a solitary occurrence, other boys having since told me that such things have often been enacted within their experience, and been allowed to pass untouched from the want of anyone bold enough to bring them to light.

" A few minutes elapsed after my attention had been attracted by Carry's appeal, then the cries seemed to be smothered, and darkness and silence once more resumed their sway, but not for much longer, though ; for now, only, in mockery of my forlornness the pale rays of the moon began to shed a fresh light upon an hitherto dark scene of horror, and enabled me to have a view of Carry—of the being whom I loved best in the world—lying like a mere log of wood not a yard from me, and apparently plunged in a death-like swoon.

" Oh ! how my heart sank when I glanced upon the closed eyelids. The dishevelled hair, upon the bleeding, swollen arms, hanging stiff by her sides—powerful tokens of a defeat dearly bought—sure sign that they had been raised in self-defence, in an unequal struggle of which I guessed the terrible conclusion.

" Had I been in a different position, it is impossible to say what 1 would have done. My blood flew to my temple—my teeth became embedded in my lips—my brow knit fiercely,—and with closed fists, I thought I could have risen to avenge the foul act of the man whom it was my destiny to call father. But that it should not be, had doubtless been ordained by that Power whose verdict has no higher tribunal, for when I tried to lift myself up, I found that my strength had forsaken me—I felt the cold creeping in the marrow of my bones—I experienced a horrid dizziness in the brain—a clammy moisture on the brow,—and, like the poor girl who lay stretched and senseless not a yard from me, I remained prostrate—still more to be pitied than she: for religion brought with it a train of thoughts, which, adding mental agony to bodily suffering, caused me to pass the remainder of the night in a martyrdom of indescribable pain, which no mortal could ever have endured for the grossest outrage that ever disgraced humanity.

"Mine is a sad story, the Arab went on; morning came, and not by word or by deed had I betrayed to father the knowledge which I possessed.

"He rose, awoke my mother, and roughly kicking me with his foot, he bid me not to remain sweating like a pig all the day long.

"I staggered to my feet; but my first care was for Carry, and so I gently stooped over her.

"Father, I said, after a moment's silence, look! look! how .pale Carry is this morning! What can be the matter with her? She won't answer me! Carry, darling—little sissy! Mother, come here! come here, I beseech you! Carry, Carry, answer! Don't you hear me?

"Like you, she is a lazy little varmint—a good-for-nothing imp, retorted my mother, heeding not my prayer, and rubbing her eyes with her left hand, while with her right she was settling up her dirty shift. Give her a good shake. Just pull her ear a bit, and see what that 'll do.

"Instead of abiding by the cruel advice given to me, I, on the contrary, gently placed my arm under Carry's form and drew it towards me.

"Carry whispered softly, and my lips met hers. But suddenly I relaxed my hold—a choking sensation rushed to my throat, and Carry's body fell heavily upon the ground.

"Her lips were icy cold, her features rigid, and the clammy cheeks, over which the dark tresses wandered, proclaimed to me the sad, heartrending truth.

"'Good God!' I exclaimed, with a shriek of terror, 'the poor girl is dead. Mother,' I pursued quickly, 'Your child is no more, and there is the murderer!'

"As I spoke I pointed threateningly to my father, whose countenance had assumed a sickly hue.

"'The boy is gone mad!' he said, derisively.

"'Mad!' I retorted. 'Father, I loathe, I scorn you! Give me the lie. Before that corpse I dare you say that you are not the murderer of my sister! Utter not so base a falsehood, or by Heavens I'll take the justice in my own hands.'

"Before the proud mien, before the threatening attitude, the father cowed, and his glance fell.

"'The chamber of death,' I pursued in one breath, 'is no place for laying bare the sore and bleeding wound. Let not desecration of the great family ties be poor Carry's burial prayer. She sleeps! Sleeps for ever in this world. I wish to Heaven my eyelids had closed ere I suffered what I did suffer, and saw what I did see. And now, unfeeling parents, farewell.'

"Quivering with rage, and yet fearful of giving vent to his aroused feelings, transfixed, confounded, and bewildered beyond description at my words, whose meaning was unfathomable to her, I left my father and mother, and hurried away from the home where I had been dragged up, and where I had never spent one minute of happiness and comfort, save when alone with Carry we sympathised over each other's sorrow, and with our tiny hands clasped in each other's we hoped for a sunshine which never came.'"

At this part of his narrative the boy stopped, and all the members of the club separated.

CONCLUSION.

Fain would we linger for a while longer with our readers; but as our story is drawing to a close, we must inform them how the different characters of this tale were treated by the hand of Fate.

Our readers doubtless will not be astonished when we tell them that Nancy turned out to be Count Duplessi's daughter, that the will was discovered, and she came in for the large fortune which was bequeathed to her. She did not forget Velvet, who had been her companion in her poverty, and she was united to him in the holy bonds of matrimony.

A year after their marriage Lady Mountcarsden died, and sad indeed was the scene which the young couple presented as they stood by the coffin where lay the remains of the patrician lady who had proved a friend to poor Nancy.

With regard to the Hallelujah Club we have nothing to say beyond that they are still in London.

Jenny, the guilty wife, had recourse to suicide on leaving her husband, and thus baffled the hangman's revenge.

THE END.

The following are the numbers of the Prizes which will be delivered per post to the lucky Subscribers with whose names and addresses we are provided:—

A Gold Watch 8599	A Gold Watch 5733	A Gold Watch 9255
A Silver Watch 6245	An Albert Guard 11335	A Silver Watch 11423
A Buckle 1405	A Gold Ring 9215	A Gold Watch 9127
A Chromo Engraving from	A Dressing-case.......... 6221	A Cigar Case 8607
Turner 6277	A Silver Watch 2332	A Meerschaum Pipe 11327
A Gold Chain 9159	An Eight-day Clock 9183	Macaulay's History of Eng-
A Set of Cricket Implements 2340	A Gold Ring 6317	land 9271
Shakespeare's Works, hand-	A Scarf Pin.............. 9223	A Splendid Engraving 6293
somely bound 11343	A Diamond Pin.......... 9231	A Meerschaum Pipe 6285
The Doomed Ship 8591	A Bracelet 11359	A Gold Ring 9175
Otway's Poems 9247	A Penknife 9167	A Gold Watch............ 9279
A Beautiful Gun 1235	A Ring 466253